All That is Left of Life

ROBERTA RECCHIA

All That is Left of Life

TRANSLATED BY
ANTONELLA LETTIERI

DIALOGUE BOOKS

First published in Great Britain in 2025 by Dialogue Books
An imprint of John Murray Press
Original Italian edition published in 2024 by Rizzoli Libri

1

Copyright © Roberta Recchia 2025
Translation © Antonella Lettieri 2025
Author licence agreed courtesy of Laura Ceccacci Agency

The moral right of the author has been asserted.

*All characters and events in this publication, other than those
clearly in the public domain, are fictitious and any resemblance
to real persons, living or dead, is purely coincidental.*

All rights reserved.
No part of this publication may be reproduced, stored in a
retrieval system, or transmitted, in any form or by any means, without
the prior permission in writing of the publisher, nor be otherwise circulated
in any form of binding or cover other than that in which it is published
and without a similar condition including this condition being
imposed on the subsequent purchaser.

A CIP catalogue record for this book is available from the British Library.

Hardback ISBN 978-0-349-70458-6
Trade paperback ISBN 978-0-349-70457-9

Typeset in Berling by M Rules
Printed and bound in Great Britain by Clays Ltd, Elcograf S.p.A

John Murray policy is to use papers that are natural, renewable and
recyclable products and made from wood grown in sustainable forests.
The logging and manufacturing processes are expected to conform to the
environmental regulations of the country of origin.

Carmelite House
50 Victoria Embankment
London EC4Y 0DZ

The authorised representative
in the EEA is
Hachette Ireland
8 Castlecourt Centre
Dublin 15, D15 XTP3, Ireland
(email: info@hbgi.ie)

www.dialoguebooks.co.uk

John Murray Press, part of Hodder & Stoughton Limited
An Hachette UK company.

To my grandmother Agata

Prologue

Awakening, 1980

Until the last of her days, Marisa Ansaldo would always retain a vivid memory of that awakening in early August.

As if it had all happened only yesterday, in her recollection she would see herself again as she plunged her face into the cold water cupped in her hands, shivering with relief. That morning, the air was still. Past the open window, beyond the beach, the sea was silent. While the sunlight progressed across the majolica tiles of the bathroom, she had brushed her hair slowly, taking in with a touch of vanity the success of her new hair colour, almost identical to the golden brown of her youth. Then, without bitterness, she had let her gaze wander over the signs of her years, which were now nearing fifty.

She was in the habit of getting up early even during her holidays at the beach house. She savoured those moments all for herself, in silence, then carried out the string of actions, always the same, that ended in the ritual coffee with which she would wake up her husband.

That day, however, as she tied her light dressing gown around her waist, she had caught Stelvio's reflection in the wardrobe mirror. He was still in their bed, soundly asleep and covered in sweat. Though it had been a while, she had had a naughty thought. Their desire for each other was no longer what it used to be, but they excused the numbness of their senses by their constant tiredness, their daughter's always being at home, and Marisa's mother's ever-watchful eye making them shy. She had turned around slowly and in the half-light of the room she had felt the urge to softly touch his naked chest, to stroke his bristly beard. Maybe it was because of the holiday which was only just beginning, or because of that silence thick with intimacy, that a tingling craving for his wiry kisses had pushed to her lips, and a pleasant heat had spread between her thighs.

Passion, as impatient as it once was, had made its appearance.

But at that moment, through the door left ajar, Marisa had heard her mother Letizia dragging her feet along the corridor. So she had smiled to herself, resigned to the missed opportunity, and left the room, casting a glance full of affection towards her husband.

That was the last time Marisa Ansaldo ever felt sensual desire.

The last awakening of the life from before.

1

The Life from Before

But when did it start, the life from before?

When she decided to marry Stelvio Ansaldo, Marisa would have replied without hesitation.

It started at the exact moment she had turned around to look at him, as they were strolling silently in Via del Moro.

'I want to marry you! Stelvio, let's get married,' Marisa said out of the blue, as if challenging him to do something crazy.

He had stared at her, puzzled and amazed. Many questions hovered on his hushed lips, all the *if*s, the *but*s, the *why*s. But then, the love he felt for this woman, for the dimples that pinned her smile to her cheeks and for her bright and open gaze that could not lie, gave him all the answers he needed. He nodded without saying a word.

The life from before started when he linked his arm through hers, holding her hand in his.

It was a Sunday in November 1956.

Before her marriage to Stelvio, there had been only her family life. The years of her childhood and early youth were gathered together in her memory in rather higgledy-piggledy fashion, like in a black-and-white scrapbook. Gradually, the scenes had started to become less vivid, as time blurred the edges and slowly eroded the details. Those were the years Marisa had spent with her sister, Emma, with their parents. A long string of days that, whether peaceful or noisy, had always felt cosy, like her father holding her tight against his round stomach, which was as big as a watermelon and perennially enveloped in his grocer's apron.

Marisa could not recall the first time she had laid eyes on Stelvio. He had appeared in her life like an extra in the movies: there, in the background of a film, watched without paying too much attention. Perhaps it had been in early 1954, when Ruggero, the delivery man for the Camastra bakery, had handed in his notice to seek his fortune in Turin. At the time, Marisa had been wrapped up in her thoughts and her work at the family grocery shop, and for a long spell she had not noticed the taciturn young man who came by early in the morning to deliver the bread in Ruggero's place. Every day before opening, she tidied the items on the shelves, affixed the signs with the various prices and noted down what needed restocking. In the meantime, her father, his apron always immaculate, arranged the perishable items in his new refrigerated counter, of which he was as proud as if it were his own son. When Stelvio arrived, he knocked twice, discreetly, on the window pane of the door, waited for her father to open it and handed him the basket with the ciriola and frusta rolls, then the one with the loaves. Her father always hurried to empty the baskets so that he could hand them back quickly. In the meantime, Stelvio went up to Marisa at the till, to have his delivery note signed. Marisa and Stelvio had only ever exchanged friendly good mornings and thank yous, and this happened every morning except on Sundays.

At the time, Marisa's head was elsewhere: she was thinking about Francesco Malpighi, her fiancé who had gone to Switzerland two years earlier to work as a waiter at Hotel Bellavista on Lake Geneva. It was a sacrifice, of course. It meant being apart and having to make do with letters; but Marisa's patient waiting was fuelled by Francesco's promises. As a consolation, he regularly reminded her that he was there for their future, to save the money they needed to open an elegant café, right there in the square, much smarter than the ones in fashionable Via Veneto. When he managed to come back to Rome for a few days, after they had made love Francesco would describe to Marisa in great detail their future Gran Caffè Malpighi: its Art Nouveau tables and chairs, its pink marble, its stuccoed ceiling, its wrought-iron windows lit from the inside and its musical events in the evening. Francesco had decided that Marisa would not work at the till nor wait tables; they would have employees for that. Instead, she would simply show up from time to time, in her furs, as befitted the proprietress. When she first heard about this plan, Marisa had laughed and objected that she didn't care if she had to work the till, for she was used to it: she had been working in the family shop since she'd left school and it was not a burden for her. Also, it would be one less salary to pay – a useful saving, especially early on. But Francesco would not hear of it: he wanted to make it up to her for all that waiting and also make amends with her parents, who, after all that time, were quite eager to see her settle down.

Marisa was young, in love and careless. After six months

spent apart, Francesco had eventually come to Rome in November 1955, for the funeral of his maternal aunt. Grieving was not their main concern at the time: they were immersed in their passion, which had been fuelled by the long time spent apart.

Then, immediately after Christmas, Marisa received confirmation that she was expecting.

That morning in late December, she had tearfully begged her family doctor to keep the news from her parents. Then she ran back to the shop and explained away her tardiness to her father. Finding yet another excuse, she went downstairs to the small storeroom and started pacing up and down. Shame, fear, and Francesco so far away ... Overwhelmed and confused, she indulged in a little cry, then delicately splashed her eyes with cold water and told herself that, after all, it was not the end of the world: a wedding could be organised in a matter of weeks. After that, she would go to Switzerland with Francesco and live there for as long as necessary. She had already suggested this course of action several times in the past, but he had always preferred to leave things as they were. At the hotel, he got room and board for free – a double room that he shared with a colleague – and that was a tidy saving. This way, apart from the money he sent to his family, he could add almost his entire salary to his savings at the end of the month. However, a baby changed everything: they had to find a solution, and fast, on any pretext, and never mind if people gossiped.

The following Sunday, Marisa pretended to go to see a friend who had been admitted to the Santo Spirito hospital so that she could call Francesco from the phone box of a city-centre hotel. The operator kept her waiting for ages. Then the man from Hotel Bellavista, who luckily spoke Italian, made her wait even longer as he redirected the call to the restaurant. Marisa prayed to herself that they would hurry up: she didn't have many tokens left, especially with the emergency surcharge. Eventually Francesco's voice rang in her ear, on the other end of the line, so beautiful, yet tinged with a worry that pleased her and somewhat relieved the anguish that had been nesting in her stomach for the last two days.

'Mimì! What happened?' Francesco had always called her by that nickname: Mimì. He had obviously taken the trouble to immediately run to the phone.

Marisa got straight to the point, since she was running out of tokens, and said, 'Francesco, something happened. You need to come to Rome; we need to talk.'

'To Rome? Now? But what happened?'

'I can't tell you. But we need to talk.' Marisa lowered her voice enough for an eloquent affection to soften her tone, as she smiled and added, 'You need to come soon, but don't worry. I am well ... *we* are well.'

At the other end, under the crackling of the line, Marisa heard a long silence interrupted only by a faraway clinking of crockery.

'Did you tell anyone?' Francesco said so quietly that she barely heard him.

Marisa shook her head slowly, caught off guard by the unexpected question. 'No, of course not.'

'I'll come down after New Year, but don't tell anyone. I'll see you on Thursday evening at six, at my aunt's. I'll wait for you there.'

And before Marisa could even finish whispering, 'Very well,' he had already hung up without saying goodbye.

Marisa walked back home, all wrapped up in her wool coat. It had turned colder. A light but persistent wind was flapping the scarf she had tied around her hair and neck. Trams were darting by at regular intervals, but she ignored them, despite the pain in her feet. She was grateful that it was dark already: it meant that she could let her disappointment and dejection spill from her eyes without having to worry about nosy passers-by. Could it be that Francesco had not understood her meaning? And if indeed he had understood her, as she believed, what kind of reaction was that? His sudden aloofness, the coldness of his response, as if the whole matter were some business that just needed taking care of ... No gentleness. No emotion. Marisa tried hard to understand. He had always been an ambitious man, with clear, defined plans in mind. He did not want for himself the life of his father, a telephone engineer with five children to feed and little means to do so. Hadn't this been part of the reason Marisa had always liked him so much? Of course, it could not be denied that having a child out of the blue, so ahead of time, changed everything. However, he had been saving for so long, and she too had something set aside in her post office savings account, not to mention the money he would inherit once his aunt's apartment was sold, since she had died a spinster. Marisa convinced herself that, once they had a chance to talk it through, they would certainly find a solution that would straighten everything out without having to give up too much. Before she eventually got home, she told herself that, after all, Francesco's coldness was understandable, and she almost felt guilty for not having been able to find a better way to tell him that he was about to become a father.

The days until the Thursday after New Year's Day felt never-ending to Marisa. To justify her gloomy mood, she invented a story that she had come down with a light flu: a slight temperature, a burning in her throat, and a headache that would not go away. She readily accepted the therapy of hot milk and honey lavished on her by her mother and the hours of bed rest imposed by her father. Thus she ended up spending a long time in her room, which she once used to share with her older sister Emma, who had got married two years earlier. Emma had never wanted anything to do with the family business: at fourteen she had gone to work in a dressmaker's shop because she wanted to become a *modiste*, and, since she was talented, in early 1951 her parents had given her the money to open a small ladieswear boutique in Via Pinerolo. Then Emma had met Emanuele Bassevi, a Jewish textile entrepreneur who, for her sake, had severed all ties with his own family, accepting to be shunned by the uncompromising social circle in which he moved and to bear the pain of having to hear his father curse him from his deathbed. Despite everything Emma and Emanuele had been through, their relationship was now untroubled. They had called their firstborn Donato, like his late paternal grandfather. Choosing that name had felt to Emanuele like a way to make amends for the wrongs he had inflicted on a father who, until his marriage with Emma, had loved him dearly and never made him want for anything. During the years of her engagement with Francesco, Marisa had dreamed of a similar bond, capable of withstanding all troubles and sorrows.

When Thursday afternoon finally came around, Marisa said that she was feeling better and that she was going to Clelia, her hairdresser, to have her hair set, although she had actually already washed and styled it herself. Clelia was also a dear friend, so Marisa asked her to cover for her and got on a tram headed for Porta Maggiore. She was an hour early but tried knocking nonetheless: at first a hesitant rap with her knuckles, then a firmer tap.

Francesco came to the door. He was in his shirtsleeves, the first three buttons of his shirt undone and his cuffs rolled up. He greeted Marisa with no joy on his face. 'Come on in,' was all he said, stepping to one side. Paralysed with embarrassment, Marisa did not even have the instinct to stretch her arms for a hug.

They had already been in that apartment several times over the past two years, given that, before passing, Zia Costantina had been spending more time in the sanatorium than at home. They had been going there in secret to be together ever since the day Marisa had decided to yield to him: since they loved each other, she did not want him to go looking elsewhere for what she herself could give him. After the very first afternoon they'd spent in Costantina's ostentatious bedroom, Marisa had already known, with even more certainty than before, that Francesco Malpighi was the only man for her. Seeing him lie next to her, his eyes full of her, had made her dispense with any modesty, with any common sense. She had been happy there; and yet, on this Thursday evening, Marisa felt that the walls covered in amaranth and the furniture dressed up with knick-knacks oppressed her and made breathing more difficult.

Francesco pointed to the drinks trolley. 'Do you want a drop of something?'

As Marisa shook her head slowly, he motioned her to sit down. She did so without even realising, sitting on the high-backed sofa with golden trim and limp worn-out cushions that made her sink into it more than she expected. She was still wearing her coat and clutching the handles of her bag with both hands.

All of a sudden, that virile, slender figure that knew how to preserve its elegance even when working hard, that body which Marisa had known with all the senses nature had gifted her, became unfamiliar to her. Francesco was still standing, his posture stiff, his hands in his pockets, his distance deliberate. He was frowning; his face was turned towards her and yet he had not looked at her at all, not even when his eyes actually rested on her. Like a blind man, he was standing in front of her without seeing her. Or rather, without wanting to see her.

Instead of despair, surprisingly, Marisa felt a great calm rise inside. She had been readying herself for tears, for pleas. She had already understood how the whole thing was going to play out: she had known ever since the day of the call, there, in that phone box at the hotel. She had been gathering the strength she needed to face that moment as if it were a battle, but instead her heart had now calmed down, her breathing had relaxed and she was staring right into his face, waiting.

'I was planning on coming down in February to talk to you, Mimì,' Francesco said, spreading his elbows out a little, though without taking his hands out of his pockets.

Marisa listened patiently.

'So much has changed...' he continued. 'What can I say?' Marisa's silence and her still gaze fixed on him were starting to make him nervous. 'Time, distance... I always loved you, but things change.' His tone was slightly upset, as if he were answering questions Marisa had never asked. 'You must understand, Mimì!'

Marisa took a long, deep breath. 'This is your child too, though.' She spoke slowly, with no emphasis.

'I know, I know.' Francesco nodded vigorously, looking vaguely annoyed. He pulled his hands out of his pockets and waved his palms around, as if to signify his despair, to show it to her. 'I wanted to tell you in another way, at another time...'

'Tell me what?'

Without even the shadow of shame in his voice, Francesco confessed, 'I'm engaged to someone else, in Switzerland.'

Marisa let her astonishment show only through a tiny movement of her eyebrows.

'The proprietor's daughter. Do you understand what that means for someone like me?' Francesco's words had burst out of his lips. Leaning slightly over Marisa, he put his hands back into his pockets. 'The proprietor's daughter, Mimì!'

Marisa barely nodded. 'The proprietress...' she said, the corner of her lip bent in a bitter smile.

Silence fell between them, disturbed only by the ticking of the grandfather clock. All of a sudden Marisa felt the need to think about something else, and let her gaze wander towards the round side table. A fine white porcelain statuette towered on it, next to an empty crystal vase; the statuette portrayed a pretty yet melancholy lady swinging, though forever still, on a swing hanging from a blooming branch blanketed with a compact layer of dust. Marisa felt sorry for Zia Costantina, who perhaps, over many years, had had no other company than the banality of these ornaments. Never before, during her previous visits, had she sensed the solitude of old age oozing from these walls.

'And what about me, now? What should I do?' Marisa asked without looking at Francesco, her eyes fixed on the pretty lady. She saw that his hand was now coming out of his pocket, with hesitation.

'Here's the address of a trusted woman, in Garbatella. Go there next Thursday afternoon, at around two, and she'll tell you what to do.'

Marisa raised her eyes to the object he was handing to her with no embarrassment, almost brusquely. It was a cinema ticket, crumpled and folded in two, on which someone had jotted down an address in an unsteady hand Marisa had never seen before. She stared again at Francesco's face, as if to make sure that it was actually him, the man she had planned to spend the rest of her life with, the man she had laughed with in their intimacy, mouth against mouth, passion shaking them from the inside. She didn't move. Francesco reached forward to grab her wrist and forced the ticket into her palm. It was the first time he had touched her since she'd arrived. The roughness of this act made Marisa pull her arm back with a start as she stood up, the piece of paper falling to the floor.

'Mimì, you must understand,' Francesco said again, pleading petulantly as he bent down to pick it up.

'What must I understand?' Marisa whispered.

'You're ruining me!'

Marisa moved further away. 'Go back to Switzerland. I don't want a single thing from you.'

Francesco grabbed her by her arm, towering over her, his face darkened by a resentment that left Marisa more speechless than his words. 'Marisa, if this baby is born, everyone will know it's mine!'

Marisa freed herself from his grip with a resolute motion of her hand. 'Why, though? You might very well be a cuckold,' she provoked him, withstanding his gaze.

'Don't be silly!'

'Just like I slept with you, I could've also slept with anyone else, couldn't I?'

Anger streamed out of Francesco's body with a blast of air from his nostrils. 'Why are you not thinking?' he shouted. 'God! What do we stand to gain by this baby being born?'

Marisa wanted to slap him, but her strength failed her. She picked up the bag that she had set down on the sofa and headed for the door. Francesco held her back once more, pulled her towards himself and bent down to grab something from the pocket of his coat, which was draped over the armchair. Marisa tried to free herself from his grip but failed. This time, Francesco pushed into her hand a small cylinder that had been wrapped tightly in newsprint and sticky tape.

'They're Swiss francs, I didn't have the time to change them. There's a big bank in Largo Santa Susanna: they'll exchange them for you in no time.' Francesco waited a moment, then put the cinema ticket with the address into Marisa's pocket and added, almost reassuringly, 'It's a tidy sum. I've already paid the lady in Garbatella – this is for you.'

Marisa stared at the roll of notes. He had prepared it with

care, maybe to be discreet or so that it would not encumber him. Or maybe he had thought that, as a grocery shop cashier, she would prefer it that way. All of a sudden, she felt as if she were holding in her hand the boundless baseness of the man she had given everything to.

'You're a smart woman,' he whispered to her with renewed gentleness, slowly easing his grip on her arm, as if wanting to give her some time to recover her good judgement before letting her go.

Staring at Francesco, Marisa read in the dark rings under his eyes the stress he had been through over the past few days: his anguish, his sleep troubled by a cowardly fear, his nagging conscience. He had found no other defence from it all than to hone his spitefulness.

'If I'd been a smart woman, I wouldn't be here today,' Marisa said evenly. She slowly pulled the cinema ticket out of her pocket and laid it in his hand, almost delicately, together with the small cylinder of notes. She lingered with her fingers wrapped around his so that he too would have enough time to feel all the weight of his insignificance, there in his palm. She wanted to tell him to never show his face again, but she knew that there was no need.

Marisa turned her back on him and felt his eyes follow her as she opened the door to the apartment and walked out.

She left him there, in Zia Costantina's dusty home.

Marisa caught the tram back home. She was feeling weighed down by a tiredness the like of which she had never experienced before. She was sitting in a window seat, her eyes obstinately fixed on the road, since she could not bear even the thought of meeting someone else's gaze. Rather than desperation, it was shame that was making her feel annihilated. Not for what she had done: that child was the fruit of a love that had been genuine on her part. And not even for what would happen when the circumstances eventually forced her to confess to her parents what was going on. What she felt was shame for herself, for having let her naivety, her blind trust in a man she had understood nothing about, cast her into that operetta. There she was, Marisa Balestrieri, just like a heroine in a Raffaello Matarazzo melodrama, the kind of film she and her mother always enjoyed watching at the cinema. She thought back to all the times she had judged those silly, gullible girls with the scorn of a modern woman who did not get how one might not recognise such an obvious deception. 'How stupid,' she had commented time and time again, between scenes. 'How stupid,' she was now repeating to herself as the tram rattled homeward.

Though she was trying to recover some clarity of mind, Marisa could not even glimpse a solution that did not come paired with sorrow. Francesco had suggested his own solution, but what was right for him would be unacceptable to her. Morals had nothing to do with it: she did not want to get rid of this child, because she loved it already. She had started loving it as soon as she had first suspected its existence and her love had not wavered for a single moment, not even now that the feelings that had connected her to its father were crumbling apart. She felt like a city shelled during wartime: on the surface there was only destruction, but a cherished life was sheltering in her womb like a treasure. All that uncertainty was wearing her down, though. What could she expect from her parents? How could she face the disappointment in her father's eyes, her father who endlessly praised her to his customers, full of pride? Marisa felt capable of withstanding her mother's screeches, her tears and her accusations. But Ettore Balestrieri's sorrow, no: the mere idea made the ground give way under her feet.

Perhaps to postpone having to meet her parents' gaze, even if just for a short while, she got off the tram two stops before hers and, walking briskly, went to find some comfort in the embrace of her dearest friend, Maria Elena Frau. While her friend's husband listened to the news on the wireless in the dining room, Marisa whispered everything to Maria Elena as they sat in her kitchen and they both wept over the misfortune that had befallen Marisa. Maria Elena supportively poured a stream of curses at Malpighi, whom, to be quite frank, she had never really liked, and promised to always remain by Marisa's side. She did not judge her, Maria Elena repeated over and over, and Marisa could count on her for anything.

To avoid being too late for dinner, Marisa stayed at Maria Elena's only for half an hour, then she walked the rest of the way home. When Marisa got in, her mother was so incensed over her tardiness that she did not even notice that her daughter's hair was not set. Letizia scolded Marisa harshly, while she mumbled one excuse or another: having them wait around for her without even letting them know that she was running late was simply disrespectful. Then she left her to have her dinner on her own, since they had already eaten. As Marisa forced herself to swallow a few spoonfuls of cold, overcooked pasta in a clear broth, her father poked his head through the door, unbeknownst to Letizia.

'Is something the matter with you?' Ettore asked softly, with solicitude.

'Of course not . . .' Marisa said with a smile. 'I popped into Maria Elena's for a chat and lost track of time.'

Ettore nodded, then disappeared again.

Meanwhile, on the Fraus' telephone, Maria Elena was recounting to her sister Ivana, who lived right opposite the Balestrieris, the tragedy that had struck poor Marisa – in strictest confidence, of course, and merely to soothe her own uneasiness. On whether Marisa had been asking for it or not, they were both in agreement: as a matter of fact, before meeting Marisa, Francesco Malpighi had had a reputation as a womaniser and one struggled to believe that a smart girl like her had failed to take this information into account. After all, being pretty and coming from a respectable family did not necessarily translate into preferential treatment. Before hanging up, they both sighed in unison to signify how certain consequences were inevitable, when a woman became too uninhibited. Less than twenty-four hours later, Marisa, the grocer's daughter, had officially become a notorious woman.

The following day, the Balestrieris gathered at Emma's for the traditional Epiphany meal. Marisa decided to say nothing for the moment so that her parents might at least enjoy what was left of the holidays. God only knew when they would be able to gather in peace around a table again, after the trouble she had got herself into. Marisa also decided not to worry too much and instead poured all her affection on to her nephew. It was already becoming natural to her to behave as if she had a new-found intimacy with babies, as if an ancestral wisdom was rising from within her as she sat him comfortably in his high chair so that he could not hurt himself. Marisa was already talking more gently to him as she stroked his velvety skin, smiling as if she was feeling an imminent joy and even wondering if she too would have a boy. Marisa was determined not to devote even a fleeting thought to Francesco Malpighi: she was certain that she could easily excise him from her head and yet, from time to time, a pain that was almost physical and pulsated in her chest threatened to thaw into inconsolable tears that she could hardly hold back.

Because of the effort of displaying a cheerfulness she was not feeling, the next day Marisa woke up tired and depressed after only a few hours of light sleep that had been unsettled by nightmares. She went down to the shop earlier than usual and got to work, looking for a distraction. Having finished arranging the items on the shelves quite ahead of opening time, she sat at the till to flick through a magazine while her father, whistling happily, put away the bread.

'Are you well, Miss Balestrieri?'

Marisa was startled: those words that were not the usual 'good morning' and 'thank you' sounded as if they had been uttered by a stranger. She raised her eyes to see Stelvio Ansaldo, who had put down his delivery note next to the till and was looking at her with a certain concern in his dark eyes.

Marisa's instinct was to cut the matter short with a dry, 'Of course,' perhaps even sounding a bit surprised. And yet, for some reason, she ended up saying something else. 'Yes, I'm well, just tired. I had the flu.'

'So I heard, from Signor Balestrieri,' Stelvio said, nodding twice, to signify that he had been enquiring about her health.

Marisa signed his delivery note and returned it to him with a faint but polite smile.

Stelvio put the delivery note away carefully, a bit more slowly than usual, then took his leave with a 'Thank you' and a 'See you tomorrow' that Marisa reciprocated half-heartedly as she went back to her magazine.

At around one, just before closing time, Marisa went upstairs to bring in the bread and help her mother set the table as usual. This time, however, rather than finding her mother busy in the kitchen, Marisa saw that Letizia was sitting at the head of the dining table, her arms resting on its surface and her hands clasped, as if absorbed in prayer. No smell was coming from the kitchen, no impatient gurgling of pans. Letizia was still wearing the suit and high-heeled shoes she had put on to go grocery shopping.

Marisa stopped on the threshold, holding the quarter loaf wrapped in paper tight against her chest.

Her mother slowly looked away from the floral Capodimonte porcelain centrepiece that lay on the table and fixed her gaze on Marisa, with no expression on her face.

Marisa held her breath.

Letizia moved her lips almost imperceptibly. 'What have you done?' It was hard to glean the emotion conveyed by her mother's forcedly low tone. More than astonishment, what was seeping through was wrath caged in frost.

'I was going to tell you tonight ...' Marisa said evenly, withstanding Letizia's gaze.

'Who did you tell?'

'Only Maria Elena,' Marisa rushed to say.

'And don't you know that she and her sister are terrible

gossips?' Letizia barely raised her tone, as she shook her head in disbelief. 'Are you that stupid?'

Marisa could only lower her eyes. There was no need to answer.

'I had to hear it from that woman, the wine-seller ...' Letizia rested her forehead on her palm, her elbow on the table. 'Every man and his dog have heard about it.'

Marisa walked into the room, set the quarter loaf down on the table, and laid her hands on the back of the chair. Only a few days earlier, her friend's betrayal would have broken her heart, but now the disappointment had drained her of all energy, including the strength she needed to feel anger.

'You've always been brazen ...' Letizia muttered in a whisper, almost as if talking to herself. 'Impudent ...' She paused, then added in a stifled voice, 'But not this! Not this!'

'I was in love with Francesco!' That bitter excuse was all Marisa could come up with.

'What will happen now?' her mother pressed on, as if Marisa had not even opened her mouth. 'What will you do now?'

Since she was brazen, Marisa Balestrieri could find no answer but a smile that bore a faint trace of astonishment. The question sounded like a provocation to her: certainly her mother must have known full well that those exact words had been throbbing in her head over the last two days. 'I don't know,' she said with a shrug, shaking her head a little.

'Ah, you don't know ...' Letizia parroted her. 'And didn't you think about the fact that you come from a respectable family, when you were doing your business with Malpighi?'

Marisa unbuttoned her coat slowly and took it off. 'No,' she said as she went to place it on the coat hanger in the hallway. She did not add another word. She simply headed to her room and shut the door behind her.

At first, Marisa sat for a while on the edge of her bed. She had not been expecting any sympathy from her mother. Letizia was like that: rigid and intransigent with herself and others, especially when it came to matters of decency. Marisa had always been puzzled by the fact that Letizia's marriage to Ettore had been born out of a mutual love that had not been affected by time. Ettore Balestrieri was a good-natured man, jovial and outgoing. Letizia, on the other hand, was reserved, closed-off and concerned with appearances. Had Emma been born only a few months earlier, Marisa would have bet that her parents had had a shotgun wedding. But no, they had met through a mutual friend, they had liked each other and they had fallen in love. They balanced each other out: Ettore smoothed over his wife's fastidiousness with his measured lightness, and she reciprocated by granting indulgence to him for manners that she found unacceptable in anyone else. Not infrequently, Marisa would hear them laugh from the other side of her bedroom wall, when they were alone in their room. Then, immediately afterwards, her mother's barely audible voice would feign vexation and order him to be quiet, while her father's laughter became even deeper.

Marisa knew that her mother would never forgive her. Emma, perhaps, might eventually understand and maybe even help her, but there were certainly hard times ahead.

She stood up and instinctively started collecting a few of her things. It did not seem so unlikely to her that, now the whole neighbourhood knew, Letizia might ask her to go somewhere else. After all, Letizia herself could go back to looking after the till in the shop.

Marisa was intent on selecting the items she might need from her underwear drawer when her father opened the door without knocking.

'Come to the other room,' he said. His tone was flat, impossible to read. However, it was certainly missing his usual tenderness when he addressed Marisa. Then he disappeared without waiting for her.

Marisa followed him unhurriedly.

Her parents were at the dining table: her mother was still sitting at its head, which was unusual, while her father was sitting to her right, a glass of water half-full in front of him that his wife had perhaps fetched out of concern that the news might prove to be too big a shock for him. Letizia was always complaining that Ettore needed to lose some weight or he risked a heart attack. Nonetheless, she did not really want to change anything at all about her husband, and always felt like the luckiest woman in the world.

'Sit down,' Ettore ordered with a slight motion of his forefinger without lifting his hand from the table.

Marisa sat in front of him. Her mother was still staring at the centrepiece, sending Marisa a clear message: had it been up to her, Marisa would not be sitting at her table.

Ettore drank a sip of his water. Obviously, not out of actual thirst: he was only playing for time. He put the glass down and clasped his hands, assuming the same pose as Letizia, then rapped the tips of his thumbs one against the other.

'You need to tell me if you still want to marry Malpighi.'

Marisa was caught off guard. She hesitated and instinctively glanced at her mother, as if looking for help, for a hint. Letizia was sitting as rigid as a statue. 'But, Papà, Francesco broke up with me,' Marisa said in a whisper.

'That is not what I asked. What I asked is whether you want to marry him.'

'He has someone else, in Switzerland.'

Ettore took another sip of his water. 'Marisa, if you tell me now that you want to marry him, I'll take your grandad's hunting rifle from the other room, get on a train for Switzerland tonight and deliver him to you tomorrow. Dead or alive, as the case might be ...' Ettore cast an expressive glance towards Marisa in which she saw, once again, the tenderness of a father who at that moment could not allow himself to be weak and yet also wanted her to know that he loved her. Despite everything. Ettore did not care about shame; perhaps he did not even know it at all. Perhaps all he cared about was his daughter.

'No, Papà.' This time Marisa spoke with no hesitation. 'I don't want to see Francesco ever again.'

Letizia scoffed nervously, staring at her husband in disbelief.

'Then we need to find another solution,' Ettore said.

'And what kind of solution do you expect to find?' Letizia burst out.

Ettore took a deep breath to steady his patience, which his wife continuously put to the test. He leaned back on his chair, crossed his arms over his bulging stomach and then spoke evenly but firmly, in a tone that Marisa had never heard before. 'Marisa, things are changing, but a bastard child will always lead a wretched life.'

Marisa lowered her eyes, hurt by that harshness which put her in front of an undeniable truth.

They all remained quiet for a moment, though the pause felt never-ending.

'Maybe she could go to Grottaferrata? Surely Emanuele won't say no,' Letizia suggested after some time, staring hopefully at her husband.

'But why? Are you worried about her belly?' Ettore asked, annoyed.

'She can give birth there ... There are nuns, in Rocca di Papa ...'

Marisa was startled and stood up abruptly. 'I'm not giving my child away to the nuns!' she shouted. The chair wobbled and fell backwards with a thud as Marisa leaned forward towards her father, her palms on the table. 'This is my child and I'm keeping it!'

Letizia too stood up. In her heels, she was taller than Marisa by half a head. 'And what kind of life will it have, with people talking behind its back, eh?'

'I couldn't care less about *people*!'

'You couldn't care less about anyone!'

'Sit down or I'll throw the both of you out of the house!' Ettore thundered, slamming his hand hard on the table, his eyes fixed on both of them.

Marisa picked up her chair. They both sat back down, hushed.

Ettore gulped down what was left of his water; if it had instead been a nice glass of Sangiovese, his mood would be much less bleak. He had never paid any mind to the fact that they had never had a son. All that worrying about carrying on the family name made him laugh: had he been a Savoy, perhaps there would have been some reason to be concerned, but who could possibly care whether there was one Balestrieri more or less on the face of the earth? He was a little sad that there was no one he could leave his business to, of course. Before Marisa met Malpighi, he had hoped for a son-in-law who might fall in love with his shop just as he had. People even came to his shop from far away; they knew that Ettore only had premium delicacies. He had a practised eye, only chose the best for his customers and knew how to make good deals with vendors, which meant that his prices were always reasonable. Even as far as Porta San Giovanni, everyone knew who Ettore was. His first name was enough, no need to say 'Balestrieri'. And yet, in that moment, he missed not having a son sitting next to him, someone with whom he could talk it through without falling prey to womanly vexation. Someone who would not insist on trying to blow against a gale. Someone who only cared for Marisa and the baby she was carrying, who was still a Balestrieri, after all.

As he fiddled with the empty glass in his hands, a thought pushed to the front of his mind, a thought that would change his daughter's life for ever and, in a way, his too.

'Stelvio Ansaldo,' he said aloud, convinced that he had not spoken at all.

The two women instinctively looked at each other to check whether at least one of them knew what he was talking about. They found only the same look of astonishment on each other's faces.

Letizia was seized by a sense of anxiety, fearing that the

news might have caused a sudden dementia in Ettore. 'Who is this Ansaldo?'

'The delivery boy from Camastra,' Marisa hurried to explain, frowning.

'And what has he got to do with all this?' Letizia asked, starting to lose her patience.

Ettore again raised his eyes to his daughter and, still half-lost in his thoughts, said, 'The owner of the Camastra bakery told me that her nephew, Ruggero, hasn't had much luck up north. He's not happy and wants his old job back.' He paused briefly, then added, 'She said that she's sorry to have to let Stelvio go because he's a good worker, but she can't say no to her nephew and so she's asked me to help her find another position for the young man.'

'So?' The more Letizia heard, the less she could make any sense of it.

Marisa, however, was starting to get the gist of it.

'I've been thinking about getting some help for a while,' Ettore continued, 'maybe part-time, and I was thinking about Stelvio. He's capable, honest, polite and hardworking.'

'But I don't want Stelvio Ansaldo!' Marisa cried out in horror.

Letizia was startled. 'Are you really talking about giving your daughter to the errand boy?' Had Letizia not been afraid that the neighbours might hear her, she would have screamed.

Ettore opened his arms. 'She gave herself to a scoundrel and now she can't give herself to the errand boy?'

His wife covered her mouth with her hand. 'You're crazy!'

'You two find another solution, then,' he replied, opening his arms as if beckoning guests to partake in a banquet. 'The fact that your daughter is pregnant is now known as far as Via Merulana, you've said so yourself. What do you think? That young men will be queuing up to marry her now?'

Marisa finally gave way to exasperated tears, her elbows on the table and her fingers clutching her hair.

'But who is this ... Ansaldo?' All of a sudden, Letizia seemed somewhat less ill-disposed to the idea, as she cautiously made her enquiry. 'Do you know his family?'

'What family? When his parents were evacuated after the San Lorenzo bombing, they settled in the shacks by the Felice aqueduct. However, within two years they were both dead. The priests took Stelvio in for a couple of years – he was just a kid – then found him a job and put him out. He rents a room from some acquaintances of the Camastras.'

'Lord,' Letizia muttered. But the invocation that had come to her lips was not compassion for Stelvio Ansaldo's misfortunes.

Ettore stood up, his chair screeching noisily on the marble floor. He looked at his daughter, who was crying, shaken by sobs, her head bent.

'That boy is sweet on you,' he told her. 'You never noticed because he's a respectful young man. As a father, I pretended not to notice either, since he's always been polite. After all, it's not his fault you're so beautiful,' Ettore said with an expressive sigh. 'I don't see any other solution,' he said conclusively. 'And now I'm going to bed to rest. You two have killed my appetite.'

Over the following hours, and through the following night, Marisa did not even take into consideration the solution that her father had suggested. She was struggling even to believe that he had actually uttered those words. Rather, she thought it absurd that he, who was so loyal and honest, could indeed consider stooping to that kind of scheming. And yet, her father's silence during the afternoon, and over dinner, had been more than eloquent. He really did not see any other solution.

Her mother was not looking at her or talking to her. She had closed the shutters in every room, feeling pursued by gossip even within the walls of her own home. The wireless, which usually brought them together for an hour or so after dinner, stayed silent. Everyone was facing dejection in their own way, and the air was so heavy that even breathing felt hard.

Marisa tossed and turned in her bed, unable to fall asleep. She was pondering how she might make a new life for herself and her child without crushing her family under the weight of her shame. She could go far away and find a job, but the thought of leaving her loved ones behind broke her heart. Moreover, she knew that a fatherless child would be followed by shame wherever she might go. 'What have I done? What have I done?' As she repeated this question over and over to herself, her anger and desperation were so overpowering that she could have ripped her pillow to shreds.

All of a sudden, Marisa started yearning for the happy years of her childhood and adolescence, which were now gone for ever. She could almost hear her mother calling out as she leaned out of the window and peered into the street to search for her daughters. Letizia used to call them in to help with dinner before their father got home from the shop. As soon as they heard her call, Emma would immediately interrupt her chit-chat with her friends in the entrance hall, while Marisa would stop her heated games of hopscotch or rope-skipping. Before they had even had the time to say goodbye to their friends, their mother's voice would echo again, impatient, quickly followed by their feet shuffling up the stairs. Family dinners had almost always stayed the same, even during the war. Nothing ever changed, apart from them. Emma and Marisa had grown up, their parents had grown old, and yet it felt as if no one had really realised it until Emma's wedding. On the first evening, Emma's empty chair had stirred up emotions in all of them. Her mother had kept her eyes low and her father had poured himself another glass of wine to help put to bed the melancholy and sorrow he was feeling over the years that were passing by and taking from him all that he held dear. It had been around that time that Marisa had started to dream of creating a family like her own, with happy times punctuated by dinners together, cheerful day trips and a summer holiday at the beach after a long year of hard work. And when Marisa's endless night eventually surrendered to the first light of dawn, rather than weeping with despair over her broken dream, she ended up weeping out of a childlike sadness.

On Sunday morning, Marisa had just fallen into a restless half-sleep when her mother walked into her room holding a small tray with a milky coffee and biscuits, put it down on the bedside table and sat on the edge of the bed, without even pretending to wish Marisa good morning. She was still wearing her dressing gown but had already combed her hair with great care; untidiness bothered her. She was the daughter of hoteliers who had been bankrupted by the First World War when she was a teenager and she did not like to have anything around her that might remind her of the poverty she had had to endure. To tease her, Ettore often said that she had only married the grocer to make sure she would never go hungry again. However, when it was just the two of them, Letizia always told her husband that she would have married him even if he had had not a single penny to his name. As long as she was with him, she needed nothing else.

'What's wrong with this Ansaldo?' Letizia said brusquely, without looking at Marisa.

Marisa tried to shake sleepiness off as she looked for an answer. She could think of many, but none was right.

'Is he ugly?' Letizia pressed her on. 'A boor?'

As she sat up, Marisa ran her fingers through her dishevelled hair and pulled it back from her pale face, showing dark rings under her eyes. 'No ...' She shrugged a little. 'I don't know ... I don't know him from Adam.'

'Your father says he's polite,' Letizia reminded Marisa.

'Yes,' Marisa agreed, after a moment of hesitation. 'He looks like a decent man.'

'So? What's wrong with him? Is he short? Fat? Crippled?'

'Of course not!' Marisa burst out, exasperated. 'He's a normal man, like many others. Nothing special.'

Letizia took a deep breath and finally looked at Marisa; her expression was serious but this time it showed less indifference, almost as if she was trying to restore some form of complicity between mother and daughter. 'Then you have to make do with him, Marisa.'

Marisa let a groan escape her lips. 'Ansaldo? Do you think it's easy? What do you want me to do? Should I just walk up to him and tell him that I got myself into trouble, that I'm expecting someone else's child and that I need a husband?'

'You have to find a way.' Letizia's tone had grown icy once again. 'You heard your father: the boy's sweet on you. After all, you've already had your practice with Malpighi, haven't you?'

Marisa hung her head under the weight of humiliation, which hurt more coming from her own mother. She held back her tears: she knew that tears would irk her mother rather than move her to compassion. Letizia had always been strict, and Marisa had never expected any sympathy from her on that subject. Letizia had raised her daughters to know that she abhorred gossip and would not countenance any taint on the manners and good name of the Balestrieris. She had accepted the rumpus over Emma's engagement only because Emanuele was an upright man who had made a choice out of love that was in keeping with her principles. And indeed nobody in the neighbourhood had dared to utter a single uncalled-for word about the Balestrieris at the time. The fact that Emanuele was Jewish was of little consequence; Emma would live in comfort, since he had already inherited most of his fortune from his paternal grandfather, who had died in America.

'Have you never made a mistake?' Marisa muttered, unable to raise her eyes.

Letizia unwittingly pulled a bitter grimace, adjusted the hem of her dressing gown, which had fallen off her knee, and slowly smoothed the fabric against her thigh with her hand. She trained her eyes on her daughter and said with a deep sigh, 'I clearly have,' then she stood up and left the room without uttering another word.

*

On Monday, as he took the bread delivery from Camastra, Ettore Balestrieri called Stelvio Ansaldo to one side and offered him a full-time job. Having already heard of the predicament the owners of the bakery had found themselves in because of Ruggero's return, Stelvio accepted with the utmost gratitude, energetically shaking Ettore's hand, as happy as ever. He promised that he would do his very best and learn fast; he was not scared of hard work. As a sign of appreciation, Ettore clapped Stelvio on the shoulder, clasping the threadbare jacket that he wore above his overalls. 'Of course, of course ...' he muttered, feeling a touch of contempt for himself. His love for his daughter did not excuse the fact that he was trying to save her honour at this young man's expense.

From behind the till, Marisa had followed the entire scene, ill at ease. She was pretending to count some coins but kept losing track and had to start over. She noticed with relief that Ansaldo was not short – quite the reverse: he was maybe even half a head taller than her father. Of course, he was a bit awkward, but his features were not unpleasant. He had beautiful, expressive eyes. Maybe his nose was a touch big, yes, but a smaller one would have looked misplaced on a face as wide as his.

All of a sudden, she realised that she had gone from dreaming about Gran Caffè Malpighi to trying to secure a husband, any husband, as if at the horse fair, and her eyes filled with tears. Not out of disappointment: she was merely disgusted by the haughtiness with which she was daring to judge that poor soul.

At that moment, Stelvio turned towards her, as if to include her in his enthusiasm. However, when he noticed that she was close to tears, his smile died on his lips.

'Are you still feeling unwell, signorina?' he said, stepping closer to the till, though not too close.

'I'm just feeling a bit poorly,' she said, playing it down.

Stelvio stared at her apprehensively. 'You're very pale,' he said, glancing at Ettore to check whether he could see it too.

Ettore nodded vigorously. 'See? She doesn't eat enough! The doctor said she needs vitamins to perk up a bit. This flu ...' Ettore started heading to his place behind the counter, then stopped halfway, smiling as if he had suddenly had a great idea, and said, 'Listen, Stelvio, why don't you take my poor daughter to have a hot milky coffee, with lots of sugar? There, at the dairy on the corner ...' He pointed in that direction.

Marisa was startled, her eyes huge. Embarrassed, Stelvio opened his arms, turning crimson. 'Well ... I wouldn't want to impose,' he mumbled.

Ettore retraced his steps decisively and went to get his daughter by the arm from behind the till, escorting her to Stelvio's side. 'Get her something to drink and have something for yourself too, and tell Berardo to put it on my tab: you're my guest!' Ettore ordered, pushing them out of the door, his hands on their backs. 'In the meantime, I'll ring Camastra and let them know that, due to my mistake, the next delivery will be delayed by ten minutes.'

As soon as they were out on the pavement, Stelvio Ansaldo turned around quickly. 'Her coat, Signor Balestrieri! You don't want this poor girl to freeze to death!' In the meantime, he had instinctively, and delicately, put his arm around her shoulders to protect her from the cold January wind.

Ettore stood for a moment on the threshold, as if in a daze, looking at them. Then he rushed to get his daughter's coat and Stelvio quickly helped her put it on.

As they walked off, headed for Berardo's dairy, Ettore Balestrieri followed them with his eyes. He was smiling.

Marisa knew very well why Berardo's wife was staring at her shamelessly as she sat at the table beside Stelvio Ansaldo.

They had ordered two milky coffees and Stelvio had insisted she should also eat a jam-filled brioche. They were not speaking, feeling ill at ease, and their heads were hanging down towards their drinks. Marisa was grateful that the dairy was still empty: she could not have endured any more eyes on her.

'Are you upset that your father hired me in the shop?' Stelvio asked, out of the blue.

'Why should I be?'

'I don't know – maybe you were hoping Signor Balestrieri would offer the position to your fiancé.'

When she pictured Francesco wearing an apron behind the counter as he sliced prosciutto, Marisa could only half-suppress a laugh, though she did not know whether it was out of nerves or amusement. She sighed softly. 'I don't have a fiancé. Not any more.'

Stelvio raised his eyes and she did the same. 'Is this why you've been unwell?'

Marisa noticed that, in his tone, there was no hint of morbid curiosity, just a sincere solicitude. 'Yes, that too,' she admitted.

'I'm sorry to hear that,' he said in a voice that was suddenly steady and warm.

'It happens.'

'But one wishes for it to never happen, isn't that right?'

'It is,' she said with a sad smile, nodding as she sipped her milky coffee, warming her hands on the glass. She nibbled at her brioche, then pointed at the small dish. 'Would you like some?'

'You should eat it up, you need to recover your strength,' Stelvio said, smiling at her.

Marisa noticed that his teeth were straight and white. 'Why are you called Stelvio?' she asked, not even knowing why, and realising only too late that her tone certainly did not show any appreciation for that unusual name.

'My dad was in the war. When they were fighting up in the mountains in 1918, sheltering in a cave on the Stelvio Pass saved him from freezing to death one night. As he was shaking with cold, he promised the Virgin Mary that, should he survive the war, he would call his first son Stelvio.' He paused for a moment; speaking about his father still made his voice crack. 'He kept his promise.'

Marisa tilted her head slightly to one side. 'What a lovely story ...' she whispered with a hint of sincere emotion in her voice.

'Well, then typhus got him when we were living in the shacks by the aqueduct,' Stelvio concluded, shrugging a little.

'I'm sorry.' Marisa put her hand on his. It happened suddenly and spontaneously. Stelvio smiled at her, appreciating her closeness, though they were all but strangers to each other.

'Now I really need to go.' Marisa stood up, wanting to escape the uneasiness that Berardo's wife's importunate stares were causing in her. 'The shop will be opening soon.'

'Are you feeling a bit better?'

Marisa paused for a second before answering. 'Yes,' she said, nodding sincerely.

Stelvio asked her to wait just a moment while he paid the bill. After he walked her back to the door of the shop, they wished each other a nice day without adding anything else. Then Stelvio and Ettore exchanged a quick wave through the window.

The following morning, Marisa and her father found Stelvio in front of the shop, freezing. He said that he lived a long way away and had been worried about being late, since the bus stop was far from his lodging. They let him in and, as solemnly as if he were being knighted, Ettore gave Stelvio some overalls, old but still in good nick, which he used to wear thirty kilos ago, and an apron. Ettore told Stelvio that Marisa would take care of the laundry and that he would need a fresh apron every morning, no ifs or buts. The following day, Stelvio would find a clean apron pressed and ready for him. Stelvio cast an apologetic glance towards Marisa, for adding to her chores, and then settled in nicely.

Ettore had Stelvio follow him around all morning like a shadow. He started from the basics, explaining to him that eyes, nose and touch were the most important tools of the trade. He warned him that it would take time, that in a grocery shop the only way to learn was by doing. Without missing a single word, Stelvio nodded, moved: after his parents' death, Signor Balestrieri was the first to teach him like a father. Stelvio had learned some notions about carpentry and fruit and vegetables from the priests, and he had worked for a long time loading and unloading crates at the wholesale market, since he was strong, but here, in the Balestrieris' shop, things were quite different. The tidiness, the neatness, the pleasant smells of fresh food, the items that Signorina Balestrieri arranged in the window and on the shelves with womanly care, her attention to colours, the boxes all facing the same direction, the prices written with beautiful penmanship. And Signorina Balestrieri herself, there on the right, smelling of roses.

When they were about to close for the afternoon, Ettore insisted that Stelvio must come upstairs and have his lunch with them. Stelvio objected, embarrassed, saying that there was no need for that, he could grab a bite anywhere, but Ettore would not take no for an answer. Marisa was sent to tell Letizia that she should add another place setting and, at a quarter past one on the dot, they were all sitting around the table at the Balestrieris'. The women were quiet, their eyes low on their plates, while Ettore was cheerful and talkative. He told Stelvio about the time his first employer – one Peppe Carpi – had hired him at the age of eight to work as an errand boy at the delicatessen in San Giovanni but then almost immediately had put him behind the counter, on a raised platform since he was so little. He had toiled fifteen hours a day, back-breaking work, and almost lost a finger once or twice. Yet by eighteen he'd already had his own shop, with customers forming an orderly queue and patiently waiting outside the door because they did not want to shop anywhere else. Ettore showed him, with pride, the forefinger of his left hand, which was lumpy, deeply scarred and also slightly wonky, proclaiming that he had poured his entire life into his shop. And had it not been for the two wars he would now own ten shops. He had almost died at the front during the first war, with a bullet in the back. And during the second war he had lost most of what he had built over nearly thirty years of sacrifice. Nonetheless, he was still standing, as firm as a rock.

Stelvio looked at him full of admiration, then, with his characteristic touch of shyness, complimented Letizia for the excellent meal. She mumbled a thank you with a slight wave of her hand that made her look annoyed rather than pleased.

Two days later, when Ruggero came to deliver Camastra's bread, Stelvio Ansaldo already looked as though he had been born and raised in the shop. He took the baskets of bread and emptied them behind the counter, complaining that the delivery was short by at least half a kilo of ciriola rolls. Ruggero had to double-check the weight and amend it on the delivery note. Then, unprompted, Stelvio cleaned a prosciutto bone to perfection while keeping in mind Ettore's instructions. It was for this reason that, at around nine in the morning, Ettore Balestrieri did something that he had never done before in forty-five years on the job: while the shop was open, he took his apron off and treated himself to an espresso at Berardo's. Stelvio, swelling with pride, watched him leave right as Signora Cavani walked in for her Thursday shop, the day when her son came over for dinner.

'Stelvio, this is an extra-special customer! I leave her in your hands!' Ettore told him, waving ceremoniously at Signora Cavani.

Stelvio nodded, politely wished her good morning and smiled warmly.

Marisa observed with surprise her father leaving the shop,

pleased with himself, his hands in the pockets of his overalls. Then her eyes fell on Stelvio Ansaldo and she let out a deep sigh.

Over the following two weeks, while looking for cheap accommodation close to the shop, Stelvio became a regular fixture at the Balestrieris' come lunchtime. After lunch, Ettore would go to rest in his room for an hour while Letizia and Marisa tidied up, and Stelvio, at Ettore's insistence, would settle down in the armchair to read the newspaper. Stelvio always felt embarrassed accepting all that kindness, since he had noticed that Signora Balestrieri was not too pleased to have him around. However, declining Signor Balestrieri's invitation would be too rude, so he always tried to be as little bother as possible. He would sit quietly in the armchair and sometimes he was so tired from his early mornings that he even nodded off. At half-past three on the dot, Ettore would reappear in the dining room, sit in the other armchair and wait for his wife to bring him his coffee. Much to his joy, Stelvio's own coffee was always delivered by Marisa, which at times made him wonder whether he was still dreaming.

One evening in late January, while Marisa was putting away her underwear in her drawers, her mother walked into the room and closed the door behind her. By this point they were barely talking to each other. Stelvio's presence at lunchtime explained why they did not feel that they could chat freely. However, they also chose to keep quiet at dinner, since every word weighed heavily on them. The Balestrieris had not shown their faces at Mass on Sundays, nor had they been to see Emma, who had been informed of the whole thing by

Letizia but had not been in touch with her sister. Marisa was terribly hurt by this: she would never have thought that her sister would add to her abandonment. Letizia and Emma, on the other hand, had been talking on the phone every day, for long spells at a time, and those conversations had resulted in the decision that Letizia was just about to relay to Marisa.

'Listen,' she said, 'I don't think you're making any progress here and you're almost out of time.'

Marisa continued to put away her silk slips, carefully.

'Your father has brought Ansaldo into the house for you. What else must he do?'

Since her daughter's gaze kept escaping hers, Letizia placed her elbow on the chest of drawers and leaned towards Marisa. 'I don't think you understand ... You have to sort this thing out!'

'But how?' Marisa burst out.

'You could have encouraged him to ask you out on a date, given him hope somehow,' Letizia scolded, her voice choking with resentment.

'He's a decent man!' Marisa protested.

'So? You don't want him?'

'Why should I ruin his life?'

'Ruin his life?' Letizia chuckled in exasperation. 'He's a beggar! Your father is giving him a trade, respectability.'

'And a bastard child!' Marisa raised her eyes and looked at her mother challengingly. 'How would you like it if a woman did that to a son of yours?'

Letizia suppressed her wrath in a deep breath, which rattled in her throat, then shut the drawer abruptly, almost catching Marisa's fingers in it. 'Now you listen to me,' she said, staring at Marisa, then continuing in a whisper. 'I told Stelvio that on Sunday afternoon I need him to take me to Grottaferrata to get the fabric I need to reupholster the sofa. We've agreed we'll take your father's van. Emma knows everything; the villa is empty and she is even going to send the custodian away until Monday.' Letizia paused eloquently. 'At the last minute, I'll say I'm not feeling well and you'll go with him.'

Marisa held her breath, her lips slightly open in disbelief.

'Do what you need to do, find a way, but you need to come back from Grottaferrata engaged,' her mother said, enunciating the last word. 'Understood?'

'So now you no longer care about gossip?'

'People are already saying that Francesco Malpighi found out that he was a cuckold and that you were carrying on with Ansaldo, which is why he broke up with you,' Letizia replied, nodding with satisfaction. Then, sneering at Marisa as she left the room, she concluded, 'You're in luck.'

Sunday turned out to be an extremely cold day, but so bright that it was almost painful to the eyes. The sky was clear and the few clouds were immediately chased away by the icy wind. Marisa got dressed without putting much care into it, lost in thought. However, she wrapped up warmly, since it was certainly going to be colder in Grottaferrata than in Rome. She had eaten little and reluctantly at lunch and her head was aching. Rather than putting on weight because of her pregnancy, she was losing it. She was lucky: she was not showing yet, just a little roundness of the abdomen, soft, that could have always been there. Her breasts, however, were fuller – almost heavier, she would have said – though this too was not noticeable.

She had wondered for a long time what she would do, on that Sunday afternoon; how she would get Stelvio to take her back home with a marriage proposal in her pocket. She had found no answers: she was a woman of feelings and this, instead, was a matter of rationality. She would need to discover Stelvio's weaknesses and think of a word, an act of seduction. However, with men she had always been unaffected, even brazen, just as her mother had said: even before Francesco, when she wanted to be courted by someone she had always made it known, with no ploys and no hypocrisies. She had won Francesco over with the most beautiful smile she could muster and the most feminine comportment she was capable of, and she had managed to convey to him that she desired him with her eyes, setting all pretence of modesty aside. But Stelvio? She felt no passion for that young man. She thought highly of him, of course, he was polite and honest, and yet that was not enough.

Nonetheless, when she heard the horn of her father's van honk twice in the street, she put on a touch of lipstick and told herself that it would have to do.

When Marisa told Stelvio that her mother was not feeling well and that she would go in her place, he seemed genuinely sorry for Letizia. As Marisa was getting into her father's cream Fiat 615, he looked at her with a strange expression on his face and reassured her that the whole trip would not take long, a couple of hours at most. Marisa had the impression that he was apologising for the time she would have to waste in his company and suddenly felt sorry for the indifference with which she had met his considerateness over the last few weeks. She wanted to find something kind to say to him, to show him that the prospect of spending the afternoon with him was actually welcome to her, but she kept quiet, her eyes fixed out of the window as they turned into Via Tuscolana. When they were more or less halfway there, to soften the embarrassment of the prolonged silence, Marisa asked Stelvio if he had ever been to Grottaferrata. He knew Grottaferrata well, he said. He had some good friends in and around the Castelli Romani and when the weather was nice he sometimes got on his old Vespa and rode all the way out there, just to have a glass of wine in good company. He smiled as he spoke about his friends; since he no longer had any parents or siblings, they were the only family he had left.

'Why? Did you used to have siblings?' Marisa asked, curious.

'One brother, younger than me. He died in the San Lorenzo bombing,' Stelvio said, his smile slowly turning from cheerfulness to a sad tenderness at the recollection of that little kid who used to follow him around on his skinny legs wherever he went.

For a moment they fell into a bitter silence, interrupted only by the dull roar of the engine, which was travelling at a constant speed.

Before they arrived, Marisa sang the praises of the villa on the slopes of Monte Tuscolo. She told him that Emanuele had inherited it from his paternal grandparents, who had left no stone unturned to save the family and that beautiful house from the calamity of Fascism. It offered all comforts and many rooms, paintings and statues, but Emma and Emanuele only lived there in summer, to escape the mugginess of the city. Marisa thought it weird that Emma and Emanuele did not feel like going there to watch the sunset more often, considering that its enormous terrace overlooked the whole of Rome. But they seemed to prefer their work and their social lives in the city centre, together with beautiful people and fashionable establishments, perhaps favouring other types of sentimentality. Marisa confessed to Stelvio that she liked going dancing, of course, and to the movies, sometimes even to the theatre, but she also felt the need for a quiet, everyday life. For her, family habits were a sort of necessity; they made her feel safe. Stelvio listened to her, nodding: he felt that way too.

Though Marisa had tried to prepare him, Stelvio was left speechless when Villa Estherina finally appeared in the distance, immersed in an endless park. As the van climbed up through the hairpin bends of the hillside, the white three-storey building felt to him as solemn as the Altar of the Fatherland. The neoclassical style of the villa was actually quite austere, but for someone who had lived in the shacks by the aqueduct it was a palace.

Stelvio's almost childlike awe made Marisa chuckle as he looked up, tilting his head to one side to see better. He chuckled with her too, at himself and at his world, which was so small that it did not extend past Gaeta, where he had been for military service. In order to make an even bigger impression on him, Marisa told him that in the basement, where the boxes for which they had come were located, there was part of a Roman road, still intact. Nobody had dared touch it, not even during the refurbishment.

They parked the van next to the side entrance, where there was direct access to the basement. The wind had abated and, oddly, the temperature had become milder. They sat on one of the marble seats that marked the edges of the garden and stopped to look at the centuries-old trees, listening to the leaves rustle. The air smelt of resin.

'This house, so alone, makes me sad,' Marisa confessed to Stelvio.

'It's not alone, it's full of memories,' he consoled her. 'Imagine all the things it has witnessed!'

Marisa did so. She thought about the many events that had taken place within those walls, in the garden, down there in the park. And what about that very afternoon? What was going to happen between them? She would only need to stretch her hand a tiny bit to touch his fingers. Or to put her lips – dried out by the cold – to his while wearing on her face the expression of a woman giving in to a sudden rash impulse after the intimacy that had grown between them during their chat in the van. Then she would only need to pretend to be confused and embarrassed, and justify so much brazenness by her solitude, and the heartbreak of having been betrayed by the man she had loved. Later, within the secrecy of those walls, she could offer herself up to him under the pretence of finding some comfort in his reassuring arms, then leave it to his sense of honour to do the rest. 'How stupid,' she had been repeating to herself over the last few weeks. 'How despicable,' she was saying to herself now that she was faced with a gaze as limpid as the sky over their heads.

She stood up all of a sudden. 'Let's go – it'll be dark soon,' she said, heading quickly for the basement door as she pulled the key out of her coat pocket.

'What about the sunset?' Stelvio joked. 'Are we going to miss it?'

'We'll see,' she said shortly as she opened the door. She turned on the light and hurriedly went downstairs, her heels clicking.

'Please be careful, Signorina Balestrieri! You'll fall to your death!'

Halfway down the stairs, she turned around to look at him. 'Please call me Marisa.'

Stelvio held his breath, dumbfounded. 'But what if Signor Balestrieri doesn't like it?'

Marisa ignored his objection. 'May I call you Stelvio?'

'What else would you call me?'

'Well, any other name would've been better,' she laughed, and resumed her descent.

Stelvio laughed too. She did not like his name one bit, that much was clear.

When they reached the storeroom, they saw, among the old furniture and trunks, three wooden boxes of fabric – two large ones and a smaller one. Stelvio picked up the first with no effort, went up the stairs and came back less than a minute later to get the other one. As he was heading towards the stairs again, the box firmly in his hands, from the corner of his eye he saw Marisa bend down to pick up the smaller box, the lighter one with all the trimmings.

'Marisa, what are you doing?' He let the box he was holding fall with a thud and grabbed her by the arm to stop her, as quick as a flash.

She was startled, confused, and scared by the loud noise.

'It's too heavy for you to take up the stairs ...' Stelvio scolded her politely. Marisa hesitated. 'You really shouldn't ...'

For some reason, Marisa was reminded of Francesco's hand grabbing her arm as he held her back to force the address of an abortionist into her pocket and a roll of notes into her palm so that she might disappear from his life. Francesco had held her back to inflict on her the worst of humiliations, while Stelvio Ansaldo was holding her back out of solicitude. Too much solicitude.

Marisa stared at him. She felt shame in uttering those words but did so anyway, her instinct telling her that she already knew the answer.

'You know?' she muttered, struggling to peer into his eyes, which he had now lowered on to the paving stones of the Roman road under their feet.

Stelvio merely nodded.

'For how long?'

'I heard Signor Camastra tell Ruggero, on the telephone.'

Marisa went to sit on the stairs. This meant that people were talking about her business as far as Acqua Santa; the thought made her legs shake.

'But I won't tell anyone,' Stelvio reassured Marisa as he sat next to her, though not too close.

Marisa shrugged, a bitter smile on her face. 'For what it's worth ... Everyone knows about it already.'

Stelvio chose to say nothing; he did not want to console her with a lie.

'I only told Maria Elena,' she justified herself.

'Of course ...' Stelvio nodded approvingly: he believed in friendship as much as she did. Then he said what followed slowly, cautiously, his heart beating faster because of the indiscreet question he was about to ask. 'Is there any hope that you and your fiancé might reconcile?'

Marisa shook her head. 'He's dead to me.' She said it decidedly, no trace of resentment in her voice. She was not the type of woman to pine away after a womaniser for too long: it was her own naivety that she could not forgive in herself, and the vile father she had given to her child.

'And what do you think you'll do?'

Marisa raised her eyes to meet Stelvio's, and what she saw there was genuine concern. Since the beginning of her story, no one had ever looked at her like that.

'My parents want you to marry me,' she confessed, unable to hold back a hint of a smile, perhaps to hide her embarrassment, or perhaps because of how absurd the whole thing was.

'Me?' Stelvio replied, placing one hand in the middle of his chest to make sure. His eyes had become enormous under his eyebrows, which were raised in surprise.

Marisa nodded.

'Why me?' He opened his arms slightly, to show that this was all there was to Stelvio Ansaldo. Twenty-six, no special skills, just enough to make a living, and an unreliable old Vespa. What kind of future could he offer her? Then, since he was no genius but also no idiot, he realised that, with all the gossip that had been going around, finding a short-term solution would not be easy. And Marisa's situation really left too little time. He thought back to the golden opportunity that Ettore Balestrieri had offered him, to the lunches in his home, to the coffee that was always brought to him by Marisa, and everything became clearer.

'I'm sorry,' was all she could say, realising that he had already found all the answers. She removed herself from his gaze by swiftly going up the stairs and back out into the open air.

Stelvio retrieved the boxes and loaded them on to the van, then went to wash the dust off his hands in the icy water of the white marble fountain that towered in the middle of the garden. He saw that Marisa had gone up to the terrace, which was accessed via an imposing outdoor staircase, and he joined her.

Sunset was drawing near.

He stood next to her and they remained quiet for a while, both leaning out, their elbows resting on the wide parapet.

'How beautiful,' Stelvio said out of the blue, his voice choked by amazement, as the sun on the horizon settled on to a thick crimson carpet, dragging behind a sharp golden strip, like a long cloak. He had never known luxury but, had he been asked to imagine it, he would have described it exactly like this. He certainly had seen many sunsets, but this one seemed to him like something else. 'And what do *you* think about this idea of getting married to me?' Stelvio asked all of a sudden, without taking his eyes off the half-globe of the sun slowly sinking behind the city.

Marisa looked at him surprised. 'I don't know,' she answered, caught unawares. She decided that she wanted to be completely honest with him. 'I don't think it would be right.'

'But, as far as I understand, you don't have any other options.'

She smiled. 'You sound like my mother.'

Stelvio pulled away from the parapet and turned towards her. He felt that he should be standing up straight to tell her what he was about to tell her.

'Signorina Balestrieri, listen, I have feelings for you. You do know that, don't you?' He preferred to go back to 'signorina' since he did not want to sound too insolent.

Marisa nodded. 'Well, I might have sensed a certain fondness,' she admitted.

'No, no, I mean real feelings,' he clarified.

'But even now that you know?'

'I had these feelings from before ... They're not altered.'

'And you would marry me even knowing what you know?'

Stelvio did not need to think about it even for a moment. 'If you wished it, yes.'

Marisa turned around and leaned with her back against the parapet, her emotions in turmoil. She crossed her arms on her chest. His gaze on her, waiting, made her feel ill at ease, making it hard to be honest.

'Stelvio, the fact that I no longer want Malpighi doesn't mean that I want to be with you. Do you understand?' Marisa wondered if there was a less brutal way to say those things, but she felt that Stelvio Ansaldo deserved sincerity more than anyone else she had ever met in her life.

'Of course I understand,' he said softly.

'I have a certain regard for you ... Well, a liking.' Marisa searched for other words, in vain.

'We can make do with that,' he ventured, slightly moving his head towards her.

Marisa fixed her eyes on to his, hoping to make herself

understood without sounding vulgar. 'But a marriage needs other things too,' she whispered.

'I know, but we'll have plenty of time afterwards. Right now, though, time is of the essence,' he said with an even wisdom in his voice.

Marisa shook her head, incredulous. 'Why do you trouble yourself so much for me?'

'Because I have feelings,' he repeated.

'Feelings for someone who threw herself away on a scoundrel?'

'At first, it was just an infatuation, like for movie stars,' he explained, looking embarrassed. 'After a while, though, I realised that I like how much you care for things, for people, the way you look after the shop, the love you have for your father. I feel that you value family as much as I do – that's it.'

'I'm not as pretty as movie stars,' she answered shyly.

'Prettier,' he muttered, not daring to look her in the face.

To her surprise, Marisa felt herself blush at the compliment, which reignited in her a womanly vanity she had thought lost for ever.

'If you want me, I can look after you and this baby, but you need to make do with me.' Stelvio hid his hands in his pockets, which felt emptier than ever.

Marisa instinctively stroked his icy, slightly rough cheek. She would have liked to thank him, but gratitude felt to her too banal a feeling, unsuitable for such priceless generosity. She surprised herself thinking about how limited her heart was, which had made it so easy to give herself, body and soul, to a good-for-nothing wretch, and was making it so hard, instead, to reciprocate Stelvio Ansaldo's feelings. However, all of a sudden, she felt a great peace inside. She had stopped feeling alone, adrift: he was offering her a safe harbour and could give a future to that child to whom, she was certain, he would be a good father.

'Should we stop for a bite, on our way back to Rome?' Marisa suggested, with her most beautiful smile, as she took him by the hand.

'Of course! You're getting so skinny ... Any more, and I'll no longer want to marry you,' he joked with unexpected familiarity.

Marisa laughed as they headed towards the staircase, without realising that she was feeling something very close to joy.

That very evening, after he had parked the van near the Balestrieris', Stelvio insisted on going upstairs with Marisa and speaking to Signor Balestrieri to ask for his daughter's hand. Though Marisa laughed and told him that there really was no need, that she would explain the whole thing to her parents and that they would be more than happy with the news, Stelvio took no heed of it.

This was how it came to be that Stelvio Ansaldo, standing in the hallway because he did not want to cause any trouble given the late hour, asked Ettore Balestrieri for permission to marry his daughter. With a certain haste, if possible, since his feelings for her were sincere.

Letizia, who was eavesdropping while sitting at the dining table, almost cried with relief.

Moved, Ettore gave his permission with a nod that was followed by an affectionate slap on the shoulder, then he told Stelvio to take the van home for the night since he was due back in the morning anyway. Or better still, Ettore added, Stelvio should keep the keys: collecting the orders from vendors was a young man's job and he was starting to feel tired. Then Ettore called to his daughter, who was sitting in silence opposite her mother, and told her to walk her fiancé downstairs to say goodbye to him. Five minutes only, he added.

Marisa put her coat back on and went downstairs with Stelvio. They were all smiling.

The following day, they settled all the details over lunch. Letizia had already gone to speak to Father Mario early that morning, setting the wedding date for the 15th of February. Both the Balestrieri daughters had an apartment in their names. However, Marisa's was rented out, and getting rid of the tenants would take some time. In the meantime, they all agreed that Stelvio and Marisa could settle at the Balestrieris', in Marisa's room, which was more than large enough for a couple. Emma and Emanuele had already promised that they would gift a bedroom suite and their wedding attires to the bride and groom. Not heeding any objection, Ettore insisted that Stelvio should receive a couple of months' salary in advance to cover the expenses that fell within his purview. Stelvio accepted, a little embarrassed, and, as soon as he had the money in his pocket he went to a small jeweller in Piazza Vittorio Emanuele and bought a modest engagement ring. The following day at opening time, when he saw Marisa at the till with his ring on her finger, he felt his chest explode with pride and was so excited that he almost cut off his forefinger.

Then the first snowfall of 1956 arrived.

The children in Appio Latino were crazy with joy. As they

chased one another, it felt as if they had trebled in number overnight, their laughter adding up to a deafening racket amid a zigzag of colourful scarves and woolly hats. In the meantime, wide-eyed and full of wonderment, the adults were taking in the city, which had become even more beautiful under that fairytale mantle, so white it glistened and gleamed in the morning light. People were shouting out with good cheer from the pavements, from one window to the other, from one balcony to the next. The people in the streets were describing in detail what they had witnessed on their way over, jostling to report to their neighbours up in the windows the most sensational anecdote or most picturesque view. Even acquaintances who had stopped talking over old grudges years earlier were now exchanging a few words.

Stelvio Ansaldo too would have had so much to tell about all that beauty: he had walked over from home, the snow up to his calves, and filled his eyes with the wonder of it. However, he was also worried, for he was running late. Almost half-past eight! He knew that Signor Balestrieri would understand, since it would have been impossible to drive the van and the buses were not running, but he still sped up even more, barely returning the greetings people were shouting at him as they waved their arms about in an explosion of joy.

When Stelvio turned around the corner and saw that the shop was still closed, he gawped for a moment. He stood stock-still, his back straight and his hands at his sides, frowning. Then he walked up to the entrance, struggling to believe his eyes.

'No one's been round this morning,' a voice croaked from above his head.

Stelvio looked up and saw an old lady, all wrapped up in a dark shawl, leaning out of a first-floor window. He remembered that he had seen her in the shop a couple of times and that she had a limp.

'I heard there's someone ill at the Balestrieris',' she continued. 'At six in the morning they even sent for Dr Gualazzi. He's been at it for two hours already. He went upstairs and never left.'

Without saying a word, Stelvio hurried towards the entrance to the building and ran three floors up, risking slipping with his wet boots on the muddy marble floor more than once. He knocked loudly for someone to come to the door right away. He was in such distress he could feel his heart in his throat: for the shop to be closed, the situation must be serious. When the door opened and he saw a neighbour's face, his breath was knocked out of him.

'What's happened?' Stelvio asked in a whisper.

The woman stepped aside to let him in. 'It's Marisa,' she whispered back as she closed the door as quietly as she could.

'What's wrong with her?' Stelvio could hardly keep his voice down.

'She has a high fever, very high; she's lost consciousness and isn't coming round ...' The neighbour looked at him with teary eyes. 'The doctor says it's serious, but the ambulance won't come with this snow and nobody can get their cars out until the snowplough comes through.' She opened her arms for a moment, as if underlining the obvious, then wrapped her woollen shawl around her chest more tightly for comfort rather than for warmth.

From the hallway, Stelvio saw Signor Balestrieri sitting

with his head in his hands and his elbows on the dining table. He walked in, frightened. 'Signore . . .' he said in a whisper.

Ettore raised his eyes, seemingly struggling to recognise him for a moment. 'I'm going to lose my daughter,' he moaned softly. 'If the ambulance doesn't come, I'm going to lose her.'

Stelvio went to Marisa's room. He stood on the threshold and saw Letizia sitting by her daughter's side. She was holding her hand and, with her other hand, she was stroking her gently as if she were a little girl, calling her name softly. Stelvio saw that they had covered Marisa up with chunks of icy snow, which, as it slowly melted, was soaking her and dripping on to the floor, turning it into a puddle. The doctor was standing in a corner, quiet, his face petrified in a tense expression.

All of a sudden, Signora Balestrieri looked towards Stelvio and Stelvio feared that she might send him away. He was about to say something, to beg to be permitted near Marisa just for a moment, when Signora Balestrieri suddenly stood up and went to throw her arms around his neck. A moment later, she yielded to a flood of tears, while she repeated in his ear, almost as if confessing a sin, 'I can't wake her up! I can't wake her up!'

Stelvio held Letizia tight, stroking her hair, which he was seeing uncombed for the very first time. Then, keeping his arm around her waist, he approached the bed. Marisa's face was as white as a corpse and she had two deep purple circles under her closed eyes. She smelt of the alcohol they had rubbed her with, to no avail.

'Her breathing is shallow,' the doctor explained to him, from the corner. 'I can barely feel her pulse.'

'But what's wrong with her?' Stelvio did not dare even touch her, so vulnerable did she look to him.

'Perhaps an infection ...' the doctor said, uncertain. 'She isn't responding to the medication. Her temperature is so high we can't even take it any more!'

'She was fine. Last night, she just said she had a bit of a stomach ache,' Letizia sobbed. 'She said she didn't want any dinner and went to bed ...' Letizia bit the knuckle of her hand; tears were no longer enough of an outlet for her anguish. 'And this morning I couldn't wake her up!'

Stelvio plucked up his courage and caressed Marisa's face. She was burning like fire, despite all that ice. I'm going to lose her, Stelvio thought to himself. He looked at the doctor. 'What can we do?'

'She needs oxygen, tests, X-rays ...' Irritated at himself, he pointed at his bag, which lay open on the chair, his instruments scattered around. 'I did what I could.'

'Signora Balestrieri, help me cover her up well; let's put her in a dry woollen blanket.'

Letizia looked at him with frightened eyes. 'What do you want to do?'

'I'm taking her to the hospital.'

'But how? The cars are all snowed in!'

'I'll carry her.'

'To the hospital?' Letizia's heart was trembling with surprise and hope at the same time.

'It's three kilometres, maybe even less ...' Stelvio stared straight into her eyes to reassure her, then added, 'I can do it, signora.'

Letizia shifted her gaze to Dr Gualazzi, to ask for his

advice. Gualazzi wavered for a fraction of a second, then barely nodded.

'Let him go, signora. We can't waste any more time.'

Among the many tales of the big snowfall of 1956, for many years afterwards the porters on duty at the San Giovanni hospital told the story of a tall, handsome young man who ran through the door of A&E with a half-dead woman in his arms, barely managing to put her down on a stretcher before collapsing to his knees. Wheezing as if he was about to die due to the icy air burning his lungs, between one breath and the next he begged, barely intelligibly, 'Please, save her!'

The porters had to help him stand, while others rushed off with the sick woman. They made him sit down and, with effort, managed to convince him to drink a hot tea to warm up, though he kept promising that he was fine and begging them to focus on Marisa.

Stelvio sat there for a while, his elbows on his knees and his head in his hands. He despaired at the thought that he might have taken too long. At one point, Marisa's weight and his weariness had pulled him to the ground in Via Appia Nuova, even though the snow plough had already been by. It had felt to him as if Marisa's breath against his neck had disappeared. He could only feel her heat, as he held her as tight as he could and begged death not to take her away. He had chased after a police car to ask for help, but in vain: they had not seen or heard him.

A long, long time went by, or so it seemed to Stelvio, before a doctor came to enquire with the nurses about the person who had brought the young woman in. Stelvio jumped to his feet and headed towards the doctor, an old man in spectacles who wore a carefully buttoned lab coat.

'She is in critical condition,' the doctor said, coming straight to the point.

Stelvio was relieved to hear that she was still alive.

'Peritonitis,' the doctor continued. Then, seeing Stelvio's confused expression, he explained in plainer terms. 'An inflammation of the abdominal organs. We need to operate to understand where it started.'

'Operate?' Stelvio repeated, his eyes wide with fear.

'Yes. But what is more worrisome is that her blood is already infected. I'm not sure she can withstand surgery, but I don't see any alternative.'

'What does it mean?' Stelvio had understood, but he did not care to look stupid: he needed some time to process the blow.

'It means that I doubt she'll make it through the surgery. However, the patient is young so it's worth trying.'

Stelvio lowered his head. 'I need to speak to her family,' he mumbled.

'There's no time.'

Stelvio raised his eyes again to meet the doctor's. 'Then do it,' he said, taking a deep breath. 'But Marisa is expecting...' he added, with a further supplication.

'It'll already be a miracle if the lady makes it,' was the only thing the doctor said before going back through the glass door.

When Ettore and Letizia Balestrieri finally made it to the hospital, Stelvio explained the situation to them as best he could and repeated what the doctor had said, his eyes swollen with tears, then in a broken voice he asked them for forgiveness, because he had decided their daughter's fate in their absence. At these words the Balestrieris sat down, subdued by dejection, and comforted each other in a messy embrace that allowed Letizia to suffocate her sobs and Ettore to hide his annihilated gaze.

A kind nurse came by to take down Marisa's particulars on a piece of paper and asked them to relocate to the surgery department waiting room. In silence, they waited there motionless. From time to time, someone somewhere would start singing a ditty, oblivious to other people's pain or perhaps in an attempt to alleviate their suffering. Holding her husband's hand, Letizia incessantly recited mute prayers at a statue of the Virgin Mary.

It was afternoon by the time the door to the waiting room opened and in came a middle-aged doctor who looked as if he was the son of the consultant Stelvio had spoken to earlier that morning.

'Balestrieri?'

They had already jumped up as soon as they had seen him. Ettore took a step forward. Dealing with the news was now his duty.

'The lady made it through the operation,' the surgeon reported, nodding slowly to signify that this was good news. 'Of course she is very weak and I can't say that she is completely out of danger, but now we can hope.'

They immediately registered the almost imperceptible smile on his face: that tiny expression was more welcome to their need for hope than air.

'You will save her, won't you?' Letizia asked, like a little girl.

The doctor opened his arms. 'We need to see how she responds to the antibiotics. Her temperature has come down and her heart is strong and healthy.' He sighed. He had reached the limit of the powers conferred to him by his profession. 'You must have faith.'

'But what was it? What happened?' Ettore shook his head; he was still struggling to believe that the whole thing was real.

The surgeon searched for a simple way to explain it. Instinctively, he looked towards Stelvio. 'The baby ...' He hesitated, since it was a delicate subject. 'It had implanted itself in the tube, outside of its natural seat,' he added eloquently.

Letizia covered her mouth with her hands, in disbelief.

'I'm sorry,' the surgeon said before taking his leave.

The Balestrieris needed a lot of faith, for Marisa seemed to have fallen into a long sleep. The doctors were struggling to explain it, because her general condition was improving, but her temperature had been high for a long time and sepsis might have caused more serious damage than they had originally thought. Emma asked the best doctors for a consultation, but their verdict was unanimous: it was hard to say when and how Marisa might come to. The most optimistic among them explained that it was as if Marisa's body had fallen into a phase of rest and was taking some time off to repair the damage. When the Balestrieris asked how long she could last in that state, the doctors sighed and raised their eyes to the sky.

When she was not at Marisa's side, Letizia found comfort in long conversations with Father Mario, while Ettore instead had withdrawn into himself. He would go to the hospital with his wife in the morning, but staring at his dearest daughter lying there, as if dead, caused him unendurable pain. While his wife was at church, he waited outside, sitting on a park bench, staring sadly at young mothers smiling as they looked after their babies in their prams by the playground. He thought about how Malpighi's baby had perhaps killed his Marisa and bitterly regretted all the silences he had punished her with after he had learned that she had gone and got herself in trouble with a scoundrel.

Stelvio Ansaldo had gone to the hospital with them for the first two days, then he had realised that Marisa would never have wanted him there, sitting idly, staring at her like a statue in a church. So he had picked up the keys to the shop and opened up, without even asking the Balestrieris. Indifferent, Ettore had let him; for the first time in his life, he did not care one bit about his shop. Stelvio did his utmost: he went to collect the orders from the wholesalers, served at the counter, worked behind the till and even took care of the home deliveries after closing at lunchtime. Keeping busy helped. The customers were kinder, more patient than usual, and would steer him in the right direction: 'Signor Balestrieri would do it like this, he would put it over there,' or 'Marisa always said that this is better! Mind, she used to put the rice on the left ...' They took a liking to him and even started coming in more often to check on him. In the evening after closing time, he would stop by at the Balestrieris' to hand over the books along with the envelope with the day's takings, hoping that Signor Balestrieri might at least glance at them. Letizia would weakly insist for him to stay for a bite to eat, but he would always leave right away, saying he was tired. Then he would dash to the van and head straight to the San Giovanni hospital, where he had made an agreement with Sister Bertilla in exchange for honey drops for the sick children. Every evening, she let him pull up a chair and sit next to Marisa for ten minutes, behind the screen. 'Ten minutes only,' she always conceded with feigned strictness, since it was outside visiting hours. Stelvio sat there and stroked Marisa's hair, which was no longer as beautiful as it used to be, thinking that, now that she was ill, he cared so very little about whether she was beautiful or ugly. He only wanted to hear her laugh again.

One Wednesday afternoon, the little boy next door ran downstairs into the shop to tell Stelvio that he was wanted upstairs, that it was urgent and that he should hurry up.

When the door opened, Stelvio found the Balestrieris abuzz, smiling, their coats already on and ready to leave.

'She's awake!' Signora Balestrieri cried, throwing her arms around his neck and kissing him impetuously on the cheeks.

'They called from the hospital,' said Signor Balestrieri, his voice breaking with emotion as he put his hat on. 'Take off that apron and come with us,' he added, shaking Stelvio by the arm energetically, as one did with family. Stelvio exploded into a joyous laugh and did just so.

Marisa's convalescence was long. However, she braved it with a smile on her face, just as Stelvio had wanted with all his heart. She did not let herself become disheartened when her strength was slow to come back, or because of the scar that branded her from her stomach to her groin and which hurt at first with even the tiniest of movements. Even eating and attempting to take a few steps were hard tasks, and the pain in her back often kept her awake all night. Her mother was always by her side, while her father and Stelvio took turns looking after the shop so that the other might come and say hello or bring her some delicious treat from the pâtisserie that might tempt her into eating. Her old friends would come by often to keep her company, always careful not to even hint at the providential peritonitis that had cleansed her reputation more effectively than Stelvio Ansaldo ever could.

Because of this, Sister Bertilla was the only person with whom Marisa found the courage to speak about her sorrow at the thought of her unborn baby. That 'out-of-place' baby, whose fate had been settled at the time of conception, made her burst into sobs as soon as she managed to find a corner all for herself in the hospital corridors. She had loved that baby whom nobody even ever mentioned any more. It seemed as if Sister Bertilla could sense Marisa's moments of dejection, as she would almost always come to find her and sit next to her, comforting her by saying that God would send her and Stelvio more healthy children as soon as she was better. Unable to lie any longer, one day Marisa confessed the truth to her. She told Sister Bertilla about Malpighi and about her shotgun wedding to Stelvio Ansaldo, her fiancé whom she was supposed to have married one day in February that no one seemed to remember.

Sister Bertilla listened in silence, stroking Marisa's hand as always. She did not come back to the topic until many weeks later, when it was finally time for Marisa to go back home and they were hugging in the medication room, promising that they would get together again very soon. As she buttoned up Marisa's coat so that she would not catch a cold, Sister Bertilla smiled and said, 'You know, Marisa, had I met a nice young man like Stelvio when I was your age, perhaps today I wouldn't be Sister Bertilla.'

Marisa too smiled at her, then hugged her one last time before leaving.

In spring, when Marisa left the hospital, it was decided that it would do her good to spend some time in Villa Estherina so that she could have more peace and quiet and take in the clean air of Monte Tuscolo. There she would be able to enjoy many comforts and take long walks, as the doctors had recommended. Letizia would go with her, while Ettore would be looked after by a trusted lady sent by Emma for a few hours every day to clean the house and cook for him. Ettore tried to object – he had never wanted help in the house – but the women would not hear of it.

Stelvio and Ettore took to keeping each other company even more than they were already doing. In the shop, Stelvio would alternate between the till and the counter. Then, at lunchtime and dinnertime, Ettore forced Stelvio to take his meals with him; he did not want to be alone, and having that stranger around the house made him feel ill at ease, like a guest in his own home.

While Marisa was in the hospital, Stelvio had found a nice furnished room in the home of an old customer of Signor Balestrieri's, a retired professor who could use the extra cash to help out his son and his large family. The apartment was only a short walk away from the shop, which meant that Stelvio could come and go in a minute. When Marisa was ill, life had been hectic and had left him very little time to think. Now that she was better, though, he was tormented by doubts and questions he dared not ask.

Visiting Marisa in the hospital, he had rarely been alone with her. They always spoke to each other with affection and she was endlessly thanking him and telling him that he should not go through so much trouble, that he should rest. Marisa had obviously been happy to have him by her side and grateful for everything he had done for her when she was unconscious, and Letizia and Ettore treated him as if their engagement had not been simply motivated by necessity; and yet Stelvio knew that, without Malpighi's child, things were now quite different.

The first Sunday after Marisa was discharged, Stelvio went to Grottaferrata with Ettore to have lunch with the rest of the family. Emma and Emanuele were also there, with their son Donato, a spoiled little blond boy who had to be scolded by his grandfather more than once. On the surface no one seemed to think that Stelvio's presence was out of place, as if he was the only one to have noticed that, despite her recovery, Marisa was no longer wearing his engagement ring. He knew that he had become so much part of the fabric of the Balestrieri family that no one, except Marisa, ever wondered if his presence there was still really justified. No one ever talked about the cancelled wedding; no one ever made any plans: everything seemed to revolve around their regained serenity and no one dared ask for more.

It was Marisa who helped him out of his predicament. On

the second Sunday after she had moved to Grottaferrata, Marisa asked Stelvio to go for a post-lunch walk in the pine woods surrounding the house. It was a beautiful day in May, a little cold but sunny. They walked side by side on the path, which was slightly damp and creaked like the lazy crackling of a fire as they went by. Light filtered through the imposing trees and there were so many aromas in the air that their lungs did not feel big enough to enjoy them all.

'Stelvio, I no longer know what I want,' Marisa said, coming straight to the point; she had realised that life was too fleeting to waste time with small talk. She looked at him with melancholy as she wrapped herself more tightly in her light woollen jacket; the sun was not strong enough to warm her through the branches.

'I understand,' he said. He'd been expecting those words.

'When we got engaged, I didn't want you . . .'

Stelvio reacted to her candour with a smile. After all, it was no secret that had it not been for Malpighi's desertion, she would never have so much as looked at him.

'But I had no other choice. We talked about it, didn't we?'

Stelvio nodded.

'Now it's different. Now I want you.' Marisa stopped walking and paused: she wanted to find simple words to express the complicated feelings that had been whirling around in her head since her recovery. 'But I need to understand why.'

Stelvio was staring at her, unable to decide whether it was good news or bad. 'You want me?' he repeated, moderately surprised.

'What more could one want than you?' Marisa let a smile slip.

He chuckled quietly. 'Marisa, you must still be ill: you're delirious!'

'No, I'm not!' Marisa said back, amused. 'However, tell me something: why were you not engaged when we met?'

Stelvio put his hands in the pockets of his jacket and shrugged. 'Until a few months before I met you, I was courting a girl from Primavalle. But her parents didn't approve, because I had no family,' he told Marisa. 'She told me that they thought I was someone who came with no references, so to speak, and they didn't like that.'

'And she left you because of that?' Marisa asked, outraged.

'Well, there must have been something else, I guess.' Stelvio sighed. 'After all, since I only went to school until I was eleven, and I was coming from the children's institute, I could only find odd jobs ... The idea of finding a good position seemed far-fetched and we had no money to get married.'

'And did you suffer a lot?' As she asked her question, Marisa realised that she was almost feeling a touch of jealousy.

'No, I didn't suffer, but I was a little hurt,' he said, after a moment of reflection. 'With you, it's different.'

'You're better off without someone like that,' Marisa mumbled as she resumed walking, all the while thinking that at the beginning the Balestrieris' attitude towards Stelvio had not been so different. Perhaps, with their opportunism, they had even been pettier.

They sat on a solitary bench in the middle of a slice of sun and remained silent for a while, until eventually Stelvio could no longer help himself. 'So, what happens now?' he asked.

Marisa let out a deep sigh. 'You need to give me some time, Stelvio,' she looked at him hopefully. 'Do you want to?'

'Of course I do,' he nodded.

'Are you mad?'

'No, I'm not,' he said with a shy smile. 'I'm happy. I thought you were going to give the ring back.' Stelvio directed his eyes at her bare hand.

Marisa chuckled, looking at her finger. 'It's too big because I've lost weight. That's why I've stopped wearing it. I'm afraid I'm going to lose it!'

'So I can hope? I can still come and see you?'

'You must!' Marisa cried out impetuously, then lowered her eyes all of a sudden. 'However, there's something that I must tell you ...' She sighed sorrowfully, not daring to look him in the eye. She felt ashamed. 'The doctor told me that it's not certain whether I'll be able to have children. There's hope, but it's going to be difficult.'

Stelvio lifted her chin slowly with a delicate gesture. 'Listen, when I ended up at the institute, an orphan, do you even know how many little kids there were there who would have wanted a mother like you?'

Marisa welcomed his gaze, moved. They stared into each other's eyes for a long time, in silence, then headed back towards the house.

By early autumn, Marisa had completely recovered. She had gone back to her job in the shop and returning to her daily routine had been a great comfort to her. People had grown tired of talking behind her back. Her engagement to Stelvio Ansaldo, whom Signor and Signora Balestrieri treated like a son, was by now so much of a given that no one had any wish to gossip. From time to time someone said, someone recalled, someone mentioned, but busybodies tended to immediately lose interest: Marisa's long illness had dampened the scandal and people were even starting to doubt it altogether. Perhaps, after all, Marisa's only offence had been that of breaking one engagement for another. And was not Stelvio a nice young man? Was he not more honest than that womaniser, that Malpighi? Some among the younger customers of the shop, those of marriageable age, even thought it a shame they had not noticed Stelvio before Marisa did.

From time to time, Ettore Balestrieri brought up the wedding again, but Marisa always deflected with vague responses. Letizia, who had intuited her daughter's hesitation, was trying to investigate discreetly. However, Marisa always clammed up, still unable to untangle the muddle of her feelings. The fact that her love for Malpighi had crumbled under the weight of his desertion did not erase the passion she had known with him. Desire, the memory of her breath being knocked out of her chest at the sound of his voice softly saying her name, the warmth of his lips against her skin . . . she had felt like a woman with him, dreamed of spending her life with him, of staring into his eyes during musical evenings at their Gran Caffè Malpighi. Little did it matter that what they had shared was all a lie, a juvenile delusion into which she had fallen out of naivety. For her, it had been real.

But what about Stelvio? He was certainly real, true, a shelter so solid that her heart might never quiver again. Their souls had met, bound inextricably by events that nothing could ever erase. He had offered her everything, eventually even the freedom to go back on an engagement born out of generosity. Because he loved her. And she? Could she love

Stelvio? Yes, she loved him. She loved him for those feelings that modesty constrained the expression of, or perhaps that he did not even know the right words for. She loved him because he was a partner and a friend, because he knew how to respect and understand silence. She loved him because, during Sunday lunches with the family, when they looked at each other they imagined the Ansaldo family around the table. Could it be enough to be happy? Months went by without bringing an answer. She had to decide whether to give up everything because of her doubts, or marry him at the risk of a marriage with no passion.

Then, one Sunday afternoon in November, Stelvio invited Marisa for a walk in the city centre. Marisa put a lot of care into getting ready in front of the mirror: Stelvio's kind compliments gratified her especially now that she could not think of herself as pretty at all, thin as she was and with her hair short. She had had to have it cut during her illness because it was too weak and damaged, but Stelvio still found her beautiful and it showed. Marisa opened the jewellery box that sat on her chest of drawers to look for a necklace and saw her engagement ring. She tried it on and was surprised to notice that it was now tight enough not to be in danger of slipping from her finger. She smiled, pleased. And then, as she stared at her hand, lost in thought, she realised that she never wanted to take that ring off ever again. This felt to her like the simplest of answers and, all of a sudden, she felt happy.

Later on, as they were strolling around Rome, she said the words that Stelvio Ansaldo had so patiently been waiting for.

'I want to marry you! Stelvio, let's get married.'

Marisa had been wearing his ring under her glove for the

entire afternoon, aware that, on that day, a new life had begun.

They got married on the following 15th February, in the church of San Giovanni Battista, with only a handful of guests. Emma made Marisa a cream suit with a jacket shaped at the waist and a fluffy skirt and, not taking no for an answer, gifted her her most beautiful mink stole. For his wedding suit, Stelvio took advice from Signor Balestrieri, who knew absolutely nothing on the subject and yet found him a tailor who made Stelvio look so smart that Marisa almost dropped her bouquet in the church. As he walked his daughter down the aisle, Ettore was chuckling under his moustache, thoroughly delighted.

They postponed their honeymoon until summer, since they wanted to go to the beach for a few days, and enjoyed the beginning of their intimacy in the apartment in Via Ilia, which had been bought a few years earlier for Marisa and had been redecorated and furnished once the tenant had left. Forty-eight hours after the wedding, busybodies were saying that Marisa Ansaldo had been seen shopping with a huge smile on her face at Federico's, the butcher's in Alberone; she was buying steak for her husband, insisting that she wanted only the best quality. Later on, the cheekiest meddlers were saying that during their first year of marriage Marisa had made Stelvio put on at least ten kilos by dint of rewarding him with the finest cuts.

Two years later, in 1959, a boy was born, whom they called Ettore. The day Marisa gave birth, at the San Giovanni hospital, she asked for Sister Bertilla to hold her hand. During labour, Marisa made everyone promise that nobody would show the baby to her husband: she wanted to be the first one to show him that child they had both wanted so much. When everything was ready, and Marisa felt presentable, they let Stelvio in, his voice and his hands shaking with emotion. Marisa was holding the baby boy in her arms.

As soon as Stelvio was next to her, she drew back the blanket his grandmother had made for him and showed him to his father, who was bursting with pride.

'It's a boy,' Marisa whispered to Stelvio so as not to disturb their child's sleep. 'Isn't he as beautiful as an angel?'

Exchanging an expressive look with Marisa, Stelvio only managed to whisper, 'More!'

In 1964, Elisabetta was born. A baby girl, all white and pink; simply looking at her made Stelvio melt into a tenderness he had never known before. Neither Emma's new daughter Miriam nor Elisabetta, whom everybody simply called Betta, ever got to know their grandfather, who was hit by a taxi and died only a short distance away from home, as he was sneaking out to pick up an anniversary gift he had ordered for his wife. Letizia never fully recovered from her grief, to the point that, when a stroke left her unable to use the left side of her body, she did not care. She was actually sad that she had not gone to him, since Ettore's death had taken away her will to live.

When Betta turned six, Dr Gualazzi diagnosed her with asthma and recommended some sea air. Marisa, Stelvio and Letizia, who had eventually moved in with them, sat around the table and decided that, for the sake of Betta's health, they had to buy a beach house. Using the insurance money from

Ettore's accident and a small loan from the Bassevis, they bought a cute little two-storey house with a pretty garden in Torre Domizia. That summer, Betta's asthma improved right away and everyone felt relieved.

Ten years later, precisely there in Torre Domizia, one morning in August would forever mark the end of the life from before.

2

From Sunrise to Sunset

On the 10th of August 1980, the last day of the life from before, Marisa left her sleeping husband, closed the door so that no one would bother him, and went downstairs into the kitchen. Despite the heat, she felt like baking a cake with lemon icing, perhaps to compensate somewhat for the sensual urge that had had to be left unsatisfied. She worked out that if she popped into the Pezzottas' bar to get some milk and butter then the cake would be ready by breakfast time, as she already had the other ingredients in the house. Stelvio always insisted on packing a box with eggs, flour, preserves, pasta and tins in the car before setting off for the beach house. Betta unfailingly complained about this, because it took away precious space for luggage, but Stelvio was not about to let the shopkeepers of Torre Domizia rob him blind. On the rare occasions he set foot in a grocery shop in the city centre, his eyes grew wide and his lips clenched at the sight of the prices: twenty or even thirty per cent more than what was fair. He always said he would feel ashamed to charge those prices in his shop.

Marisa was bent over the oven, fiddling with the matches, when the slight silhouette of her niece Miriam in a T-shirt and shorts appeared on the threshold.

'You're up already?' Marisa said, greeting Miriam with a surprised smile as the crackle preceded the flame on the head of the match by an instant.

Miriam returned the smile, slightly embarrassed. 'I always wake up early ...'

Marisa detected an apologetic tone in Miriam's voice that filled her with tenderness.

Though Miriam and Betta were the same age, Marisa was always surprised at how different they were. Miriam was still childish, both in her looks and in her manners, while Betta, at sixteen, already looked like a woman. Betta and her cousin had seen little of each other over the years because since elementary school Miriam had been sent to Switzerland, to a boarding school in Lugano, and only came back to Rome for the Christmas holidays and for one month during summer. That was what Emma had decided for her children: having kids and nannies around the house irritated her, and she needed peace and quiet after long hours of work in her atelier. Marisa had always thought it absurd that Emma would willingly choose to miss out on the joy of seeing her children grow up, but over time it had become more than evident that she and her sister did not see eye to eye when it came to motherhood. Of the two, Emma was the one who more closely resembled their mother, both in appearance and in character – tall, slim and elegant in her bearing. However, Letizia's sense of family had been passed down only to Marisa.

Miriam had inherited her supple figure and innate

refinement from her mother and grandmother and, on the whole, was quite pretty. Yet her mother was impatient to fix the small gap between her middle upper incisors. This was an imperfection that her dentist had called a 'diastem', something which Miriam would be able to correct later in life, once her wisdom teeth had come through. That flaw bothered her mother so much that in family portraits she always told Miriam to smile without parting her lips.

That summer, Emma and Emanuele had decided to go on a cruise around the Norwegian fjords, so they had allowed Miriam to spend the last week of her holiday at the beach with her cousin, aunt and uncle. The family driver would come by in a few days to pick her up so that she could pack her things for Switzerland, since school started early over there. Emma was proud of the fact that her children were independent, whereas Marisa still missed her son dreadfully. Over the past couple of years, Ettore had been performing in concerts all over the world. Sometimes Marisa thought that she would have preferred it if Ettore's talent as a pianist had never been discovered, if that might have meant getting to keep him by her side. And yet, she only needed to remember all of the passion and effort he had put into music to tell herself that a mother's yearning was nothing in the face of her son's happiness.

In a way, Ettore's destiny had actually been decided by Emma and her husband.

When the children were little, they would sometimes have Sunday lunch all together at the Bassevis'. On these occasions, Donato often butchered a tune or two on the piano to entertain the guests and show off the scant progress he had made with his music teacher. Ettore would stare at him, bewitched, and ask Donato to teach him. Then, one Christmas Eve, while the grown-ups were engrossed in their conversation, Ettore had sat down at the piano and played as if he had never done anything else in his life, and they had all stopped to listen, somewhat ill at ease. When Ettore finished playing, Emanuele had looked at Marisa and Stelvio and asked, 'Was that Bach?' But it was hardly a genuine question: there was no doubt that the only thing Marisa and Stelvio knew about Bach was his name. Or rather, his last name. Two days later, Emma and Emanuele had insisted Ettore have an audition with Professor Carracci, Donato's teacher. When Professor Carracci had heard Ettore play, he had said that not only was he willing to teach him, but also that he would do so for free.

Even before he graduated from the Santa Cecilia conservatory, Ettore was already performing as a soloist all over Europe, with his teacher acting as his impresario. So the world had gained a pianist and Stelvio and Marisa had found themselves with an empty chair around their dining table much earlier than expected, and with a piano in the living room that no one played any more.

Now they were lavishing all of their attention on Betta, who was very different from her brother: outgoing, loud, with little interest in school, and cheeky, but not in the same way Marisa had been. Betta, in fact, displayed all the impertinence of her generation. Her behaviour especially threw Stelvio, who generally struggled to be strict because it was not in his nature, and, as a result, the restrictions he imposed on her were of little consequence. Marisa had a more no-nonsense approach, and from time to time tamed Betta by dint of grounding her, or even occasionally wielding her slipper. However, without fail their arguments ended in big hugs and mutual apologies. Despite their clashes, the Ansaldo home was full of love.

This was why, seeing Miriam's shy face that morning, Marisa could not help but think that she really did not understand how Emma could have decided to voluntarily deprive herself of her children.

While the oven was heating up, Marisa said to Miriam, 'Now, would you like to help?'

Miriam nodded. 'Of course.'

'Great!' Marisa went to get her purse and handed it to Miriam. 'Take Betta's bike – it's the red one under the porch – and go and get us some milk and butter.' Then she explained exactly where Miriam needed to go. The only bar that was already open at that time, even on a Sunday, was just a short distance away on the right – Miriam could not possibly miss it.

Marisa noticed that before setting off Miriam had beamed at her happily, without worrying too much about her diastem.

Up until the age of sixteen, Miriam Bassevi had only had one bad habit: that of strongly believing that happiness was right there, just within reach. The more she wished for it, the closer it felt.

As she pedalled along the uneven pavement, the deserted beach catching her gaze from time to time, Miriam thought that, after all, happiness was not too unlike a mosquito that lands on your sticky skin on a summer evening. It just stands there, hard at work and placid. A quick, firm blow is enough to leave its imprint on your hand. Gotcha! Then a rush of adrenaline surges through your body. However, Miriam actually never splatted mosquitoes like that. First off, it was not polite, but there was also always the inevitable pang of sorrow stopping her, mingled with repulsion. What she did do was shake it off, a little too late, receiving an itchy bump in return for her scruples.

Betta on the other hand was phenomenal at it, which always made them laugh: she never missed a single one.

As she pedalled along past the orderly expanse of blue sun umbrellas of the Florida Beach Club in Torre Domizia, Miriam wondered why she would ever imagine happiness as a mosquito rather than as, say, a butterfly. But a mosquito seemed more fitting, since it was only right for a butterfly to fly away, free. Betta always said that Miriam was weird, with all those big thoughts of hers that Betta struggled to follow. Once, her cousin had burst into laughter and said, 'Being smart must be so hard!' Betta usually spoke of herself as if she was stupid, yet Miriam was firmly convinced that that was not the case: she just preferred doing other stuff, rather than pondering things over and over as Miriam did. But her cousin was also sharp, and funny too. In the little time they spent together, they never got bored. Betta would tell Miriam all about her group of friends, the boys she dated and her life at that secondary school that was so different from the one Miriam attended. When Miriam told Betta about boarding school, Betta gave her cousin an anguished look and said, 'I swear, I'd kill myself!' But Miriam was used to it, and she would not feel at ease in a life like Betta's.

Nonetheless, Miriam would have liked to be like her

cousin: cheerful, beautiful, bright. She wondered whether her mother would have appreciated having a daughter like Betta. As the years went by, Miriam was becoming more and more convinced that Emma Bassevi had quite simply realised that she did not like being a mother. She was not like Zia Marisa, who could show you what a mother's love was just by touching your face. Or like Zio Stelvio, who always protested only half-heartedly, smiling when Betta jumped on him, boisterously hugging him with the strength of a bear cub. Miriam wondered what her mother would think if she ever got wind of the fact that in Torre Domizia her niece Elisabetta was known as Elisa-Tetta – due to her large breasts that she did nothing to hide – and that she loved it when someone called her that.

Miriam almost laughed out loud at that memory as she got off her bike in front of the Pezzottas' bar.

Betta came down to the kitchen exactly as she had woken up, wearing her pyjama shorts and a thin, tight vest that made her grandmother turn up her nose. Letizia was sitting in a corner, one hand over the other on the handle of her walking stick, the end of which rested elegantly on the floor beside her legs as if she were a Hollywood movie star from the twenties.

In the middle of the table there was a triumph of cake, its icing smelling of lemons from the garden. Betta bent forward, closed her eyes and took in a deep breath, letting the smell inebriate her. A few of her curls almost brushed the icing as they escaped the hair tie that gathered her golden locks in a heap on the top of her head. She quickly pulled back with a smile and protested to her mother that all that sugar was making her fat. They squabbled a little, with Marisa saying, as she washed the baking tin, that Betta was under no obligation to eat it. Nevertheless, Betta hugged her mother from behind and wished her good morning, then went to kiss her grandmother, who ignored her.

They had breakfast together, under the porch. Their holiday cat, a regular summer fixture, received his bowl of cat food, which, like every year, Marisa had packed in the hope of seeing him again. After preening itself, the cat lay basking in the gentle eight o'clock sun.

They chatted about this and that, and then, while the girls got ready for the beach, Stelvio set about tidying up the garden, which had suffered in their long winter absence. Their neighbour, who lived in Torre Domizia permanently, let herself in once a week to do the bare minimum, but there were weeds that needed pulling out and the hedges needed trimming. Marisa in the meantime started preparing the tomato sauce for lunch, while Letizia stared out of the kitchen window, reminiscing about the holidays they had had during the early years of her marriage, when the girls were little and played kneeling on the sand while Ettore dozed by her side.

That day, only Miriam and Betta went to the beach. They asked a kind young man to help them with their sun umbrella and he immediately started flirting with Betta. She pretended not to notice and dismissed him with a big smile, then dashed into the water, splashing and squealing because it was cold. Betta shouted to Miriam to come in and they spent a long time standing there together, shivering, until the lapping of the waves eventually became more pleasant and they started chatting. Betta told Miriam that over summer weekends, and on the Ferragosto bank holiday, young holidaymakers usually lit bonfires on a beach called Torre del Fratino, which was only a kilometre away from there. They would gather on the beach late at night and build bonfires so big that they would light up the old tower that rose out of the sea, some twenty metres away from the shore. Betta told Miriam that it was a sight worth seeing: people playing the guitar, singing, dancing, or simply kissing or disappearing to make love. Then Betta laughed at seeing Miriam's eyes grow wide. Betta confessed to her cousin that she had been going to the bonfires since she was thirteen, unbeknown to her parents. She sneaked out in the middle of the night through the French windows in the sitting room and reached Torre del Fratino from below, walking along the beach to avoid being seen from the street above and returning home just before sunrise, since her mother usually woke up early. She had never been caught, she boasted.

'And ... you do all those things?' Miriam asked, a hint of shy curiosity in her voice.

'Of course!' Betta laughed and splashed Miriam. 'It's not like I go there to watch!'

Miriam laughed too, and remembered that you had to catch happiness as if it were a mosquito.

'Today is Sunday,' Miriam pondered aloud. 'Are you going?'

Betta did a couple of backstrokes. 'Don't know, don't think so. We only just arrived – I don't even know who's here yet ... ' Betta stood up again. 'Why?'

'No reason ... ' Miriam shrugged a little.

Betta glanced at her sideways. 'Do you want to go?'

'No,' Miriam rushed to say, blushing faintly. 'You know I get shy.'

'Why?' Betta teased her, naughtily. 'God forbid you should snog someone, Miriam!' she said, laughing.

Miriam shook her head, irritated at her own embarrassment. 'You're so stupid,' she mumbled, moving away with graceful strokes.

Betta laughed, standing still in the waves and letting the August sun kiss her skin, her eyes closed and her blonde curls wet, shining as if diamonds had just rained down on her from the sky.

For lunch, Marisa made one of Stelvio's favourites: tomatoes stuffed with rice, the sauce smelling of fresh basil that their neighbour had given her when they had bumped into each other earlier that day. They ate with gusto and chatted lightheartedly, as one did on the first day of a holiday. They were all in a good mood, except for Letizia, who for many years now had been experiencing cheerfulness as something to feel guilty about. Letizia always ate in silence, though from time to time she failed to hide her annoyance at Betta's language or at Marisa and Stelvio's conspiratorial jokes, which only made the loneliness she carried inside more bitter.

In the afternoon, while Stelvio snoozed on the sofa and Letizia dozed upstairs, the girls watched TV for a while and then went back to the beach.

Marisa did not go with them: instead, she did the washing-up and tidied the house. The night before, they had arrived late and she had only managed to do the bare minimum so that they could go to bed. So now she dusted, emptied the shelves and tidied them, checking the expiration dates on the tins left over from the year before, then she swept and mopped the floors and, when Stelvio woke up, she made coffee. She carried the cups to the porch and sat down next to him, exhausted. Stelvio affectionately scolded her for tiring herself out by doing more than what was needed and announced that for dinner they would all go for pizza at the Frattali place and he would not take no for an answer. Marisa smiled at him and did not object. She kissed him on the cheek, then went to take a long, cool shower and fix her hair. The girls came back at around seven, their skins reddened by the sun and their eyes shiny with seawater. As they went upstairs they left a fine trail of sand but Marisa did not protest, happy to see them smiling, cheerful and chatty. She quickly swept up the sand and then went to get ready to go out, wearing a necklace and a touch of lipstick so that Stelvio would be proud to have her by his side.

As they sat at their table in the pizzeria, waiting to be served, they watched the sun set in the distance, the sky a dark canvas ripped by tears in all shades of grey. Gloomily Letizia announced that rain was on its way, while Stelvio smiled and let the girls have a drop of cool beer from his bottle. It was already dark by the time they had had pizza and then a gelato on the square. At home, they wished each other good night on the landing and went straight to bed. It had been a full day.

A little after eleven, the Ansaldo beach house was already quiet. Music, cackling and the occasional chimes of a bicycle bell could be heard from the bars and the restaurants of the beach clubs along the coast. In the dark, Letizia listened to life and cursed it because it deprived her of peaceful sleep, her only consolation. As he waited to fall asleep, Stelvio let himself be lulled by the discreet breathing of his wife who, lying next to him, had fallen into a deep slumber almost right away.

The last day of the life from before was over.

Miriam woke up with a start, convinced that she had had a nightmare. She put on the small bedside table lamp and let her dazed eyes wander slowly around the room that had once been her cousin's. There was almost no trace left of Ettore, only a couple of old books on the desk and an Elvis poster. Miriam thought it odd that a pianist should have a poster of Elvis with his guitar hanging behind his bedroom door, but she knew so little about Ettore that she would not have been surprised to learn that he wasn't as boring as she imagined.

Miriam lay still. She was feeling drowsy and yet she was unable to go back to sleep, her mind hard at work to remember the nightmare that had woken her up. Then, all of a sudden, Elvis disappeared and Betta appeared, one forefinger against her lips to signal to Miriam to be quiet. Miriam sat up. Betta closed the door carefully and jumped on to Miriam's bed.

'I can't sleep; let's go to the bonfires!' Betta whispered, cheerful.

Miriam's eyes widened with surprise. 'To the bonfires? Now?' she asked, her voice catching slightly. 'Are you crazy?' She looked around for her watch, which she had put down on her bedside table before going to bed. 'It's already past two.'

'So? Some friends of mine stay out as late as four, and others even sleep directly on the beach,' Betta said, and smiled at Miriam cheekily. 'Things only begin to get really interesting around this time.'

'No!' Miriam shook her head resolutely. 'I'm not coming.'

'But why?' Betta complained.

'It's the middle of the night. I'm scared,' Miriam said, shrugging a little. 'And it doesn't feel right towards Zia and Zio.'

'And who's gonna tell them? Papà is snoring like a trombone and Mamma is wiped out. She won't be up before six.' Betta gave Miriam an eloquent look. 'And Nonna is deaf...'

Miriam wavered for a moment. She imagined herself at Torre del Fratino; she imagined the bonfires, and guitars playing under a starlit sky. She thought that maybe one of Betta's friends would find her pretty and invite her for a walk while someone strummed Claudio Baglioni's *Sabato pomeriggio* in the background. She blushed at that silly thought but told herself that maybe, for once, she too would have something extraordinary to tell her friends when she went back to Lugano.

However... 'No,' she surprised herself by repeating, shaking her head with conviction.

Betta snorted. 'You're such a bore!'

Miriam lay back down on her bed to avoid any further temptation and Betta stood up, looking disappointed.

'Are you going?' Miriam asked Betta, hugging one half of the pillow as her head rested on the other half.

Betta considered the idea for a moment, then shrugged, as if Miriam's saying no had dampened all her enthusiasm. 'No... I wanted to show you the bonfires. I'll go next week,' she whispered.

As Betta was opening the door carefully so as not to make any noise, Miriam thought about the fact that this time next Sunday she would be in Villa Estherina, alone with the maid, waiting for Monday morning when she would have to leave for Switzerland.

'Okay, fine!' She laughed softly, suddenly euphoric. Her eyes were shining with fear and excitement.

Betta's face lit up with glee. 'I'll be back in ten minutes. You get dressed and take a jacket, it can get a bit chilly.' As Betta was about to leave the room, she turned around and stared at Miriam for a moment, closing the door again. 'Miriam?'

Miriam looked at her, waiting.

'Don't you ever get rid of it, the gap in your teeth,' she mumbled, almost as if enraptured by a sudden thought.

'Why?' Miriam asked, smiling with surprise at the words that had come from nowhere.

Betta tilted her head to one side, looking at Miriam with tenderness. 'Because you're beautiful the way you are.' Then her expression quickly turned to playful naughtiness. 'And very sexy,' she chuckled, stifling her voice, as she disappeared into the corridor.

3

The Night

Miriam had never realised that a beach could be so dark.

They had come out of the house through the French windows and Betta had left the front gate ajar, blocking it with a stick so that it would not close behind them. Then she had motioned Miriam to follow her, quickly crossing the road and heading down the slope towards the shoreline. Miriam had trotted behind her, the espadrilles she had stupidly put on immediately filling with sand. In fear of losing sight of Betta, Miriam was keeping her eyes wide open; in that darkness her cousin looked like Mowgli in the jungle, and the whole thing felt to Miriam like a foreign land.

Betta stopped to wait for her. Miriam could not see her face clearly, but she knew that Betta was smiling at her, the night breeze making her short orange skirt flutter about. Over her bikini top Betta was wearing only a long-sleeved shirt, undone and tied at the midriff.

Miriam caught up with Betta. She was breathing fast from the effort, and out of nervousness. She had worn a denim jacket that was way too warm for the temperature and she was already feeling hot. 'Will you wait for me!' Miriam protested.

Betta laughed and took Miriam's hand. In her other hand, she was carrying her flip-flops.

Their long walk towards Torre del Fratino started like that, hand in hand.

At times, they could hear the music, the faraway buzz, the occasional screams of excitement and the sudden explosions of uproarious laughter coming from the disco bars along the road, just past the fences of the empty beach clubs. The utter darkness was broken only by a few glimmers of faint light that reached as far as the shoreline.

Miriam looked up and saw the moon appear behind a sky that looked like a sheet of frosted glass. The jumbled transparencies in black and grey revealed its blurred shape, but its light seemed trapped. It was a captive moon, melancholy.

Miriam squeezed Betta's hand harder as they stepped up. They were not making any noise as they walked, apart from their rapid breathing and the rustling of the breeze on their light clothes.

Miriam smiled as her anxiety slowly subsided, turning into a childlike hunger for adventure. She realised that her canvas shoes had filled with sand and grown heavy, and were slowing her down, so she asked Betta to stop for a moment while she quickly bent down and lifted her feet up to take them off with her free hand, not daring to let go of Betta.

Maybe it was because of the incessant noise of the wind, or of the waves breaking lazily and persistently on the shoreline, that neither Miriam nor Betta noticed anything at all until their mouths were clasped firmly by unknown hands.

It was surprise, rather than terror, that paralysed Miriam for a few seconds. She had to let go of Betta, who was wiggling her fingers in vain while an overpowering strength pulled Miriam away. She dug her nails into the arm that grabbed her, trying to free herself from a grip that was almost stopping her breath. She tried to scream, but neither air nor voice could filter through the palm over her mouth.

Miriam let out a stifled groan as she felt her back sticking to the body of the stranger who had lifted her up and was now carrying her away. She kicked, wriggled and writhed. The grip keeping her mouth shut had now been supplemented by an arm around her waist, a vice so tight that it forced her to double over. Miriam heard a laugh explode in her ear. 'Gotcha!' it said. It was a laugh that had the same smell as the drop of beer that Zio Stelvio had let her taste for the first time, only stronger.

Miriam searched for Betta, her eyes wide in an attempt to counter all that darkness, and saw that there were two strangers tackling her cousin. They were carrying her away towards the fence of the beach club the girls had just walked past. One was keeping her legs still, the other her torso and her head. Betta was thrashing, in vain, just as Miriam was. The men were laughing. Amid hoarse exclamations of mutual encouragement and an indistinct muttering, Miriam caught her cousin's stifled screams. Loud screams, louder than her own. And yet, just like hers, voiceless. Though her screams were trapped in her throat, Betta kept on screaming, incessantly. And Betta's screams were not just louder: she was also trying to say something. She was pleading, perhaps, but also something else. What was she saying? Eventually Betta was too far away for her to see, or maybe her point of view had changed, since the stranger who held Miriam was moving her around as if she were no more than an insect kicking its legs. Now Miriam could only hear her cousin's voice, stifled by hands just like the ones that were stopping her own breath. Miriam darted her eyes around wildly, looking for Betta in the few glimmers of light where the darkness had barely faded. She called out for Betta, but the sound that came out of her mouth had nothing to do with her cousin's name. So she tried to cry, 'Help,' but immediately realised that there was no point.

The stranger dumped Miriam like a sack, face down on the sand, removed his hand from her mouth for a moment, then slammed her face hard into the damp sand, pressing on the back of her neck and crushing her head so hard that breathing became even more difficult. Miriam gave up on any attempt to scream and struggled for a breath of air instead. Taking advantage of the little movement allowed by the hand that was gripping her hair, she rummaged in the sand with her nose, digging a little hole. Then, pushing down her forehead, she filled her lungs enough to be able to snap backwards. This action however was met with a brutal shove in the middle of her back that pinned her down once again. When she landed violently on the compacted sand again, Miriam felt an explosion of pain in her ribs that made yet another scream gush out of her, though this one too was lost in the sand. She remained still, desperately rubbing her face in the sand and searching for air once more. When she found it, she greedily filled her lungs. Then she had to slow down: the pain in her ribs was turning her stomach at every breath, driving her crazy. Even while Miriam felt the stranger pull down with one tug both her trousers and her bikini bottoms, she could only worry about not suffocating. She let him fumble all over her, as he panted with the violence of a hungry beast, then, when he entered her furiously, she barely noticed the other pain, different and new, that he caused her. She knew what was happening, of course, and yet the brutality of that act was so strange, so outside of her notion of horror, that she did not even fight back; she did nothing to avoid it. She only cared when, in the unrelenting urge of his violence, the invader of her body suddenly dropped the entire weight of his torso on to her back. Then pain swallowed her up, together with one last groan that died in her chest.

Suddenly she felt exhausted by all that unendurable suffering, by the pointless struggling, by the bestial, obsessive movement that was still raging inside her. Miriam gave up. While she abandoned herself to what she accepted as a welcome loss of consciousness, the wind, or maybe her imagination, carried one more stifled scream from Betta, this time feebler. It sounded as if Betta was calling out for her mother. But she was not pleading, no. It was a desperate, yet angry scream. Then, before the world finally went dark, Miriam understood: all this time, Betta had been trying to scream her name, Miriam.

She was woken by a volley of small, icy drops plummeting sparsely from the sky. She could feel them stinging her half-naked body, tick-tock on her head.

Miriam opened her eyes just a crack, enough to realise that it was no longer night but not yet day either. She listened to the silence. No more voices, sounds. The music was over. No one was laughing. No one was screaming. Everything was silent, except for the sound of the sea and of the icy drops now pummelling her skin and the beach. She moved her neck slowly, like an old turtle, her body rigid and heavy like a shell. She looked up. From the crack in her eyelids, she could see that the sky was looming over her, low, compact and leaden. A thin strip of light was rending the horizon and moving forward over the sea, headed towards her like a carpet of dull glow that was revealing the world to her anew. A new world. The invaders had gone.

Miriam gathered her arms, which were starting to tingle after the long stillness, and dug the palms of her hands into the sand to push herself up as she bent her knees. The twinge in her ribs hit her like a knife and made her collapse forward with a groan which this time was voiced. She strained to tear the silence by calling for Betta, but the sound came out feebly, like the squeaking of a broken thing. It took Miriam a minute to learn how to coexist with a pain that, when she remained still, pulsated more mildly, tolerable, only to then whip at her savagely every time she moved. She kept her torso stiff as she held her breath and sat up, whimpering, her legs bent to one side. She sat in that pose for a moment, still, facing towards the sea like the Little Mermaid that she had once seen on a summer's day, looking out on to the Copenhagen harbour.

Miriam studied her turquoise cotton trousers and her bikini bottoms, which lay coiled around her ankles, then slowly covered her nakedness, putting her clothes back on more out of instinct than modesty. As she went through these motions, she learned how to control the pain in her ribs. The breathing, the inclination, the best level of tension in her muscles. Miriam licked her lips, which were covered in sand, then the wounds that her incisors had left inside her mouth. She swallowed a paste of saliva, blood and sand that crunched under her teeth. She got up on her knees and remained on all fours for a while, then she turned around and looked away from the sea to scan the beach, which the rain was now pelting with little polka-dots.

Then she finally saw her. Betta. Miriam's sore lips curved in a faint smile. Betta was not as far away as she had believed when it was darker. She was relieved. Betta had not left. She was lying there, on her back, right next to the light blue fence of the beach club.

Miriam stood up, but she had to stoop as she walked: in that position, new pains exploded all over her. Her arms, her legs, the back of her neck hurt. She felt a fierce burning between her thighs and pangs so deep that they made her instinctively tense the muscles in her lower abdomen. As the rain became heavier, she stepped up and reached Betta.

Confused, Miriam stopped a short distance away and her eyes narrowed, focusing slowly. On closer inspection, Betta was not lying down, not exactly. She was looking at the sky in a ballerina pose, her left leg bent in a triangle, her foot pointing to her right knee; one of her arms was elegantly arched above her head, while the other instead was fully behind her back, at an angle that looked wrong and slightly lifted her off the ground, making her pirouette look awkward. She was too tall and curvy for ballet, Miriam thought. Betta too was naked from the waist down: her orange skirt was hiked up and they had ripped her bikini bottoms off. Her breasts had fallen out of her bikini top under her undone shirt.

Miriam slipped into the small space between Betta and the fence so that her back would be covered. She knelt next to her, no longer noticing any pain.

'Betta?' she whispered to wake her up gently. 'Betta?' she called out again softly.

She looked at Betta's body, which was wrapped in the blue light that came before dawn, and took heart at the fact that they had not hurt her so badly. Betta was still as beautiful as ever. Miriam pulled her orange skirt down and carefully tied up her shirt.

'Betta, shall we go?' she whispered, pleadingly and at the same time somewhat impatiently. She was cold. Betta must be cold too. Miriam moved enough to be able to take her cousin's hand into her own and realised that it was icy, that it had none of the softness she had felt earlier, at night, as they were running towards Torre del Fratino.

Finally, she looked at Betta's face. In the pale glow of the day drawing near, Miriam forced herself to look at Betta's eyes. They were staring at the sky, glazed over. In her half-open mouth, Miriam could see sand sticking to the inside of her lips, to her teeth, to her tongue. The rain was falling on her still body and her eyes remained fixed; they were letting themselves be flooded, defenceless. As she stroked her cousin's blonde hair, heavy with rain and the sand, Miriam realised that Betta would no longer know pain.

Betta had decided that she preferred to stay there, in peace. Miriam told herself that she was not wrong, after all. She kept

Betta company for a while longer and then, when she felt ready, she decided that it was time for her to go.

The rain was now pouring, washing sand and blood away. Barefoot, Miriam went up the large steps of the beach club's wooden boardwalk, making the carpet of abandoned beer bottles clink as she walked by. She reached the road and headed back towards the Ansaldo home, which was only a few minutes' walk away. Miriam was surprised to realise how little progress they had made, and how far from the bonfires at Torre del Fratino they still had been.

No one saw Miriam. On the beach, Betta Ansaldo was looking at the sky while Torre Domizia slept its last hours of restful slumber.

Miriam went in through the gate, which she left open, closing the French windows because it was raining. She went upstairs, holding on to the handrail, and left the door to her room ajar, as it had been earlier. Soaked in rain and moving slowly so as not to feel too much pain, she lay down on her bed. As shivers shook her body, she thought back to her nightmare, the one she had not managed to remember. She closed her eyes. All of a sudden, everything seemed so clear that she felt comforted. Simply, she inferred as she dozed off, she had never woken up.

When Stelvio Ansaldo opened his eyes, he was surprised to see that although it was almost seven his wife was still deeply asleep next to him. The days when Stelvio was not woken up by Marisa tapping gently on his shoulder and handing him a cup of coffee were rare. However, towards morning the storm had brought with it a pleasant coolness, so much so that

Marisa had wrapped herself up tightly in the sheet and slept in a little longer, perhaps without even realising it.

Careful not to wake her, Stelvio got up and put on his shorts and his vest, then went downstairs, happy to have the chance for once to return his wife's daily kindness. In the kitchen, his mother-in-law was boiling water to make herself a cup of tea. He wished her good morning and Letizia asked him whether Marisa was unwell, since it was unusual for her to still be in bed. Stelvio smiled and whispered, 'She's asleep,' as if Marisa were close by, then he started making coffee.

While Stelvio Ansaldo carefully filled the little funnel of their old moka pot, Mauro Sattaflora was crossing the road that separated him from his family's beach club, Le Dune. He was still feeling sluggish: he had been up until the wee hours with the others, at the Fratino, and had hoped that the storm might last at least through to the morning so that he might have a lie-in. But no such luck. Now that it was letting up a bit, his father had made him get out of bed to go and sort out the sun umbrellas. Mauro wondered if he would ever get to go on a real holiday. In his twenty years of life, his summers had all been spent here at the bar, or breaking his back with deckchairs, loungers, sun umbrellas and pedalos, from seven in the morning to seven at night. His father liked to repeat that he was building a future for him, but Mauro felt that, in the meantime, he was eating up his present. Mauro went down the large wooden steps, huffing and puffing and cursing the nasty people who came to sit there at night to gulp down beer and smoke filth, leaving a heap of rubbish for him to pick up the next morning. As he turned towards the back of the bar to get a bin bag, he caught a glimpse of something that looked so odd that he froze, his feet digging in the sand.

Stock-still, he stared on.

Next to the right-hand side of the fence that marked the boundaries to the beach club, and which he himself had re-painted light blue three months earlier, a woman was lying down. She looked as if she was sunbathing with her clothes on, but the sun was not out. On the contrary, the sky kept opening up, clearing up for a moment, only to then darken again. Mauro did not think there was going to be much in the way of good weather that day.

There was also something familiar in her appearance, though it was hard to say from so far away. Mauro approached her slowly, curious, stretching his neck.

It only took him four or five more steps to recognise her. There was no mistaking Betta Ansaldo. As soon as you set eyes on her she was imprinted on your brain; she teased your dreams, made you smile like a fool just at the thought of taking her out for a Coca-Cola.

Mauro sped up. Had it been someone else, he would have assumed that she had drunkenly flung herself down to sleep it off, but Betta was not like that. What on earth was going on?

He got as far as a few steps away, then froze again, his body suddenly crossed by an icy shiver that he would never forget. His head bent backwards, as if he had been smacked right in the face.

Over the years, he had seen two dead people on that beach, both drowned. And what he remembered of those blood-curdling scenes was enough to make him feel confident that, though Betta Ansaldo might not have drowned, she was certainly dead. As he raised both his hands to his head, a torrent of entreaties came streaming out of his mouth, addressed to all the saints, virgins and martyrs in the calendar as well as the baby Jesus. He could not believe that, of all people, he had to be the one to stumble upon something like that. Why him? All he had ever wanted to do that morning was sleep in!

He looked around for help. Not for Betta – nothing could be done for her now – but for himself. What was he supposed to do?

Mauro called out for his father. The lights in the bar were still off and he remembered that when he had left the house his parents had been fighting in the dining room. Confused, he took a step back, suppressing a sigh that contracted his features. He reflected that he had to call the police, the authorities, maybe an ambulance. Eventually, instinct took over and he started running at breakneck speed towards the Ansaldos', to tell Betta's father that his daughter was there, at Le Dune. As he ran, Mauro already started calling out for Signor Ansaldo without even realising it, waking up Torre Domizia with his screaming.

Mauro found the gate open, crossed the garden and flung himself against the door, thumping on it with both palms as if he were asking to be let out rather than in. He called out for Signor Ansaldo at the top of his lungs. He thumped and shouted, causing an enormous racket.

Stelvio Ansaldo came to the door followed by a strong smell of coffee, his eyes wide with surprise. 'Mauro!' he exclaimed, frowning, as if looking at a madman.

All of a sudden, Mauro was lost for words. He stood

speechless for a few seconds, staring at Stelvio Ansaldo: he realised that he could not say what he had come to say.

'It's Betta,' he muttered. He had been screaming until that very moment, but now all of a sudden his voice had become weak.

'Betta?' Stelvio repeated. 'What do you want with Betta?' He sounded more intrigued than angry.

Mauro stared into his eyes and swung both his arms in the direction of the road behind him. 'She's at Le Dune! Betta, she's at Le Dune,' he said, his voice cracking.

At the top of the stairs, Marisa, who had woken and heard everything, ran to open the door to Betta's room. When she saw that her bed was empty, she stifled a scream in her hand.

Stelvio followed Mauro without any more questions, leaving the front door wide open, Letizia standing stock-still and speechless on the threshold. He ran after Mauro with all the strength he could muster in his legs, just as he was, in shorts, vest and slippers, eating up the road as if he were starving, stretching his stride as far as his build and height would allow. The air whipped his lungs as it entered his throat with excessive violence, but he pushed through the pain, bending his arms to his sides and clenching his fists. He felt unable to think, yet he was remembering how, as a kid, he used to race his little brother, letting him win to see him smile. He was thinking of how, from under the sun umbrella, he used to run into the water holding Betta in his arms, just to hear her laugh as she clung on to his shoulders with her little hands. All the times he had run in his life were flashing before his eyes, like someone looking back at the time of their death.

When they reached Le Dune, Mauro leapt down the first two wooden steps, then suddenly stopped, as if struck by lightning, and turned around to look at Stelvio: it was only at that moment that it dawned on him how foolish he had been in bringing a father to see his dead daughter's body. Mauro instinctively tried to stop him by putting both his hands on Stelvio's chest, almost as if wanting to send him back home. 'Signor Ansaldo,' he groaned with sudden contrition. 'Maybe it's best if you don't,' he mumbled, his eyes filling with tears.

A din was already rising from the beach: people had heard Mauro Sattaflora scream and someone had gone down to see what was the matter. Mauro heard his mother invoke the Virgin Mary, her voice broken by dazed desperation.

Stelvio flung Mauro to one side with a shove so powerful it made him lose his balance, then pushed past him and resumed running. He no longer needed Mauro to show him the way: he just had to follow the voices. He hurtled down the steps, towards the shoreline, and did not stop until he saw a small crowd standing a few steps away from the fence.

Then he caught a glimpse of his daughter on the sand. She was lying motionless while all those people stared at her in dismay, keeping at arm's length. Eventually, someone noticed him and everyone fell silent: they only needed to exchange quick glances to know that Stelvio Ansaldo had arrived.

He moved closer, though he was no longer running; his strength had deserted him and his legs felt as heavy and stiff as cement.

Giulio Sattaflora quickly walked up to Stelvio, his hand open to stop him. 'No, Stelvio!' Giulio said. 'No!'

Stelvio pushed past him too and headed towards his

daughter. The crowd opened to let him through without him uttering a word.

Then Stelvio saw her, his baby.

As he fell to his knees next to her, he considered bitterly that people had just been standing there, staring at her, without helping her, without giving her a kind word. 'Daddy will fix it,' he whispered to her. Stelvio slowly and gently straightened her leg and moved her arms to her sides, brushing a few grains of sand off her face.

Then he realised that there was nothing else he could do.

As he slid his arms under her body, he heard a choral lament behind him, a painful, 'No! No!' But no one dared to move. Signora Sattaflora was sobbing.

Stelvio stood up and lifted his daughter in his arms, stooping with the effort. He realised right there and then that it had been so long, too long, since he had last picked her up in his arms. She had become a woman and he had not noticed. Stelvio remembered a light weight, a little girl. Now, instead, he felt that he could hardly carry her, a feeling that reminded him of the day he had carried Marisa to the hospital, to save her life. To save her life ...

With a gentle jolt, he rested Betta's face on his shoulder, bending his head sideways to hold it there. Then he turned around and started walking unsteadily on the sand, losing his balance.

Mauro came up beside him. 'Signor Ansaldo ...' He put a hand on his arm. 'Where are you going?' he asked kindly, tears streaming down his tanned face.

'Home,' Stelvio said, his eyes fixed on the road. 'I'm taking her home!'

'You can't,' Mauro keened. He knew the rules.

Stelvio did not answer. He continued to walk towards the road.

All of a sudden, Marisa appeared at the top of the wooden steps, panting. She was in her nightgown, barefoot, her dishevelled hair ruffled by the wind, which was now picking up.

They stared at each other.

She shook her head violently, her eyes wide. Swiftly, she came down to him, pouncing like a predator. She tried to force her hands in, to turn Betta's face around, but Stelvio stepped away, swerving towards the shoreline. Then Marisa tried to grab Betta, to take her from Stelvio, but he held her tightly to himself.

'Give her to me!' Marisa shouted at the top of her voice. 'Give her to me!'

Stelvio was holding her back, speechless, his eyes shut tightly so that he would not have to look at his wife.

'You must take her to the hospital!' Marisa shouted so loud that it felt like she might be heard at the ends of the earth. 'You must save her!'

Stelvio collapsed to his knees, his soul burst. All his love – it was no longer of any use.

'Stand up!' Marisa grabbed him by the arms in an absurd attempt to pull him to his feet, then she tried again to take her daughter from him. 'Stand up!' Desperation had turned her voice shrill, strange. She knelt in front of her husband and stared at him, her features contorted.

Stelvio opened his eyes. 'We can't save her!' he muttered as he held his daughter's face tighter against his neck for a moment, then he gave in and let Betta slide on to the sand, propping her head up in the crook of his elbow.

Marisa dug her nails into her own face and opened her mouth to scream. But no sound came out, only a broken breath. She stood like that, the fixed image of grief, a grief that she could not voice.

Later, the rumour in Torre Domizia was that, before stepping in, the crowd had stood there for a long time, staring at them dazedly, almost as if lost in contemplation of a twisted nativity scene.

When Maresciallo Tommaso Nardulli arrived on the scene at around eight, Signora Sattaflora had Betta Ansaldo covered with a white embroidered linen sheet from the dowry she had prepared over the years for the daughter she had never had. Carla Sattaflora had known Betta since she was a little girl, and it had almost felt like giving her one last gift.

Marisa Ansaldo had collapsed and someone had shouted out to call an ambulance. But right at that moment Giovanni Di Lillo, a family doctor who had retired over twenty years earlier, had happened to be passing by during his morning constitutional along the coast. The elderly doctor had taken Marisa's pulse and ordered for her to be put in a car and taken home; there was no cure for despair. 'Just leave her alone,' he had muttered as he headed back home, exhausted by all the suffering he had had to bear witness to. So Mauro and his father had helped Marisa to her feet, sat her in their car and taken her home. They had found Signora Balestrieri on the threshold, the door open wide. Seeing her daughter in that state, babbling nonsense and barely able to stand, Letizia had goggled with the watery eyes of a sickly old lady. 'What happened?' she had asked in a whisper.

Mauro and Giulio Sattaflora had exchanged a hesitant glance, fearing another stroke. Then Giulio had plucked up his courage. 'Betta was in an accident, Signora Balestrieri,' he had whispered gingerly as he held his breath. 'I'm so sorry.'

Against all expectations, Letizia had just clenched her jaws and tightened her lips. 'Put her on the sofa, please,' she had muttered, showing them the way with her stick. Then she had seen them out with a curt thank you while they offered to help in any way that might be required and overstressed their sympathies.

Stelvio, on the other hand, was still sitting next to his daughter, on the sand. From time to time, the bravest among the onlookers walked up to him to ask if he needed anything, if he wanted a glass of water. Stelvio always merely shook his head, a faraway look on his face.

Maresciallo Nardulli was shocked to hear that the dead girl was Stelvio Ansaldo's daughter: over the past ten years, he and Stelvio had been playing bocce every summer. The death of a young woman was always a tragedy, of course, but having to witness a friend sit next to that white sheet was more than he felt he could bear. That morning, he was wearing his dress uniform because he was due at a ceremony in Civitavecchia later that day. Blaming the heat, he took his jacket off in irritation and handed it to his colleague to put in the car. He even took the liberty of loosening his tie, the challenging grimace on his face openly daring anyone to say anything about it. Stepping ahead of his two subordinates, he went down to the beach, towards Stelvio and his daughter. He slowly walked around the sheet, unable to find the courage to lift it, then he crouched next to Stelvio and put an arm around his shoulders. Having failed to find anything to say, he set about the task of being a carabiniere, especially thankless at a time like that.

When his colleagues Bazzi and Faragna caught up with him, he stood up and ordered them to carry out the preliminary investigation, then he headed towards the small crowd of onlookers that were standing under the bar's pergola, sheltering from the sun: despite it being still partly overcast, it was already getting quite hot.

'Who found her?' Maresciallo Nardulli asked.

Mauro Sattaflora, who had come back from the Ansaldos' house, raised his hand as if he were in school.

'So, tell me,' Nardulli ordered, wiping his neck with his handkerchief.

'She was over there,' Mauro said, pointing towards the fence.

Nardulli looked towards the light blue fence, then at the sheet. 'You moved her?' he asked, his voice sounding more surprised than annoyed.

'Her father ...' Giulio Sattaflora rushed to explain.

Nardulli knitted his thick eyebrows at the top of his nose, turning towards the sea. 'And how did she get all the way up to the fence?'

'I don't think she drowned, sir,' Mauro said expertly.

'What do you mean, she didn't drown?' Half an hour earlier, back at the station, Faragna had reported that the switchboard had a woman on the line who lived right opposite Le Dune: she was screaming like a mad thing that a girl had jumped into the sea and that the body was now on the beach. The maresciallo turned around and looked at the sheet as if he was seeing it for the first time. Bazzi was holding it up with two fingers, studying the body intently.

Nardulli raised his hand to his forehead, then saw Faragna heading towards him briskly, unconcerned with the sand getting into his dress shoes. Faragna motioned to Nardulli to step to one side and spoke into his ear with circumspection. 'Maresciallo, she certainly didn't drown,' he whispered.

They exchanged a meaningful glance.

Nardulli looked at Stelvio Ansaldo again. 'I'll ring the magistrate,' he said, his face grey. 'You make all these people move along. Including the father.' And, cursing under his breath, he went back up towards the road, leaving behind the most compromised crime scene he had ever seen in his life.

When the mortuary police were finally permitted to take the body away, the medical examiner already felt more than certain that Betta Ansaldo had not drowned. Only a gang of incompetents like the fools from the Torre Domizia station could take as gospel the words of an hysteric over the phone, he complained to the investigating magistrate, adding that the post-mortem report would take at least a week. However, the magistrate should consider himself warned: it was already shaping up to be an ugly business indeed. Elisabetta Ansaldo had certainly died after midnight, perhaps at around two or three in the morning – it was hard to be more precise given the rain and the overnight drop in temperature. She exhibited unequivocal signs of violence, but the medical examiner was reserving his conclusions until after he had run all the tests.

Suffocation, he was inclined to say, was the cause of death, but there was something that still puzzled him. He suggested the magistrate make it a top priority, unless he wanted to spend the Ferragosto bank holiday hunting down a pervert.

The officers managed to gather very little evidence that could be useful, as half the population of Torre Domizia had been toing and froing across the scene after the body was discovered. They found the bikini bottoms in the sand next to the fence, recognising them because they matched the top that the victim was still wearing. They also found a pair of flip-flops some ten metres further from the fence, between the shoreline and the stretch of public beach. And so much rubbish. Cigarette stubs, litter and those little wooden sticks from ice lollies. They did not find any traces of blood – the rain had washed away everything.

Giulio Sattaflora had already cleared away the rubbish on the wooden steps. He did not want it known that people had been hanging around his beach club the previous night, smoking that muck.

No one noticed the pair of espadrilles that the tide had first grabbed and then returned to the beach, one a short distance from the other. The following day, a red-headed girl picked them up and, realising that they were not only pretty but also quite expensive, washed them carefully in fresh water, let them dry and put them on, feeling quite pleased with herself as she showed them off.

Unaware of the summary that the medical examiner had already given to the investigating magistrate, the holidaymakers of Torre Domizia took to speculating about the details of Betta Ansaldo's tragic death. People were saying that as soon as she had arrived in Torre Domizia she had been heartbroken to see that Rocco, the son of Fausta from the bakery, was now engaged to a nice girl from Santa Severa. Over previous summers, many of them had noticed that he and Betta were on intimate terms, and girls her age were known to sometimes lose their heads and do something rash over such disappointments. By the early afternoon people had returned to their sun umbrellas, amid much sighing and head-shaking. Not the patrons of Le Dune though, who were forced to make other arrangements, since Giulio Sattaflora's beach club had been cordoned off until the magistrate authorised its reopening. Mauro and Giulio tried in vain to persuade anyone who would listen that Betta had certainly not drowned herself. At first, people made fun of their theories, then they started glowering at them: many things might happen in Torre Domizia, but the murder of a sixteen-year-old girl was not one of them.

It was almost noon when Maresciallo Nardulli accompanied Stelvio Ansaldo home.

Marisa was lying on the sofa while her mother watched over her, sitting on a chair nearby. Marisa had been shaking so much that Letizia had had to cover her with a blanket before phoning the emergency services: on arrival they had told her that it was normal, that it was shock, and they had prescribed Marisa something for her fever and some drops to calm her down.

His feet dragging and his eyes glazed over, Stelvio went to stand next to Marisa and bent down to stroke her hair. Then he let himself drop into the armchair.

Nardulli asked Letizia if there was anything he could do to help and she said no, shaking her head slowly.

'I'll come by in the evening to check on you,' he told Stelvio, putting a hand on his shoulder.

'When will we get her back?' Stelvio asked, his voice hoarse.

The maresciallo opened his arms a little; he had no way of explaining to Stelvio that he had very little experience with this kind of business. 'In a few days. The medical examiner needs to complete his investigation ...'

Stelvio looked him dead in the eyes, for the first time since they had met earlier that morning. 'They murdered her,' he whispered.

Nardulli could only nod slowly.

That day, after Maresciallo Nardulli had left and she was alone with Marisa and Stelvio in the small living room, Letizia Balestrieri stored her stick in the umbrella stand and began doing without it. It was not that tragedy had worked a miracle on her, of course not. But that new sorrow had removed any shame she might have felt in showing to the world the limp with which she had been left after the stroke a few years earlier. So she started walking around unaided, no longer caring about the pitying glances people might cast in her direction because of her struggling gait and her twisted, almost useless left hand. After all, people would now pity her for the rest of her days.

Letizia pulled the address book out of Marisa's bag and called the Bassevi residence. The newly hired maid told her cordially that the housekeeper had gone home to Salento for her holiday. Letizia asked for her number and phoned her. Rosaria, who was more or less the same age as Letizia but certainly in better shape, was deeply upset at hearing about the incident. She reassured Letizia that she would immediately notify Signor Bassevi's personal assistants so that they could get in touch with the cruise ship and ask them to return as soon as possible. She asked after Miriam, and Letizia, sounding slightly uncertain, said that she must be in her room. Miriam must have seen and heard everything from the French windows in her room, which overlooked the garden, and Letizia was not surprised in the least that she had felt so devastated at the news that she had decided to remain upstairs. Rosaria decided that it would be better for the poor girl to leave Torre Domizia. Since the family driver was on holiday until Friday, she would send the custodian of Villa Estherina to pick up Miriam and take her home. He would be there in a couple of hours. Rosaria assured Letizia that the new maid would certainly be able to look after Miriam until her parents returned. Then she added apologetically that she had no way of coming herself, as it was her turn to look after her bedridden mother.

'I understand, Rosaria. Thank you,' Letizia mumbled.

'My most heartfelt condolences,' said the other woman, sincerely moved.

As soon as Rosaria hung up, Letizia dialled the number of the hotel in Australia where Ettore was staying. Marisa had noted everything down thoroughly, as usual, and so, although the stranger on the other end of the line did not speak Italian, eventually Letizia was put through to Ettore's room. Luckily, Ettore's clear, kind voice answered right away.

'Ettore, dear, it's Nonna,' Letizia said in a whisper to her favourite grandson.

Ettore froze. The simple words and tone of that greeting were already the herald of tragedy. 'Nonna,' was all Ettore could say.

'Your sister, Ettore. Your sister. You need to come back.' Letizia did not manage to say any more.

Putting the address book back into Marisa's bag, Letizia went upstairs with a great effort, grabbing on to the wooden handrail. She pushed open the door, which had been left ajar, and found Miriam in her room, sitting on the edge of her bed, already dressed in a pair of crumpled trousers, her palms resting on her lap. The girl's paleness made the red of her lips stand out, and her eyes, which were dark-circled and hollow, conveyed to Letizia that, just as she had suspected, Miriam already knew what had happened to Betta.

'Someone will be here shortly to pick you up. He'll take you home.'

Miriam nodded slowly.

Letizia realised in that precise moment of her life that, at some point a long time ago, she had become a woman unable to offer any comfort. 'Do you need anything?'

Miriam shook her head without looking at her.

As anticipated by Rosaria, less than two hours later the custodian of Villa Estherina was already outside the Ansaldos' gate. He honked twice: he had heard about the incident and felt that ringing the doorbell might not be appropriate.

Miriam walked down the stairs slowly, letting her fingers drag over the handrail. No one noticed that she had not packed her things, that she was uncharacteristically dishevelled and untidy, that she was walking rigidly, as if trying to keep her balance on a tightrope, and that her shoelaces were untied. She stepped into the living room, where Letizia had closed the shutters almost completely to shelter it from the light and any prying eyes. Zio Stelvio was sitting in the armchair, staring at the void that had opened in front of him, while Nonna had gone to let the driver know that Miriam would be out in a minute.

Miriam went to stand next to Zia Marisa. The drops that the emergency services had prescribed for her had made her fall into a strange drowsiness that caused her to utter words at random, as if she was in a peaceful delusion. Every so often she was shaken by shivers. Miriam adjusted the blanket on her aunt's shoulders, bent down to kiss her on her warm temple, and put her mouth to Marisa's ear, so that no one but her could hear what she was about to say.

'We will wake up eventually, Zia,' she whispered. 'Don't be scared.'

Then she went out into the blinding light of the day.

4

The Damage

The following day, Rome's local news section had a short article, just five lines long and signed M.R., detailing the discovery of the body of a sixteen-year-old girl, E.A., on the beach of Torre Domizia, a small resort on the coast. The working hypothesis was suicide, but the magistrates were waiting for the post-mortem report before making any official statement.

Ludovico Castagnoli, who was the investigating magistrate for the case and whose in-laws owned two small hotels in Torre Domizia, had not deemed it necessary to inform the press that it was already established that Elisabetta Ansaldo had been raped before her death. And that she had not drowned. He was prevaricating in the hope of postponing any official statement until after the Ferragosto bank holiday: people were shaken enough by the terrorist bombing of the Bologna Centrale station only ten days earlier, on the 2nd of August, and everybody needed some breathing space to calm down. Torre Domizia was a resort for families, where people went to unwind after a year of hard work; news like this would upset the holidaymakers and attract all sorts of morbid attention, including TV reporters. There was a concrete risk of a general exodus that would ruin the entire season. And for what? A brief chat with the mayor had been enough for Castagnoli to find out that the Ansaldo girl had been quite precocious and not necessarily always that well behaved: after all, she had gone to the beach in the middle of the night while her parents believed she was asleep in bed.

Maresciallo Nardulli had been bothering Castagnoli with endless phone calls, his opinion being that people needed to know that the carabinieri were investigating a murder and a rape. Should families not be on the lookout? Torre Domizia was full of children and other young girls the same age as the victim; what if they were in danger? Eventually Castagnoli had to put Nardulli back in his place by reminding him that he and his men had already done a terrible job and that, once the whole business was finally out in the open, they would also have to explain why, on the morning of the discovery, there had been everything but a marketplace at the crime scene. Nardulli did not dare answer back; he knew full well that there had been some unforgivable oversights that day due to naivety. After all, Torre Domizia had never known much more in the way of crime than a few drunken brawls and some night-time altercations among neighbours.

The maresciallo had been discreetly asking around, chatting with the beach club owners and the people who had known Betta Ansaldo, hoping to find out whether she had been seen talking with anyone unusual. Yet, so far, Betta had not been seen out and about that summer, neither in the square nor at the Fratino; she had only just arrived. She had gone to the

Frattali pizzeria with her family the night before her death and witnesses had confirmed that she had walked back home arm in arm with her disabled grandmother. The witnesses had also recalled that she looked even prettier than the year before.

After clocking out in the evening, Nardulli went to check on the Ansaldos, as he did every night. Just for a moment, his eyes low. The investigating magistrate had ordered him to keep quiet on the details for the time being. Stelvio thanked Nardulli for having stopped by and then immediately went back to looking after his wife.

Stelvio had put Marisa upstairs so that she would have a bit more peace and spent almost all of his time by her side. Letizia instead sat downstairs by the window, looking through the slats of the shutters, and opening the door if someone came by. The neighbours kept on bringing heaps of food; Letizia always thanked them politely, then set it all down on the living room table without even opening the lids. For two days, no one ate at the Ansaldos'. When the pangs of hunger eventually became more insistent, Stelvio and his mother-in-law dined in silence. Then he put some rice salad on a plate and went upstairs to his wife, who was always asleep, numbed by the drops. While Marisa protested weakly, Stelvio helped her sit up and wheedled and coaxed her into eating a few spoonfuls and drinking some water.

After he set the glass down on the bedside table, Marisa, in a moment of relative lucidity, put a hand on his wrist.

'Where is she? Where is she now?' she mumbled.

Stelvio stared at her, unable to decide what kind of answer his wife was looking for, before giving her the only reply he was certain of. 'At the morgue,' he said.

Marisa tilted her head slightly to one side. 'I want to go there, I want to be with her.'

Stelvio sighed. 'You can't.'

'I can't?' Marisa said, sounding like a confused child.

'No. You can't.'

She lay back down slowly and buried her head in the pillow. Then she closed her eyes again and waited for the deep slumber to come and get her.

It was only by chance that, one day, as he was having his postprandial coffee in a bar only a short distance away from the Ansaldos' house, Maresciallo Nardulli overheard a blond young man boasting to his friends about seeing Betta Ansaldo on the public beach the day before her death, and even helping her set up her sun umbrella. He also said that it was the first time he had ever seen her, but that he knew it was her from a photograph taken the year before which an acquaintance had shown him. According to him, they had exchanged looks and smiles and she had not seemed sad in the least. On the contrary. He sighed and added that he could not make any sense of it, since she had looked so happy not even twenty-four hours earlier.

Nardulli walked up to him and took him to one side, touching his elbow lightly and motioning to him with his head. He asked for his details and the young man started to fret.

'Look, I didn't even know her,' he repeated defensively, his eyes fixed on Nardulli's khaki uniform. He said that his name was Lollo – that was, Lorenzo Calbiati – and that he was staying with his parents at the Sant'Elena guest house, in Via Matera.

'I understand that you didn't know her,' said Nardulli, looking annoyed. 'But what I want to know is whether she was on her own or with someone else.'

'She was with a friend. A girl smaller than her. A skinny one.'

'And you didn't know her either?'

'Never seen her before.'

'You sure?' Nardulli stared at him. 'Try to remember.'

The young man did not need to. 'Never seen her before,' he repeated. However, his face then lit up and he added, excitedly, 'Miriam! I heard Betta call her Miriam!'

Nardulli made a note. 'Very well. How long are you here for?'

'Until the end of the month.'

'Make sure you remain available for questioning.' Nardulli motioned him back to his friends and went to pay for his coffee.

It was Signora Balestrieri who came to the door when Nardulli arrived at the Ansaldos'. At that moment in time, she seemed to be the only one with whom it was still possible to have some semblance of a conversation, since Stelvio was always upstairs with his wife. Nardulli and Letizia sat down in the kitchen and she offered to make him coffee, but he said that he had just had one. Eventually, he accepted an orzata, though enjoying a cold drink felt somewhat tactless, given the circumstances.

'Signora Balestrieri, have you ever heard of a girl called Miriam? She was a friend of your granddaughter's.'

The old lady stiffened. Then she got up, took the fruit bowl from the table to the sink and picked through some rotting pears and peaches. Nardulli noticed that the fingers of her good hand had started shaking more than usual.

'Please, try to remember,' he encouraged her. Puzzled by the sudden tension, he kept his eyes on her bony back, which the stroke had left lopsided.

With the help of her bad hand, Letizia cut off all the rot from the fruit and set aside what could be salvaged, only to then crossly put it all in the bin since there really was nothing salvageable.

Nardulli waited, patiently.

'Miriam is my other granddaughter,' Letizia said without looking at him.

Nardulli was startled. 'And is she here? May I talk to her?'

Letizia turned around, her eyebrows arched in a hostile expression. 'Why? What does this have to do with Miriam?'

'What do you mean?' Nardulli said, unable to hold back a faint smile of incredulity. 'She might have met someone; Betta might have confided to her that she had a friend, or a date . . . '

'Miriam comes from a family that is in the public eye. She had little familiarity with her cousin,' Letizia responded curtly. 'Anyway, she's left already.'

'Where did she go?'

'I told you. She comes from a family in the public eye.' Letizia carefully washed and dried the empty fruit bowl, then put it back on the table and sat down again. She took a deep breath, staring at Nardulli. 'You need to leave my granddaughter Miriam out of this. She's not like Betta: she's a reserved girl.'

'But Signora Balestrieri, you understand—'

'No, Maresciallo, *you* need to understand,' she interrupted him. 'Miriam must not be involved in this business in any way. I'm sure that her mother, my daughter Emma, would agree with me.' Letizia looked at him eloquently. 'Please, leave her alone.'

'But we must find out who did those horrible things to Betta!' Nardulli tried to explain. 'It would be just a couple of questions ... And her parents would be present, of course.'

'We must protect her,' Letizia retorted sharply.

'Protect her from what?'

'From gossip!' Letizia snapped, her voice hoarse and strict.

Nardulli stood up, though he had not yet finished his drink. Suddenly, the cloying, slightly vinegary smell of the rotting fruit in the still-open bin reached his nostrils. Though the fruit bowl had been sitting right in front of him on the table, he had not noticed the smell until Letizia had stirred its contents, nor had he noticed the swarm of fruit flies that had now migrated into the bin. As he headed towards the corridor, lost in thought, Nardulli also noticed that Signora Balestrieri seemed oddly at ease in that very dim light, while he found it oppressive.

'Give my greetings to Stelvio and Marisa,' he said as she walked him to the door, dragging her leg, her gait slow but determined.

'I will,' she said, coolly seeing him out.

That very afternoon, Nardulli phoned the investigating magistrate in Civitavecchia and reported the matter of the cousin, who had already left Torre Domizia and who might know something useful. 'You know,' he commented, 'girls talk to each other; maybe this Miriam knows something about a rejected suitor or a peeping Tom who might have been bothering the victim.' The owner of the Frattali pizzeria had also confirmed that the girl had come in for pizza with the rest of her family, the night of the tragedy. The two cousins had seemed to be getting along very well, he said, though they were so unlike one another. So Nardulli formally asked Castagnoli permission to track down this Emma, i.e. Betta Ansaldo's aunt, to obtain her permission to interview her daughter. Castagnoli, who was about to leave his office to spend half a day in the sun by the pool, vexedly retorted that he would think about it: they needed to proceed carefully when approaching minors as witnesses, and assess how important the impressions of a young girl might actually turn out to be. Before hanging up, Castagnoli scolded Nardulli for being slapdash once again.

Nardulli apologised. 'So, may I bother you again tomorrow?' he insisted, with a certain stubbornness that was unlike him.

'I'll call you, Nardulli,' Castagnoli said dismissively before hanging up.

The following day, the investigating magistrate did not call.

However, towards lunchtime, Ludovico Castagnoli received a phone call from a dear friend, Counsel Custureri, the owner of a legal practice by the same name in Rome, in the Prati neighbourhood. They reminisced about the good old times at university and about a sailing holiday with their families off the island of Elba, then told each other off for having fallen out of touch over the last few months. They lamented the obligations, the frenzy of modern life, then absolved each other with mutual indulgence. Eventually, Ennio Custureri apologised and admitted that his was not just a social call, as it should have been: he was ringing also to discuss a professional matter. Custureri said that he had received a phone call from an important client of his, Emma Bassevi, who had asked him to deal with the delicate matter of the death of her niece Elisabetta in Torre Domizia.

'You mean Emma Bassevi the designer?' Castagnoli asked, impressed: his wife squandered the best part of her allowance in Emma Bassevi's boutique.

'Yes, and wife of Emanuele Bassevi,' Custureri said, adding to the sense of prestige.

'Ah, I see.'

'Ludovico, I understand that you're in a difficult position, but if you could give me some more details ... Signora Bassevi is rushing back from a cruise and is very worried, as well as saddened, of course. The matter was even talked about in the news, and the family cares a great deal about discretion.'

With a deep sigh, Castagnoli leaned back in the large leather chair behind his office desk into which he had nestled his stout body. 'What can I say? There isn't much I can share ... It's a nasty business. Worse than it might seem, Ennio. I'm waiting for the post-mortem report, but it's a real mess.' His tone had become progressively lower as he spoke. 'As if the Bologna bombing had not been enough already, now this too ... '

Custureri did not speak for a long time. 'But how nasty?'

'First-page-and-headlines-in-the-tabloids nasty.' The magistrate sighed eloquently. 'We're trying to play for time. It's a difficult investigation, with very little evidence. However, I can guarantee you that we're doing our very best, Ennio,' he added as he opened his drawer to look in his address book for the phone number of that moron Nardulli, who did not even know who he was investigating.

'Of course. I know how you work.' Custureri paused for a moment, looking for the right words before continuing. 'Listen, Ludovico, I know that I'm asking a lot, but given the delicate circumstances ... can't we contain it somewhat, limit the publicity around this accident?'

The magistrate frowned. 'Contain it?'

'These are the kind of people who don't like to advertise their business,' the lawyer explained.

'Ennio, unfortunately this is one of those stories with which the press will have a field day.' Though he was alone in the room, Castagnoli waved his hand in the air to signify that they were at the mercy of the wind on that matter.

'But if we could soften it a little ... '

'Soften it how? This is a very serious crime,' Castagnoli said, rocking in his chair: he too was annoyed at the idea of the inevitable. 'My dear fellow, the reputation of Torre Domizia is also at stake. It's a real tragedy!'

'Indeed. We all want justice. But there's no need to throw respectable people to these vultures.'

'Custureri, when the post-mortem report is released, it's going to be a bombshell, do you understand? I've spoken to the medical examiner; it's a nasty business,' he repeated.

'But you're the investigating magistrate. You decide when and how,' Custureri replied, his tone halfway between adulation and admonition.

Castagnoli rolled his eyes: his friend was putting the screws on him. 'Look, I'll do what I can,' he promised, given that he too was in no rush to kick the hornet's nest.

'Thank you. May I reassure Signora Bassevi as far as her daughter Miriam is concerned?'

Castagnoli wavered, stunned. It was one thing to play for time with that nonentity of Nardulli, but ignoring a possible key witness was something else. 'But talking to the girl could prove useful . . .' he muttered.

'Yes, but the girl barely knew her cousin. She's led a very sheltered life. We don't want to go and upset her, now do we? Her grandmother has spoken with her and assures me she knows nothing about it.'

Castagnoli opened his arm, surrendering. 'Very well, then,' he said as he stroked his tie, which was resting on his round stomach.

For the rest of the phone call, they planned a long-overdue get-together on Elba, like the good old days. When they eventually hung up, Counsel Custureri immediately called Signora Balestrieri, who had contacted him the day before on behalf of her daughter Emma. He told her about the phone call he had just had with the investigating magistrate and tried to reassure her as much as he could.

Ettore Ansaldo could have travelled from the airport to Torre Domizia in a taxi or a hired car, but he had chosen to take the train. Even his endless trip from Melbourne to Fiumicino Airport had not been enough for him to prepare for that homecoming. Though he had tried and tried, he just didn't feel ready. How could he add his mother's grief to his own? What would he say to his father? And then there was his grandmother, whose spirit had already been so heavily eroded by the loss of her husband and by her illness. They were all there, waiting for him to join them in that unfortunate embrace of grief.

He had to prepare himself for the fact that Betta would not be there. For the absence of that explosion of vitality, colour and vivacity which overwhelmed him every time he got back from one of his trips. He had almost always felt ill at ease when met with the expansiveness of Betta's affection: that cheerful welcome came naturally to his sister, while he, on the other hand, felt more and more of a stranger at home as the years went by. Now she would not be there. Never again.

As he walked on the busy high street that led from the station to the road along the seafront, Ettore tried to convince himself that Betta, who had been the most alive of them all, was truly dead. That she had disappeared from their lives on a summer night. And that thought had shattered all the music in his head, as if it was impossible for him to find harmony again in a world where such terrible things could happen. During his long journey, he had tormented the buttons of his Walkman in search of something that might help ease the chaos which had exploded inside him. But nothing seemed to work. For the first time in his life, music had brought him no comfort whatsoever: his sorrow was stronger. And he could barely imagine the grief of his mother, who had been so viscerally close to Betta that at times he had experienced a little pang of jealousy, feeling excluded from their feminine bond. After all, he also shared very little with his father. Now there was only Ettore left to support his mutilated family in all that emptiness.

When he reached the house, he stood in front of the gate under the sliver of light from the lamppost, trying to muster his courage. Suddenly, he heard the lock click and saw the front door open. He stepped into the garden and quickly walked towards the door, taking shelter in his grandmother's arms.

In the kitchen, Ettore exchanged hugs with his father, hungry for comfort. There were no tears; tears would have seemed banal in the face of what had happened. Stelvio and his son looked at each other, finding confirmation in one another's eyes that it really was true. That Betta really was gone. Ettore was almost struggling to recognise his father: he was unshaven and had deep circles under his eyes and a lost expression on his face. His voice, usually virile and deep, sounded weak and hoarse. As they sat at the kitchen table, Stelvio explained to his son what little he knew about his sister's death: she had left the house in the middle of the night, perhaps on one of her usual capers, and had met someone who had hurt her. Getting himself into a bit of a muddle, Stelvio reported that Maresciallo Nardulli had said that there were no suspects at present and that the investigation in Torre Domizia was difficult because people were always coming and going, particularly over the weekend. Many young people roamed around in their cars and on their scooters, especially at night, coming from San Giorgio and Tarquinia and going maybe even as far as Santa Marinella. They bar-hopped, club-hopped, drank. It was hard to know if Betta had known that monster.

His grandmother was listening, her expression etched in stone.

Ettore was about to ask how she had been killed, but could not bring himself to do so. He was not ready to know; he was already devastated enough at the thought of what his sister's last moments might have looked like. He wondered if he would ever be ready. Instead, he only found the courage to ask, in a whisper, 'And Mamma?'

Stelvio lowered his eyes to his hands, which were resting one on top of the other on the table in front of him. 'Mamma is not well,' he muttered.

Ettore could see his father's affliction become more tangible. He could see it in his gaze, in his fingers which were tensing slightly, in his breathing that now seemed unable to leave his throat. 'I'll go upstairs and say hello,' Ettore said, standing up.

'She might be asleep,' Stelvio warned him. 'We're giving her something to keep her calm ...'

Ettore nodded as he went upstairs followed by his father, while his grandmother remained downstairs.

When Ettore walked into his parents' bedroom, he saw in the light from the bedside lamp that his mother was asleep, resting on three pillows: one in the middle and the other two on the sides, slightly askew, as if to keep a child safe. Her hair was uncombed, and one strap of her nightgown had slipped off her shoulder. When Ettore went to stand by her, he was surprised by the pungent smell of sweat. Over his twenty-one years of life, he had never imagined that his mother might smell like that. His stomach knotted, not out of repulsion but rather from sorrow at seeing her in that state.

He sat carefully on the edge of the bed and stroked her hair. 'Mamma?' he whispered. It was not enough. 'Mamma?'

Stelvio bent over her and delicately shook her naked shoulder. 'Marisa, Ettore is here,' he told her with a hint of merry melancholy in his voice. 'See?'

Marisa opened her eyes very slowly and focused them on Ettore and Stelvio. She sat up sluggishly, digging her elbows into the pillows. 'Ettore?' she asked in a whisper.

Ettore took her in his arms, as if she were a little girl, and she clung on to him, her fingers like hooks on his shoulders. 'Ettore!' she cried out with joy.

'Mamma!' Ettore pressed his lips into her uncombed hair.

'You came,' she said, holding him tighter with the little strength she had left.

'Of course. I'm here with you now,' he comforted her.

Marisa pulled back to look him in the eye. 'Betta is gone,' she murmured as if all of a sudden her joy in seeing him had disintegrated into the awareness which followed every awakening.

'I know.' The only thing Ettore could do to console her was to stroke her cheek.

'She's gone,' Marisa repeated, letting go of her grip and sliding back down, wrapping her arms around her chest as if to hold on to the emptiness of her daughter's absence. 'Betta is dead,' she said to herself, closing her eyes.

When his father eventually persuaded him to leave the bedroom where his mother had plunged herself back into sleep, Ettore saw that his grandmother was busy making up his room for the night. He thought that she looked worried, preoccupied. She had gathered the sheets Miriam had slept in into a big heap and was now quickly sweeping up sand from the floor, as if his cousin had gone to bed without showering or changing her clothes after the beach.

Letizia made his bed carefully and promised that the next

day she would move the stuff that Miriam had left lying around out of his way. Then she apologised, nervous: she had had so much on her mind that she had not realised that his room needed readying.

Ettore reassured her that he did not need anything and did not want her to tire herself out. Letizia offered to fix him a bite to eat, but he promised her that he had already eaten on the plane. He just needed some rest.

As Letizia was leaving the room, dragging away the heap of Miriam's sheets, Ettore looked at the girly accessories that his cousin had tidily arranged on the desk, turning it into a small dressing table. An open holdall was still on the chair, overflowing with colourful clothes.

'Where is Miriam?' Ettore asked.

'Miriam has left,' his grandmother said without looking at him. Then she closed the door behind her without another word.

Serenella Bonsanto had little experience working as a maid in a wealthy household, but Signora Bassevi had hired her anyway, in haste, before leaving for the fjords. The one who had come before her, a Peruvian lady, had suddenly decided to go back to her country, so Rosaria, who had been a dear friend of Serenella's mother's, had put forward her name, vouching for her discretion. Therefore, in August, she had found herself all on her own looking after the Bassevi villa in the Olgiata neighbourhood, her only company being the custodians and a mean dog with a flat muzzle that lived in the back garden and snarled at her, frothing at the mouth every time she looked out of the window or stepped out on to the terraces.

Even from that empty house, Serenella, who was a smart woman, had already figured out all there was to know about the Bassevis: she had figured out that in that house no one cared about anyone else. Donato lived in Milan, where he was a student at the Bocconi University, and spent the whole year there. Signor and Signora Bassevi slept in separate rooms. Finally, their younger daughter was a snooty cow. When Miriam had come back from the beach house after the horrible accident involving her cousin, Serenella had tried to show her some kindness, to give her a few words of comfort. But Miriam had barely said a word in return, instead spending her days holed up in her room, sleeping and uncaring. Serenella had not seen her shed a single tear. More than once she had offered to run the girl a bath – she looked like a tramp, her trousers and jacket all crumpled, her feet bare – but every single time Miriam just said that she would do it herself, without a word of thanks. Miriam did not want any lunch. Nor any breakfast or dinner. Nothing. The day after her arrival, she had gone down to the kitchen, grabbed a bottle of water and a bag of sliced bread and disappeared again. She tidied up her own room, or at least so Serenella believed. Serenella even wondered whether she was shooting up drugs, in that room upstairs; she looked so skinny, pale and brutish that she might have been taken for a junkie. Moreover, she was all out of kilter when she walked.

Serenella had been a bit surprised that Rosaria had not said a single thing about the girl being problematic. However, for her discretion she was being paid a more than respectable salary, and with room and board, so she would do well to continue minding her own business.

Miriam spoke to her mother two days after she returned from the beach house. It was actually Serenella who picked up the phone, and Signora Bassevi said that she was in a hotel at the end of the earth, waiting to find a flight to come home to Italy. Her voice was hoarse with exhaustion. Signora Bassevi asked to be put through to her daughter, so Serenella went upstairs to tell Miriam to take the call on the phone in her room; and, since the door had been left open, Serenella listened in. Miriam told her mother that she was well and that she need not worry. She was resting, as she was tired. Then Signora Bassevi spoke for a long time, and Miriam listened without saying a single word. Only at the end did she say, 'All right.' After that, Signora Bassevi asked Miriam to put Serenella back on, so Serenella went back downstairs to take the call in the dining room. Signora Bassevi informed Serenella that Miriam would return to school in Lugano a little earlier than expected, as being back at school would be good for her: attending summer classes and seeing her schoolmates again would help her take her mind off things. Of course, Serenella thought to herself, her cousin has just died – not a big deal! She can play the piano, play some tennis, and she'll be right as rain in no time! That thought made her mouth bend in an indignant grimace. Signora Bassevi told Serenella that the family driver would be kind enough to come back from his holidays for a couple of days to take Miriam to Switzerland. Then she thanked her and hung up.

Less than forty-eight hours later, Miriam was gone. Serenella watched her leave the house without saying goodbye, but at least she had washed, changed and combed her hair. She had no luggage, just a shoulder bag. And, when

Serenella finally went into Miriam's room to tidy it, she was overwhelmed by a surge of nausea at the smell of sweat and urine. She opened the window and the shutters to change the air and the mean dog leapt up as soon as he saw her at the window, barking and frothing at the mouth. Serenella drew back with a start, cursing him for the fright he had given her. When she turned around again, she let her gaze roam around the room in the daylight. Everything was perfectly tidy and clean, apart from the unmade bed, the bag of sliced bread half-empty on the rug, and the bathroom door, which had been left open and through which Serenella could glimpse a pile of towels on the floor.

It was as if two different girls had lived in that room.

All of a sudden, and without realising why, she felt so ill that she had to leave immediately.

Two days later, Serenella Bonsanto handed in her letter of resignation and left without giving notice, because she never wanted to set foot in Miriam Bassevi's room ever again.

5

Goldilocks

Though the outcome of the toxicology screening would take a few more days, the medical examiner submitted his postmortem report just before the Ferragosto bank holiday. He briefly met with Magistrate Castagnoli and Nardulli to clarify some of the more complex points, then he assured them that he would let them know whether the girl had taken any substances of interest as soon as possible. He also added that the body would be returned to the family for the funeral the very next day.

Nardulli felt very distressed when he returned to the station after his meeting with the medical examiner. He locked himself away in his dusty little office, leaving the roller blind down; he could not stomach the idea of daylight shining upon the monstrosities that Dr Frasca had just siphoned into his head. The medical examiner had explained the whole thing as if he were talking about a crash between a motorbike and an articulated lorry, using that technical jargon which seemed to have been invented specifically to discuss the matter without actually saying that what they were talking about was a sixteen-year-old girl who had been grabbed by two or three people, immobilised, and raped repeatedly as she choked to death. For Nardulli, who had only chosen to become a carabiniere as a way to escape the endemic unemployment that plagued his native Campania, this was rather more than he felt he could bear. Castagnoli had asked him to report the post-mortem results to the parents. How was he supposed to tell Stelvio Ansaldo that his daughter had been grabbed from behind? That they had torn out locks of her hair, that she had skin fragments from those bastards under her fingernails and that her own skin bore bite marks from one of those animals? How was he supposed to report that they had pushed her face down as she died? And in the meantime ... in the meantime, they had raged upon her like beasts, like stray dogs turned vicious by hunger. How was he supposed to tell him, man to man?

And there was more, of course. That was also not easy to say. The medical examiner had called them 'the assailants' since it was not his place to call them murderers; the experts and the judges would decide that in court. It was true that Elisabetta Ansaldo had a large haematoma at the base of her heart, caused by a knee that had pinned her down while someone else took his time with her. It was true that the pressure and constraint of her arms as they were held behind her back had made her hypoxic. But Elisabetta Ansaldo's airway had mostly been obstructed due to a seizure caused by a devastating asthma attack. To cut a long story short, she had been suffocated by her own mucus. Someone had probably left her there to die as she begged for air with the last glimmer of consciousness still left in her. The assailants. There was no doubt that they were rapists, but whether they were also murderers was still to be ascertained. 'Of course they were,' Nardulli had said immediately, staring at Castagnoli and the medical examiner as if it was obvious. However, the two men had exchanged a knowing glance: they clearly knew well the infinite ways of injustice, loopholes, reasonable doubt. Nardulli had felt small and stupid as they looked at him as if he were a simpleton.

Moreover, they did not really have any evidence that could be of actual use in identifying the assailants. Some skin fragments, body fluids, their blood type. When caught, they would of course be able to match that evidence against them. But in summer Torre Domizia turned into a madhouse. On that cursed night, nobody had seen or heard anything. Many young people had been partying in Torre del Fratino, or dancing in clubs, or drinking in bars. Some had even flung themselves down to sleep it off on the beach, but the area where the attack had taken place was quite isolated, just before the last beach club, towards the mouth of the river. And what role might the code of silence play? The solidarity of predatory males? Nardulli had been going around for days, asking questions. Many knew Betta Ansaldo, but few were aware that she had already arrived in Torre Domizia, since they had not yet seen her around that summer. Women answered his questions reluctantly, feeling as though they were gossiping about a dead girl. Men collaborated sorrowfully, and yet from time to time they accompanied their words with sly glances and smirks – everyone knew that Betta was easy.

Nardulli had even talked about it with his son Maurizio,

who was just a few years older than Betta and had only known her by sight. He knew, like everyone else, that she was after older boys. He had told his father that last year she had even got together with a guy who was twenty-two or twenty-three and who sometimes would take her in his car as far as Bracciano, where his parents had a house. She was a pretty girl, Maurizio had said, but not his type. Nardulli had smiled, somewhat pleased. His son shared his taste in women: he too liked shy brunettes. Betta instead was a girl of bubbling beauty, which left the insecure baffled.

At any rate, they were definitely in the dark with the investigation. Like Nardulli, the medical examiner and the magistrate were also convinced that she had known her assailants: all that violence smacked of retaliation, of subduing a woman you could not forgive for being too much. But how many males in Torre Domizia had felt these feelings towards Betta Ansaldo?

After all that, Maresciallo Nardulli needed to swing by his house to stealthily drink a couple of fingers of whisky before going to talk with the Ansaldos. Luckily his wife was not in, and his sons were also out and about, maybe at the beach, so he was able to take his time in the dim light of his sitting room. As he sat in his armchair, he looked for the right words, in vain. When he treated himself to a glass of something, he usually liked to be lulled by the faraway noise of trains going through the station. Instead, that day, the muffled clatter almost made his anxiety worse. Since the day when they had found Betta's body, indistinct faraway noises distressed him: they felt to him like voices he did not know how to listen to, signs he did not know how to interpret. Never before had he had to face his own inadequacy to this extent.

Eventually, he resolved to go. He went to freshen up, since the humidity had made his shirt stick to his back, then took a long walk in the direction of the Ansaldos' beach house, which was a couple of kilometres away from his home.

This time it was Ettore, the firstborn son, who came to the door. He was a tall young man, with dark hair and a slim, elegant figure. He looked nothing like his sister or his parents. Ettore let him in with a formality that somehow clashed with his young age. Letizia appeared behind him right away and asked Nardulli if he would like something to drink. Nardulli declined politely, then asked to speak with her son-in-law. There was no need to call him: Stelvio came downstairs within seconds. He was even paler than before, his grey beard hiding his face and his T-shirt already looking roomier than the previous week. Stelvio and Nardulli clasped their hands on each other's forearms for a moment, then went to sit at the kitchen table.

Before he began to speak, Nardulli glanced at Letizia, then at Stelvio and Ettore, enquiring with his eyes whether it was appropriate for the old lady to stay.

Letizia sensed what was going on before anyone else and merely said, 'We're listening, Maresciallo.'

She was the only one still standing while Nardulli informed them of what he had learned, tactfully choosing his most delicate words. The family would eventually be able to read the court proceedings, and he didn't want them to hear the most gruesome details in his voice. He reported, as Castagnoli had asked him to do, that Betta had been immobilised and brutally assaulted by at least two people, perhaps three. His eyes dropped as he told them that her body showed clear signs of constraint and violence. He explained the question around the cause of death, which had been brought about by a series of tragic circumstances. He told them about the asthma attack, which had caused the asphyxia, and asked if Betta had ever suffered from it.

'As a child,' Stelvio said with a hint of desperate tenderness in his voice. 'But the sea air had cured her,' he added softly.

When there was nothing else to say, they stared at each other for a long time, as still as statues.

The first to crumble was Ettore. His elbows on the table, he hid his face in his hands and finally surrendered to the uncontrollable tears that for some reason had not yet managed to erupt. His grandmother comforted him by putting a hand on the back of his head and stroking his hairline with her thumb. She kept her eyes low, her lips tight in a wholly private grief that she was trying hard not to let show on the outside but was nevertheless making her scrawny figure shake almost imperceptibly.

Nardulli looked at Stelvio, who just sat there, unable to move, unable to ask. A man in shambles, a man who overnight had lost a daughter, his peaceful life, the innocence of being a decent man. Who could even fathom what kinds of thoughts were going through his head as he comforted his grief-stricken wife? How did it feel to drag oneself around a house where day never broke, where everyone whispered so that nothing might disrupt the too-fragile balance? Nardulli had no idea. He did not know what it felt like having to live knowing that your daughter had been violated so brutally as to cause her deep lesions. Having to imagine that she had suffocated to death, her lungs and chest clenched in a grip of fire, her throat scraped by her vain efforts. Nardulli did not even have a daughter.

'Stelvio,' he muttered as in a brotherly gesture he put a hand on the other man's. He felt that he had to find a word. Something. Then he added, with a voice that seemed on the verge of breaking, 'She fought back like a lioness, to the very end.'

And then, finally, having tormented himself for days imagining his baby being murdered while he slept peacefully in his bed, Stelvio Ansaldo felt his eyes slowly fill with tears and pride. He let the sobs he had been repressing for too long explode in his throat, his chest shaking violently. In the end he cried just like that, composed, sitting with his hands on his lap. And, as he wept, he had the hint of a proud smile on his lips at the thought that his daughter had only given up in the face of death.

What was left of the Ansaldo family went back to Rome the day after Ferragosto. Ettore drove the car just slightly ahead of the hearse that carried Betta's white coffin. From time to time, Marisa turned around to look and asked her husband, in a whisper, 'Is she really in there, Betta?' Stelvio nodded each time, speechless.

As soon as she got back to Italy, Emma tasked a funeral home to organise the service for the following Tuesday. To save her sister from an excruciating task, Emma went to her atelier late one night, unprompted, and chose an outfit for her niece. She had Betta's hair set and the hairdresser cried bitter tears: in thirty years on the job, she had never seen more beautiful curls.

To avoid prying eyes, Emma decided that there would be no chapel of rest, and hired a security company to provide personnel so that access to the church of San Giovanni Battista would be granted only to those authorised. Though Counsel Custureri continued to apply pressure on the investigating magistrate to ensure as much privacy as possible, Emma was obsessing at the thought that the press might become relentless, now that the details of the case were starting to become known.

Emma did not go to see her sister until the evening before the funeral. Though she had been speaking often with Letizia on the phone, Emma had kept postponing going with the excuse that she was trying to sort out all of the formalities as quickly as possible in order to spare Stelvio from having to worry about bureaucracy. However, the truth was that she had been procrastinating because seeing Marisa would be both painful and awkward for her.

Over the past few years, she and Marisa had drifted apart. This was not due to lack of affection; rather, the profound differences in their lives had reduced to a minimum their ability to share in the events of the family. Marisa had chosen to live comfortably in a nest that Emma found limiting and stifling, by the side of a nice man who was irritatingly banal. Unlike hers, Marisa's and Stelvio's marriage was of course happy. There was no doubt that they loved each other. However, Emma struggled to believe that her sister might find any kind of personal fulfilment in a routine that lacked all aspiration. In short, that she could be happy in her mediocre life. Now, this tragic event in Marisa's life was a wound for which Emma could not find any words of comfort, neither as a sister nor as a mother herself. Betta's death had opened a chasm in Marisa's world, and Emma felt as if she were powerlessly witnessing a nest of sparrows ravaged by predators.

On the phone, her mother had told Emma about Marisa's nervous breakdown and the fact that she had to be medicated into a stupor. Though she'd thought she was prepared, Emma was nonetheless deeply shaken on seeing her sister's dismay, expressed through the alarming fixity of her gaze. Stelvio was sitting next to her, and in the light of the bedside lamp he looked as pale as a corpse. Emma and Stelvio only exchanged a firm handshake, their eyes misty, before Stelvio stood up to leave the two sisters alone. Emma sat on the edge of the bed and stroked Marisa's hair, just as they used to do when they were girls, to console each other over the pains and injustices that from time to time had perturbed the calm flow of their lives. Marisa was awake but was not looking at Emma. It was impossible to tell whether she was even aware that Emma was sitting next to her. Emma called Marisa's name softly as she tucked a stray strand of hair behind her ear and did up the buttons of her cheap nightgown, so different from the ones that Emma had often gifted her over the years. Emma wondered if Marisa had ever even worn the elegant lingerie that for the longest time she had insisted on buying her. She felt sorry that her sister, who was still young, had forgotten how attractive she was, despite the extra weight she had put on her hips and her generous bosom. And yet Marisa had always seemed happy the way she was, perhaps because she felt confident that her husband only had eyes for her. Something that Emma could not say of her own husband. But she did not care: Emanuele was welcome to do whatever he pleased as long as he left her the freedom to live the life she wanted, devoting herself to the atelier that was the very essence of her existence. She poured all of her soul into it: into the folds, into the rustling of the fabric as it was kissed by the light. Marisa was different: for her, family was everything.

Emma felt a vice clamp around her heart at the thought of Betta. That niece of hers, so extroverted, so loud, so naturally sensual – the truth was that Emma had never liked her. She had always found her coarse, her frankness bordering on rudeness a little too often. And all the rumours, the gossip about her that Marisa and Stelvio did not heed. All that coming and going of boys – Emma had always found it in bad taste for a teenage girl. With all due respect, she had even spoken about it with Marisa. Her sister had smiled at her misgivings. 'Let her have her experiences. As long as she's careful . . .'

Facts demonstrated that Betta had not been careful. Counsel Custureri had examined the post-mortem report together with his experts and, without going into too much detail, he had told her things so ghastly that Emma hoped the whole thing would never come to trial, so that she would not have to hear them again or, even worse, read them in the newspapers. Emma was not blaming Marisa for what had happened, let alone Betta, who had paid with her life for the recklessness of her young age. However, Betta had trotted through the world like Goldilocks through the forest. Like the protagonist of the fairytale that Emma used to read to Miriam when she was little, her niece had trespassed, without a single care in the world, and, failing to recognise the perils, had pushed onwards into experiences that were not appropriate for such a young girl. And the consequences had been horrible. Maybe that ending was inevitable. Nonetheless, Emma could not help but wonder in her heart of hearts if Marisa, as a mother, had really done enough.

And now, it would not only be Betta who would pay, but all of them. The events of that tragic night would weigh heavily on their lives, together with all the garbage that was bound to come out in the newspapers, in the housewives' weeklies, in everyone's minds. Betta was the victim, of course, but her death had brought to the surface all of her scorn for the rules and for common morality. Magistrate Castagnoli had told Custureri that she had been sneaking off at night to go to Torre del Fratino for at least the past three years, and that there she had been seen drinking, smoking weed and slipping away with God knew who. Someone had even recounted the story of how, the previous summer, a group of boys had grabbed her and thrown her to the ground as a joke, taking turns to mime intercourse with her and feel her up. And she had laughed with them, making only feeble attempts to get away and joining in the general cackling. The boys from that episode had been identified and deemed to be unconnected to the crime, but who knew how many more might have taken her complicit enjoyment of the whole thing as encouragement?

Lost in her thoughts, Emma was stroking Marisa's hair, which was clumped in strands, damp with sweat, when all of a sudden Marisa seemed to notice her. They stared at each other and Emma smiled at her in a sad but comforting way, as she would with a child.

'Emma,' Marisa muttered in a thick voice, raising her head slightly from her pillow.

'I'm here, dear,' Emma said, squeezing Marisa's hand.

'Betta is dead,' Marisa said in a dull voice.

Her sister merely nodded, tears of grief clouding her vision.

'She died on the beach ...' All of a sudden, Marisa was lost in thought. 'Her thighs were bruised.'

Emma felt her stomach clench in a knot, then felt a sudden pang of guilt at the severity with which she had been judging her niece only a moment earlier.

'Don't torture yourself, Marisa.'

Marisa ignored her, 'She died alone, at Le Dune.'

'I know.'

'They murdered her,' Marisa said, resting her head back on her pillow.

'You need to be strong. Betta wouldn't want to see you like this.' Emma squeezed Marisa's hand a little harder.

Marisa arched her eyebrows. 'And what do *you* know about what Betta would want?' she asked Emma, a hint of hostility and genuine surprise in her voice. 'You know nothing about her. You don't even know anything about your own daughter.'

Emma lowered her eyes. Though uttered in the bitterness of desperation, there was some truth in those words. 'Betta loved you very much, I know that,' Emma muttered.

Marisa laboriously sat up and stared at her sister. Emma looked so much like their mother when she was her age, though with the refinement of wealth that corrected any excesses. Marisa knew that Emma needed her pills. To lose weight, to sleep, to work, to delude herself that time was leaving its mark only on other women. Maybe Emma already had a pill for the excruciating sorrow of losing a daughter. Marisa's doctor too had prescribed her many pills, but hers only sapped her energy. They prevented the pain that was gnawing at her insides from making her crumble like a statue made of salt. They simply prolonged her torture, damning her to an endless agony.

'It should have been you,' Marisa said all of a sudden, staring at Emma.

Emma was startled inside. She loosened her grip on her sister's hand.

'Why didn't it happen to you?' Marisa wondered again, lost in her thoughts. 'You never cared one bit about your children.'

'You don't really think that,' Emma muttered, her eyes full of tears.

Then Marisa remembered Miriam. All of a sudden, she saw her again as she smiled on the threshold of her kitchen in Torre Domizia. Her skinny legs poking out of her shorts, her green stripy T-shirt. *I always wake up early*, she had said. Marisa brought the back of her hand to her mouth and bit on her knuckles, choking a sob, overwhelmed by the terrible words she had just uttered.

Emma stroked her face. She knew her sister's kindness, knew that even in her deepest desperation she could not be so cruel. 'No,' Emma repeated with conviction, speaking instead of Marisa, 'you don't really think that.'

Marisa shook her head violently, unable to speak for the sobs trapped like prisoners in her throat.

Emma held her tight.

*

On the morning of the funeral of her second child, Marisa Ansaldo rose at daybreak. Following the doctor's advice, her mother had reduced the dosage of her drops the night before so that she would be able to leave the house and go to the church. Feeling more lucid, Marisa was able to stand up and go to the bathroom on her own.

Everything ached. Her bones, her muscles, her skin. She felt as if an endless fever was burning inside her. Bending with effort over the sink, she washed her face, just as she had done on the last day of the life from before. Then she looked at her hair. Her mother and Stelvio had bathed her the night before leaving Torre Domizia, but her hair was glued to her head again, eternally damp with sweat. She brushed it, just as she had done on the last day of the life from before. That morning, Betta had been peacefully asleep in her room, waiting to be woken by the smell of cake with lemon icing. She had protested – Betta, that was: she'd wanted so badly to look slimmer in her bathing suit. And yet she had eaten a generous slice, smiling and licking the icing from her fingers like a little child. Everything had been a game for her: she said one thing and then its opposite; she provoked then retreated. She explored the world with no hint of false modesty. Her daughter had not had an ounce of hypocrisy in her, and liked to be exactly who she was: beautiful, bright, beloved and happy. And why should she not be happy, considering that life had given everything to her?

Marisa dragged her bare feet to her daughter's room, which was neat for once, since she had demanded that Betta tidy it before they left for the holidays. Marisa felt sorry at that thought: without its messy heaps of clothes – dirty, clean, old, new, summery and wintry – the room did not look sufficiently like Betta's. Everything was always in a jumble with her. Since everything was a game for Betta, she would dress and undress herself the way she did with her Barbie dolls, until she was pleased with the result. Her empty desk – the books from the previous year already put away – lay in wait for new ones that would never come.

Marisa sat on the neatly made bed, the bedspread nicely tucked in and, on the side, the plush cushion in the shape of a heart that Betta had received from her first boyfriend when she was twelve. They had broken up soon afterwards, but Betta had continued to cherish that cushion. On the shelf, Marisa saw the records Betta would never play again as she painted her nails, putting the varnish on and taking it off ten times, never happy. Eventually, Betta always shouted for Marisa to come and help her with her right hand. And so Marisa would go, pulling up a stool to take off the utter mess that Betta had made of it and putting it back on properly as they exchanged confidences. Betta had always opened her heart to Marisa about everything.

Everything apart from the fact that she was sneaking out to go to Torre del Fratino. She had not told Marisa about that. She had kept it to herself. And what else? At night, on that beach, who had she been intending to meet? Had she actually been headed to Torre del Fratino? Marisa wished to have Betta right there, in front of her, to ask her and then slap her with all her strength. Not to cuddle her, brimming over with love, but to shake her, Betta's hair clenched in her fists, as she yelled all her anger at her. Only afterwards would she hold her tight, forgiving her and asking for forgiveness.

For having been blind and inattentive. Inadequate. Absent. Where had she been, Marisa, as Betta lay dying? She'd been deeply asleep, relieved at the unexpected coolness brought about by the looming rain. Her daughter had lain dying and maybe calling out for her mother, as she always did when she needed her. This time, though, her mother had not come. She had left her there, waiting under the leaden sky until it was too late. Now, they were lost to each other for ever. Betta – the child Marisa had held in her womb, then in her arms like a tiny bundle, then by her hand as she walked her to nursery, then arm in arm as they spent the afternoon shopping – was no more. She had dissolved. A short life of which nothing remained but an empty room, unusually tidy, with posters on the walls and a faint smell of vanilla that had survived her but would surely fade before long.

Ettore appeared on the threshold of Betta's room, wearing his pyjama bottoms but no top. He looked at his mother but did not dare go near her. Marisa stared at him for a long time – her son, whom she had wished for with all her heart and who had left the nest too soon – and held out her hand, beckoning him to come and sit next to her. Ettore walked through the room slowly and sat on the bed by her side, his hand squeezing his mother's. They did not speak, lost in the memory of Betta in that room. Her voice echoed in their ears as if trapped by the walls; it bounced in the air, was caught on the objects on display on the little wardrobe shelves, slid off the girlish pictures that perhaps Betta would have soon taken down to make space for something else. But not yet: after all, childhood had ended only yesterday.

Outside of their memories, everything was quiet. There

was something monstrously unnatural in the silence of that room. Ettore and Marisa felt it, distraught, as it slowly devoured Betta's sound, her existence amid those walls. The nothing that was left loomed over their memories: everything was already starting to look a little further away, a touch less sharp.

'When are you leaving?' Marisa asked. It was the first time since her daughter's death that she had addressed him with words that made sense.

Ettore took a moment before answering. 'I'm waiting to hear back from my professor in Santa Cecilia.'

Marisa looked at him, failing to understand.

'He might find me a teaching position, for this year.'

Marisa tilted her head slightly to one side, confused. 'What about your tour?'

He avoided her gaze. 'I can't right now. I need to spend some time at home, with you and Papà.'

'To do what? To mourn the dead?' His mother's tone had suddenly turned dry.

'No, Mamma. I've been away for so long. Being together will be good for us,' Ettore said, feigning excessive conviction. As a matter of fact, he was lying: this house that reeked of death was driving him crazy. It was not just his sister who had died – they all seemed dead. Everything was dead. Music sounded broken inside him: it screeched and did not give him a moment of peace.

His mother knew it; she knew him better than anyone else, perhaps even better than himself. With an effort, Marisa pulled herself up and went to the door. Before leaving the room, she turned around.

'Get on a plane tomorrow and go. I don't want you here.'

Ettore opened his mouth to reply but she left him no time to do so.

'Go away,' she repeated, as if chasing away a dog that was bothering her, before disappearing into the dark corridor.

When Stelvio woke up, he found Marisa sitting in the armchair by the window, intent on looking outside. He said, 'Hi,' since wishing each other good morning had stopped making sense. He went to make her a cup of barley coffee and brought it to her with two biscuits. Marisa ate and drank in silence. Stelvio went to take a shower, shaved carefully and got ready. He wore the dark suit and the tie he had bought for Betta's confirmation the previous year. Only Marisa would know that he had chosen it because on that day their daughter had said, brimming with pride, that he looked so handsome in his smart suit. She had insisted on having their picture taken and now that photograph stood on the bedside table in her room, in a fluffy frame that was the same orange as the skirt she had been wearing on the night she died.

When he was ready, he opened the wardrobe again and picked out an outfit for Marisa. He went up to her and took the small breakfast dish from her hands.

'Come with me,' he said to her. 'I'll help you wash and then we can get you dressed.'

'I'm not coming,' she said with conviction as she kept on staring at the street and its occasional passers-by.

'What do you mean, you're not coming, Marisa?' Stelvio asked her, as if speaking to a little girl who was having a tantrum.

'Why should I come?'

'Because we need to be by Betta's side today.'

'We needed to be by her side while they were murdering her. There's no use now.'

'And you want her mother to not be at her funeral?'

Marisa half-smiled, bitterly. 'The last place she'd have wanted me to be is her funeral.'

Stelvio nodded, patiently. 'However, today, this is all we can do.'

'You do it. I'm not coming.' Marisa went back to staring outside; as far as she was concerned the conversation was over.

Stelvio insisted until he felt exhausted, trying to persuade her in every possible way he could think of and rummaging through all the words that felt or at least sounded right to him. Letizia too came to lend her support, in a less accommodating way, telling Marisa that she could not miss her daughter's funeral. For once, she was not concerned with what people might think. Rather, she told Marisa that over time she would come to regret not having been by Betta's side one last time, while what was left of her took her leave of those who loved her. It was not a matter of faith, nor of propriety. It was an act of love.

But Marisa was not even listening. She was staring across the road at Valerio, the upholsterer, who was walking into his workshop, perhaps to take care of some urgent errand since the shop was meant to be closed for the holidays. The city was empty, asleep like in the early hours of a Sunday. What day was it instead? Monday? Tuesday? Marisa no longer knew. After all, what did it matter? Everyone had been afraid that once the dosage of her sedatives was reduced her mind would be overcome with grief. That she would alternate between hysteria and delirium as she had in the first few hours. On the contrary, oddly, she had woken up feeling like an empty vessel in which everything that happened around her echoed, leaving her indifferent. It would seem that in the half-consciousness of those days her grief had been at work in her, relentlessly stripping the flesh from every feeling. It had killed her without her even realising. Without anyone realising. She was calm, far removed from the things of life.

Not knowing what else to try, Stelvio asked his wife's dearest friend of twenty-five years for help. Marisa used to say that 1956 had taken away a child from her and given her the two best people she had ever met: Stelvio and Sister Bertilla. Sister Bertilla had retired from her work at the hospital and lived with her sisters near Via Appia Pignatelli. Since then, Marisa had got into the habit of visiting her most Sundays. They would chat and chat, confide in each other and exchange little presents. When Stelvio phoned her, the elderly nun was just about to leave to go to the church for the funeral. She told Stelvio that she would come right away, and asked Sister Caterina, the younger nun who was accompanying her, to hurry up.

When Stelvio came to the door, Sister Bertilla took his face into her knotty hands, just as she would with the dearest of her sons, and did not say a word. Stelvio closed his eyes and for a moment abandoned his face in her palms, the way he would with his own mother, whom he had lost too long ago. He, too, did not say a word.

Sister Bertilla found Marisa where her husband and mother had left her, looking out of the window without actually seeing a thing. Sister Bertilla asked Stelvio for a chair, sat down in front of Marisa and asked to be left alone with her.

'Marisa, you must get ready,' Sister Bertilla ordered with a kind but firm voice.

Marisa did not so much as look at her. 'Did you see what your God has done, Bertilla?'

'It wasn't God.'

'Then where was he?'

'The same place he was when his own son died on the cross,' Sister Bertilla muttered.

'You say he's omnipotent and yet he left her to die alone, at Le Dune.'

'No, she was not alone. He held her in his arms while she left this world, as lovingly as you would.'

Marisa looked at her for the first time. 'Poor Bertilla,' she whispered with a certain commiseration in her voice. 'Even you don't believe it.'

Sister Bertilla remained by her side, keeping her company. They were looking outside, together. The morning sun was now high in the sky and it was already setting the air on fire as it filtered through the half-open shutters.

'You know, Bertilla...' Marisa searched for the right words to explain what she felt. 'I looked at myself in the mirror this morning.' She aimed her eyes at Sister Bertilla to make sure that she was following. 'And I've seen that I look... normal.' Marisa was leaning forward a little as she spoke. 'Malpighi's child left me with a scar on my body up to here, almost to the middle of my chest.' She slowly followed with her fingers the outline of the scar above the light cotton of her nightgown, which was now sticking to her, damp with sweat. 'I lost it and my body is disfigured for ever because of it. And it felt right, because that was how I felt. Disfigured.' For a moment, Marisa abandoned herself to the memory of the emptiness left behind in her by that unborn child whom nobody ever mentioned. 'With Betta, though? When your child dies, grief should maim your body, don't you think?' Marisa looked into Sister Bertilla's eyes for a sign of understanding. 'It should deform you, leave you with your insides out, bleeding.' She opened her hands to show herself as she was, whole. 'All that pain ... And instead ...' The rest of her words dissolved on her lips.

Sister Bertilla took both her hands. Marisa pulled back instinctively, but the nun's grip was stronger. 'I see your pain, though,' Sister Bertilla told Marisa to comfort her, to do justice to her desperation. She interlaced Marisa's fingers with her own. 'Do you remember the day Betta was born? I was there. I was holding your hand just like this.' She lowered her eyes. '*Help me, Sister Bertilla!* you said,' she reminded Marisa in the tone of a mother talking to her little girl.

The shadow of a tender smile appeared on Marisa's lips.

'I was there,' the nun continued. 'I held Elisabetta even before you did.'

Marisa remembered. It was true. Sister Bertilla had put Betta on her chest, as she had done with Ettore.

'I have to go to say goodbye to Betta,' Sister Bertilla told her, her voice choking with a grief that was similar to Marisa's yet different.

'I don't want to,' Marisa said back, softly.

'Help me, Marisa.' Sister Bertilla tightened her grip so much that it hurt her. 'I can't do it without you.' She paused for a moment, the air loaded with the unspoken. 'Help me: my faith is wavering, and, without my faith, I have consecrated my life to nothing.'

Marisa looked at their hands clasped together, so tightly that their knuckles were already turning white.

'We'll go like this,' the nun reassured Marisa. 'We'll help each other like this.'

They held hands while Father Mario, who was so old he could barely stand, spoke about God's plan and how it escaped human understanding, and about the cruelty of miscreants who one day would find themselves before Our Lord and would have to answer for their actions. He spoke of redemption and forgiveness. He reminded everyone that 'unto dust shalt thou return' and that Elisabetta, a most beloved daughter and sister, had gifted them with joy and love over her short journey in life. Unhappy with his own arguments, he reassured the congregation that they would all meet again one day, in the Kingdom of Heaven.

Sitting between Stelvio and Sister Bertilla, Marisa was staring at the framed photograph of Betta that had been placed on the coffin: her hair loose on her tanned shoulders, the open smile between the little dimples that softened her cheeks giving her a childish expression. Her eyes shone, though the photograph could not show the tiny specks of gold that brightened her brown irises. It felt as if she was looking straight at her mother, from out of the explosion of flowers of all colours that surrounded her. Every arrangement came with a white sash. Emma really had thought about everything: pink and white roses from Mamma and Papà; white roses, lilies and chrysanthemums from Zia and Zio; mixed flowers from her cousins; carnations, gerberas and sunflowers from Ettore; only white roses from Nonna. But there were also a great number of colourful bouquets, truly magnificent. Others still were more modest, small, with cards tucked among the stems.

However, Marisa's gaze was fixed on an arrangement of red roses and white orchids with no sash. It was the most beautiful of them all, and she had recognised it. She had received an identical, breathtakingly lavish bouquet on the day of her twenty-first birthday, delivered at home by a messenger in livery. 'For Signorina Balestrieri,' he had said to her politely as she looked for a tip, her heart beating wildly in her chest.

'That one there is from Malpighi,' Marisa whispered to Sister Bertilla with a slight movement of her chin.

Sister Bertilla looked at the arrangement that carried no sash or card. She said nothing and carried on listening to Father Mario.

Marisa, on the other hand, was plunged into the nostalgia of that day so many years ago when, holding that bouquet close to her chest, she had tasted the naive certainty of a happy life. Although in fact, Malpighi truly had given her a happy life in a way. His desertion and their unborn child had put Stelvio Ansaldo in Marisa's path. Now, all of a sudden, night had fallen and everything was over, but Malpighi could not be blamed for that. Sincere forgiveness towards Francesco Malpighi poured out of Marisa's heart. Right now, as she sat in front of her daughter's white coffin, the pain he had inflicted on her seemed like a small thing indeed. Marisa thought that he deserved her forgiveness, if only for the thoughtfulness he had shown towards her daughter: not a homage to the dead but an act of gallantry towards a young woman whose life had been cut short. Just like that, with no need for words or cards, since he knew that her mother would understand and that was enough for him.

Smiling, she stood up, walked up to the coffin and placed Malpighi's arrangement in front of the photograph of Betta, who had never received flowers in life. The people in the church looked at Marisa pityingly.

Being so weak, she swayed a little. Stelvio caught up with her, surrounded her waist with an arm and helped her arrange the flowers the way she wanted, then took her back to her seat.

On the day of Elisabetta Ansaldo's funeral, Gaspare Mannino left home early. He got on a coach at the bus stop in the square in Genzano and sat at the very back even though he was the only passenger and all the seats were empty.

The driver was humming 'Porta Portese'. At every verse, he raised his voice a little, cheerful, as the following day he too would finally be on holiday.

Gaspare's head was splitting. He could not even remember the last time he had slept. Maybe two days earlier, but he could no longer tell night from day, cold from heat. From time to time, he collapsed for a few minutes out of sheer exhaustion, only to then wake up with his heart in his throat and his stomach clenched in a vice that made him throw up the little food he had managed to get down. Gaspare had told his mother, who was planning on spending a few more days in Torre Domizia, that he had come down with the flu. His mother was upset that he had not stayed with her for the whole month as he had promised. However, she was happy that he had been hired to work at the tourist office. She had not had high hopes for Gaspare since he had dropped out of secondary school, but evidently his late lamented father had interceded for him from Heaven and found him a job. As a matter of fact, though, there had never been a job at the tourist office, and Signora Mannino would only later find out that her son had lied to her.

Gaspare looked at the quartz watch that his mother had given him for his eighteenth birthday. She had spent a fortune on it, but she had told him that he deserved it: even though he had given her reason to worry from time to time, as all children did, he was a good son after all. Over the last few days, Gaspare had stopped wearing the watch on his wrist. Instead, he kept it clenched in the palm of his hand. It had stopped telling the time after he had spent hours washing and scrubbing it under the tap. He had ruined it for ever, and to no avail: the blonde curls were still stuck between the links of the wristband. They seemed to be melded into the grooves of the metal, and the harder he scrubbed, the more they shone like gold threads against the steel of the band. He had scraped at them with his nails, but they did not break, so tightly were they wound. This morning, Gaspare actually had the impression that they had increased in number. He felt like standing in the middle of the town square and screaming at the top of his lungs, 'My watch is growing hair, see?' Gaspare thought about chasing down passers-by and friends to show them. But no, he could not do that. He had to keep the matter of the golden locks to himself. He had to keep many things to himself. Too many.

The driver was still singing when Gaspare got off the coach. It was already stiflingly hot though it was not even eight in the morning but Gaspare was no longer capable of feeling warmth, not even in the long-sleeved shirt he had worn to hide the scratches that Betta Ansaldo's nails had left on his arms. He began walking along Via del Pometo. Not a single car went by; there was not a living soul around. The grit on the asphalt crunched under his trainers in the stillness. That emptiness scared him. He felt as if he was the only person left on the face of the earth, until a stray dog, a female with a long golden coat, appeared next to him, startling him. She lifted her young, lively muzzle and swung her head, as if motioning him in the right direction. Gaspare followed her as far as the monumental bridge that had brought him there in the first place. When they stopped, he held out a hand to stroke her, but the dog pulled back, suspicious, her tail between her legs. It was as if she could see right through him. Then, all of a sudden, she scampered away as if someone had called her.

With hardly any effort, Gaspare pulled himself up on to the wide parapet. He knelt and then stood up, filling his lungs with air. Feeling a light gust of wind, a smile of relief on his face, he let himself fall into the void.

With a thud, his body landed in the dense undergrowth seventy metres below.

6

Normal Life

Elisabetta Ansaldo was buried in the Campo Verano cemetery, in the Balestrieri family vault, next to her grandfather. The vault was a small chapel that Ettore Balestrieri had bought, at great cost, because he needed to know that one day he would somehow be surrounded by his loved ones again. Ettore would have never believed, when he was alive, that the first to join him would be the granddaughter he had not even met.

On the first Monday of September, Stelvio Ansaldo got up early to go and open the shop. He left Marisa in bed, unable to determine whether she was still asleep or merely waiting for that day too to be over one way or another.

His customers started poking their heads in right away, looking uncertain and even almost timid. They asked, 'May I?' and let themselves be served without making too many demands. They waited patiently to pay until Stelvio had a chance to go to the till. Only a few dared ask, 'How is Signora Ansaldo doing?' Stelvio would nod slowly, without raising his eyes. 'Better. Much better. Thank you,' he lied each time.

No one ever mentioned Betta. No one dared to. Losing a daughter, especially one so young, was a devastating loss, but the details they had read in the newspapers had left them all speechless. Not a single word had been uttered in the neighbourhood on the matter, not even a comment in the privacy of one's own home. Even the most inveterate busybodies were filled with uneasiness in the face of that tragedy.

During the first few weeks, Letizia looked after the house on her own, as much as her health allowed. Then, one day, a day like any other, Marisa got up, got dressed in her house clothes and started cleaning. Stelvio took care of the groceries. He would bring her what she needed and she would cook the simplest fare: pasta, stew, salad, vegetables, chicken and potatoes. It was careless food, unimaginative, only good to fill up the dishes on the table and satisfy what little appetite they had left. The clattering of the tableware amplified their silence as they ate. Marisa no longer had any interest in the outside world and Stelvio had become taciturn, always lost in thought. On Sundays he accompanied his mother-in-law to Mass, listened distractedly to the priest, then went to the cemetery with her, to tidy up the chapel and bring fresh flowers. They exchanged a few words about the marble, which was turning yellow in one corner; about the light, which was perhaps too dim; and about the early signs of rust on the grille of the wrought-iron gate. Each time, Stelvio promised that he would take care of it soon.

Marisa did not go. She stayed at home. She had not left the house at all, not since the day of the funeral. In the morning, she never got out of bed before eight even though she was always already awake. She slept in short spells throughout the day: half an hour in the armchair while the TV played a documentary about the fish of the Pacific Ocean; ten minutes with her head on the arm of the sofa while Stelvio watched the news; some scraps of rest in the darkness of nights that felt never-ending. From time to time she would go into Betta's room and lie on her bed, dozing off only to awaken with a start, convinced that she had heard her come in, open her wardrobe and leaf through a book at her desk while huffing and puffing at the thought of doing her homework. The pain of waking up was always the same or, rather, ever more atrocious. 'Betta is dead,' Marisa repeated to herself over and over again.

Months went by without Marisa even noticing, until one day she realised that her hair had grown and that a great number of white strands were shining through her natural colour. So she grabbed her scissors and chopped off all that was left of the golden-brown dye, which had turned dull over time. She cut her hair short, as she had seen her hairdresser Clelia do over the past forty years, then combed it, tucking in as best she could the few natural waves that were left.

When Stelvio returned from the shop at lunchtime, he stared at Marisa for a while, confused, then he smiled at her with a tender sadness. 'You look good,' was all he said.

When the holidays drew near, Letizia announced that she wanted to go and spend some time at Emma's to see her grandchildren, who would be home for Christmas. Marisa said that it was fine by her. Once Letizia was packed up, she went to join her daughter in the kitchen, where she was peeling potatoes, as she waited for the Bassevis' driver who would be there shortly to take her to Emma's.

'Are you sure you won't need me?' Letizia asked.

'And what could you do? Go. There are no grandchildren here.'

'Ettore is coming, though, isn't he?'

'It's still to be decided. He is busy with the rehearsals for the New Year's Day concert in Germany.'

'Won't you come to Emma's?'

'No.'

Letizia sat down. She always felt exhausted of late. 'Marisa, one day Ettore will have a family of his own,' Letizia consoled her daughter. 'Grandchildren will bring you some joy.'

Marisa stopped peeling potatoes and scoffed at her mother. 'Ettore?' she said, staring at Letizia. 'Have you really not worked it out?'

Letizia looked at her. 'Worked what out?'

'Ettore is not the type to go after women, Mamma,' Marisa said eloquently.

Letizia froze, stunned.

Marisa seemed to be lost in thought for a moment as she stared at Letizia. 'You *hadn't* worked it out ... That's why you've always doted on him so much.' She smiled, as if disclosing that information to her mother had brought her some unhoped-for comfort.

'It isn't true!' Letizia muttered.

'Of course it is,' Marisa replied, standing up and turning her back to her as she soaked the potatoes.

'Did he tell you?'

'I'm his mother. He doesn't need to.'

This time it was Letizia who scoffed. 'As if you have ever been any good at knowing the first thing about your children!'

Marisa turned around abruptly. 'Don't you dare!'

'It seems obvious to me that you failed to raise them properly. You always allowed Betta more freedom than you should have,' Letizia said, then took a deep breath and added in a tone loaded with insinuation, 'And what you didn't allow her, she took the liberty of doing anyway.'

'I don't want to hear you utter Betta's name in my presence ever again,' Marisa said, her voice choking with anger.

'Why? Because I'm speaking the truth? You reap what you sow.'

Marisa shook her head in disbelief.

'If she'd stayed at home, like a decent girl, she'd still be alive,' Letizia carried on. 'Everybody thinks it, but no one dares to say it to your face.' As she said this, she pushed herself up on her good arm and stood up.

Marisa peered into Letizia's eyes, still unable to believe that her mother had really uttered those words. 'You think she had it coming ...' This was not a question, merely a statement that was leaving her breathless.

'I didn't say that.'

'But you do think it. You've always thought it.' The frost Marisa felt inside prevented her from saying any more.

Letizia Balestrieri chose not to answer; instead she went back to her room to wait for the Bassevis' driver, then left without exchanging even a parting word with her daughter.

When Stelvio returned home in the evening, he asked after his mother-in-law and his wife told him that she had gone to stay at Emma's. Then Marisa added that she would not be back, and left it at that. Stelvio studied Marisa's expression and realised that Letizia had been unable to hold her tongue even in the face of a mother's grief. He knew what people thought of Betta. He had read it in Emma's eyes, in Emanuele's, in Counsel Custureri's. When he had gone with Emma and Emanuele to the legal firm for an update on the investigation, the lawyer had hinted at the fact that, during the preliminary inquest, it had emerged that Betta was acquainted with many young men – and that word, 'many', had sounded like 'too many'. And many of these relationships were not just friendships – and that 'many', too, had sounded like 'too many'. People were talking, telling, alleging. Yet Stelvio had also realised that nobody seemed to actually know who all these young men were, or where they lived. Only a handful of names had emerged, and they were all decent boys, above any suspicion. It seemed that there were only nice boys in Torre Domizia. And if that was so, Stelvio had asked, why was it a problem if Betta was in the habit of wandering around on her own at night? Why did Custureri insist that she had been reckless? If they were all nice, as they kept on saying, why should Betta have been afraid?

Custureri had writhed in his plump leather chair. 'You see, Signor Ansaldo, the investigating magistrate is convinced that they were criminals just passing through, young men involved with a bad crowd ... Are you following the investigation of the Bologna bombing? All hell has broken loose ... ' Custureri had said, casting a sad but eloquent glance in his direction. 'Over the last few years, organised crime has been increasingly active, even on the coast, as you will certainly know ... '

'But didn't you say that Betta was perhaps meeting someone?'

'It's possible, it's possible,' the lawyer had said as he nodded quickly.

'And when would she have made this appointment with organised criminals? She had been to the beach with her cousin the day before and Miriam says that they didn't speak to anyone.' Stelvio had turned towards Emma to confirm that Miriam had indeed said that.

'Maybe she went to the bar to have a soda, or maybe she rang someone in secret. You know young people these days ... They act thoughtlessly; they don't think about consequences.' Custureri had looked at Stelvio with a gaze full of insinuation. 'Maybe in her naivety she had been too familiar with some shady characters.'

Stelvio had taken a deep breath. He was buckling under the weight of sorrow and had very little energy left, even to speak. 'Look, are we trying to ascertain whether my daughter was a fool, or are we trying to find these bastards?' He had leaned imperceptibly towards Custureri. 'Because I still can't tell.'

'Of course we're looking for the culprits, of course!'

'So why is the magistrate enquiring so much about Betta?' Stelvio had said, narrowing his eyes. 'Betta was who she was, but she was not an idiot. She had friends everywhere, everyone loved her, she went to the cinema, she went dancing and she didn't like school. Her mother and I reined her in with words, punishments and, when necessary, even the occasional slipper. Even if she had been seeing the whole of Torre Domizia – and Marisa and I know that this is not the case – what would that have to do with what happened to her?'

'To find the culprits, we need to understand the dynamics,'

the counsel had said, his eyebrows arching at the banality of the question as if he were talking to some poor bumpkin.

'Dynamics of what?' Stelvio's tone had risen ever so slightly, made coarse by the anger slowly mounting in him. 'They murdered my daughter and left her there like a dog, tossed her away.' His voice had cracked and he had needed a moment to collect himself. 'We're here, talking, debating whether she was respectable or not ... What difference does it make? Why do you care?' Emanuele Bassevi, who was sitting to his right, had put a hand on his arm to calm him down. Then Stelvio had added, 'I want justice for my daughter!' His voice, choking, had sounded like a scream.

'Of course, of course!' Custureri had agreed, raising his hands condescendingly: there was good reason to fear that that man was at madness's door – his eyes sunken in his dark sockets, his hands shaking, his voice hoarse. The counsel had glanced at Emma Bassevi, looking for her support.

Emma, who was sitting to the left of Stelvio, had stepped in right away. 'Stelvio, Custureri and his counsels are doing their very best to find the people who did those horrible things to Betta.'

'And what are they doing? What *are* they doing? Even if my daughter had promised herself for money, what would it be to you?' Stelvio had snapped. 'Tell the magistrate that he needs to turn Torre Domizia upside down. No out-of-towner nor a single car goes by the river mouth without the entire town noticing!'

'Stelvio, calm down,' Emma had whispered.

'The bar at Le Dune was already closed for the night. The back of my daughter's hair smelled of beer but she had not had anything to drink! The medical examiner said so!' Stelvio had slammed his hand on the desk and Custureri had flinched. 'Who sold the beer to those animals? Where did they buy it, these out-of-towners you talk about?'

'This is impossible,' the counsel had complained, shaking his head towards Emma.

'I want a new counsel!' Stelvio had said, standing up.

Custureri had thrown up his hands again.

'To what end, Stelvio?' Emma had interjected. 'To put yourself in the hands of unscrupled people who are only looking to gain publicity off the back of Betta's death?' she continued as she followed Stelvio, who was headed for the door.

'I want to see those animals behind bars!' Stelvio had said as he opened the door. Before leaving, he had turned towards Custureri. 'As long as I don't find them sooner and kill them with my own hands.'

On the way home, Emanuele, talking father to father, had convinced Stelvio that he needed to let Custureri's counsels do their job since they were the very best, they had the most reputable experts and they could access the most favourable consultants. Emanuele had told Stelvio that, father to father, he understood his anger: if someone had done to Miriam what they had done to Betta, he would have reacted just as he had. But they ought to remain rational and try to reconstruct in full what had happened that night in order to better understand whether Betta really had known her murderers. As Stelvio himself had said, Betta had had friends everywhere. At this point Stelvio had looked him in the eye and understood that Emanuele Bassevi actually had no clue about how

Stelvio felt: he was so certain that something like that could have never happened to his daughter.

Marisa, who had been questioned briefly just a handful of times, never asked her husband about his meetings with the counsels and with Magistrate Castagnoli, or about the phone calls with Maresciallo Nardulli, who could not deny that those animals really seemed to have appeared from thin air and disappeared back into it. Nardulli had told Stelvio that everything was back to normal in Torre Domizia even before the end of summer. The holidaymakers had gone back home firmly convinced that a horror like that could have never been perpetrated by someone from the area. As if the monsters had come from the sea and gone back the same way. As months went by, Stelvio became increasingly convinced that they would never find his daughter's killers, since they had never really been looking for them in the first place. Or, if they had tried, like good old Nardulli, they had failed. Even the newspapers were talking about the case less and less, and with more resignation. 'The Torre Domizia murder' had turned almost immediately into 'the Ansaldo case' and was slowly slipping into the hotchpotch of crimes about which no one had much to say. A victim but no culprit. An inquiry that was going nowhere. It happened. Maybe his wife's silence, her apparent indifference, stemmed precisely from that. She had realised before anyone else that they were impotent in the face of that night that had swallowed up everything and left only Betta's violated body behind, like scraps after an abundant meal.

So, after the night that had taken their daughter, the silence of everyday life slowly took over everything else. During the week, Stelvio spent his days at the shop. Then, in the evening, Marisa wished him good night after dinner and went to bed, knowing full well that she would not sleep a wink. In the morning, she had nothing to say to him apart from reminding him to take out the rubbish, pay the bills or buy groceries. He looked after normal life outside the house; she looked after normal life within the walls of that home that she had turned into a shelter from everything and everyone outside it. She cleaned, ironed, cooked. The phone hardly ever rang any more; the doorbell was always silent. All that happened beyond the door to the apartment had ceased to exist.

Stelvio stopped going to church on Sunday mornings after Letizia moved out, but nevertheless he kept visiting Betta every week. Marisa never went with him; she had not been to her daughter's grave since the day of the funeral. On Sunday mornings, Stelvio caught the bus to the Campo Verano cemetery and chose a little bunch of flowers from the kiosk by the entrance, taking care to always pick a different one; then, after a long walk along the paths of the cemetery, he went to spend some time in the Balestrieri mausoleum. He chatted aloud with his daughter about this and that. While he arranged the new flowers with great care, he explained to Betta that her mother could not make it because she was not well. But she was thinking of her. Always. All the time. When dejection spilled over, he asked Betta for advice: 'What should I do? How can I help your mum?' His daughter smiled at him from the photograph and did not answer. There was no answer. What might she know about any of it, at sixteen? So Stelvio asked his father-in-law instead, with tears in his eyes. 'Ettore, what should I do? I'm not as strong as you!' All that silence made him feel lonelier than ever before. Everyone had abandoned him.

Then, in February, the day of Betta's seventeenth birthday arrived. Neither Stelvio nor Marisa said a word that morning, pain nailing their breath into their chests as they stood in the kitchen and drank coffee that had never tasted so bitter. Before going to open the shop, Stelvio asked Marisa if she wanted to go to the cemetery at lunchtime. He could not find the strength to say his daughter's name. Marisa said no and then headed to the bathroom to load the washing machine.

That evening, when he got back home, Stelvio saw that Marisa had left his dinner in the oven. He went to look for her and found her in Betta's room, lying on the bed under a throw. His wife told him that she was not hungry, that he should go ahead and eat and not wait for her. Stelvio came closer, hoping to exchange a few words, to ask her whether they could try to see if their grief might become a bit more tolerable by bearing it together. But he did not dare open his mouth, like a doctor giving up on a patient who was sick beyond hope.

As he went back to the kitchen, his eyes fell on the old upright piano and he headed towards it slowly. They had put the stool away many years ago: after his son Ettore had left, it had become simply a useless encumbrance. Even the missing stool broke his heart now. Over time, he had got used to the distance between himself and his son, but now, knowing that he was far away exacerbated his bewilderment. Marisa had driven Ettore away from that bleakness so that he might breathe in life and save himself, without taking account of them. It had been the right thing to do. His need to have him close instead, even only for a comforting glance, made Stelvio feel selfish and weak. What mattered was that Ettore followed his path, despite the pain of the phone calls, of the rare visits without Betta's cheerfulness to welcome him back.

Stelvio lifted the lid of the piano and pressed a key at random with his forefinger. A sharp, annoying tone echoed through the silence. He closed the lid carefully so as not to make any more noise.

He sat down to eat, not even turning on the TV for the news. He was struggling to swallow his food, so tight was his throat after the desolation of a day that, in another epoch, would have been a boundless celebration. Stelvio took a bottle of wine from the shelf that had been there for ages and that night he – who had always drunk so little – accompanied every forkful with a sip or two of wine. When he had drunk half the bottle, he realised that he was feeling better. He was breathing again and his chest felt lighter. The scream of pain from deep down inside him was so dampened that he could almost no longer hear it. On the contrary, he felt a pleasant, drowsy euphoria tickle him within, almost a lull. He washed his plate and went to bed, where he passed out.

The following evening, Marisa told him that she had decided to move into Betta's room at night, so that her insomnia would not bother him. Stelvio said that it had never bothered him and that she could keep her light on as long as she wanted. He insisted, but she had made up her mind: it was better this way; she would feel free to get up when she could not sleep. So she stopped sleeping in their bed. Again he looked for something to say to her, a word that might penetrate the loneliness Marisa had walled herself into, leaving him on the outside. It was to no avail. All he got from his wife was an indifference that he felt he did not deserve but which he excused because of a desperation he understood all too well. Since neither his daughter nor his father-in-law, whom he had loved like a father, had managed to give him any good advice, Stelvio Ansaldo found no other relief for his sorrow than the bottle he took home every night – though only after ringing it up at the till, since he was an honest man even in his vice. During the string of purposeless days that was his normal life, he started to live only for the consolation of the wine that he drank alone with his dinner. When the first anniversary of his daughter's death came around, he went to the cemetery on his own and cried tears of sorrow and shame because, in order to survive, he had had to become a drunk.

Emma Bassevi only realised how much her daughter had changed when she saw her get out of the car one day in December, a few months after Betta's death. The driver had gone to fetch Miriam from the airport and drive her to Villa Estherina, where the family was spending the holidays. It was the early afternoon of Christmas Eve. Over the previous months, Emma and Miriam had spoken on the phone at least once a week and Miriam had always sounded cursory, evasive. She made it seem as though nothing ever happened, as though everything passed her by inconsequently. Academically Miriam was as successful as ever, her teachers had reassured Emma, but she rarely took part in extracurricular activities, did not socialise much, and often looked tired. After a brief fainting spell during PE, the school doctor had found her appetite lacking and her sleep insufficient. So, with her parents' permission, he had prescribed her vitamins and homoeopathic drops that would help her sleep a little better. They had all agreed that this was a normal consequence of the trauma Miriam had experienced due to her cousin's death. However, Emma and Emanuele had not deemed it necessary for their daughter to see a therapist, despite the doctor's strong recommendation.

But when Emma saw Miriam walk towards her in her cream coat across the patio of Villa Estherina, she had the feeling that her daughter was a stranger. Miriam's face was almost completely hidden behind a chunky scarf that only revealed her eyes and Emma thought, feeling slightly uneasy, that she had the gaze of a grown woman. It had lost the light of adolescence, as if twenty years had gone by since they had last seen each other. And she was so thin: Emma almost feared that Miriam might be blown away by the December wind, so insubstantial did her body look.

'Darling!' Emma said, smiling joyously from the threshold and opening her arms to welcome her in.

Miriam returned her mother's hug with no feeling and lowered her scarf to cursorily kiss her cheeks. 'Mamma . . .' she said, then walked past Emma and into the house.

While Miriam was at Villa Estherina, her presence instilled in her family a subtle sense of unease. She was as kind as ever but she smiled very little. She listened to the conversation around the table without saying a word, and if someone addressed her directly she let out half-formed sentences that quickly dispersed among the voices of others. It was like having an uninterested guest who was prone to becoming distracted by thoughts that took her elsewhere. She spent a lot of time in her room and declined her brother Donato's invitations to check out this trendy bar or that one, now that she was a bit older.

Emma shared her worry with her mother, but Letizia played the whole thing down. She complacently reminded Emma that Miriam had always been a sensible girl. Then she added eloquently that there were more important things to worry about.

One afternoon, while the sun was still high and it was unseasonably warm, Emma tried to persuade her daughter to go for a walk in the park. Miriam accepted unenthusiastically.

'The headmaster told me that you're no longer riding,' Emma said, after they had walked in silence for a long while. Her daughter had always been an excellent rider and the previous year had won prizes in all the competitions she had taken part in.

'I'd rather focus on my schoolwork.'

'But you adore riding!' Emma objected petulantly.

'Not so much any more.'

'You should eat more. You're skin and bones.'

'I'm fine.'

'Are the vitamins helping?'

'Very much.'

They walked in silence for a while longer before Emma decided it would be okay to ask, 'Do you miss your cousin?'

Miriam walked on without saying a word, as if she had not heard a thing.

'We never spoke about it . . . ' Emma insisted, ill at ease. She hated the idea of bringing up this subject with her daughter. Emma waited, in vain, for a word, a sign. 'Miriam?'

Miriam stopped and stared at her mother over the top of her scarf, her curious doe eyes making her look like a little girl again. 'What is there to say?' Miriam asked, as if Betta were just a futile memory from a long-gone past.

Those words sent a shiver through Emma: for a few seconds she felt as if someone had told her that, in a parallel world, it had been her daughter and not her niece who had died on that beach. She looked at Miriam as she resumed walking, her hands in the pockets of the fuchsia jacket that Emma had given her, her two flamingo-like legs poking out at the bottom. Her mother's instinct, which was usually unreliable, told her that she had to ask more, that she had to understand. And yet, she did not speak. The walk ended and they went back inside.

Over the following months, Miriam became a constant concern for Emma.

At first she tried to call her more often on the phone, but the aseptic cordiality of their conversations disquieted her. Emma no longer noticed the impatience that had been creeping into her calls to Donato over the years, but Miriam's indifference distressed her. Her daughter defused her worry with perfunctory words, reassuring her with banal arguments that resembled closely the platitudes Emma herself used with her most prestigious and most petulant customers. This attitude hurt Emma, of course, but what she was sensing mostly frightened her. That sense of detachment, which was so grown-up, could not be further from Miriam's nature prior to Betta's death. After the tragedy, Emma had instinctively sent Miriam back to the sheltered environs of her school, certain that physical distance would protect her from any kind of involvement in the matter of her cousin. She had believed silence to be the solution. Denial, almost. Because she would not have known how to explain to her daughter, who was still so naive, the brutality of the violence to which Betta had been subjected, the cruel end that had overcome her. And yet, Miriam *knew*. What had Sattaflora's son said when he'd knocked at the door that morning? And what had Marisa screamed in her desperation? But, more importantly, how far had Miriam's imagination gone when confronted with all that had been left unspoken?

Letizia insisted that her granddaughter would have been able to hear very little or nothing at all from Ettore's room. Then she would become irritated, say that they needed to leave it all alone, that people of Miriam's age changed their moods all the time. She knew it all too well, having raised two daughters of her own. The more Emma asked and tried to understand, the more her mother became upset and ordered her to let her granddaughter be, to stop tormenting her. Emanuele was on his mother-in-law's side and accused his wife of being obsessed with the whole thing. At times Emma wondered whether she should ask Marisa for help, but then she always ended up thinking that it would be cruel to seek advice about a living daughter from her sister who was mourning a dead one. The mere idea made Emma feel guilty, and deeply ashamed of her inability to be a good mother, despite having had the privilege of seeing Miriam turn into a woman.

Towards spring, as she relaxed after an intense day at work, Emma had an idea that lit her up inside with an almost childlike enthusiasm. While she browsed through a photoshoot on the latest trends in equestrian fashion, she remembered a competition Miriam had taken part in two years earlier. At that time, a breeder they knew had shown her daughter an English thoroughbred of rare beauty and Miriam had fallen in love with her. For a long time, she had stroked the horse's streamlined muzzle and her black coat, on which the morning light drew streaks of gold. Emma could not remember ever seeing such marvel in her daughter's eyes. Eventually Miriam had pulled herself away from the horse – reluctantly but with resignation, like a meek child whose most longed-for doll has been taken away. Emma and Emanuele had smiled at this, touched. Then they had immediately forgotten all about it.

Using Miriam's former riding teacher as a broker, Emma negotiated for the young thoroughbred for over two weeks. But the breeder was not interested in selling; he deemed the mare priceless. She was perfect and had already proved herself in international competitions. He called her his gem. Eventually, though, Emma got her way, buying her for a price that made her head spin. But she told herself that if Emanuele could squander a fortune on the vulgar bimbo he kept, then she had every right to buy her daughter the horse of her dreams. At any price.

After her school graduation in June, when she came home for good, Miriam noticed that her mother was possessed by an unusual euphoria. Emma could sense her daughter's hostility and worried that she had got it all wrong once again. She remembered that Miriam was no longer interested in riding and told herself that her gift would just prove a further demonstration of the fact that she did not know how to listen.

All of a sudden, she hated both herself and the thoroughbred that was about to become the symbol of her yet another failure as a mother.

Still, Emma decided to take Miriam to the riding ground with an excuse the day after her return, still hoping deep down that her gift might open a breach in the wall her daughter had surrounded herself with. Miriam agreed to go along reluctantly, reminding her mother that she was no longer interested in riding. Emma plaintively begged her to be patient. When they got there, the stable manager escorted them with ceremony, all the while casting conspiratorial smiles at Emma: he had been around horses long enough to realise the momentousness of the occasion.

Eventually, Miriam saw the mare grazing under the tepid sun.

'Indira!' she murmured in a whisper, her gaze enraptured by a memory that for a moment called her back to the life from before.

'She's yours,' Emma said, stopping a little behind her.

Miriam moved forward deliberately and Indira lifted her muzzle. She slowly surrounded the horse's neck with her arms and the thoroughbred let her, docile. Then Miriam pulled back just for a moment, glanced at her mother with eyes full of tears and moved her lips in a voiceless *thank you*.

Emma nodded, in tears. Though she managed to persuade herself that she was weeping out of joy, instead she was feeling an infinite sorrow and did not know it.

Emma thought that Indira's arrival in her daughter's life had brought back a certain normality that felt reassuring. Though

Miriam was adamant that she would no longer compete, she still spent all her days at the riding ground: the fresh air had returned a slightly healthier complexion to her skin, and the long rides she took had brightened her eyes. She was still quiet but less lost in her world. Her mother noticed that none of her friends from school called her or invited her out. Emma asked her why and Miriam told her that she no longer had much in common with her schoolfriends: they had grown up and, though they had spent many years together, it was now time for them to go their separate ways. Instead she felt the need to meet new people. All the same, Emma could not see any new friends on the horizon – let alone any aspiring boyfriends, even though Miriam was pretty.

One day, while they were having breakfast on the veranda, Emma suggested that Miriam should go to see their new family dentist to find out whether it was finally time to fix the diastem between her incisors. Almost startled, Miriam raised her eyes from her cup as if she had heard a voice from somewhere else, far away from there. Her face turned glum all of a sudden. 'No,' she said.

Her tone had a resoluteness that disconcerted Emma. 'Why not? It wouldn't take much ...'

'I said no,' Miriam repeated, going back to sipping her tea.

As she studied her, Emma realised that Miriam's rigid diet went well beyond womanly vanity: she barely nibbled at food and refused to eat any kind of sweet things. Emma decided to speak about it with Dr Mineo, a psychiatrist who had been helping her face some weaknesses of hers that had been troubling her for years now.

'Very well,' Emma said, sighing accommodatingly and

forcibly pulling herself away from a train of thoughts that was making her feel terribly uneasy. 'After all, the gap has already become so small ... You know, it actually suits you. Maybe you're right, maybe you should keep it.'

Miriam stood up all of a sudden, noisily pushing her chair back. 'Please don't mention it again,' she said curtly, and then, having put an icy end to the conversation, went back upstairs.

That summer, Dr Agostino Mineo and Indira helped Miriam carry the weight that was crushing her.

Indira made Miriam feel less lonely, and Dr Mineo introduced her to barbiturates.

Like Emma, Agostino Mineo thought that psychoanalysis was a fashionable waste of time and that it had come about only to satisfy the voyeurism of certain gasbags who were unfit to become doctors. Therefore, he met Emma Bassevi's revelations with gentle reassurances and recommended she send her daughter to see him instead. Dr Mineo deemed it unnecessary to stir up the obvious grief that the girl was feeling over the loss of her cousin. Why harass her? All they needed to understand was how they could make her feel better. He promised that he would help her without fail.

Emma had quite a struggle convincing Miriam to let herself be seen by Dr Mineo. Miriam's excessive thinness and her constant tiredness worried Emma more and more every day, but her daughter obstinately refused to go, and spent entire days locked in her room to avoid having to talk about it. Eventually, when pleading failed, Emma went as far as threatening to get rid of Indira if her daughter still refused to indulge her.

Miriam gave in, on condition that Emma would leave her alone afterwards.

So, one muggy afternoon, Miriam went on her own to the top-floor apartment of the elegant building in the Fleming neighbourhood where the consultant saw his patients. Dr Mineo's elderly mother acted as his secretary, since almost all his income, which was sizeable, was squandered on young women, gambling, and excellent whisky. The doctor subsidised his vices by liberally prescribing certain substances to the ladies of Rome's higher echelons. His patients adored him because he showed as much indulgence towards their weaknesses as he did his own. He wrote out his prescriptions with the discretion of a gentleman of a bygone era and handed them out like freshly cut flowers. The ladies smiled and paid, grateful: they needed the pills to keep their figures, sleep peacefully, dampen the sorrow of a cheating husband or feel a touch bubblier at a dinner party with friends.

Dr Mineo agreed that Miriam was actually quite underweight. And pale. However, he thought that the Bassevi girl seemed serene. Surely she could not be blamed for being somewhat lazy by disposition, uninterested in social life, not at all keen to be involved in certain pastimes of questionable taste that were very common among girls her age. Actually, he found the refined and ethereal young girl to be exceedingly pleasant, her immature body tickling one of his own weaknesses. When Miriam explained to him that her only issue was insomnia, Dr Mineo knew for certain that their friendship would be long-lasting. Of course the lack of sleep was sapping her energy away, turning her apathetic: a good night's sleep would have her blooming like a rose, he thought. Mineo could almost already smell that rose as he stared smugly at her with his large smile, his eyes narrow under his heavy lids.

Naturally, the Bassevi girl was much too young for a regular prescription. Nonetheless, the psychiatrist dipped heavily – just for her – into his personal stash of a particular sleeping pill that was much loved by his patients who suffered from anxiety. He started by giving her enough for one week, just what was necessary for her to appreciate its benefits and come back to see him. It was a gift, on condition that it would remain their little secret and that she would eat more regularly. To amuse her, he told her that he would test her little finger like the witch in *Hansel and Gretel* at every appointment to make sure that she was putting on a little weight.

Miriam did not smile.

That very evening, Dr Mineo's pills revealed to her the secret of oblivion.

Oblivion. As time went by, oblivion tormented Marisa Ansaldo. At these times, her grief became less palpable and let normality filter through, like light through a worn patch of curtain. The spontaneous pleasure in smelling freshly baked bread just out of the oven. The comfort of a warm mug in her hands on a cold winter morning. A little tune, hummed absentmindedly as she hung the laundry on the shared terrace of the apartment building, under the spring sun. The smile that rose to her lips when Ettore rang. Life beckoning. But, when Marisa involuntarily responded, she was then immediately plunged into an agonising guilt. Because she had chosen to survive her baby, who had become dust. So, to escape oblivion, she remained locked in her solitude. She opted to spend her time entirely within the walls that guarded the memory of Betta. The idea of leaving that place, even for a short while, pained her and made her feel as if she were abandoning her daughter.

Sometimes Marisa studied her husband and felt that, for him, oblivion was not as terrible as it was for her. On Sunday afternoons she observed him watching the football on TV, getting angry at a missed goal and muttering curses under his breath. His daughter was not by his side, as she used to be in the life from before. In those moments Marisa hated him: she could see oblivion in his eyes, and it added to her own like the most terrible of sins.

Little by little, they were letting normal life pervade them. The distance and the silence that Marisa had put between herself and Stelvio were all she had left to testify to the irreversible damage that had devastated their lives.

It was true. Stelvio too had to deal with oblivion. When he greeted with a joyful good morning an old customer who had recovered from an illness. When he laughed at the delivery boy telling a lighthearted joke. When he handed a sliver of pizza bianca to a restless toddler in a pram and caught the mother's delighted gaze as she waited to be served. The affliction was the same. But his affliction was added to by his wife becoming more and more disconnected and standoffish every day. Stelvio knew that he had failed to save Betta and now he had failed to save their marriage too: without her daughter, nothing else mattered for Marisa. Not even him.

7

The Girl with the Diadem

Miriam Bassevi, instead, sought oblivion compulsively.

To her, memory was an endless torture: it beleaguered her when she was distracted; it shredded her sleep with recollections that became sharper and sharper every day, moving closer to her, against the natural flow of life, which usually tended to fade with time. The hoarse voice of a stranger, a smell, a sudden flash of light, the first few notes of the song of the summer: any of these was enough to take her back to that beach, under the black sky. Regardless of where she might be at that time, the events were revived in her head right there and then. Air would leave her lungs and crush her against the ground; all of a sudden it was dark and the invader was digging inside her again and again, while Betta stared at the sky in her ballerina pose. Though it all took place in her head, these recollections would leave Miriam physically devastated. People around her noticed only the briefest spells of absent-mindedness, a momentary loss of interest, yet she was fighting to not succumb to her demons every single time.

The first one to guess that Miriam Bassevi was not just a

stuck-up bitch was Cristiana Massiroli, in the winter of 1982. Miriam and Cristiana attended the same design academy in Piazza Colonna but had never spoken to each other. Miriam kept to herself. She often went to class wearing chic riding clothes designed by her mother and was so reluctant in her note-taking and drawing that it was obvious she was only there to please someone else. Moreover, she was evidently anorexic: as the daughter of two physicians, Cristiana had a sixth sense for that kind of stuff. Then one January morning Cristiana observed Miriam trying to drink some tea in the café near the academy: her hands were so shaky that the contents of her cup were spilling all over the place. Cristiana watched Miriam put the teacup back down on to its saucer and wipe the scalding tea from the back of her hand, then massage her neck as if it had turned into marble. She was pale and had deep circles around her red eyes, as if she had not been able to find any peace in days.

Cristiana Massiroli went to sit at Miriam's table unbidden, a surge of sympathy rising inside her, and asked, 'What do you need?'

Startled, Miriam stared at her as if she had never seen her before, and perhaps she had not. 'Excuse me?'

Cristiana lit a cigarette. 'Amphetamines?'

Miriam opened her mouth in indignation, ready to put that stranger who was blathering about drugs back in her place. Instead she surprised herself by answering, 'Phentatyl,' suddenly feeling less hostile.

Cristiana Massiroli grimaced in surprise. 'Phentatyl?'

Miriam nodded quickly. A week ago, Dr Mineo had had a near-fatal heart attack that had put him in a coma and left Miriam out of pills and prescriptions overnight. Her diminishing supply had alarmed her, so she had been to see another consultant. However, he had categorically refused to prescribe Miriam the only medicine that made her feel better and helped her to sleep for a few hours. In its place, he had offered her alternative therapies that had sounded ridiculous to her. What could that man possibly know about the nightmares that tortured her? Miriam had tried to ration the pills she had left while she looked for another solution, but now she was out, and in withdrawal, and she still did not have a bloody prescription. Twelve more hours and she would go insane.

'Do you know someone who sells it?' Miriam pressed Cristiana, trying to sound nice.

Cristiana Massiroli shrugged. 'I wouldn't know, to be honest. Maybe Leo.'

'Where do I find him? At the academy?'

'Who, Leo?' Cristiana laughed in a puff of smoke. 'As if!'

'Where, then?'

'On Fridays you can find him outside Blue Alien, the club on Via Aurelia. By the watermelon kiosk that's shut in winter. He's usually there between midnight and about two or three in the morning.'

'And how do I recognise him?'

'How many pricks do you know who spend their time in front of a watermelon kiosk in the middle of winter?'

Miriam stared at her. As she took this stranger in, she felt like an alien: she was struggling to follow her, to get her sarcasm. It was only then that Miriam noticed that Cristiana had a small ring through her left nostril to which she had attached a thin chain coming from her earlobe. Cristiana's dishevelled mane of black hair with faded blue tips made her look belligerent, but her features were delicate, like a young girl's.

'Do you know him well, this Leo?' Miriam asked.

'I used to buy weed from him. I know he's with a different crowd now.'

'Is he trustworthy?'

'He's a dealer,' Cristiana said with a shrug, to signify the absurdity of Miriam's question.

'Where on Via Aurelia?' Miriam looked for a pen in her handbag.

'In the Montespaccato area. Just ask around, everybody knows him.' Cristiana Massiroli looked at Miriam with a certain pity in her eyes. 'Don't come to class in this state, though,' she advised her.

Miriam lowered her eyes. 'Okay.'

'Do you want some weed?'

Miriam shook her head and stood up. She left her cup of tea unfinished in the middle of the flooded saucer, slung her bag over her shoulder and looked at Cristiana with gratitude. 'I'll see you around.'

Cristiana remained at the table and ate the butter biscuits that had come with the tea and which Miriam had not even touched. 'See you,' she said as she watched Miriam walk away.

Miriam went back home, headed straight for the bathroom and vomited bile, shaken by spasms. She quickly took off all her clothes and stepped under the icy stream of a cold shower. That was what she did when she could no longer breathe – the shock of icy water forcibly pushed air into her lungs and helped her catch her breath again. Then she slid down slowly, hugged her knees with her hands and stayed there for a while, naked and shivering.

Things had taken a rapid turn for the worse ever since Miriam had moved into the apartment in Via Barberini. While she was still living at home she had been forced to try to keep the situation under control: although her mother was now living between Rome and New York, and her father had basically moved out, the watchful, prying eyes of her grandmother and of the help followed Miriam around everywhere. Now she spent the great majority of her time on her own instead. The apartment, which the Bassevis had owned since the fifties, had been vacated the year before, so Miriam had asked her parents to let her move in, and they had agreed, since she did not want to learn how to drive and the apartment was only a short walk from college. Her parents were paying for the academy and had allocated her a sizeable monthly allowance for her expenses, only ringing her from time to time to check in. Miriam had no other worry in the world but to stay alive.

However, over the past few months she had often wondered why she put so much effort into it. Apart from the time she spent at the riding ground, when she was well enough to go, life was becoming more unbearable by the day. She had hoped that time might eventually soften her obsessions, her panic attacks, her terror at the nightmares that tortured her. Instead the exact opposite had happened: it was like desperately swimming towards the shore only to realise that the water was getting deeper, while tiredness crushed her arms, weighed down her legs and took her breath away. She had been clinging on to that phantom life, though now she no longer knew why. Or maybe she did. She stayed alive because death, too, terrorised her. She would have preferred to disappear, rather than die. She had already looked death in the eye; she had seen the abyss of nothingness that it left behind, and the mere memory of it made her want to scream. What if death was not just nothingness? She no longer trusted even the idea of death. There was no shelter.

Miriam turned off the tap, got out of the shower and went to bed, wrapping herself up in the blanket without drying herself off first. She was shuddering. She would not die that day either, she thought, as her mind suddenly gave in like an overloaded switch. She shut off without any of the slow struggle usually associated with sleep. Maybe she fell asleep, worn out by the insomnia of the previous days; maybe she passed out. In the apartment, which had been elegantly refurbished before she moved in, her presence became imperceptible. Not a breath. This was Miriam Bassevi now: a fragile balancing act between living and dying.

When Miriam eventually regained consciousness, she shot upright in bed, gasping gutturally as if she was finally catching her breath after prolonged apnoea. As if she had just resurfaced from deep water. Or maybe as if someone had been pushing her face downwards, smothering her. It was dark and she did not know where she was. She felt all around her, moving her hands frantically, and sensed damp sand underneath, above, all around her naked body. She turned to run away but the sand had tentacles that were holding her back. Her eyes widened, paralysed with terror. She tried to scream but her voice was dead. Just like Betta's. She wriggled free and fell through the air. On impact, the pain in her elbow and then on her forehead gave her the strength to let out an aching groan from her throat, which returned to her enough lucidity to realise that she was at home.

Miriam freed herself from the sheets that had coiled around her and lay on the rug on the floor. Her eyes had now got used to the darkness, returning to her the comforting outline of her bedroom. Once she had recovered her strength, she stood up, fighting back against dizziness as best she could, and went to get dressed. She put on a pair of knickers, gym socks, a sweatshirt and some blue jeans. She gathered all the cash she had in the house as well as a few pieces of jewellery and then called a taxi, wrapping herself up well before leaving the house.

Miriam asked the taxi driver to stop at the end of the road, in front of the kiosk.

The man, who was bald, chubby and roughly in his sixties, did so.

Miriam paid the fare and added a generous tip. 'Please, wait for me here. I'll be back in ten minutes.'

'No, sweetheart, I'm done for the night,' said the taxi driver as he combined the money she had just given him with the wad he had pulled out of his pocket.

'Please! I'll pay for waiting time.' Miriam stared at him helplessly, leaning forward a little more from in between the seats.

'I got a home too, you know?'

'But where will I get another taxi at this time? How will I call it?' Miriam said in frustration.

'And I care?' The taxi driver nodded towards the young men by the kiosk. 'Ask them, you'll find a ride.'

'But it's only ten minutes.'

'I only live around the corner and I'm not going all the way back to Via Barberini.' The taxi driver pointed at the door. 'Come on, girlie, get out now.'

Miriam let out a deep sigh of misery as she got out of the car. The taxi driver started the engine again, disappearing within seconds.

Miriam stood stock-still. From the warehouse, she could hear the muffled sound of music blasting at a volume so high the ground was shaking. The car park was teeming with young people. Car doors were being opened and closed all over the place, motorcycles were being revved up, and there was a constant buzz of screams and excited laughter.

Miriam's head started spinning again so badly that she staggered. When she felt steady enough on her feet, she started to make her way falteringly towards the kiosk, which was enveloped in darkness compared to the brightly lit car park. Miriam saw a sort of unruly queue. However, even in that scattered formation, it was obvious that everyone was waiting their turn. They were all orbiting around a young man of medium height with dark hair, short on the sides and a bit longer at the top, who was braving the cold of the night in a light jacket worn open over a knock-off branded sweatshirt. From time to time, when people were crowding him too much, he raised his voice to keep them at bay. Then someone in the queue would immediately start relaying his words and gestures to impress on the others that they needed to be cool or he would lose his patience.

At first Miriam kept slightly to one side, then she realised that others were getting closer and cutting in, so she moved forward. By the time it was her turn, she could feel that the guy behind her was so impatient that he was almost on top of her. She did not manage to say a single word and stepped aside, consumed with anxiety. No one was talking: everyone went up to the young man, handed him one or more notes and then he, depending on the money, put his hand in his pocket, pulled it out and quickly slid the contents of his palm into that of the other, who then left in a rush, their fist clenched. It was like a well-oiled machine into which Miriam could not slot. She looked on for a while, shivering with cold despite her puffa jacket, scarf and woolly hat. She realised that this was not the place for her, but she had no clue how to get back home.

She walked away from the kiosk and sat down on the pavement, in the light of a lamppost. Her muscles were spasming all over her body. Her head was throbbing like a huge abscess and she felt as if she was going to be sick. Moreover, the elbow that she had knocked upon waking was hurting a lot. Breathing in the icy air soothed her nausea but also heightened the burning feeling that was setting her throat on fire. Miriam wanted to lie down, to close her eyes and never move, never hear, never see again. Like a rock.

She folded over and stayed still for a long time, until a sudden jolt of anxiety made her jump to her feet. She set off, not knowing where she was going. Maybe she could get herself home; maybe she was not as far away as she thought. Once she had left the cone of light of the last lamppost, Miriam walked past the watermelon kiosk and saw the young man in the knock-off sweatshirt. He was the only one left.

She walked up to him.

'Are you Leo?'

He raised his eyes from his shoes, which were also knock-offs. 'And you wanna know this why?'

'Do you have any Phentatyl?' Miriam said, only managing a whisper.

He stared at her for a long time, his eyes narrowing. 'I don't handle that stuff.'

'Who does?'

'You can try Wheels, near the rehab at the San Giovanni hospital, under the statue of the Virgin.'

'And what do you handle?'

'Come again?' he snapped, gruffly. 'If it's Phen you're after, I got nothing for you.'

Miriam wrapped herself tightly in her jacket as she looked for something to say, to ask. Maybe something that could help her, help in any way at all. But nothing could help her. She had come all the way here, to no avail, and now she didn't know how to get back. She turned around and resumed walking on the dark pavement, at times more slowly and at times speeding up. For a moment she mistook the road she was on for the one to the river mouth, in Torre Domizia. The road that led to Zia and Zio's. Maybe she was not that far. After a while, the pavement ended and Miriam had to continue on the dirt along the side of the road. From time to time, the headlights of cars zooming past in the opposite direction dazzled her. She would narrow her eyes, waver a little and then speed up. Her steps started overlapping. She stumbled, fell to her knees a couple of times, then got back up. All of a sudden, the headlights of a larger vehicle blinded her completely. She brought one arm up to her eyes. Then the darkness sucked her in.

When she came to, light lashed against her pupils so painfully that she had to shut her eyes again with a groan as she instinctively shaded them with her hands.

'How you feeling?' someone asked from the dark.

'Fine,' Miriam muttered. She couldn't tell whether she was lying down or standing up. Then she breathed in a subtle smell of dusty earth and coughed twice, shaking.

'Fine my ass. You were frothing like a snail.'

Miriam forced herself to open her eyes. She saw a figure looming over her: the young man in the knock-off sweatshirt was squatting next to her, and the lights blinding her were the headlights of a car parked just behind him.

'You were convulsing,' he grumbled, wiping her mouth with a corner of her scarf. 'You out of your mind, walking around in this state?'

Miriam tried and failed to push his hands away, muttering half-sentences that made no sense. Eventually she managed to keep her eyes half-open while he lifted her head delicately and put the cool glass of a small bottle to her lips.

'Drink.'

Miriam hardly managed to swallow a few sips. Now her throat was hurting even more than before. She pulled back. 'I don't want sparkling water,' she protested, annoyed.

'My apologies, I'm fresh outta rosewater,' he taunted her.

Miriam slowly managed to sit up as he brushed the dirt off her shoulders and hat as best he could. 'I want to go home,' she muttered.

'At your service!'

Miriam stared at him without understanding. 'Can you find me a taxi?'

'Where d'ya think you are, Roma Termini?' He tried to help her stand up but she collapsed to the ground a couple of times before actually managing to get to her feet.

'I'll walk, then.'

'Sure, straight to the cemetery,' he quipped, holding her up only by her thin arm as he guided her to the car and opened the door.

'No, I'm not getting in,' Miriam said and flung her arms around, trying to wriggle free and escape his grip.

'And how're you getting home? You know someone inside?' He nodded in the direction of the huge warehouse where Blue Alien was. 'I'll go look for 'em.'

'No, I don't know anyone,' Miriam said, backing up a bit more. 'But I'm going home on my own.'

He gulped down what was left of the water and flung the small bottle away. The glass exploded on impact, somewhere in the dense darkness. 'Suit yourself,' he said, irritated. Without closing the door, he walked around the car and got in. 'So? What's it gonna be?' he asked from inside the car.

Miriam looked around. The warehouse was far away, the car park was half-empty and the road was almost deserted. Miriam could see only darkness in front of her. Given that every option terrified her, she gave in. She got in the car and closed the door, though too weakly for the lock to actually latch. He grumbled, climbed out of the car again, slammed her door shut and got back in. He noticed that she had pushed herself right up into the corner of the seat, against the door, and was staring at him, barely breathing.

'Look, no offence, but on top of everything else you're also kinda ugly,' he reassured her, then started the engine.

Miriam relaxed a little. She waited a few minutes, then asked, 'Where did you say I can find the guy who might have some Phentatyl?'

'Forget about Wheels – you gotta go to the hospital all right, but to A&E,' he said without peeling his eyes off the road. 'Another fit and you're done for. You understand?' He was speaking as if he were much older than he looked, and sounded almost paternal.

Miriam put her hand in the inside pocket of her jacket and pulled out a few 100,000-lire notes, two gold chains and a bracelet with filigree decoration. 'Please,' she said, showing him the lot in the palm of her hand. 'I'm going to be sick otherwise.'

He shook his head.

'Please,' she insisted imploringly, stretching her arm further towards him.

They did not speak for the rest of the journey. Miriam had let her open hand fall on her lap, the money and the jewellery still in her palm.

'What's your name?' he asked.

'Miriam,' she said, after a long moment of hesitation.

He looked at her. 'What, you from abroad?'

'Of course not!' Miriam said, vaguely annoyed. 'It's a Jewish name: it means Maria.'

He chuckled, amused. 'Maria?' he repeated.

'Why are you laughing?'

'My name is Leo De Maria.' He winked at her, smiling meaningfully. 'Must be fate ... '

In her bewilderment, Miriam's lips moved under her scarf to form an invisible smile.

Leo De Maria drove on for a long while. He took her to a place that reminded her of the urban scenes she had seen in Donato's comic books – places that she had never even suspected actually existed. The bumpy roads, which were barely lit by mostly broken or dim lampposts, were lined with high-rise buildings, all identical, that seemed built with Lego blocks by a child with no imagination. Miriam, who had only known the art and beauty of Rome, felt flung into one of the distressing visions from her dreams.

'Where are we?' she asked, peering through the windscreen, her heart thumping fast.

'In Heaven,' Leo said sarcastically as he pulled over. He stopped the car, then collected in his fist what Miriam had been holding in her palm. She did not object. Leo searched her eyes to make sure that she understood. 'Stay here and don't move. Lock the door and, if someone comes up to the car, don't roll the window down.'

'Where are you going?' Miriam asked, consumed by anxiety.

'To look for your Phentatyl.'

Miriam wavered for a moment, then took a deep breath. 'Okay,' she whispered.

Leo got out of the car and locked the door with the key, motioning her to also lock it from her side.

Miriam did so and watched him disappear. She opened her eyes wider and laid her forehead against the icy-cold window, hoping to see him for a bit longer, but he vanished into the dark mouths of those huge buildings. Only a few windows on the façades were still lit, scattered among the many blind ones. Shivering with cold, Miriam thought that this was a kind of solitude she had never known before. She could not remember ever feeling so far away from any familiar reference point. Not even on the beach. And yet, in that silence, locked in a car that only Leo had the keys to, her fear was different. She could not have explained how. Rather, in her confusion, in her panic that did not relent even for a moment, Miriam felt certain of one thing only, beyond any rational explanation: she was not afraid of Leo De Maria.

She buried her face deeper in her scarf, which was still wet with the saliva Leo had wiped from her mouth, and closed her eyes. She knew that what was taking place that night was the preamble to an unavoidable ending. The blame was not on that depraved psychiatrist who prescribed to his patients – her mother included – everything they wanted. Miriam was no fool: she had known right away that she was not going to make it out of this addiction alive, and that the relief the substances gave her would eventually kill her, one day or another. Sooner or later, her need for respite would become stronger than her fear of what death might be. Like a finger suddenly poking her on the shoulder, it would push her off the tightrope she was balancing on. That was how it would end. And, after all, she was fine with it. Nonetheless, she was now sobbing in her dirty scarf, her body shaken by all kinds of pain. Bitterness poured out of her eyes in warm tears that stung her skin at the thought that, once, she had been a normal girl, daydreaming about happiness as she pedalled along the beach.

Leo found her dozing like that, her face entirely hidden in her scarf. Worrying that she might have died right there, in his car, he shook her by the shoulder.

Miriam was startled and her face poked out of her scarf.

Leo showed her a little square of tissue paper. 'I found this. Someone I trust said it's the same,' he told her.

Miriam took the tiny parcel and opened it, though with effort, since her fingers were shaking so much. 'Mine are a different colour,' she observed, staring at the pills uncertainly.

'This is all I could get,' said Leo, while she took two to her lips. 'Wait a moment.' He motioned her to hold on as he stretched his arm behind the seats and pulled another half-litre bottle of water out of somewhere. He uncapped it with a key and handed it to her.

Miriam swallowed the pills and this time drank almost half the bottle.

'Just so you know, this is expensive water: I nick it from the trattoria where I work,' Leo pointed out with a half-smile.

Miriam wiped her lips on the back of her hand. 'If you have a job, why do you deal drugs?'

Leo stared at her pensively, then shook his head.

Miriam did not give up. 'Isn't the money you make enough?'

'I'm greedy,' he said, curtly and sarcastically.

Miriam buried her face in her scarf again as she handed the bottle back to him. Just like the first time, he finished its contents, opened the window and flung it outside, causing a clanging of broken glass once again.

'You know, bins do exist,' Miriam scolded him.

'You wanna teach me how to live now?' Leo asked, turning the engine on.

Miriam did not answer and just looked out of her window.

'Where d'you need to go?' Leo asked.

'Barberini.'

Impressed, Leo arched his mouth downwards and raised his eyebrows, then set off for the other side of Rome.

Now Miriam could finally float into a deep, dreamless sleep. Pain evaporated from her body and her mind, while the dull noise of the engine lulled her. When Leo De Maria eventually pulled over in Via del Tritone and asked her more than once with increasing insistence where he should take her precisely, Miriam was only able to say that she wanted to be a rock. Leo barked at her that he did not care one bit, he only wanted to know the house number, since he too was tired. But Miriam pushed him back, annoyed, and plunged back into her peaceful sleep. She even thought that it was a beautiful night, a beautiful night to die.

Leo had to knock on the door with the tip of his shoe, since he was holding Miriam in his arms; although she weighed next to nothing, he had no way to get his key out of the pocket of his jeans.

It took a while before Corallina came to the door. As she stepped aside to let him in, she let out a cry of surprise. 'What happened?'

'Nothing. She's just a mate of mine who's had too much to drink.'

'And where do we put her?' Corallina surveyed all the forty square metres of their apartment; with the three-quarter sofabed where Leo slept pulled out, there was even less space.

'I'll put her in my bed. We'll fit,' Leo reassured her.

Corallina pulled back the blankets and helped him set her down. They took off her shoes, her woolly hat, her scarf and her jacket.

'She's skin and bones,' Corallina said, casting an unconvinced look at her brother. 'And what's this bruise on her forehead?'

'Corallina, she's a mess,' Leo said curtly.

Corallina covered Miriam with care. 'Well, then, welcome,' she sighed with a bitter smile.

It was morning when Miriam opened her eyes. All was quiet. The sunlight was pouring into the room through a double-casement window with white lace curtains. Still dazed, she let her eyes wander around. She was lying on a bed, all wrapped up in a matted wool blanket. The bed was in a tiny sitting room attached to a minuscule kitchenette with little blue flowers painted on the yellowed white of the tiles. On the opposite wall, there was a colourful curtain drawn under a small arch that led into the rest of the apartment. The walls were painted in a faded aquamarine that was peeling in several places, and canvases of flowers painted in childish strokes were dotted here and there.

And then there was Leo De Maria, sound asleep next to her, his face almost completely buried in his pillow. He was so close that Miriam could hear his breath. She could not remember the last time she had been so close to someone as to hear them breathe. Or maybe she could. She also could not remember how and why she had got to this apartment, but she did know that she had collapsed into a deep sleep soon after taking the pills. So, while she slept, Leo had taken her and brought her here. All the inexplicable trust of a few hours earlier was immediately dispelled: how could she have let Leo take her? She was overcome by a strong nausea and decided that she had to go. Go home.

She slipped out of the bed and, with unsteady steps, gathered her things, which had been piled tidily on a chair. She put them back on, fighting against her sore limbs that were making every movement arduous. Then she opened the door softly, praying that Leo would not wake up at the click of the lock, and only pulled it to as she left so as not to make any more noise.

A few minutes later Miriam was in the street, in another world that she did not know. She found herself among dilapidated buildings that were surrounded by run-down playgrounds and derelict flower beds. She took a few steps, read the name of the street on the corner and went to study the timetable at the bus stop, hoping to be able to figure out where she was. But everything was completely unfamiliar to her. Miriam walked as far as her strength let her but she could not find her bearings. Eventually, she got on a random bus and remembered that she had no money: Leo had taken everything, including her jewellery. She didn't have a ticket, and she didn't care.

It took her two hours, a long stretch on foot and three different buses before she got home. As soon as she stepped into her apartment, she stripped off and rushed to wash under the stream of the shower, scrubbing away the thought of Leo

De Maria's hands on her body while she slept. Deep down she knew full well that he had not touched her, but it didn't matter: her imagination horrified her more than reality did. She could hear him breathing nearby. She rested her forehead on the majolica tiles and waited, in vain, for the water to wash away a smell that existed only in her head.

That very night, Miriam went to look for the place near the hospital that Leo had mentioned. The effect of the pills he had found for her had waned hours earlier. Miriam could not remember the name of the man, so she looked around, asking everyone who looked shady enough if they knew where to find medicines without a prescription. Then she said that she was looking for barbiturates to a stranger who looked like a junkie and he offered her some methadone instead, insisting nervously. She dithered for a long while, then declined, since she had never heard that word before. At eleven, she took a taxi from Piazza San Giovanni to Blue Alien, but there was no sign of Leo there. Miriam went back in the same taxi to the spot where she had met the guy with the methadone, but he too was gone. She got back home in the middle of the night, exhausted and empty-handed. She knew that in just a few hours the pain would drive her mad and her head would explode, her thoughts thumping harder and harder. She collapsed on to the living room rug with a wail of desperation.

At three in the morning, after a few fragments of fitful sleep, Miriam woke with a start, Leo's address clear in her head. She could not have explained how, but amid all the confusion it had resurfaced in her memory, together with the verse of a poem she had learned in elementary school that was now persistently echoing around her head. Miriam called a taxi and left home once again, asking to be dropped off somewhere on the correct street. She wandered for a little while, since she had no clue of the house number, then started reading the names on the buzzers. This took some effort since almost every single one of them had been vandalised and the names were often illegible. She had almost lost all hope when she found a De Maria, house number 26, apartment 12. She recognised the hall and, since the lock on the main door was broken, she went directly upstairs. The walls in the stairway were peeling and covered in graffiti and obscene drawings. In the corner of a dimly lit landing, there was a half-dead plant that smelled of urine. Amid all that squalor, Miriam remembered how clean Leo's apartment had smelled.

It was only when she arrived in front of his door that she realised she was under the assumption that he lived on his own. What lay behind the curtain under the arch? Who had painted the mediocre canvases with the flowers? The cramps in her arms and back made her decide that she didn't care. She did not care about a single thing. She only wanted him to help her find Phentatyl or something similar, just like the previous night.

At first, she knocked softly. Then, without waiting, she knocked again, louder. Some time passed before she heard a noise from inside, through the door made of a honeycomb wood so thin that it had amplified the rapping of her knuckles on the panel. She noticed some movement behind the peephole, then the door inched back just for a moment before being thrown open.

Miriam gaped. She couldn't help it. She stared at a light silk turban with tropical prints surrounding a virile head that must have been in its thirties and bore on its cheeks the indelible marks of having suffered from acne earlier in life. The lack of eyebrows, which had been completely waxed off, clashed with the very light shadow of morning stubble that had not yet been shaved. The slim yet big-boned body was wrapped in a light dressing gown in a floral pattern that sported a deep neckline on the chest and reached down to mid-calf.

'I'm sorry. I must have the wrong door. My apologies,' Miriam said, bewildered and unable to move.

'You're Miriam!' The voice was deep, slightly hoarse, but made gentler by a smile of surprise. 'What are you doing here, so late at night?'

'I was looking for Leo,' Miriam said apologetically, taking a step backwards.

'Leo is not back yet. He works at night.' The statement sounded like a reminder rather than information.

'Right.' Miriam took another step backwards.

'Do you want to come in?'

Miriam shook her head resolutely. 'No.'

They stared at each other for a while longer, then Miriam turned around to head down the stairs as she muttered yet more apologies.

'I'm Corallina, Leo's sister,' Corallina said in a loud tone that carried a hint of sadness, the words sounding like a long sigh.

Miriam stopped and looked at her again. Corallina was staring at her, her head delicately tilted to one side and a hand with nails varnished in red now clutching the neckline of her dressing gown.

'I am terribly sorry, I didn't mean to inconvenience you, truly,' Miriam repeated.

'Come on in, I'll make you something hot to drink while you wait for Leo.'

Miriam hesitated.

'You can trust me,' Corallina reassured Miriam with an elusive smile. 'And you don't need to be so formal; I'm not that old.'

Miriam dragged her tired legs into the apartment.

Derision did not hurt Corallina. Not any more. And neither did diffidence, which at times was even understandable. What Corallina would never get used to was the uncomfortable feeling that she could see in the eyes of strangers. It looked too much like her own, when she sometimes absentmindedly met her reflection in a mirror or a shop window and it gave her a start. She did not recognise it. She was even disquieted by it. It had nothing to do with the Corallina who lived in her head and who she imagined walking down the street in her high heels and billowing skirt. That body that was a stranger to her was glued on to her person, on to her face, under her clothes, beneath the colourful turbans that hid her baldness. Without the filter of imagination, even she could see her grotesque ugliness. So Miriam's reaction had not hurt Corallina, not at all; it had simply saddened her for a moment. How could Miriam understand? Despite a body drained away by fasting, Miriam was still a woman in all her refined beauty. As she asked her to sit down, Corallina yearningly observed Miriam's thin waist, which was accentuated by her pretty double-breasted wool coat that was fitted on her chest and then flared out in an A-line. Corallina even let out a sigh of admiration for its beautiful duck-egg blue and forgot to ask Miriam if she wanted to take it off.

'Shall I make you some milky coffee?' Corallina offered.

Miriam was sitting a bit rigidly at the kitchen table, her hands in her lap. 'No, thank you.'

Corallina had the impression that Miriam was shivering lightly. 'Are you cold?'

'I'm fine,' Miriam said, lowering her eyes.

'You know what? I'll warm up some milk for myself anyway.' Corallina smiled at Miriam even though Miriam was not looking at her. 'Maybe you'll change your mind. Lately I've been having this annoying little cough, especially at night.' Corallina delicately tapped her fingers on her flat chest. 'As soon as I drink something warm, I immediately feel better.'

Corallina fumbled at the hob in silence. That young woman reminded her of the injured animals Leo used to bring home as a child. One time it was a swallow, next a pigeon, then a cat that was more dead than alive, and once even a hedgehog. However, he only kept them until they were better, since their parents had no intention of taking in a pet. When he was little, Leo used to say that he wanted to be a vet, but a lot had happened since then, Corallina thought with some regret.

Without saying a word, Corallina put a glass of hot milk in front of Miriam together with the sugar jar, then sat down to drink hers. They did not speak for a long time. Corallina could sense that Miriam had stopped feeling ill at ease. Nonetheless, she remained clammed up in her silence. And Corallina could feel all of Miriam's hostile vulnerability in the air. She could actually sense a lot about that stranger just by looking at her. Corallina was like that: she could feel other people's pain within herself, even when they did not share it. Perhaps it was because she had experienced so much pain herself.

'You know, your hair is just gorgeous!'

Miriam barely lifted her eyes.

'And if I say so, you'd better believe it: I've been a hairdresser for the past twenty years!' Corallina touched her silk turban, which in her imagination gathered hair as blonde as ripe wheat and as long as Farrah Fawcett's. 'However ... am I allowed to say? You don't nourish it enough!' Corallina told Miriam off sweetly. 'Without vitamins it loses all its shine.'

Miriam did not budge from her obstinate silence; she wouldn't have known what to say.

'Just look at it, though: thick and light at the same time ... You must have a thousand billion silk threads in there!' Corallina smiled with satisfaction. 'And your bob! So *charmant*! Who cut it?'

Miriam hesitated, shaking her head slightly. 'I don't remember. It was my mum's hairdresser.'

'What a hand! Bobs can be so tricky ...' Corallina waved a hand to signify how much tribulation a wrong bob could cause, then very subtly pushed the glass of milk closer to Miriam. 'Have a sip, before it gets cold.'

Miriam raised her hand to the glass, clenched her fist for a moment to control her shaking, then slowly brought the milk to her lips. It was barely lukewarm now.

Corallina nodded slowly, in silence, though in her head shouting encouragement to Miriam.

'Leo was upset this morning when he realised that you had

left without even having breakfast,' Corallina confessed in a whisper, as if her brother were in the room, ready to protest against her indiscretion.

Miriam drank on without looking at Corallina. The first few sips had been hard but now the liquid was sliding down her dry throat without her even realising.

'Would you like a little slice of pie? I made it myself.' As she spoke, Corallina had already got up to fetch a dish covered with a chequered tea towel.

'No,' Miriam answered decidedly, then thanked Corallina politely.

'You don't like it?'

'I don't eat sweet things.' Miriam paused. 'Not any more.'

Corallina seemed in shock. 'You don't?'

Miriam shook her head.

'Why not?'

Miriam looked at Corallina. She had never really asked herself that question, perhaps because she had always known the answer. The decision had matured on the first morning back at the Swiss school, two summers earlier, when the smell of lemon icing coming from the beignets on display in the cafeteria had reached her nostrils. On that day Miriam had learned that, rather than comforting her, sweetness punished her with the memory of things that were gone for ever.

'They make me feel sick,' she said, aloof.

Corallina stared at her, one hand on her side and the other under the dish with the pie. 'Imagine that!' she muttered as she put the pie away. 'What about some bread?' she ventured, encouragingly.

Surprisingly, after a moment of hesitation, Miriam nodded.

Corallina quickly took a rosetta roll left over from the day before out of a paper bag, placed it on the most beautiful dish she owned, and covered it with a linen handkerchief that had come with a housekeeping magazine a long time ago, then presented it to Miriam, setting it down in front of her with the same caution one might show when offering a treat to a diffident stray and then waiting with bated breath.

Miriam took the roll and started nibbling at it without even breaking it up with her hands. At every bite, Corallina nodded almost imperceptibly.

When Leo let himself in, he remained stock-still for a moment, staring at them, before closing the door again. He looked at Miriam with a frown, then at his sister. They had both turned in his direction. Only Corallina was smiling.

'What you doing here?' Leo asked Miriam.

'I'm sorry.' Miriam lowered her eyes. 'I needed to talk to you.'

'At this time of night?' Leo was clearly annoyed: he was looking at Corallina with a tension in his eyes that he could barely hide.

Corallina stood up all of a sudden. 'Darlings, I must really go to bed. I can't keep my eyes open,' she announced, adjusting the sides of her turban. Then she said to Miriam, 'You'll forgive me, won't you?'

Miriam nodded. 'I'm sorry I bothered you,' she murmured.

'Nonsense!' Corallina rushed to answer cheerfully. 'A girl with such a nice coat can call in on us any time she wants!' She waved aristocratically to them both before disappearing behind the curtain.

Leo tellingly motioned at Miriam with his head. She joined him at the door and they both stepped out on to the landing.

'You crazy, coming here?' Leo asked under his breath, his anger choking in his throat as he quietly pulled the door to.

'I didn't know what to do.' Miriam was on the verge of tears as she massaged her arms.

'And I care?' Leo snapped, barely managing to keep his voice down. 'What didya say to my sister?'

'Nothing, I swear,' Miriam whispered desperately.

'You sure?'

'I only told her that I needed to talk to you.'

Leo seemed to relax a bit. 'And she didn't ask you anything?' Miriam shook her head.

Leo leaned on the door jamb with a sigh, suddenly feeling guilty for having been so harsh to Miriam – a feeling which irritated him even more. 'You can't just come 'ere to my place!'

Miriam nodded several times, quickly.

Leo nodded as well, to signify that that was a hard and fast rule. 'You even left the door open this morning! What were you thinking? Were you raised in the Colosseum? What if a burglar sneaked in? Or a rat?' Leo pressed on, peeved.

'I'm sorry ... I'm sorry.' She did not dare raise her eyes.

'Yeah, sure, you're sorry ... ' Leo parroted her, vexed.

Miriam pulled the money she had withdrawn from the bank that morning out of her coat pocket. 'Can you find me some more Phentatyl?' She stretched a handful of notes towards Leo, imploringly. 'Please.'

'You need to quit that shit!' Leo said, exasperated.

'Please!' Miriam's voice sounded like a sob. 'I'm going crazy without it. I can't cope.'

At first, Leo put his hands in his pockets and looked up in a huff. Then he opened his jacket and, from an inside pocket, pulled out a little square of tissue paper like the one he had given her the previous night. 'Last ones, though. Understood?'

Miriam took it from his palm, astonished, wiping a tear with the back of her hand. 'How do you have them already?'

'They're from last night. You coulda bought a pharmacy with the kinda dough you gave me. I didn't give 'em all to you cos otherwise you'd just go and off yourself and then I'd be in real trouble.'

Miriam handed him the money.

'Keep it. I also have the change from last night in the house.' Leo popped back in and came out a moment later with what was left of the money he had taken the previous night, and her jewellery. A chain with a small charm was missing, but Miriam did not notice.

'Could I have some water?' Miriam asked him, letting the pills fall on to her palm.

'You take 'em at home,' Leo said, nodding towards the stairs. 'And don't come back here!'

'But I couldn't find anyone by the rehab! Where do I find the guy you mentioned?' Miriam whined.

Leo's eyes widened in surprise. 'You went to the rehab on your own?'

Miriam nodded.

'You're completely nuts! Best if you just go ahead and off yourself with those pills!' Leo pointed at the stairs again, this time tensing his arm, barely able to suppress the anger in his voice. He could just picture her, in her suede ankle boots and her light blue coat, looking for Wheels. Leo could have slapped her; he didn't even understand why he cared so much about her, considering that he had met her no longer than twenty-four hours earlier and that she had only brought him trouble and taken precious hours of sleep away.

Miriam put the pills into her pocket and mumbled a goodbye along with some more words of apology. She slowly started going down the stairs, leaning against the peeling wall with her hand. The bread and the milk Corallina had given her had made her feel a little better, but her head was still spinning and her legs were shaking.

Leo huffed, rolling his eyes. 'Where d'ya think you're goin'? Come back here,' he grumbled all of a sudden from behind her, still irritated but using his special tone that meant that he was there for her, that he was not going to leave her alone.

Miriam turned around to look at him. She realised that those words, though brusque, made her feel better. Like Corallina's bread and milk.

She went back up the stairs and he guided her inside, threading an arm behind her waist to support her, since he could see that she was very weak.

It was almost six in the morning when, at the end of a long negotiation, Leo finally persuaded Miriam to wear to bed an old tracksuit that no longer fitted him. Miriam went to change in the small bathroom that was just past the colourful curtain and then got into her side of the bed under the matted blanket. The pills were starting to work and she felt they were giving her an unusual sense of wellbeing that morning. Sleep came on slowly as she looked at Leo, who lay opposite her, still awake. Miriam had begged him to leave the light in the kitchenette on since she did not like being in the dark and he had agreed. He always grumbled but, when all was said and done, he was not unkind.

'Why didya leave like that, this morning?' he asked her all of a sudden. This time there was no reproach in his voice, only a hint of resentment.

Their heads were on their pillows opposite one another.

Miriam considered an infinite number of lies. 'I was scared,' she confessed instead.

'Of what?'

'Of you. I got scared because you had brought me here and I couldn't remember it.'

'And where was I supposed to take you? You were asleep! I couldn't just leave you in Via del Tritone, could I?'

Miriam wrapped herself up tightly in the blanket. 'I know. The thing is, I'm always scared.'

'You stroll around looking for dealers and then you're scared of me,' he taunted her with a half-smile.

For a moment, the other half of that smile rose to Miriam's lips. 'I'm like that,' she said with a sigh.

'Like what?'

'Like that,' she repeated with resignation.

Leo stared at her for a long time in silence. Though the light coming from the kitchen was dim, their eyes found each other. 'I lied to you,' he whispered to her.

'When?' Miriam moved imperceptibly closer to him, pushed by curiosity.

'It's not true that you're kinda ugly.'

Miriam smiled again as sleep fell over her like a benevolent cloak. 'It doesn't matter anyway,' she murmured.

*

Leo was no longer there when Miriam woke up towards noon, and Corallina was hard at work in the kitchen. She was gently fluttering here and there in an apron with a bib worn over a floral woollen dress that had a high neck and a flared skirt. She had made her face up, drawing her eyebrows on with a pencil, and was wearing garish pendant earrings and a turban that matched the brown of her dress. Miriam felt as if she could grasp Corallina's essence in the sunrays that were filtering through the curtains, just like when, as a little girl, she could see the drawing she was about to trace on a white sheet of paper through a lit window. Miriam felt as if she could just see Corallina's graceful figure, her long blonde hair, her silky skin, her tapering fingers that were kneading the dough on the small square table. Miriam smiled because Corallina was beautiful to look at – if you were lucky enough to see her.

Right then, Corallina lifted her gaze from her dough and looked towards Miriam, her face opening up in a smile.

'Good morning!' she greeted Miriam cheerfully.

'Good morning,' replied Miriam as she sat up. 'I'm sorry I slept so much!'

'Like a rock,' Corallina laughed. 'Good for you, my dear.'

'Where's Leo?'

'Leo went to the trattoria, love. He works on Sundays.' She seemed once again surprised that Miriam had forgotten.

'Of course,' Miriam said, looking away.

'You're staying for lunch, though, aren't you?' Corallina asked in a whimsically pleading tone, pausing her kneading for a moment. 'I'm making bread just for you.'

Miriam stared at her. Corallina tried to soften Miriam up with a playful expression, her head tilted to one side.

'Okay, then,' Miriam said, the hint of a resigned smile on her lips.

Corallina got back to work, graceful and energetic. She put the bread in the oven and turned off the gas under the tomato sauce which, upon tasting, she had deemed to be ready, then she hurried to heat some milk and poured it into a glass.

'There you go.' Corallina came up to the bed and handed it to Miriam as if she had been patiently waiting for it since the moment she had woken up.

Miriam could not bring herself to say no. She felt that Corallina's spontaneous kindness deserved as much kindness in return, even if she did not feel like drinking the milk. 'Thank you,' she mumbled.

Corallina sat on the edge of the bed, feeling that she should keep Miriam company as she had her breakfast. Loneliness was twice as tough during meals, Corallina had always thought. And she felt that this girl who was all skin and bones knew something about it too: a woman could be desperately alone in many ways and at all times.

Miriam took a sip. Corallina had not put any sugar in it. She drank again, comforted.

'Why are you called Corallina?' Miriam asked.

Corallina's eyes brightened at a question that brought up her most cherished memory. 'Leo gave me this name. Isn't it wonderful?' She spoke slowly, her voice choked with emotion.

'It is. It's beautiful.'

So Corallina too answered kindness with more kindness, and told Miriam the story of her name.

Not being Corallina had been horrible for her. Actually, in the beginning, she had not known what her name was, though it certainly was not the name her parents had given her, the name everyone called her by. Nothing belonged to her. They dressed her in clothes that were not hers and the toys she was allowed to play with were so crude that she preferred spending time on her own, daydreaming. It was then that imagination had become one of her closest friends. She had understood early on that she should look for what she was missing right there, in her imagination. She collected all sorts of things that might prove useful to her: the fairytales she heard at nursery, the memory of the knick-knacks that little girls brought to school, the softness of skirts with floral patterns that no one would ever dream of dressing her in. She would spend her time on her own and satiate her need for beauty as best she could, stealing with her eyes. She had started cutting out pictures from mail-order catalogues and making a notebook where she pasted all of the things that she coveted. Dresses, handbags, heels and costume jewellery. The notebooks had later become two, then five, then ten. Eventually, it was as if she had an entire encyclopedia of beauty. However, over the years, the more beauty she poured into her notebooks, the more the mirror reflected back to her an image that was as crude as the boyish toys that were forced on her. The little girls in her class were blooming into creatures that she thought were all breathtakingly beautiful. Whether fat or thin, short or lanky, they all made her sigh with envy. They all had something that was completely missing from her.

When Leo was born, she was twelve. It had not been hard for her to realise that this second child, a son, was seen as a great relief, especially by her father. Her mother too was happy, knowing that Leo was a way to give her marriage another lease of life. Though she had got one child wrong, everything would be all right with this one: she was not going to let it happen twice. Leo was a darling – cheerful, happy and wonderfully naughty. Their parents encouraged his impetuosity ecstatically, sharing knowing glances. She too was relieved: she loved Leo with all her heart and would have never wanted nature to play on him the same practical joke it had played on her, a joke that was becoming crueller year after year. Her bones were stretching, her shoulders were becoming wide and stocky, her neck was thickening and with each passing day her face was losing more and more the gentility of features she had had in her childhood. Adolescence was well under way and her hair was becoming increasingly wiry and curly, while facial hair had started to prick through the skin of her face, which was now rough and plagued with acne. She desperately fought against it, keeping her posture straight in an attempt to emulate the elegance she so yearned for, while in the meantime nature was shaping her body into that of a brute. She used to cry bitter tears over her notebooks, imagination having ceased to be enough for her.

So, when she was at home alone with Leo, and he was watching TV or playing with his toy soldiers, she would go into her parents' room and try on some of her mother's clothes. Just as a little comfort. A nightgown, a pretty skirt, tights, although everything was too small for her. She especially liked to put on a raw coral necklace that someone had gifted her mother after a trip to Sorrento. She would wrap a scarf around her head, put on the necklace and a touch of red lipstick and look at herself in the mirror. Somehow, as if by magic, that necklace made her forget all her sorrows for a moment. Wearing it, she felt more feminine. She would then sit there, at the dressing table, and look at herself, flaunting first her right side, then her left. She even dreamed that, dressed like that, she might make a breach into the heart of a young man at her hairdressing school, a gentle fair-haired boy she pined for.

Then, one day, she had seen Leo reflected in the mirror. He was spying on her, hiding clumsily behind the door jamb. She had taken off the turban and the necklace in haste, her heart racing, since her brother was only six and famously could not keep a secret. She was about to promise him the world as long as he did not mention a word of what he had just seen to anyone, but something in his eyes had stopped her in her tracks.

'The necklace suits you,' Leo had said, to relieve her from all her worry.

'It does?' She had smiled vainly, tempted to put it back on.

'A lot.' Leo had nodded seriously.

'Thank you, love.' She'd felt as if her heart was about to explode with tenderness.

Leo had stood pensively for a little while. 'If you want, I can call you Corallina. Do you like it?'

It was then that Corallina had been born. Every cell of her body had opened up to life and she had felt so happy that she was shivering with emotion. 'Very much,' she had said, her eyes so veiled with tears that she could no longer see her brother.

'Okay,' Leo had said in a firm voice, like a grown-up, almost as if he was sealing a deal.

Corallina had stopped him as he was going back to watch

TV. 'Leo?' She had waited for a moment for the tears that were preventing her from looking at him to dissipate, since she wanted to make sure that he quite understood her. 'Only when it's just the two of us, though, okay?'

Leo had nodded, and there had been no need to say any more.

Miriam listened in silence, holding the empty milk glass in her hands. Corallina's story had pulled her into a flow of emotions that, for the first time in a long time, had distracted her from herself. Her words had delicately pushed Miriam into a dimension that was hard to imagine and now everything seemed magically clear in its complexity. Corallina was a trapped woman and, though damned to live a life in between, she had nonetheless brought all of her incommensurable beauty into it. Miriam then realised that it would be hard to find a comment that might be appropriate. Feeling sorry for Corallina would imply a level of pity that she did not deserve. On the contrary, Miriam really admired Corallina's strength, which was so generous. It was then that Miriam realised what to say.

'I'd like to be like you,' she murmured.

Caught off guard, Corallina let out a surprised laugh. 'Heavens!' She brought her hand to her chest. 'What on earth are you talking about?'

'I mean it.' Miriam nodded with conviction.

'And I'd like to be like you, instead.' Corallina smiled at Miriam with complicity.

For the first time in a long time, Miriam's face opened up in a smile.

Corallina's eyes immediately widened and she stared at Miriam, open-mouthed with astonishment, while she pressed her hand harder on her chest, as if to contain too strong an emotion. 'I can't believe it!' Corallina murmured in disbelief. 'Just like Brigitte Bardot!'

Miriam frowned. 'What do you mean?'

Corallina pointed a varnished nail in the direction of Miriam's lips. 'That . . .'

'Oh. My diastem.'

'Diadem?' Corallina's eyes widened even more.

Miriam laughed, then corrected Corallina. 'Diastem! A diadem is what princesses wear on their heads.'

'Diastem, diadem . . .' Corallina shook her head and waved her hands about to signify a certain intolerance for such minutiae. 'It looks wonderful on you!' She looked at Miriam with dreamy eyes, then added, 'So *charmant*!'

They both laughed as the smell of bread imbued them like a balm.

Leo returned home that afternoon and was surprised to find Miriam still there. Corallina had persuaded her to have her hair washed and set. She had made it look shiny and flowing but kept insisting that it really had taken her no effort at all since it was already naturally beautiful. Leo did not comment – he was not one for compliments – but stared at Miriam as she went to the bathroom to put back on the clothes she had been wearing the night before.

'Isn't she lovely?' his sister whispered to him.

Leo replied with a shrug as he dipped a piece of bread into the leftover sauce and bit into it.

'I managed to make her eat, you know?' Corallina boasted. 'Give me a month and she'll be as good as new.'

'Leave her alone, Corallina. I told you, she's a mess.'

'So? I can tell you like her.'

'Sure, as if!' Leo griped as he chewed.

When Miriam came back into the room, she took her coat from the rack next to the door and put it on. 'Thank you for everything,' she said to Corallina.

'Don't mention it. I should be thanking you; I always find myself eating alone on Sundays,' Corallina complained, looking vexedly at her brother.

'Can I call a taxi?'

'From the phone box. We don't have a phone,' Leo said with his mouth full.

Corallina glared at her brother, incredulous. 'You really want her to get a taxi?'

'A taxi is perfectly fine,' Miriam interjected.

'You heard her.' Leo looked at his sister. 'She can get a taxi,' he added provokingly.

'Leo will take you.' Corallina cut the matter short as she handed her brother a tea towel to wipe the sauce from his hands. 'Where are your manners? You look like a pig!' she reproached him.

Grumbling, Leo cleaned his hands. 'I'll be out late tonight,' he muttered to Corallina, his mouth still full. He put his jacket back on and went to open the door. 'Princess, after you …' he teased, indicating the way to the landing with a chivalrous sweep of his arm.

Corallina laughed, putting her hands on her hips, then said to Miriam, 'See?'

Miriam stared at her, struggling to understand.

'I knew it was a diadem!' Corallina said, looking at Miriam conspiratorially.

Miriam smiled as she shook her head and followed Leo outside.

In the street, she watched Leo open the padlock on the chain he had locked up his scooter with. Then she saw him get on the saddle and kick the stand back. 'So?' Leo asked, revving a worryingly hiccoughing engine a couple of times to warm it up.

'So what?' Miriam asked.

'Are you getting on or what?'

'No, I'm not!' Miriam said, flabbergasted.

'So how're you getting home?'

'Where's the car?'

'The car is not mine. Someone lent it to me cos I was on foot.'

'And we're supposed to go on this thing?' Miriam looked horrified at the run-down scooter, which was all dented and had cracks in its tyres.

'What can I say? My horse just died.'

Despite herself, Miriam let out a little laugh that was a mix of nerves and amusement.

'So?' Leo urged her on. 'Don't tell me you're scared.'

Miriam shook her head. 'Not at all,' she said defiantly, undoing the buttons of her coat from the waist down so as to be able to get on.

Leo drove a short distance, then jammed on the brakes. 'Sweetheart, you need to hold on, or you'll be flying off at the first corner,' he shouted at Miriam from over his shoulder.

Miriam timidly put her hands on his hips.

'What's this, some kind of ballet nonsense?' Leo laughed, grabbing her hands and wrapping them around his waist.

As they zoomed off, Miriam leaned her body on to Leo De Maria's. All of a sudden, in the cold winter wind, she felt as if she had found a great warmth.

When they reached her apartment, Miriam got off the scooter. Leo remained on the saddle, unable to decide whether to speak or merely say bye and drive off. Miriam, on the other hand, knew for certain that she had something to say, but this felt like the wrong place and the wrong time. For a while, they exchanged glances only to then immediately avert their eyes; they both felt that the topic was too complicated to handle.

Eventually, it was Miriam who started talking. 'Thank you.'

'What for?'

'For helping me.'

'That's not helping.' Leo fixed his eyes on Miriam's. 'Look for a good doctor, Miriam.'

She let out a deep sigh. 'Corallina is lovely.'

'I know,' Leo muttered, his eyes low on the handlebars.

'You have a great bond.' Miriam paused for a long while. 'You need to stop dealing that stuff, Leo. If you end up in prison, it will kill her.'

Leo took to polishing the headlight with the cuff of his jacket, which he had pulled over his fingers. 'You think I don't know that?'

'So?' Miriam pressed him on. 'You can quit.'

'I need the dough.'

'To do what? It doesn't look like dealing is doing much for

you anyway!' Miriam pointed at the peeling paint on his old scooter.

'It's not like we were all born with a silver spoon in our mouths,' Leo snapped. 'You live in Barberini and I live in San Basilio. You think you have something to teach me about life?'

Miriam shook her head. 'No. I can imagine it's hard. But your sister doesn't deserve that kind of heartbreak.'

'I'm doing it for her too, so she can reopen her salon.'

'Why did she close it?'

'Some fuckers set it on fire three years ago. She'd put into it everything she'd earned in ten years working for other hairdressers for a pittance, and now she's still paying off the debt.'

'I'm sorry,' Miriam said in a whisper.

Leo kept his gaze fixed on the road to hide the anger that was clouding his eyes.

'Quit, Leo. You'll find another way. Don't throw your life away; she'd never want that for you.' Miriam spoke slowly but with a resoluteness that she too found strange in herself. 'What if you end up killing someone with the stuff you sell?'

Leo shrugged. 'I only deal with the light stuff . . .'

'Are you serious?' Miriam said in a huff.

Leo started the engine again, revving it loudly. 'Right, I'm off.'

Miriam took a step back, waiting, not knowing what for.

'You got enough pills?' Leo asked, feigning nonchalance.

'I think I'll be okay,' Miriam said.

Leo nodded, an expression impossible to define on his face. 'See you around, then.'

Miriam too nodded without saying a word.

They looked at each other and this time it was Leo who found the courage to say something. 'I'll quit if you quit,' he suggested, not even knowing where those words had come from.

Surprising herself, that day Miriam smiled once more as she stared at him, vaguely incredulous. 'Swear!'

Leo too smiled a little, almost feeling puzzled at himself. 'I swear.'

Miriam nodded. 'I'm in.' Her heart was racing out of fear, and panic was already making her breathing weaker, but she felt a subtle happiness spread inside.

Leo stared at her for a long time, then dashed off without another word, tearing the silence with the croaking but oddly cheerful roar of his old blue scooter.

8

The Girl with the Corals

That night, Corallina was struggling to fall asleep. She had had her passion flower and valerian tea, but still felt that nature was set against her even when it came to sleep. She tossed and turned in her bed, tormented by bad thoughts again as she had not been in a long while.

Sharing her memories with Miriam had been lovely. Corallina had never done that with anyone else before; she felt protective of her most intimate thoughts. However, this afternoon she had, instinctively, just like that. Despite Miriam's ostensible aloofness, Corallina had recognised in her a sensitivity that somehow was akin to her own. Perhaps her agitation stemmed precisely from there, from that kinship. Miriam's silences, the gloom she seemed trapped in, her diffidence, her constant need for non-verbal reassurance – these things reminded Corallina of the symptoms that had afflicted her too, in a past that everyone would have called remote but which she carried within herself, as sharp as if it had been yesterday.

Sadly, it had all begun with the name Leo had given her. But that was another story, a story of pain.

She had just turned nineteen at the time and was feeling proud of herself because a hairdresser in Torre Maura had hired her as a trainee. Corallina was already quite good – perhaps even better than the owner herself – but as a trainee her employer could get away with paying her a pittance. Corallina was happy all the same. Of course her body was still devastated by the wrong hormones. Of course she still felt frustrated at not being able to wear what she wanted. And of course, as far as her hair was concerned, a few highlights were the most she could get away with, and even that had made her father turn up his nose. In the end, though, by using a little bit of imagination, she still felt able to enjoy life: as long as she did what she loved, she could bear being something she did not. Her customers adored her and from time to time a neighbour or two even asked her to visit them at home on her days off for a blow-dry, a perm, a dye or a manicure. Corallina would take her bag and go, since each little bit made a difference. And indeed, she had been nursing a plan for a while: a salon of her own, yes, but also something else, a dream she did not even dare to confess to herself. A few months earlier, she had discovered that there actually was a way to fully become Corallina. She had even seen some other Corallinas and her heart had exploded with joy. These women were beautiful. Corallina had cut out their pictures and pasted them in her notebooks.

One Sunday afternoon after lunch, she had got ready and left the house for her appointment with Signorina Garbati, an eighty-year-old lady who only wanted to be styled by Corallina because she made her grey hair shine like silver. The usual dodgy types were hanging out in the playground next to the main door of Corallina's building. They spent their time drinking beer and blowing out stinking smoke at all hours of the day. Whenever Corallina walked by, they elbowed each other and made guttural noises, squealed, sniggered and shouted at her – 'Pietro the fag, you're a vile old hag!' – all the while cracking up with laughter and piling up on top of each other like apes. Corallina always held her chin up high and tried hard to look proud of herself in front of those nonentities. On that day specifically, she remembered hearing her mother close the window to block out the voices from downstairs. Corallina had set off at a brisk pace when, all of a sudden, she had heard the pitter-patter of feet running after her and Leo's voice calling aloud, 'Corallina! Corallina!' Corallina had turned around abruptly and suffocated a scream within: her little brother was holding out the manicure case that she had left behind on the console in the hallway. A roar of laughter had exploded as loud as a bomb.

Leo had stopped in his tracks, frozen, as if a bomb really had gone off. He had stared at Corallina, his eyes wide with guilt, sorrow and fear. His quivering lips had opened to look for a word that could repair his involuntary betrayal, his broken promise. Leo had realised that asking for forgiveness would not help anything: the damage was already done.

Corallina had run towards him and hugged him. 'Thank you, love! Thank you!' she had said as she frantically ruffled his hair so as to have an excuse to cover his ears. She knew that it wouldn't change a thing, but how else could she protect him from all that cruelty? Then she had hugged him tightly and taken the case from him. 'I'd be in trouble if I went to see Signorina Garbati without it,' she had said, slapping her forehead to signify how serious a blunder Leo had saved her from.

In the meantime, Leo's eyes had filled with tears of genuine sorrow. And that sorrow had crushed Corallina's heart more than any humiliation. 'You go home now, sparrow, go.' Corallina had given him a gentle nudge of encouragement on one shoulder, reassuring him with a nod of her head. 'Go!'

Leo had had to march past the commotion he had unwittingly caused. Overwhelmed with dejection, he was almost dragging his feet. Corallina had followed him with her eyes until he had disappeared into the hall, then she had set off again, her head now hung low. That evening, not a single word had been uttered on the matter at home and they had all eaten dinner in a graveyard silence.

The following Tuesday evening, Corallina had locked up the salon as usual, since her employer only trusted her to do so; then she had caught the bus and got off at her usual stop on Via Casilina, which was just a short distance away from her home. As she walked through her neighbourhood, the streets became dark and deserted. She had barely noticed the light blue van. When its back doors were flung open, she had been startled, but it was surprise rather than fear: until that day, she had never really believed she had anything to be scared of. Six people had jumped on her. As they grabbed her, her instinct had reached deep inside her, discovering a physical strength that had felt as unfamiliar to her as the hands that were dragging her into the van. To subdue her, they had kicked her brutally in her thighs, yanked at her, punched her in the face and head and finally dragged her inside by her hair.

Corallina had cried and pleaded as she screamed in pain and asked why. Their only response had been to laugh in her face, as if only a fool might fail to understand. They had stripped her naked, amid a hail of spit and kicks in the testicles, so that the atrocious pain they were inflicting on her would remind her of who she really was – or, rather, who she was not. Then they had urinated on her so that their piss would remind her of her worth. Eventually, they had raped her however they could, taking turns, and beating her all the while because she had forced them to stoop to such a repulsive act, because she was not a female.

Finally, they had dumped her on the asphalt, throwing her belongings on top of her, and driven off with a squeal from the tyres. Someone had found her a few hours later and called an ambulance. Corallina had spent many weeks in the hospital healing the wounds in her body. The other patients in the male ward had looked at her warily and hardly ever talked to her. Her parents had come to see her only a handful of times; the hospital was far away and visiting times did not align with their shifts. These visits were always full of embarrassment. After a while, her father had stopped coming altogether. Her mother continued to carry out her duties, bringing her a few changes of clothes, some magazines, a packet of crispbreads and a few bottles of water. Leo could not go, because children were not allowed in the ward. However, a volunteer called Giuliana had taken a liking to Corallina and often kept her company. They chatted and chatted and, when Corallina was able to stand again, she had given Giuliana a lovely haircut. Giuliana had liked it so much that she had asked Corallina how she might return her kindness. Corallina had smiled and asked her for a blouse and a skirt with a floral pattern, one of those skirts that fluttered about like leaves as you walk. Something second-hand, from the flea market, nothing expensive.

One day in May, Corallina finally left the hospital. She was on her own, wearing a blouse, a white skirt with a print of red roses in bloom and the coral necklace that Leo had sent her in a parcel, hidden among some clean underwear. At home, she learned that her father had not only skipped the hospital visits but had actually packed his bags and gone off to who knew where. On seeing what Corallina was wearing, her mother had explained, full of resentment, that there was a limit to the indecency a family should be expected to bear. Corallina had understood and asked her for forgiveness, with no resentment of her own. So she had gathered her things and her beloved notebooks in an old gym bag. Then she had lowered her eyes to Leo, who was staring at her motionless from the threshold, shaken by tears. She went up to him to pat him on the head, drying his eyes with the chiffon scarf she was wearing around her neck for the first time, after keeping it hidden for years and years.

'I'll call you every day. I promise,' she reassured him.

Leo nodded.

'I'm going to set up a house full of flowers. It'll take me a little while.'

'How long?'

'I'll let you know when it's ready. But in the meantime you need to behave. Do you promise?'

'Okay,' he said, perhaps wondering whether Corallina still put any stock in his words.

Corallina had kissed him on the forehead, as lovingly as a mother would. 'Being Corallina is amazing,' she whispered to him. 'Thank you, Leo.'

Crying harder, Leo had sobbed, 'You're welcome,' as he hugged her.

But it was not just what she could glimpse in Miriam that was keeping Corallina up. There was also another strange fixation: the feeling that she had already seen her somewhere. There was definitely something familiar in Miriam's small face, in her delicate features, in her brown bob that emphasised her long neck. But what could Corallina have in common with someone who wore such elegant clothes? Corallina reckoned that on the night Leo had brought Miriam home asleep she had been wearing designer clothes worth at least two million lire, what with her jacket, blue jeans and shoes. And her cashmere jumper, as light and soft as silk, with the logo on its satin tag sewn into the edge of the cuff.

All of a sudden, Corallina sat up straight, jumped out of bed clumsily and ran into the small sitting room. There was a magazine rack next to the sofa where she kept glossy periodicals, weeklies and photo-romances she bought to keep her customers entertained while they waited. She spilled its contents on to the floor and sat down, flicking through the magazines wildly and huffing every time she set one aside that had yielded no results. Then she found it, the picture that had been keeping her awake. *Bassevi Style Lands in New York*, read the headline. Last year, Corallina had pored over the article with dreamy eyes: she always found Emma Bassevi's designs so elegant and they never failed to give her a shiver of pleasure. The idea that she could not even afford a Bassevi belt in a sale broke her heart. However, it had not been the pictures from the opening of a new showroom on Fifth Avenue that had been niggling at her, nor the designer's successful autumn/winter collection, but rather the only image in the feature that portrayed Emma Bassevi and, one step behind her, her children: a stocky young man, utterly charmless, and her then-eighteen-year-old daughter, Miriam, who was as elegant as a swan.

'Jesus!' Corallina exclaimed as she pressed the palm of her hand on her chest, trying to calm her racing heart. 'Lord!'

Corallina studied the picture until she was sure that it could not be a coincidence, a mere resemblance. No, of course not, she couldn't be mistaken. So, how had a billionaire's daughter ended up in her home in San Basilio? And what did Leo have to do with that kind of world? Corallina stood up, the magazine still in her hand, and went to drink a glass of water to settle the anxiety churning in her stomach. Then she dabbed cold water on her forehead, since all of a sudden she had a headache. What was Leo up to? And in what way was Miriam a mess?

For it was obvious that she was a mess. Then Corallina's heart suddenly skipped a beat: she might have just discovered the answer she was looking for. Of course! How could she not be a mess, considering what had happened to her cousin? Two years earlier, Corallina had read in the newspapers that Emma Bassevi's niece had been found dead on a beach, the victim of a horrible crime. Her name was Elisabetta. Corallina had never been able to forget the picture of that beautiful blonde girl, in the prime of her life. The idea that those monsters were still free, still out there somewhere, had distressed her for months. Corallina knew what it was like, and it had taken her a long time before she could accept that she had been lucky to survive. That kind of trauma must weigh like a boulder on a young woman like Miriam: no wonder she felt burdened by the tragedy that had struck her cousin.

Corallina sat down at the kitchen table with her glass of water, mulling over how life could be both beautiful and cruel. As far as she was concerned, she had decided that she did not want to yield before the ugliness of life. But she had realised that she was strong: the more they tried to crush her down, the higher she held her head. She stared at the picture in the glossy magazine for a long time. Miriam was not like that. Miriam's sorrow had made her fold into herself, you could tell just by looking at her.

When Leo got back home, he found Corallina still up, sitting at the table. He walked into the room with cautious steps, to avoid treading on the magazines scattered all over the floor, and looked at his sister with worry on his face.

'What happened?'

'Come here and sit down,' Corallina told him calmly but firmly.

Leo took his jacket off, went to sit to Corallina's right and stared at her for a while, slightly alarmed. Something must be quite wrong for Corallina not to have a smile on her face.

Corallina slid a magazine, folded back, across the table. Leo looked at it, his eyes narrowing and a slight frown forming on his face. It took him a moment before he recognised Miriam, and the astonishment left him speechless.

'You didn't know?' Corallina asked.

'No.' Leo shrugged, trying to feign that it did not make a lot of difference to him.

'You're friends with someone like that and you don't know?'

'Well, I had a sense that she wasn't from Torbella.'

'And how come someone like her – a mess, as you say – comes here looking for you in the middle of the night?' Corallina was now staring at him with enquiring eyes.

'I'd helped her out the day before ...'

'With what?'

'I told you. She was feeling sick at the club; she'd had too much to drink.' Leo realised that Corallina knew full well that he was lying.

'Last night she was sober, though,' Corallina pointed out, still evenly, though it was obvious that Leo was on dangerous ground.

Leo moved the magazine to one side, irritated. 'Corallina, you've met her, right? She's weird.'

'Leo, look me in the eye!' Corallina waited in vain for her brother to lift his gaze. 'What was Miriam Bassevi looking for, here in our home?'

Leo's silence turned the room to ice.

'What kind of stuff are you giving her?' Corallina asked, her consternation turning her voice into a hiss.

Leo stood up all of a sudden and went to lean with his back against the kitchen cabinet, following an instinct to put some distance between himself and his sister before she flew into a rage.

'What are you dealing, you fool?' Corallina too stood up

and waved the magazine around in front of him. 'What are you giving this poor girl?'

'Nothing, Corallina! She was convulsing cos she was in withdrawal from some pills of her own.' Leo rattled off his confession. 'I was only helping her out!'

'Help?' Corallina cocked an ear, flabbergasted: she could not believe she had heard him right. 'And since when are you an expert with this stuff? A girl is convulsing and you, rather than taking her to the hospital, help her find some filth?'

'She's a mate – what was I supposed to do?'

Corallina laughed hysterically. 'A mate? Do you think I'm stupid?'

Leo fell silent, his head hung low, his mind crowded with a thousand thoughts: Corallina had no clue how hard it was to make do with the next to nothing they paid him at the trattoria, and without a contract to boot. Leo had never told his sister this, but during his last year in secondary school, when he was still living with his mother, who had been terminally ill with cancer, they would not even have had enough to eat, let alone for the rent or her treatments, if it hadn't been for the weed he had dealt at school. His mother had categorically refused to ask for any help from Pietro, as she had continued to call her daughter until the very end. Instead, she had insisted on making do with what they had, at least until she could see Leo graduate secondary school. He had asked people for loans and pawned off some items of little value, but he could not work miracles, and his evening job as a waiter paid very little. After his mother's death, Leo had moved in with Corallina and stopped dealing drugs, making ends meet with what he earned at the trattoria. All until Corallina's salon had been set on fire and things had once again taken a turn for the worse.

'And how did you end up mixed up with all this?' Corallina asked, still staring at him in disbelief.

Leo made one final attempt. 'With all what?'

'With dealing drugs,' she snapped. 'How did you end up dealing drugs?'

'I used to play football with a guy from Tor Sapienza who was in my year at school. He ended up making friends with some guys from Magliana, and when he heard that things were tough he helped me out.' Leo desperately looked for some words that might reassure Corallina as she glared at him. 'But it was always light stuff ... None of that junkie dope!'

Corallina had to sit down; her legs were about to buckle. 'A drug-dealer ...' she was muttering to herself, still struggling to reckon with the idea. 'A drug-dealer,' she repeated, her eyes staring into nothing.

'I swear I'm through with it!' Leo put his hands on the table and leaned towards Corallina. He wanted to put a hand on her shoulder but did not dare touch her. 'I'm done with it, Corallina!'

'How could I be so naive?' Corallina was too focused on her inner monologue to hear him. Her fingers were clutching her silk turban, which was now lopsided, exposing the fuzz of hair on her temple and behind her left ear. But she did not care. After a sorrow like this, what could she possibly care about being ugly and bald? 'And now what?' she asked her brother, though actually still talking to herself.

'Now that's it,' Leo promised once more.

'I should go to the carabinieri. Right now. Tell them that there's a criminal living under my roof.' Corallina stood up as she spoke her thoughts out loud – she needed to make herself some camomile tea. All of a sudden, she addressed her brother. 'That way, you'd end up in prison with even worse criminals,' she snapped. 'See how you like it.' Her voice had lost all of its kindness; she was too weak to tame her throat at that moment.

Leo remained quiet – he had run out of arguments. His actions could not be explained away with some noble motivation. He had got himself mixed up with exactly the kind of riff-raff Corallina despised so much, and only because he had not been able to do any better: at the end of the day, he was just a guy without talents who had broken bread with some very nasty people. Even if he had had some ambition when he was younger, he had been a mediocre student who had been unable to land anything more than a dead-end job after graduation. He had seen people from working-class neighbourhoods just like San Basilio prove that it could be done. But not him. He was risking going to prison for peanuts. At least his friend Federico Nardi had made a name for himself in Tor Sapienza and could even afford to give Leo his own turf just for old times' sake.

'I'm sorry,' Leo muttered. It was the only thing he could think of at that moment. And yet, somehow, he also felt relieved that this was finally out in the open. Deep down, he had always known that lying to Corallina was a rotten thing to do: it was not right that she should keep loving someone who did not deserve it.

While Corallina waited for the water to come to the boil,

they did not say another word to each other. Leo had sat back down, as if waiting to be sentenced. He was staring at his fingers, which were interlaced on the table, and from time to time he glanced at that stranger in the magazine who had shown up just to throw his life off balance. He was not angry at her, though. Rather, he felt a great sense of disillusionment at the idea of all that distance that separated them, which went far beyond the kilometres between her home and San Basilio.

'She's quite pretty, isn't she?' Corallina said all of a sudden from behind his back, her usual sweetness back in her voice.

Leo was startled, his sister's sudden change of mood catching him off guard. 'This again? No, she isn't!' Leo moved the magazine to the side.

Corallina let out a cheeky smile. 'Look at you!' she taunted him.

'Who? That bag o' bones?' Leo said, annoyed.

'Just so you know, you're a handsome young man too,' his sister reminded him with pride.

Leo shook his head, amused. 'What's wrong with you? One minute you wanna send me to the tank and now you lookin' to marry me off?'

'So what? You can do both!' Corallina challenged him.

Leo burst into a sincere laugh that lifted a cloud from his face. 'Can you imagine her queuing up in Regina Coeli for visiting time?'

Corallina too laughed out loud, despite herself. 'No, not really,' she sighed, shaking her head as she readjusted her turban. She poured boiling water into the cup – the one with daisies had felt appropriate – and put the camomile teabag in to steep, then she carried the cup to the table on its porcelain saucer and sat back down and sighed. 'I guess I can't send you to prison.'

'I guess not,' Leo echoed, opening his arms. Clearly that girl was the only thing standing between him and prison.

'I'll put you on probation, though,' Corallina said, now serious again. 'Starting from tomorrow, you'll find yourself a real job: if they don't pay you enough at the trattoria, go to a building site, down a mine ... wherever, really!' Corallina fixed her eyes on Leo's. 'But you must promise me that ...' She didn't manage to finish her sentence as tears choked her. After all, she knew that Leo was not a bad guy.

Impetuously, Leo squeezed her hand tightly in his. 'I'm sorry, Corallina,' he muttered, the guilt weighing on his chest just like that time so many years ago.

Corallina nodded quickly a couple of times to indicate that she forgave him. She waited for her tea to be ready, squeezed the teabag carefully, stirred in some sugar and started sipping at it. She was persuaded that, in life, even the things that were nasty, even the things that were wrong, all happened for a reason. Otherwise, one would simply lose one's mind out of desperation and let oneself dry up like a plant without water. Even Leo going a bad way, for example, had perhaps happened for a reason: now he was on Miriam's path before she could crumble to pieces completely.

'Leo, this girl needs help,' Corallina said, as she stared lost in thought at Miriam's picture.

Leo shrugged, nodding towards the magazine. 'Corallina, when people have everything, they're never happy. Anyway, she promised me she's gonna quit too,' he reassured Corallina.

'But how?' Corallina shook her head. 'Do you realise that she's Elisabetta Ansaldo's cousin?'

At first Leo looked at Corallina without following. He had to dig deep into his memory for a moment before he could link that name to the picture he had seen all over the newsstands, on the first pages of the newspapers, right below the articles on the Bologna bombing. 'The girl who was killed in Torre Domizia?' Leo seemed perplexed. 'You sure?'

'Positive. She was Emma Bassevi's niece, and Emma Bassevi is Miriam's mother. I even saw her in the pictures from the funeral.' Corallina remembered a photograph taken from afar, where Emma Bassevi had been supporting her sister alongside a nun.

Leo leaned against the back of his chair with a deep sigh. He had not followed the news closely at the time, but he remembered that it was an ugly story. Those bastards had ganged up on her and left her dead on a beach in God knew what state. As far as he could recall, no one had ever been arrested for it.

Of course, he now understood Miriam a lot better. And yet, beyond her diffidence, beyond her almost childish fears, it seemed to him that there was a contradiction of sorts between her guardedness and her tendency to self-destruct.

'And you think she's the way she is just because of that?' Leo asked with scepticism.

Corallina stared at her brother pensively for a long time as she slowly sipped at her hot camomile tea. 'Such a man's thing to say . . .' she whispered, a cloud of bitterness veiling her voice. She had never told Leo about the violence she had experienced herself. She had protected him as best she could from that sorrow, with silence. That grief had been only her own to bear.

Leo looked at her, failing to understand.

Corallina smiled sadly and took another sip of her tea. 'Remind me to lend you the necklace some time.'

9

Rocks

Over the next four days, Leo hoped in vain that Miriam would get in touch. At the peak of childish selfishness, he even wished she would be sick enough for her to seek him out again. Not that he had any intention of finding her any more pills, but he would have welcomed the chance to be indispensable to her somehow. But Miriam had not been in touch with him.

Despite this, Corallina felt quite hopeful, even though she did not say so openly. She was like that, an optimist by nature. Meanwhile, Leo dealt with his growing disappointment by putting on a sulk that he explained away to his sister as the worry of having to find a decent job, and quickly. He was even a little embarrassed at the thought that he had believed he and Miriam had shared some level of intimacy. In his previous relationships, he had always been focused entirely on the physical side of things; emotions made him feel vulnerable. The complex mechanism of gazes and precarious balance that he had shared with Miriam was new to him, and intrigued and scared him in equal measure. He almost felt a certain uneasiness when he recalled how he had watched her sleep without even wondering if he desired her, since he had felt that somehow Miriam's insubstantial, distressed body was already his. It had only taken him two nights, just two, to convince himself that, for reasons he did not understand, they were right for each other. Right, but definitely ill-matched. At the end of the day, he had decided that he did not care if he was unsuitable for her: he knew he could give Miriam what she was missing. The fact that the Bassevis were rich did not scare him one bit – Miriam needed him.

It was because of all these thoughts, mulled over during several evenings spent in a bad mood while watching TV on the bed with Corallina, that one afternoon Leo decided he had waited more than long enough, and showed up at the building where he had dropped her off a few days earlier. The doorman politely stopped him in the lobby, informing him that he had to let Signorina Bassevi know that he was there before he could let him through. Leo took a liking to him, since he had not questioned for a moment whether Signorina Bassevi would even want to see him. Indeed, the signorina said on the phone to let him through, and Leo ventured cockily into the ground floor of the building. However, the building itself was so big that Leo had to return to the doorman to ask how to get to the penthouse, since there were more staircases than in a hospital. Leaving his booth for a moment, the doorman quickly escorted Leo to the correct lift. Leo thanked him, somewhat dejectedly: all of a sudden, he felt like a mere fool from the outskirts.

When the doors of a lift that was as big as the apartment he shared with Corallina opened on to the landing, he saw Miriam on the threshold and immediately felt better. However, his relief was short-lived. She looked terrible, enveloped in a tracksuit that was so big on her that it looked like a sack. The blue circles under her eyes stood out on her pale skin and her lips were dry and cracked, scored by reddish lines. Miriam was staring at him without smiling, her eyes swollen and reddened, whether by tears or insomnia it was impossible to tell.

'I've changed my mind: you are kinda ugly,' Leo greeted Miriam as he came up to her. Miriam barely smiled, but he could tell that she was amused. Nevertheless, she was clinging on to the door jamb, her head tilted back against it. 'At least you're not frothing at the mouth.'

'What do you want?' Miriam said, still smiling. Just a little, but it was a smile.

It was not the kind of reception Leo had been hoping for: though he sensed no real hostility, she did not look as though she was planning on letting him in. He tried his best not to lose heart. 'Are your folks in?'

'No. My parents live somewhere else.'

'How're you doing?' Leo asked softly, trying to mask the worry in his voice. He had got close enough to see that it was a miracle she could stand.

'How it looks.' Miriam lifted her little shoulder in her giant sweatshirt.

Leo studied her with an expert eye. 'Are you using again?'

'No. I promised,' Miriam said, slightly miffed. 'What about you?'

'No.' Leo showed her his open palms defensively.

They stared at each other, ill at ease for a moment.

Leo looked around. 'You gonna let me in, or do you usually entertain on the landing?'

Miriam sighed. 'Better not, Leo.'

The disappointment at her refusal was compensated by the thrill of hearing her say his name. 'Why?' Leo said, trying to make a show of detachment.

Miriam did not answer.

'You're scared ...' He punctuated his words with a resigned nod.

She only hesitated for a moment. 'No ...'

Leo put his hands in the pockets of his jacket and swayed slightly, stirred by a surge of satisfaction. *No*, he repeated in his head in the same tone she had used. All of a sudden, he felt like a giant. 'Why, then?' Leo pressed on with a kindness that surprised even him. 'Come on.' He smiled at her compellingly. 'I've come all the way from San Basilio and you keep me out here on the doormat? Your doorman is gonna get ideas ... That's how you'd treat your dealer.'

Miriam stepped to one side, not quite convinced. 'Five minutes only, though,' she said, moving just as far as she needed to let him past.

'Of course ... Two, three minutes tops,' Leo taunted her, squeezing into the apartment and closing the door behind him.

It took Leo only a second to realise that Miriam did not really live in that place. She did not live there, nor anywhere else. Her name was on the doorbell, her stuff was in the wardrobe, but that apartment that seemed as big as a hotel to Leo bore no trace of her. There was not a single object that was personal: a photograph, a book. A flower. Having been surrounded by Corallina's flowers for years now, Leo was convinced that the homes of all women were always full of flowers, one way or another. Not here, though. Miriam lived in a place where, despite the large windows overlooking the Roman skyline, the light showed no colour. Everything was fake, like the rooms in furniture shops with shelves full of cardboard books. It seemed as if she were just passing through, crashing with a thick blanket and a pillow on one of the two white leather sofas arranged in an L-shape in the living room. There were some bottles of medicine on the crystal coffee table, together with a carton of milk, a glass, and a half-empty bag of sliced bread. Leo looked at her as she snuggled back under the blanket despite the stifling heat of the apartment and thought, with great sorrow, that he was not enough to help Miriam. He felt stupid for having believed he could, even for a moment.

'What's all this stuff?' he asked, nodding towards the pills.

'I need to take it instead of Phentatyl until I'm over the withdrawal.'

Leo looked at the bottles sceptically. 'All of it?'

Miriam nodded.

'What a bargain!' he quipped sarcastically.

'A consultant prescribed it to me. They gave me injections for the first two days, but now I can manage on my own.'

'You feeling better?'

Miriam had to think for a moment. 'I'm no longer in pain or all the other stuff . . . ' She shrugged. 'I'm not convulsing either.'

'That's good.' He nodded.

She nodded too, though not with conviction.

Leo came closer and cautiously sat on the sofa without asking permission. Miriam still looked at ease, so he felt that he could take his jacket off; he was starting to sweat. 'So what's wrong?'

'What's wrong is that ...' Miriam muttered, rolling her eyes in exasperation. 'That I can't sleep. That's what's wrong.'

'And what does your guy have to say about that?'

'He only talks bullshit!'

Leo widened his eyes, pretending to be impressed. 'Would you listen to her! Two nights in San Basilio and Bambi turned into a badass!'

'Stop treating me as if I'm two,' Miriam protested.

'Why? How old *are* you?' Leo taunted her, laughing.

'Stop it already!' She wrapped herself up more tightly in her blanket and sank her dishevelled head into the pillow she had placed on the wide armrest.

Leo sighed. 'Miriam, you need some serious help.'

'I'm getting it.'

'But if you can't sleep and you don't eat, then it's not helping enough. Like hell you're gonna quit Phentatyl like this!' Leo pointed at the bag of sliced bread on the coffee table. 'What on earth is this rubbish? You call this food? You really do wanna die an ugly death!'

'Come on, now, go back home,' Miriam said with annoyance, slowly pushing her bare foot on his thigh.

Leo delicately grabbed her icy foot with his hand and Miriam instantly pulled it back, prising herself up on to her elbows. 'Don't touch me!'

'I'm sorry,' Leo said, raising both his hands.

Miriam lay back down again. Suddenly she looked too exhausted even to be angry.

'Miriam ...' Leo leaned towards her, stretching his arm along the back of the sofa. 'I can't bear to see you like this. You understand?'

Miriam closed her eyes, curling up with a deep breath.

'Why don't you sleep a little now? I'll be here, right next to you.'

'I don't want to sleep if you're here.'

'But you did sleep at mine.'

'I'd taken pills.'

Faced with the depths of Miriam's indifference, which stripped him of even the modicum of self-respect he still had left, Leo huffed. 'Well, I was still there, though,' he reminded her, offended.

Miriam narrowed her eyes and looked at him. The afternoon light had given way to the shadows of the evening. She stretched her arm to turn on the floor lamp that hung over the sofa. In its diffused light, she saw that his open hand was resting on the blanket, waiting. At first, she did not understand. They looked at each other and Leo attempted an encouraging smile. Miriam was moved by the realisation that Leo believed he could heal her pain with that childish gesture. However, though hesitantly, she still placed her hand on his. All of Leo's contradictions, rather than bothering her, made her curious: he could be right and wrong at the same time. She let him squeeze her fingers just a little. His hand was big, warm, and as welcoming as a shell. All of a sudden, Miriam had the impression that she had become tiny. So tiny that all of her could fit into his palm. She felt his thumb stroking the inside of her wrist, then the back of her hand, while his grip became indiscernibly tighter. She thought about pulling her hand back: that feeling scared her a little. But before she could do so, she fell into a sudden, deep and dreamless sleep.

Leo did not move. He sat there motionless, only allowing himself to breathe. Even when his neck became stiff, his arms got pins-and-needles and his eyes threatened to close, he did not move a single muscle, as if the rest of Miriam's life depended on him. As if only he could hold her back with his hand, only he could stop her from drifting away. He would not get another opportunity, he could feel it: if he wanted to give himself a chance, he needed to show her that he could make a difference. Hours went by and he did not allow himself a single moment of sleep, bartering his own rest for Miriam's, whose need was so much greater than his. She too was motionless in sleep; she too merely inhabited the silence with her almost imperceptible but regular breathing. Leo realised that he loved hearing her breathe peacefully like that: it was the only treasure he could offer her.

At daybreak, Miriam opened her eyes, then closed them again for a moment instinctively; the light from the lamp, though dim, had blinded her. Then she looked up at Leo. He was still there, just where she had left him the night before, before sleep had taken her to who knew where. It felt as if only a moment had passed, but it had been many hours. Where had she gone? She closed her eyes to try to remember and knew with certainty that she had been nowhere else but right there. She had not been on the beach, not that night. Nor on the road that led to Zia and Zio's. Nor in Betta's eyes, as she looked up at the sky laden with rain. She could not find in her head any trace of her usual nightmares, only the feeling of quiet, benign darkness enveloping her.

'You held me in your hand,' she whispered, attempting a dazed smile.

Leo smiled back with pride and nodded, exhausted.

'Like a rock,' she added, without taking her eyes off his.

When Miriam wriggled away to the bathroom, Leo stretched and then rang his neighbour to ask her to let Corallina know that he was not dead nor in jail, but at she-knows-who's place. Given the early hour, the neighbour told him to fuck off and only after much insistence promised to knock at his sister's door. Leo looked for another bathroom – it seemed obvious to him that there must be dozens in that apartment – and, feeling out of place, urinated carefully, making sure to clean up after himself, unlike at home. All that mirror and marble sent a chill through his spine that he had never felt before. He thought it absurd that someone might like living in a place like that, and wondered whether maybe he did not understand luxury because he had always been penniless. Had he had any money, the first thing he would buy would be a sailboat like the one he had once seen moored in the Anzio harbour. What the fuck was the use of all that marble for someone who was still alive? He really could not wrap his head around it.

Leo washed his hands and face, looked at himself in the mirror and found himself to be not quite as handsome as usual, perhaps due to his stubble, which did not suit him, or because of the circles under his eyes from the sleepless night. 'You'd better rely on your personality today,' he recommended to himself aloud as he energetically dried his face on a towel that felt too soft to actually use.

Leo was so hungry that when Miriam returned to the living room she found him eating the sliced bread from the bag as he sat on the rug with his back against the sofa. She laughed.

'What you laughing at?' Leo protested, then added, 'You only keep foil in your kitchen!' He studied her and realised that she was oddly dressed, with tight velvet trousers, a heavy tweed jacket and knee-high boots. 'What you doin', goin' fox-hunting?' he asked with his mouth full.

'I'm going to the riding ground. I'm feeling better today.'

'And what do you do at the riding ground?' Leo asked as he stood up and shook the crumbs off his sweatshirt.

'What do you think?'

'Really? You ride horses?' Leo's tone was halfway between curiosity and amusement.

Miriam handed him his jacket. 'Thank you for last night.' She wanted to say more but struggled to name or find the words for the emotions she was feeling.

Leo let a cheeky grimace slip. 'I swear I can do better than that,' he joked as he stretched out a hand to brush back a stray strand of hair that had escaped from behind Miriam's ear.

She took a step to the side, blocking his hand with the back of hers. 'Leo, no,' she said firmly, serious all of a sudden.

Leo stared at her, confused. 'But I haven't done anything...'

'And neither should you!' Miriam said curtly.

'I was only gonna touch your hair!' Leo tried to explain, puzzled.

'And I don't want you to!' Miriam pushed past him, headed for the bedroom.

Leo followed her, annoyed, throwing his jacket on to an armchair. 'That's not how it works, though! Who do you think I am?' He raised his voice. 'I'm a decent guy!'

Ignoring him, Miriam pulled her riding bag out of the wardrobe, put it down on the chaise-longue at the foot of the bed and packed it with everything she needed. Leo stood beside her.

'Did you hear what I just said?'

It seemed as if Miriam was not even listening to him as she put on her coat quickly, zipped up the bag and flung it over her shoulder.

Leo intercepted her as she headed for the door and grabbed her by the arm, blocking her. 'Miriam!' He needed her to know that he had absolutely nothing in common with the animals who had raped and murdered her cousin; that she could trust him and he had already demonstrated as much to her. He put an open hand behind her neck instinctively, to force her to look him in the eye.

But it was as if a stranger had touched her, as if he had not been at her side for hours as she slept, had not held her hand for the entire night. Miriam flew into a rage, wriggled free with the roar of a caged animal and hit him square in the face with all the strength she could muster – a strength that would have been impossible to imagine in a body as delicate as hers.

The impact and the pain that exploded in his nose left Leo breathless, stunned and unable to react. Then other, less powerful blows reached him in quick succession. Instinctively he grabbed her by the wrists, trying to hold her still as best he could. 'Miriam!' Leo screamed, but she screamed even louder, wriggling. Suddenly, Leo could see in her eyes a terror that threw him more than anything else – the terror of a woman expecting to be hit back, and even more ferociously. So he let her go and stepped back, defending himself with his arm. As soon as she was free, Miriam disappeared through the door in a flash. Leo tried to call after her, followed her and saw her leave the apartment without even closing the door. His vision was blurring as the burning in his nose made his eyes well up. He realised he was bleeding from one nostril and ran into the bathroom, suppressing a stream of expletives.

Standing in front of the mirror, Leo tried to stop the nosebleed, then cleaned up everything as best he could. He was shaken and needed some time to calm down. He wandered around the apartment, bloodied towel in hand, looking for a washing machine, until he discovered that there was an entire room devoted to laundry. He threw the towel into the washing machine and shut it. Then he turned around and leaned against the drier, his hands in the pockets of his jeans, staring ahead as he reflected on the absurdity of what had just happened. He felt such a sense of uneasiness that for the very first time he wished he had never met Miriam Bassevi. He had done many things wrong in his life, yet he felt that only now had he lost his innocence, in that handful of seconds, right in front of his eyes. And he didn't even know why. He felt like crying and didn't even know why.

He went back into the living room to retrieve his jacket, put it on and zipped it up to hide the bloodstains on his sweatshirt, then left the apartment, closing behind him the door that Miriam had left wide open, as if she had been fleeing from who knew what.

He was about to press the button to call the lift but then realised that the idea of getting into it oppressed him, so instead he took the stairs. It was between the fourth and the third floors that he saw Miriam sitting on the steps, a heap of nothing piled on the wide marble tread. She was all curled up and pressed against the wall, her arms wrapped tightly around her chest. Her bag had fallen down two steps below her.

For a moment, Leo considered whether to stay clear of her. Get in the lift. Just leave. Instead, he decided to stay, and descended the few steps that separated them, slowly, to give himself enough time to try to find something to say. When he sat next to her with a deep sigh, he still had not found the right words, and realised that he never would.

'I made a mistake,' he said softly, lowering his eyes. He was not sure he was being sincere, but this felt right.

Miriam was staring into nothing, towards the huge window that was starting to glow with morning light.

'I'm sorry,' he added, looking at her.

Miriam shook her head imperceptibly and took to tormenting the fabric of her coat with her fingers.

'I'm sorry, Miriam,' Leo insisted.

'It's not your fault,' Miriam muttered in the weakest of voices. 'It's my fault.'

Leo took a deep breath. He rested his elbows on his knees and started looking outside. The large window overlooked a big inner courtyard with trees, carefully tended flower beds, marble benches and what looked like a small well right in the middle. It was a lovely day, and lovely days always improved his mood in no time. 'It's no one's fault,' Leo resolved, calmly.

Then Miriam abandoned herself to a quiet weeping. Her chest was shaken by deep sobs as she tried to keep them inside, while tears started brimming over her lower eyelids as if they would never stop.

Leo let her cry for a while, then stretched out to open her riding bag, rummaged inside and found a pair of cotton socks. He folded one of them and with gentle movements wiped her face and nose.

With eyes full of sadness, Miriam noticed the purple swelling at the root of Leo's nose and under his right eye, which he could not open fully.

'You're always a state,' Leo complained with a half-smile. 'Either frothing at the mouth or dripping with snot ...'

Miriam lowered her eyes and a deeper sob coursed through her. She shook her head, taking the sock from his hand with exasperation, and blew her nose. She glanced at him and a hint of a smile came to her lips as she curled back up against the wall still sobbing.

Leo stretched a hand over her legs, offering his palm.

Miriam deposited the sopping sock into it.

Leo gave her the other one so that she could cry to her heart's content.

Miriam took it with hesitation and shakily rested her icy hand in his palm.

Leo squeezed it.

They sat there for a long time, until Leo suggested they go back in. He felt that the horses could wait, at least for one day. Dejectedly, Miriam told him that she had left the keys inside the apartment. Then, as they were trying to come up with a solution, she remembered that the doorman most likely had a copy.

Leo was not impressed by this.

'What if he sneaks in?' he asked, worried.

'Of course he wouldn't,' Miriam reassured him.

She went downstairs to ask for the spare key, then they went back into the apartment. Leo watched her take off her coat and boots, scattering everything on the living room rug, then swallow two pills from one of the vials on the crystal coffee table without even taking a sip of water.

'You haven't eaten a thing,' Leo reproached her.

She nodded towards the bruise on his face. 'You ought to have that checked out.'

'No need. It's nothing.'

Miriam forced herself to look him in the eyes. 'I'm sorry,' she muttered.

Leo shook his head to mean that it did not matter, then took a deep breath.

'Corallina recognised you in a magazine. I know who you are. She also told me about your cousin,' he rattled out in one breath. The fact that he had not told her already was making him feel guilty.

Miriam did not look surprised. She knew that she had been in a few magazines since she had turned eighteen, and she also knew that there was a part of Betta's story that belonged to the world: what was left of her had been chopped into tiny pieces and fed to strangers to satisfy their morbid, bored curiosity.

'I'm sorry,' Leo added.

Miriam avoided his gaze, turning around to fiddle with what was left of the bag of sliced bread.

Leo looked for a way in, a word that could make her see that, though he did not know how to make her pain lighter, he could still listen, understand. However, faced with Miriam's discomfort – she could not even bear to look at him at that moment – he felt that all he could offer were stupid words.

'I'll go, then,' he said, feeling as if he had no other choice.

Miriam nodded.

He waved at her a quick goodbye that she did not see, and left without saying another word.

To explain his bruised face, Leo told Corallina and everyone else that he had been in a fight during a five-a-side match. No one had any reason to doubt this, and actually the lie earned him the respect of many: in his neighbourhood, coming to blows was always an attestation of character, regardless of who had come out on top.

Not only had Leo not come out on top in his fight with Miriam, he also felt empty. Over the following two days he lazed about, pretending to his sister that he was looking everywhere for a new job. However, he could not get anything done: the thought of Miriam was draining him. He knew that somehow she would manage without him, and yet he could not help but wonder: for how long? It was only a matter of time, this much was obvious to him. He felt impotent, which he did not like: despite all his limitations, he was not someone who could just do nothing. He went back to hoping, in vain, that Miriam would get in touch with him. It seemed to him that she should now be the one to send a signal. He went through her neighbourhood a couple of times, wondering if it would be appropriate to call in for a quick hello, but eventually he decided to leave her alone. He felt out of place in her life. Actually, he was convinced that she did not even have a life. She was at the bottom of a deep hole: if you leaned over, you could get a glimpse of her, and maybe she would even let you pull her up a little, so that she could breathe just enough to stay alive a little longer. However, she would then plunge back down into the pit, and the worst of it was that, if you were not careful, you risked falling in right behind her.

Over the years, Leo had befriended the local newsagent in San Basilio, where Corallina sent him from time to time to get gossip magazines. When he was not in a rush, Leo always liked to spend a few minutes chatting with the guy, since he was quite a bit older than him and knew a lot of things. So, one Thursday morning, Leo asked him if there was a way to get hold of a newspaper that had come out a couple of years earlier. The newsagent put his glasses on – not without some affectation, as the topic fell within the scope of his specialism – and explained to Leo that he could either order back issues, which would take time, and money, or he could go to the newspaper archive in the National Library in Castro Pretorio. Leo was surprised to hear that there he could find not only one but all the newspapers he might need, and the magazines too. And it was all free. The newsagent made a point to say that he thought it an excellent thing, since before ending up in school textbooks history was first and foremost told in the newspapers. The only thing was that people did not know it yet. Then, as it was his habit, he shifted the topic to one of the many awful events of the Fascist period, which was where almost all of his conversations led. Leo listened politely for a while, to show that he was grateful for his help, and then went back home, his head full of thoughts.

The following day, he went to the library. He was told that he needed to get a card and with trepidation he agreed. In truth, he was a little embarrassed about the whole thing: it almost seemed disrespectful for him to be there, since he had only ever read *Pinocchio* and a few chapters from *The Betrothed* back when he was in school. He waited for the card to be ready, then explained that he was looking for the place where you could read the newspapers. The lady who had issued his card shook her head and said that he needed an appointment for that, since he had to be taken to the archive and receive all the necessary training on how to use the reader. Dejectedly, Leo said that he hadn't known he needed an appointment and that he was carrying out some urgent research for his university professor. Staring suspiciously at his face, which was still bruised, she asked if he had a letter from the professor. Leo cursed in his head and said that he did but that he had left it at home, not realising it would be needed. He was still in his first year, he explained, and did not know how everything worked yet. The lady pretended to be impressed and, sounding sardonic, said that it was really remarkable that a professor had asked a first-year student to help him with his research. Leo said evasively that it was just a small thing, nothing worth mentioning. Still not satisfied, the lady asked him what he studied. 'History,' he said, a wave of anxiety rising within him. He felt as if he was back at school, where he used to hope fervently that the teacher would ask him a question about the Fascist period, since that was the topic he knew best.

The employee sighed, slowly shook her head from left to right and picked up the phone. Leo held his breath, sure that she was calling the cops to have him thrown out and banned from all the libraries in Rome. Instead, she talked to someone and asked for a favour, for them to make an exception. When she hung up, she explained to Leo where he needed to go and wished him luck. They exchanged a conspiratorial glance and he thanked her, then dashed off, relieved that the woman had realised that his intentions were not bad after all.

Leo spent the entire morning in the library. Seeing him so focused on the newspapers and absorbed in reading them, someone who did not know him might have thought that he really was a student. The only detail that gave him away was the fact that he was not taking any notes. He didn't need to – he would remember every word he read that day for the rest of his life.

The first thing he would never forget was the fact that Elisabetta Ansaldo and Miriam had the same eyes. They were completely different in every other respect, but they had the same eyes. There were only three pictures of Elisabetta in circulation, which the newspapers and magazines had printed over and over again, enlarging them, shrinking them, changing the colours, flipping them in a mirror image. Those pictures all said the same thing: that Elisabetta was breathtakingly beautiful and that, in all likelihood, a pack of animals had made her pay for the frustration of having no other way to have her. Because of the bond he shared with Miriam, looking at Elisabetta now left him stunned, as he processed his grief all at once. Elisabetta was no longer just a stranger in the news, and reading those articles felt like a ton weight on his chest. He found some grainy pictures of the place where the body had been found, and of the Ansaldos' beach house, but there were very few personal details. The counsel acting as the spokesperson for the family had kept asking for privacy, given how tragic the event was. Rather than reporting on the facts, the articles seemed to be attempting to reconstruct them. Some journalists had tried to stir up controversy by saying that the investigation had been carried out ineptly, with no respect for the most basic procedures. This was why so little was known about the Ansaldo case. Too little.

In the early morning, a sixteen-year-old had been found dead on the beach and they did not even know for certain whether the crime had actually taken place there or not. Traces, evidence, witness statements: it was all insubstantial, vague, meaningless. Rape had been confirmed, but there were still doubts over the number of assailants. Moreover, it had been impossible to confirm whether the victim knew them or not. No one had seen or heard a thing. In Torre Domizia, everyone seemed to think the world of everyone else, so the gang must have come from elsewhere. It could be no other way. The nice boys from Torre Domizia had all been out dancing in the clubs, lighting bonfires on a beach well known to the local youth or at home, sleeping peacefully.

And what about Elisabetta, or rather Betta, Ansaldo? That night, she was in none of those places where the nice boys were. Her parents had no clue when she might have sneaked out and where she might have headed. The editor-in-chief of a weekly magazine had written a very harsh editorial criticising her mother, Marisa, for having been unable, or unwilling, to watch over her teenage daughter, who in summer was accustomed to frequenting places that were ill-suited for a girl of her age, exposing herself to risks that had eventually doomed her to a 'preventable' death. However, the people from Appio Latino, the neighbourhood where the girl lived, all said that Betta was a bright and self-confident young woman who was not prone to excesses and had a kind heart. The Ansaldos were good people, the interviewees made a point of underlining, and they did not deserve the tragedy that had struck them.

In another weekly magazine, one of those with more headlines than articles, Leo found an interview with a certain Frattali, the owner of a pizzeria where the Ansaldos had dined just a few hours before the tragedy. Signor Frattali, who was pictured outside his pizzeria, had told the magazine that the entire family was there that night, and that Betta had laughed and joked with her cousin, who was visiting Torre Domizia for the first time. Here the journalist explained that Miriam, who was the same age as Elisabetta, was the younger daughter of Emma Bassevi, fashion designer and wife of the famous textile entrepreneur. In the same article, Emma Bassevi was pictured in her atelier and also, in another shot, grainy and taken from afar, from the day of the funeral. The caption explained that the funeral had also been attended by the victim's mother Marisa, her father Stelvio, her brother Ettore, her uncle Emanuele and a nun. The victim's cousin

Donato was also there, arm in arm with his grandmother. A little group gathered in their sorrow behind the white coffin on the hearse, the hatch still open. Everyone was there except the Bassevis' younger daughter. However, the caption did not mention this explicitly.

Leo continued his search, reading other articles. Many hypotheses and theories had been put forward in the Ansaldo case, and it had been reported that a few bottom-rung members of organised crime gangs had been taken in for questioning, seeing as they had been spotted in the area in the days immediately before and after the crime. There was not a single word about Miriam, who had been laughing and joking with her cousin just a few hours before the tragedy, and who that night had been asleep in the same house. As if she had never existed. After all, the family counsel had asked for privacy and, as far as Leo could tell, this guy was a respected professional who could wield a certain authority.

Leo forced himself to read more closely one of the rare articles that contained more details on how Betta had been attacked. Grabbed from behind most likely, silenced with a strong pressure applied to her mouth, held by her wrists, beaten, bitten, and raped in a particularly brutal way. This was the story that the deep excoriations and the bruises on her thighs, buttocks and breasts told. Then she had been left to suffocate following an asthma attack brought on by oxygen deprivation made worse by a weight in the middle of her back, perhaps a knee. A death that had not been necessarily intended but still caused, an expert had explained. And all of this had happened during a fragment of the night, maybe on a dark beach, in the deserted expanse of Le Dune beach club, under a black sky, a storm approaching, about to wash down and wash away every trace, leaving behind only Betta's body, which could no longer give any answers.

Leo could not stop thinking about Frattali, the pizzeria owner, who had remembered seeing Elisabetta and Miriam together. He rested his elbow on the desk he had been assigned to and ran his fingers through his thick hair: a doubt was eating away at him. To him the whole thing seemed so obvious that he wanted to scream, and yet he kept telling himself that it could not be.

Exasperated, he eventually stood up and left with a specific image in his head, one he had not seen in any of the newspapers but which was perfectly clear in his mind as if he had taken it himself: Betta and Miriam, sitting next to each other in the restaurant, their pizzas in front of them. They were laughing and joking together. The following day, only one of them would still be alive.

After he left the library, his thoughts throbbing in his brain, Leo circled aimlessly on his scooter in the area around the Roma Termini station, exchanging little nods of acknowledgement from afar with a few of the soldier ants from the drug-dealing operation that he had met in the past, and even with some former customers. He went as far as Piazza Vittorio and wandered through its porticos. He bought a sandwich, which he had to force down, and a bottle of sparkling water. He tried in vain to silence his bustling brain until mid-afternoon, when he finally made up his mind. He dashed towards the nearest phone box and called Federico Nardi, his old friend who had helped him make ends meet when times were tough. They hadn't spoken for a while: after promising Miriam and Corallina that he was done with dealing drugs, Leo had told Nardi that he was positive a plain-clothes cop had been watching him the last time he was outside Blue Alien. Nardi had said that if Leo was feeling nervous it was better for him to lie low for a while.

Lucio, Nardi's younger brother, came to the phone and told Leo that Federico was out, at the dogs, by which he meant a former warehouse in the outskirts, towards Finocchio, where they organised illegal fights between people or animals, depending on the day. So Leo got back on his scooter, filled it up and drove off at full throttle, heading towards Finocchio.

When he got there, he had to hang around the warehouse for a while until a junkie who was also a dealer recognised him and vouched for him. When he got in, Leo realised that it was dogs day and felt like screaming at this fucking life that never gave him a moment of peace. He made his way through a thick blanket of cigarette smoke and the baying and whimpering coming from the middle of small, overexcited crowds. The smell of sawdust, blood, dog shit and piss turned his stomach. A bookie came up to him, beguiling, but Leo brusquely motioned to him to keep moving. Leo asked two guys who were smoking off to one side if they had seen the Sapient, as Nardi was known among that crowd because he came from Tor Sapienza. One shook his head, the other said, 'Maybe,' and pointed his sharp chin towards the throng of people at the back, where the fights with the best dogs took place.

Leo pushed his way through the crush, then asked a friend of Federico's, whom he only knew by sight, if the Sapient was there. The guy was short and had to stretch his neck and jump up a little, like a chicken, just so that he could watch the dogs tear each other apart.

'He came by but he's gone now. He went to the gym. He has a fight tomorrow,' the guy shouted to make himself heard over the din, pointing towards the area with the ramshackle boxing rings to the right. Leo was relieved to leave that place, even if that meant dragging his ass all the way to the gym in Tor Sapienza where Federico had been training for years.

When Leo finally got to Boxing-Bo, he took in the smell of sweat and feet with a certain relief: it replaced in his nostrils the smells that had followed him there all the way from the warehouse. As Leo made his way through the gym, looking left and right, he risked being hurled against the wall a couple of times as the punching bags swung around. He bumped into one of the trainers, a toothless guy with a watermelon gut, and asked him whether he had seen the Sapient. The guy mumbled that he had left already, but then someone else, from the boxing ring, told Leo that the Sapient was still in the locker room, then bounced his glove off the palm of his other hand a couple of times, puffing out his pecs in a display of strength. Leo smiled at him mechanically, nodded to show how impressed he was and in his head told him to fuck off as he headed for the locker room.

Federico Nardi greeted Leo warmly, despite the brusqueness with which they had parted ways the last time. Nardi finished getting dressed, putting on his Moncler and drawing a woolly hat on to his shaved head, then he flung his bag over his shoulder and told Leo that he needed two steaks, a beer, a fuck and a joint, in that order. Then he explained with resignation that he had to pass on the fuck since he needed all his hunger for pussy in his muscles for the following day. However, he could still indulge in the other three. So, putting an arm around Leo's shoulders in a friendly embrace, he invited him to dinner. Leo said yes.

They ate in a trattoria where the air was almost impossible to breathe because of the grill, fryer and cigarette smoke. There was such a racket that they only managed to exchange a few words by shouting themselves hoarse. Nardi told Leo that he had got his hands on a Polish girl who was a real gem, and was also bringing him some good luck, since things had been going pretty well for him of late and he was making important friends who had a lot of time for him. Nardi explained that he had bought a plot of land in Borghesiana and was planning on having a villa built there soon, including a basement with a bar as well as enough space for a pool table and a poker table, just like in the movies. Then he added that he also wanted a pole put in so they could have strippers. As he gulped down his second beer, he laughed, pleased with the thought, and invited Leo to come over: the two of them had been through thick and thin together and he would never forget that. Feigning enthusiasm, Leo accepted the invitation.

When they left the restaurant, they went to sit on the steps that led to a dark portico. A strong smell of cat piss was coming from the column next to them. Someone close by was listening to Claudio Baglioni in their car with the doors wide open. Nardi opened his gym bag and, cursing the dim light, expertly rolled two joints.

Leo took his joint and inhaled for a long time, his eyes

closed. After a day like the one he had just had, he deserved some quality hash.

Nardi looked at Leo smugly. 'Moroccan. What you think?'

Leo replied with a deep nod of agreement as he exhaled.

'These days I'm only dealing the good shit, Leo!' Nardi took a toke. 'Smack is on the way out. That stuff is for tramps; it's a thing of the past.' He shrugged to signify that he had left all that mediocrity behind. 'I could really use someone like you. Someone trustworthy. Bro, you need to change your circumstances too.'

Leo remained quiet for a while. He was staring ahead, lost in his thoughts, trying to assess when and where to roll the dice. 'Federico, you know I told you about that cop following me around at Blue Alien?' he asked all of a sudden, without looking at Nardi because he knew that he was not good at lying.

'Sure.'

'This morning, they called me in for questioning at the Aurelio station.'

Nardi stopped, alarmed, with the joint mid-air. 'What for?'

'They wanted to know where I was the night of the Torre Domizia murder.'

'What murder?'

'Elisabetta Ansaldo.'

Nardi laughed heartily. 'Must be two years now.'

'Almost.'

'Right. The fuck do they want, then? And with you, of all people ...'

Leo had to inhale again to gain time. He was making it up as he went along and could not afford any mistakes.

'She was a hottie, that one,' Nardi said, thinking back to the pictures he had seen. 'Must've ended up in the way of some randy perv.'

Leo nodded.

'You knew her?' Nardi looked at Leo enquiringly.

'As if!' Leo said.

'So what? Why they looking into you?' Nardi pressed him.

'Fucked if I know ...'

'Fucking pieces of shit!' Nardi shook his head, slapping his hand on his thigh. 'And what did you tell 'em?'

'That I don't remember. What else?'

'Bastards!'

'Thing is, I'm losing my mind over it,' Leo complained, feigning worry in his voice.

'For sure,' Nardi agreed. 'You need an alibi?'

'Dunno. Let's see how it pans out.' Leo hesitated for a moment, then carried on, 'Your mates – the seaside is their turf, right?'

'North of Fiumicino, it's all ours,' Nardi qualified with pride. That 'ours' encompassed the fruit of all his efforts, all the shit he had had to eat before things had taken a turn for the better.

'Have the cops been to see *them*, by any chance? Why just me?' Leo took a quick toke, looking worried. 'You heard anything at all?'

'They came round all right, to bust our balls about the bomb in Bologna, but not for blondie. As far as I know, anyways.'

'See? Fucking bastards!' Leo cursed with almost childish irritation. 'Just me! Can you believe it?'

'But what you got to do with her?'

'Someone musta been spreading some bullshit around, to drag me into it.'

'Bro, you need to calm down, though.' Nardi comforted Leo with a gentle squeeze on his shoulder. 'You really need to chill.'

Leo nodded in a way intended to signify that that was easier said than done, especially when he was the one being called in for questioning.

They smoked in silence for a while, feeling deflated. Nardi, too, knew that it was easy to lose your sleep when the pigs were on your back for this kind of stuff. As much as you tried to stay squeaky clean, they were always there, sniffing up your asshole. After a while, he let out a deep sigh brimming with sympathy. 'Anyways, I'll let you know if they've been looking at us for that shit,' Nardi told Leo. 'And I'll ask around,' he promised, then added optimistically, 'So you can forget all about it.'

Leo stretched his lips in a smile of appreciation and nodded hopefully. They finished the joint, then unceremoniously went their separate ways.

The following morning, Leo ate his breakfast in silence. He was only in his boxers and T-shirt, and looked tired: he had slept poorly. He did not realise that Corallina, who was sitting in front of him, was staring at him inquisitively, not only because he had not had a shower yet and smelled of fried food, cigarettes and something else unpleasant, but also because it was obvious that he was consumed by some kind of sorrow that he did not feel he could share with her.

'You were out late last night,' she pointed out with a loaded tone, reminding him that they had a deal.

'I went to grab a bite with Nardi,' Leo reassured her, listlessly dunking his biscuits in his milk.

Corallina took a sip from her own cup. She did not like to meddle, but after the business with the drug-dealing she had realised that she needed to keep Leo on a shorter leash. Also, she was not buying that tale of the brawl at the football match. 'What were you up to yesterday?'

Leo shrugged. 'Out and about.'

'Did you meet up with Miriam?' Corallina asked hopefully, though her brother's mood indicated that he had not seen her in days. Something must have gone wrong between the two of them, and Corallina knew that Leo did not have enough experience with girls to know what to do.

He shook his head to mean no without lifting his eyes from his cup.

'Did you fight?'

'Sorta.'

Corallina sighed. In some ways, Leo was still immature, even somewhat primitive. 'What did you do to her?'

'Nothing, Corallina,' he said, irritated.

Corallina put a hand on his arm to comfort him. It was obvious he was upset. 'She'll get over it and come looking for you, you'll see.'

Leo took the last sip of his milk, which was mixed with all the biscuit crumbs at the bottom of the cup. 'Don't think so,' he said, accompanying his words with a sceptical grimace.

'Why? She doesn't like you any more?'

'When did she ever like me? She liked the pills, not me.'

Corallina looked at him with a cheeky glint in her eye. 'Of course she likes you, Leo—'

'Miriam doesn't like anyone,' he cut her short. 'And stop treating me like a schoolboy!' he snapped, standing up.

Corallina stared at him, dumbfounded: he had never been so brusque with her. She peered into his gloom and realised that there was something more in there than mere disappointment over an unrequited interest. Leo disappeared into the bathroom to shower, though he mostly wanted to remove himself from the conversation, and Corallina pottered about in the kitchen, lost in thought. She was a romantic by nature and had really believed that Leo could save Miriam from all the loneliness and vulnerability that was crushing her. She could picture someone just like her by his side – such a refined girl, sensitive, without an ounce of vulgarity in her body. Corallina was convinced that Miriam could bring out all the tenderness Leo was hiding. Her brother had a lot of tenderness inside. The problem was that he was ashamed of it: he had been brought up to be a man with no weaknesses. In the eyes of the world he had to be Corallina's manly brother, but Corallina was sure that Miriam could heal this damage, forcing him to express the delicate feelings he was capable of. But her brother was so confused, insecure and conflicted that maybe Miriam had failed to understand him, caught up as she was in her own sorrow. However, Corallina still believed that they might find each other after all: she had seen how they looked at each other and it had made her heart flutter with a pinch of envy. Maybe, Corallina told herself with a mischievous smile, she could even draw a treasure map for them – she who had no experience of that kind of love and yet knew all its secrets.

When Leo came back into the kitchen, dressed, shaven and

even smelling of cologne, he found Corallina kneading energetically and looked at her, puzzled. 'What you up to now?'

'I'm making bread,' Corallina announced.

Leo knew it was almost time for her to go and see her customers. 'Now?'

'Yes, now. I'll leave it to prove. Then, when it's ready, you can bake it.'

'Me?' Leo pointed at himself, widening his eyes with incredulity.

'You'd better.' Corallina looked at him eloquently. 'Since you need to take it to Miriam.'

'No way!' Leo made a sharp motion with his hand and walked away, mumbling to himself in half-sentences, vexed questions and exasperated answers, pacing around the house as if its square metres had suddenly trebled. He disappeared into the other room for a while, then came back and leaned against the low wall separating the kitchenette from the small sitting room, which was almost completely taken up by his extended sofabed.

Corallina had put the dough in a bowl and was massaging it with oil.

'I'll explain everything you need to do,' she reassured him.

'You'll explain nothing! Me? Bread?' Shaking his hands in his pockets, Leo protested again but with less vigour.

'Do you want to see her or not?' Corallina challenged him, certain that she would come out on top.

Leo rolled his eyes and Corallina smiled triumphantly.

Seeing Corallina give the dough its final touches and carefully cover the bowl with a tea towel while she addressed it with kind words as if it were a baby under a blanket made

Leo burst into laughter despite his bad mood – his sister was as mad as a March hare. Yet Leo still managed to mess up Corallina's loaf: he misjudged the cooking times, perhaps misled by the colour, which took longer than expected to turn the golden hue Corallina had described. Leo was very pleased with himself when he took the loaf out of the oven, certain that it was perfect, but it took him only a moment to realise that it was in fact as hard as a rock. He pushed his knuckle into it several times: there was no denying that only an axe could cut through that crust. And, as sure as his name was Leo De Maria, had he had an axe to hand he would have gladly destroyed the entire apartment like the madman in *The Shining*. Instead, he left the bread on the table and went to throw himself on to his bed, sulking, his arms crossed behind his head. He blamed Miriam for his bad moods, which were not giving him a moment of respite, and for the fact that before meeting her he had felt at home in his lousy life, quite comfortable. Now, instead, he was out of place everywhere.

Eventually Leo gave in: he stood up, put on his trainers and his jacket and left the house, telling himself that he did not need a fucking loaf just to go to tell a girl that he cared for her.

As long as he lived, Leo would never forget the surge of emotion he felt when Miriam came out of the building in Piazza Colonna where she had her classes and walked straight up to him as if they had made a date. She did not smile, of course, but neither did she look annoyed.

In the distance, Leo noticed that punk girl, Cristiana Massiroli, who was smoking a cigarette and staring at him inquisitively, and he averted his eyes, feeling awkward. He could never fathom that she was indeed the one who had brought Miriam into his life.

'How did you know I was here?'

'The doorman told me you were at school and I remembered the name of it from the folders you had at home,' Leo explained.

Miriam wrapped herself tighter in her coat: the wind was icy despite the sunshine. 'I don't know if you're more of a dogged detective or a deft stalker.'

'I'm certainly daft,' Leo mumbled.

Miriam let out a little girl's laugh, 'I said deft!'

'I know! You think I found my diploma at the bottom of a bag of crisps?'

Miriam stared at him intrigued. 'And how did you know what time I finished?'

Leo shrugged. 'I didn't. I've been standing here waiting.'

Miriam looked at him with some tenderness in her eyes. 'You're right, you are daft.'

'If you're done being a bitch, I can take you home.' He was smiling too.

This time, Leo did not have to insist too much to convince Miriam to get on his scooter. However, she did grumble as she got off: what with her bag, her folder and the encumbrance of her coat, it was a miracle she had made it back home in one piece, despite that wreck he called a scooter.

'And why d'you care?' Leo provoked her. 'It's just another way to kick the bucket, after all.'

This time Miriam did not laugh. She lowered her eyes, holding the folder tight to her chest. 'Thanks for the ride.'

Her tone implied that he should leave, but Leo pretended

not to notice. He pushed the scooter on to its stand, got off and took out a scrunched-up plastic bag from under the saddle.

'What is it?' Miriam asked, taking it from his outstretched hand. She peered inside and saw a paper bag.

'Bread. Corallina said you like it.'

Miriam opened it. 'But this is not Corallina's.'

'Don't be a drag, just eat it!' Leo protested. He was still in a bad mood because of that loaf that had turned out as hard as a rock despite taking up the best part of his morning. 'This is also good.'

Miriam handed him the folder, took the bread out of the bag and started eating it in silence, amid the comings and goings of passers-by. 'Do you want some?' she asked him after a while.

Leo shook his head, unable to stop staring at her. Watching her eat was already making him feel better – obviously he was just as crazy as Corallina.

Miriam swallowed another bite. 'But did you come just to bring me some bread?'

'No ...' Leo looked at her cheekily. 'I came cos I care for you.'

This time, Miriam laughed, shook her head, and brushed off the flour and the crumbs from her lips with a childish movement of the back of her hand that took Leo's breath away.

'Why're you laughing?' Leo carried on with a half-smile. Hiding behind that ambiguity made him feel less vulnerable. 'What? You don't like me?'

Miriam thought about it for a moment. 'I don't know,' she said with a slight shrug.

'Who is your type, then?'

Miriam's eyes filled with a sudden melancholy. 'Dunno,' she muttered, then slowly ate the last piece of bread.

'Don't you wanna have a boyfriend?'

This time Miriam did not show even a moment of hesitation. She shook her head quickly, though almost imperceptibly.

'Going into a convent, eh?' Leo teased her.

'Might do,' Miriam said shortly, scrunching up the bag once more and handing it to him as she took her folder back.

'You're welcome . . .' Leo opened his arms sarcastically, to show his readiness to help, then put the bag back under the saddle.

'Thank you,' Miriam said, clutching the folder to her chest again.

Leo let out a deep sigh. 'How's it going with your medicine?'

'Okay.'

'And are you sleeping?'

'A little.' Miriam nodded reassuringly. Then she pointed at the bruise under his eye, still visible though the swelling was gone. 'And how are you doing?'

'Tip-top.' Leo waved his hand about to signify that it was all water under the bridge, then nodded towards her apartment at the top of the building, which to him looked like the cartoon tower of an unreachable princess. 'You not inviting me in for coffee?'

Miriam narrowed her lips, hesitating for a moment. 'Better not,' she murmured.

'Got a degree in good manners, haven't you?' Leo laughed, disguising yet more disappointment.

Miriam smiled bitterly. 'Leo, it's not you . . . ' She was looking for the right words. 'I know you're a decent guy.'

'Is it because you're . . . the way you are?' Leo looked at Miriam expressively. He had actually not yet fully understood what that meant, and was only just now starting to get a sense of it. However, he knew for certain that he was happy to accept her as she was.

Miriam nodded, her eyes veiled with sadness.

Leo bent his head slightly towards her. 'But when two people . . . care for each other . . . they also face their problems together.' Actually, he would have liked to say it in other ways, but he had stopped in a sort of middle ground, in a land of dusk, because the path ahead looked long and hard. He needed to tread cautiously, if he wanted even a hope of reaching his destination.

Miriam bent her lips slightly in a smile of gratitude. For a moment his words had made her feel normal, as if there was a remedy for nasty things and evil could be healed by just having someone who cared for you by your side.

'Forget about it, Leo.' Miriam shook her head a fraction as the sentence formed on her lips in a tone that was halfway between a plea and thoughtful advice.

'No.' Leo shook his head more decidedly. 'Not gonna happen!' He fixed his eyes on Miriam's: he wanted her to know that he was going to take it slow, but would not be taking any steps backwards.

In another dimension, Miriam saw herself taking one step forward then another, putting her head on Leo's shoulder, trying to understand what it meant to abandon oneself for a moment to the certainty of support, to the steady hold of an embrace. But she stood still, as if her body was made of stone. Without saying a word, Leo sensed her vision and shared it with a part of himself that went beyond the usual senses. That contact moved him: it was an intimacy that challenged space, time and all that was spinning around them, in that city street where the entire world was rolling by. When he felt her cold fingers all of a sudden on his cheek, it took him a few seconds to understand that it was really happening, that Miriam was really stroking his face. So, before that instant was over, he stopped her hand with his. Then, as delicately as he could, he closed his eyes and touched her palm with his lips, putting all his love into that gesture, because he didn't know whether he would ever get another chance.

Unafraid, she observed that moment of beauty that was giving her her first instance of true oblivion. Leo De Maria's dark hair, which was fluttering slightly in the light afternoon wind; the discreet touch of his warm lips on the palm of her hand; his fingers holding hers in a grip that caused her no pain. She smiled at her heart beating fast in her chest, as if inviting her to wake up. Then the bitter echo of what was lost took over again, and all she could do was pull back her hand, already feeling nostalgic.

'Bye, Leo,' was all she said before turning around and disappearing into the vast lobby of her building.

Leo stood there, not knowing whether to feel joy or despair.

The following day, outside the academy, Miriam instinctively looked in the direction of the oval fountain in the middle of the square and saw him there again. She headed in his direction, ready to protest against his obstinate pushiness, but instead she found herself smiling at him and simply saying, 'Hi.'

Leo said, 'Hi,' back, and that was enough to decide that, for once, they were in agreement.

10

The End of Winter

Unbeknown to Miriam Bassevi, Leo De Maria became her boyfriend during those last scraps of winter. So, with the help of his girlfriend, who was the practical type, he started looking for a job in the classifieds, as he sat next to her on a bench under a barely lukewarm sun. Miriam ate the bread and the fresh fruit that he brought her and, in the meantime she read the listings, evaluated them, scolded him and circled those that were a good fit. At first, Leo almost always failed to make a good impression during his interviews: he was self-conscious and his grades had been mediocre. However, Miriam always knew how to find the right words to cheer him up afterwards. She made him feel clever, always wanted to hear all the details, told him where she thought he had gone wrong, and got angry when people were rude and dismissive to him. Eventually Leo found a job as a sales assistant in a large sports shop, where he was first taken on for a trial and then hired. Even with no previous experience, he was a fast learner, had an excellent memory and really had a knack for dealing with customers. People liked him; his employer told him so. Miriam was so enthusiastic at hearing that he had been hired that Leo felt slightly embarrassed when he had to tell her that he was just selling trainers, sweatsuits and swimming costumes. But Miriam was genuinely happy for him.

In the mornings, Miriam continued to attend the academy. She struggled to focus and, unlike her mother, was not at all convinced that this was her path. Even from New York, where Emma had been based for several months now, she insisted that Miriam should stick with it at least until the end of the year. Since studying was no longer as burdensome to her, Miriam did not feel the need to drop out just yet. Moreover, Leo said that her drawings were beautiful and that she could do whatever she wanted, if only she went into it with the right attitude.

During the week, Leo called her every evening from the phone box near his house, even when he worked late. They chatted for the duration of a couple of tokens and he made her laugh and checked whether she had eaten enough and slept at least a little. He was sorry that they could see so little of each other and told her so. Miriam remained quiet at the other end of the line. Then, at one o'clock one day, he found her waiting outside the shop, which was closing for the afternoon. She had a bag with their lunch in one hand and her folder in the other. Taken by surprise, Leo stood still for a moment, staring at her, almost as if struggling to believe that she was actually there, for him. Miriam was smiling at him, so he came up to her and hugged her. She let herself be hugged, a bit rigidly but with no hostility, and to Leo that felt like the best day ever.

The only day of the week when Leo was able to go and pick her up after class was Mondays, since his shift did not start until four. They would spend some time together and eat a bite, then he would take her back home on his scooter and they would chat for a little while longer outside her building, until he eventually had to dash off because, as usual, he had stayed overlong. And it was on one of those Mondays that, as they chit-chatted, Miriam smiled somewhat mysteriously and said that she had a present for him.

Leo felt uncomfortable and worried, since he had nothing for her. 'It ain't my birthday ...' he protested, almost embarrassed.

'Well, I don't know when your birthday is,' Miriam pointed out with a shrug.

'And I don't know yours,' Leo added in his own defence.

Miriam put her hand in the pocket of her coat and handed him two keys on a metal ring. For a moment he thought that they were the keys to her apartment, which he would have not minded having one bit, seeing as even the doorman had a set. Then he took them and realised that they were car keys.

Leo was speechless for a few seconds. 'What are these?' he asked, confused.

Miriam pointed with her chin to an ivory Fiat Panda parked along the pavement to her right. 'The keys to that.'

Leo directed his gaze to the car, frowning. 'You outta your mind?' he muttered.

'A little. But you already know that, don't you?'

Leo took a deep breath: he wanted to make himself crystal clear without sounding rude. 'Miriam, I can't possibly accept it.'

'Why not?'

'Cos you have to be a gold-digging lowlife to have your

rich girlfriend buy you a car,' he explained paternally, as if teaching a daughter the basic principles of life.

'First off, I didn't buy it, it was a present.'

'Even more so!'

'But I have no use for it. I don't even know how to drive.'

'So what? You can learn.'

Miriam shook her head. 'No chance. I get anxious just at the thought.'

'You telling me you can drive a horse but not a car?'

Miriam burst out in a ringing laugh. 'I don't *drive* the horse.'

'What d'you mean? It doesn't go on its own.'

'But it's different.'

Leo watched her laugh and she looked so beautiful to him that for a moment he had to try hard to push some air down into his lungs. 'Don't think so,' he said, also laughing.

'Trust me, it's different.' Little by little her seriousness returned, but the spark of cheerfulness lingered in her eyes. 'It's been parked downstairs in the garage for a year. No one uses it.'

'Then you can sell it, or give it back to your folks.'

'They don't even remember that they've given it to me.'

Leo sighed, unable to even imagine how someone might forget having spent millions of lire on a car. 'Miriam ... I just can't.' Leo handed her back the keys with a hint of a smile. 'But thank you anyway.'

'Please ...' Miriam begged him with that little whimsical voice of hers that never failed to send a shiver down Leo's back.

Leo rolled his eyes with exasperation: when she pleaded

with him like that, he became a wimp. 'Come on, Miriam,' he grumbled.

'Then use it just for a little while; when you can buy your own, you can give it back,' she suggested with conviction.

He spun a hand in the air. 'Sure, a matter of days!'

'But you have a job now ...'

'With my salary, I'll be lucky if I can get a new scooter in three years.'

Miriam stared at him, disheartened: Leo's financial struggles always left her without argument. The more she got to know him, the more she was starting to realise how hard life could be without all the privileges she had always taken for granted. She felt guilty because he always put an enormous effort into trying to understand her problems while she took too little interest in his.

'I was just hoping this might mean we could see each other more often,' she sighed, stretching out her hand to take the keys back.

Hearing those words, Leo instinctively tightened his grip on the keyring.

They looked at each other.

'You're such a smartass ...' Leo muttered, looking at her sideways, while his lips spread out in a smile.

'Sorry, I don't speak your language,' she said back.

'You're a bitch,' he translated concisely as they got into a gentle struggle over who should get to keep the keys, unable to peel their eyes off each other.

'You mean you're taking it?' Miriam could already taste the thrill of having come out on top.

'You know how long a car like this is gonna last in San

Basilio? Come morning, even the tyres will be gone,' he warned her.

'It's insured,' she reassured him. 'And if someone tries to steal it, the alarm goes off.'

'They eat alarms for breakfast in San Basilio.'

Miriam laughed again as she let go of the keys.

'If we break up for any reason, though, you will take it back right away,' said Leo, forgetting that she did not yet know that she was his girlfriend.

'Okay,' Miriam said. As if, unbeknown to her, she was his girlfriend.

Sundays were the days when they got to spend the most time together. Leo would go to pick Miriam up in the morning and take her to his place to have Sunday lunch with Corallina, who was in charge of the cooking. Corallina always welcomed them euphorically because she had realised that her brother had slowly conquered the heart of the girl with the diadem – as she kept calling Miriam. In the face of his sister's excessive cheerfulness Leo always felt a little sad: he did not dare to discuss, not even with Corallina, what was tormenting him about his relationship with Miriam. In the afternoon, Leo and Miriam would go for a walk in the centre of Rome or stay in at hers and watch TV, listen to records or play chess. Miriam had taught Leo how to play and he had discovered, not without a certain pride, that he definitely had a knack for it.

One Sunday, they stayed up later than usual, lay down together in Miriam's bed and talked at length, their fingers interlaced. Leo told Miriam about his difficult childhood and his parents' separation because of Corallina; Miriam told Leo about her years at boarding school, which was not as sad a thing as he had imagined, and about her family, which had been crumbling apart over the past few years and of which, apart from her grandmother, nothing was left but a huge, empty villa in Olgiata. However, she talked about it with a certain detachment, resigned to the bitter course that things could take in life.

Then Leo plucked up the courage to ask, 'Why did you start with the Phentatyl?'

Miriam got lost in thought for a moment, then said, 'To stop thinking.'

'About Elisabetta?' Leo mumbled, his heart beating so fast in his chest that he feared she might hear it.

Miriam slowly disentangled her hand from his and put her fingers on his lips. 'Betta. We called her Betta,' she said in a whisper. Then nothing more, and Leo did not find the courage he needed to work his way into yet another silence.

When Miriam fell asleep, he stayed awake and started thinking. He thought about how her body – apart from some brief, cautious contacts – was instinctively hostile to him. As much as it hurt him to admit it, even just to himself, it was obvious that the natural desire he felt towards Miriam was perceived by her as a threat to the relationship they had built. And this, for Leo, was an insurmountable obstacle, since he knew how to have sex but not how to talk about it. He had tried bringing the issue up a few times, when the right opportunity arose, but Miriam just clammed up, in a form of mutism that was as hostile as her body. So Leo kept quiet, out of fear. Fear of losing her, of course. And what else? Just of the absurd idea, which was actually not so absurd, that she would never make love to him? Maybe, and yet there was something else. Leo joined up the pieces of everything he knew about Miriam: the tragedy that had struck her cousin, of which so many details still eluded him; her addiction to sleeping pills; her fear; her complicated relationship with food and her own body, towards which she showed no vanity whatsoever. He had never caught her looking at herself in the mirror or carefully choosing what to wear. Miriam did not like herself; rather, she hated herself. Over the past few weeks she had put on some weight, and the outline of her breasts, which had become slightly rounder, was causing her visible discomfort. She disguised it, even mortified it, with exceedingly tight sports tops that she wore under her clothes, as if femininity was something to be ashamed of. Leo observed all this and said nothing, but Miriam's distress was tangible. He knew that the consultant who had helped her overcome her addiction to Phentatyl had tried everything in his power to persuade her to start seeing a therapist but she had not buckled. Leo was sure that she would go back to the drug sooner or later, if he failed to understand her. And then maybe even Phentatyl would no longer be enough.

When he received his first salary cheque, Leo decided to take another step forward. Though he could not really afford it, given their bills and Corallina's debt, he bought a gift for Miriam and waited with a certain impatience for the following Sunday evening. After they had pizza bianca with mortadella for dinner, a speciality to which Leo had introduced Miriam, and after he had beaten her twice at chess, he managed to persuade her to snuggle together under a blanket on the sofa while they listened to a record that Miriam's brother had given her who knew how long ago and which she had not even taken out of the shrink-wrap yet. It was a Doors LP and by the second track Leo had already decided that it was totally cool. Miriam smiled and said he could have it.

'Thank you, but I've got no record player.' He smiled. 'Where would I play it?'

'Well, then you'll have to come over to listen to it.'

Leo stared at her, happy. When she said things like that, it was as if she was swearing eternal love to him, and he always felt an earthquake shake him from the inside. 'I have a present for you too,' he announced, feigning nonchalance.

'You do?' Her face lit up with curiosity.

'Come on, close your eyes.'

Miriam hesitated, ill at ease.

'Never mind, keep 'em open,' he rushed to say, having learned to read her signals right away, though he still could not make much sense of them. He stretched over to take his jacket from the armrest and rummaged in his pocket. 'Gimme your hand,' he added, stretching out his so that she could lay hers on top.

Miriam did so and Leo put something in her palm. When she lowered her eyes, she frowned, puzzled. She immediately recognised the thin chain she had given Leo the first night, to pay for her Phentatyl. He had given back only one of the two but she had not noticed. This was the white-gold chain with a small charm in the shape of a cursive 'M' that had little diamonds set in the corners. It had been her parents' present for her sixteenth birthday. Now, however, there was a silver heart next to the 'M'.

Miriam touched it and smiled. It was a round, full heart. 'This isn't mine,' she said, faking surprise.

'I know, it's mine,' said Leo, becoming immediately overwhelmed with embarrassment at that show of romanticism. Luckily, it was just the two of them.

'Can you help me put it on?' Miriam asked, her voice cracking with emotion. She had stopped wearing that chain a long time before and had not cared that she no longer had it, but now it was different.

Leo fought with the catch for a while: it was small and his fingers were too big. And his hands were shaking, but he did not want Miriam to notice. They stood like that, their faces almost touching, for a long time, and he did everything in his power not to look at her. He felt the need to kiss her and in that moment, right in that moment, he could not bear even the thought of being rejected.

After a while, she laughed and did up the catch herself, teasing him for being so clumsy. Leo understood that her joking was merely an attempt to hide her mortification at denying him what he so wanted, so he put a hand on her cheek and slowly stroked it. It was already a lot, he knew it. But it was no longer enough, and now Miriam too had realised it.

'Hey! You know that my intentions are serious, don't you?' he muttered, shaking her face ever so slightly. He desperately wanted her to believe him.

Miriam put her head on his shoulder, all of a sudden looking exhausted.

'Miriam,' he said softly in her ear. 'Why won't you talk to me?'

Miriam surrounded him with her thin arms and pressed herself against him, rigid and awkward, as if something had been paralysing her for too long, emptying her of all strength.

Leo hesitated for a moment, then hugged her carefully, almost as if he was scared of hurting her, so vulnerable she was. He put his cheek against hers and listened to her cry her usual bitter tears, which once again remained wordless.

Leo De Maria learned how to walk on a tightrope around Miriam Bassevi, a real balancing act. Normally impatient when faced with complicated issues that made him feel inadequate, he started to let Miriam's silences point him in the right direction, one day at a time. Thus he kept her anchored, as best he could, to that strange life in which their existences had met. It was a path full of emotions that were both intense and exhausting, but the only alternative was to let her go. Leo was certain she would not try to keep him: she was not ready to offer anything more and knew that time could not stay still, as if their relationship were child's play. But Leo was determined not to take a single step backwards. There was a time before Miriam and a time after her; taking care of her had put him in touch with the best part of himself, and made him feel strong and vulnerable at the same time.

But what about Miriam? Miriam had placed him at the centre of her world, which had no reference point, and she was keeping her balance only for him, eating only because he fed her. From her he had to accept both the hours of joy, in which he could glimpse the carefree teenager she had been, and the time of sorrow that could not be spoken of. Those were the times when she shut him out as if he was her worst enemy, the invader of a pain that only concerned her, and so she chased him away, as cruelly as the desperation that tore her apart from the inside. Leo took it all, remaining by her side. Every single time. Because, when Miriam looked at him and apologised, he saw in her eyes the reflection of the man he wanted to be, someone who was much better than he was. When a girl looks at you like that, she loves you, he thought to himself, and felt encouraged.

In his own way, Leo De Maria was feeling happy this Saturday evening. He had popped into Miriam's for a quick hello and then gone back home, devoured the two schnitzels and the salad that Corallina had left him and flung himself on to his bed, exhausted. He had the impression that his boss at the shop was happy with him: as soon as a customer walked through the door, he always called for Leo, even when there were other assistants available. 'You look after them,' he would say to Leo with a knowing look, motioning towards the customers with his head. And Leo would almost always make a sale – he had a way with customers. Things were a bit better with Miriam too; of course – not even a hint of what he actually wanted, but she no longer went all rigid every time they were close to each other. On the contrary, it was often she who sought him out. She would take refuge in his arms and let him hold her as if he were warming her up from a big chill. Sometimes, she even let herself be stroked, like a diffident cat who was too lazy to bolt away. Leo had learned how to walk the tightrope without falling: he knew when it was time to stop and take a deep breath. Let time do its thing. Because he believed that time healed everything.

Over the following years, Leo would sometimes wonder what would have happened to him and his relationship with Miriam Bassevi if things had followed their course, if time had been left to decide the fate of their relationship. If Federico Nardi had not rung his doorbell well after midnight to wake him up and ask him to come downstairs.

Leo had put his clothes back on in haste, cursing, and Corallina had poked her head through the curtain to ask what was going on. Leo had reassured her by saying that it was just a friend popping by to say hello, and she had said that his friends were crazy, circling her finger next to the side of her head.

When he got downstairs, Leo looked around: Nardi was nowhere to be seen. Then someone honked once briefly to attract his attention. Leo waved at Nardi and quickly headed towards his friend's new car.

'What're you doing here?' Leo greeted him.

Nardi took a drag of his cigarette and tapped the ash off with his forefinger into the ashtray on the dashboard. 'Gotta talk to you.'

Leo hoped that he had come on some drug-related business, maybe for some deal he was involved in. He had certainly not forgotten their conversation from a few weeks earlier – quite the contrary. But now he was too scared, and if that was indeed the reason why Nardi had come to see him, maybe he no longer wanted to hear him out. Sometimes, at night, a certain suspicion had been thumping in his brain like a headache that nothing would shift, and only went away when sleep finally became stronger than anything else – stronger than any fear, even the most irrational.

'That Torre Domizia business, Leo,' Nardi said, offering him a cigarette.

Leo hardly ever smoked cigarettes but he took it nonetheless and let Nardi light it up. He had to take a deep drag before he could speak. 'You heard something.'

'Eh. Something weird.'

'Meaning?'

'You ever know a certain Mannino? Gaspare Mannino.'

Leo thought about it for a moment, then shook his head. 'Never heard of him.'

'You sure?'

'Sure,' Leo replied, trying hard to appear aloof.

'Basically, this Mannino guy used to buy dope for his girlfriend from Knight, one of ours in Fiumicino. Then, all of a sudden, he disappears. Nothing at all for a few months. Maybe they broke up, or she bought it.' Nardi cut the air with his hand to underline the hiatus. 'Then Mannino reappears all of a sudden, around Ferragosto. He's looking like shit, talking nonsense, and asks our guy for something cos he's going out of his mind. But he's got no money. He even tries to give him a watch that don't work any more. Cheap stuff.' Nardi stubbed out his cigarette and immediately lit another one. 'Knight don't wanna hear it, tells him to make himself scarce.'

'So?' Leo was staring at him, frowning.

'So hear me out: all of a sudden, the guy totally loses his shit and starts saying he's gonna go to the cops or he'll go crazy. And what does he say?' Nardi paused for effect. 'That he's one of those who did over Elisabetta Ansaldo!'

Leo stared at him, frozen. Then he quickly rolled down his

window for a moment and threw what was left of his cigarette out. 'Mannino?' he asked in a whisper.

'Who else?' Nardi replied, a flash of satisfaction in his eyes. 'But there's more: the guy says that there was three of 'em that night. He says that he and some guy from Torre Domizia messed up with blondie and that they didn't want to kill her ...' Nardi lowered his voice to signify that the matter was becoming delicate. 'It sounds like the other guy, the one from Torre Domizia, was the only one of the three who actually knew blondie, and that he has friends in high places ...' Nardi added eloquently.

'And who is he?'

'No clue. But he's untouchable, at least according to Mannino. So much so that he says to Knight that he's even scared to go to the cops about it.'

'And the third one?'

'So now here's the weird thing that makes me think this Mannino guy was wrong in the head: he mentioned someone, some bloke called Leonardo, mate of his.'

'Leonardo?' Leo repeated.

'Leonardo,' confirmed Nardi. 'Weird, ain't it? I think that's why they called you in.'

'But my name is Leo. Just Leo,' Leo said, dismissing the explanation with some annoyance, since he had lied to Nardi about the cops visiting him in any case.

'Yeah, but I told you: Mannino was out of it,' Nardi said, drumming his forefinger on his temple. 'He even says that there were two chicks that night: Elisabetta and another one, a skinny brunette that this Leonardo did over. Two on blondie and just one on the skinny one.'

Leo stopped breathing but Nardi did not notice.

'Anyways, Mannino says he thinks she's dead too, cos this Leonardo guy had gone at it like crazy. But they didn't find her body in the morning. It wasn't on the beach where they'd left 'em. Gone. How can a chick disappear just like that? Mannino says to Knight that he thinks the sea took her, cos they left her closer to the water.'

Leo stared at Nardi, expressionless.

'You followin' me?' Nardi pressed on, proud of the result he had achieved for Leo. 'So it could be that eventually this Mannino guy really did go to the cops, or maybe he called it in, and so they're looking for a Leonardo. This could be why they came to bust your balls: maybe they heard about the weed you used to handle in Ostia.'

Leo moved his lips, but it took him a few moments before he could articulate any sound. 'This Mannino, where is he now?' he whispered.

'Nowhere. He jumped off the Ariccia bridge a week later.'

'And Knight said nothing to no one?'

'The fuck was he gonna say, Leo? He told me in confidence cos he knew I was asking for a mate who'd happened to get caught in between. You think he was gonna sing to the pigs?' Nardi laughed in disbelief. 'I told you already: Mannino was out of it. Stands to reason the whole thing was just something cooked up in his head ... Maybe he too had started partaking ... '

Leo sat stock-still, paralysed, staring at a point ahead of him, beyond the dim light of the lampposts that barely punctuated the darkness.

'Leo, mate, you need to chill.' Nardi slapped him on the

knee. 'They woulda called you back in if they had their hands on something real.'

Leo nodded, opening the door. 'Thank you.'

'What for? Come and see me: you know I got plans for you,' Nardi said encouragingly. He could see Leo was much too worried.

'Sure.' Leo got out of the car and shut the door without another word.

On the way from Nardi's car to the main door of his building, Leo De Maria suddenly became an adult. At the age of twenty-two, he had believed himself a man already. He had a job, was helping Corallina pay off her debt, and took care of his troubled girlfriend. But he had been wrong. Until that moment, he had yet to know life in all its harshness. He had never felt the weight of sorrow so unbearable that it bent your back. He had dealt with his father taking off, his mother's death and the pain of his sister, from whom life had taken much and given little. But now it was different. He was no longer the same man who had left home with the laces of his trainers undone and his jacket cockily open over his T-shirt in the middle of winter. He was now going back home with his eyes lowered, his arms wrapped tightly around his chest against a cold that was making him shiver. He was fighting back tears since adults could not afford to cry, adults could not yield to pain: rather, they must face the consequences, decide, choose. Do something. And he felt as if he was dying. He was an adult and he didn't know what to do. He went up two flights of stairs and then felt that he didn't have enough strength in his legs. So he sat down on a step, his elbows on his knees and his head clutched in his hands while his fingers tormented his hair, which was short at the sides, the way Corallina always cut it, believing it suited him best. Eventually, he melted into sobs, since he had been just a boy until only a moment before.

When he got back in, he tried hard not to make any noise so as not to wake up Corallina. Nevertheless, she immediately appeared under the arch, though she was not wearing her usual turban. Something in the sound of Leo's steps as he walked back in had filled her with anxiety and she had come out of her room as she was, forgetting all silly vanities. She could feel her brother in her own blood and her blood was telling her that something was wrong.

They stared at each other for a long time, in silence. Corallina waited for Leo to find the right time, the right words, as he stood still in the small sitting room. His eyes were red and swollen and he looked as if he was facing the kind of desperation that gripped your chest and clenched your throat to the point that you feel you could no longer breathe. Corallina knew that kind of desperation well, and would have never wanted to see it in her brother's eyes.

'That night, Miriam was on the beach with her cousin,' Leo said in a hoarse voice veiled by a stifled calmness.

Corallina's eyes narrowed in surprise: she was struggling to understand, to catch the meaning of his words. Or, perhaps, she was merely struggling to admit to herself that she had understood perfectly well and could not believe what she had just heard.

'Did she tell you?'

Leo shook his head.

'Who, then?'

'Nardi.'

'And how does he know?' In her consternation, Corallina seemed to be grasped by a sudden anxiety.

'He spoke to someone he knows.'

'Someone he knows?' Incredulity was making her voice shake. 'What kind of people are you dealing with?'

Leo went to sit on his unmade bed, his head hanging low.

'How can he say something like that?' Corallina went to stand in front of him. 'I've never read anything of the sort, never heard anything on the news. I'd remember if Miriam had been with her cousin ...'

'There's nothing in the papers,' Leo muttered. He knew all too well, having spent hours in the library reading through them. 'Miriam is nowhere to be seen in this business.'

'So how can you know it's true?'

Leo did not speak for a long time. Answering was hard and painful. He would have had to explain to Corallina the picture of Miriam and Betta in the Frattali pizzeria, that picture which he had taken in his mind, sharp, and which had made him wonder a thousand times why Elisabetta would go out on her own that night. Sure, it was certainly possible that she had. Maybe she wanted to meet someone, spend some time with him behind the dunes. But she could have also asked Miriam to go with her, after they had laughed and joked together in the pizzeria that night. And then? What had happened then?

'I know that it's true,' Leo just said. Even before the facts and the articles in the newspapers, his instinct told him.

'But did Miriam ever say anything?' Corallina asked, lost.

Leo shook his head. 'No,' he said, lowering his voice. 'But I've never touched her, Corallina,' he said without looking at her. Sometimes, fewer words were enough to explain difficult things.

Corallina stared at him, stunned.

'Never. Not even a kiss. You can't touch Miriam,' Leo said with the bitter resignation of someone who had come to terms with an irreversible course of events.

Corallina slowly went to pour herself a glass of water. She drank it in small sips, struggling to swallow with her clenched throat. For Corallina too, instinct came before facts. And her instinct had always told her that Miriam's vulnerability hid an affliction that was quite familiar to her. She had the soul of a creature who had been violated, humiliated and trampled, and who was trying to escape the horror of what had been. And the horror she felt towards herself. Corallina knew it.

'What are you going to do now?' Corallina asked Leo without turning around.

'I don't know.' Leo too had been asking himself the same question incessantly.

'You need to talk to her.'

Leo did not speak and Corallina went to sit next to him. 'Leo, you need to understand what happened. If you don't understand, you can't help her.'

'She doesn't speak about it, Corallina.'

Corallina put a hand on his arm, gently. 'Miriam doesn't speak about it because she doesn't want this thing to come between the two of you.'

'But why?' Leo looked at Corallina. He had given

everything to Miriam, but it had been all for nothing: he had had to learn the truth from Nardi.

His sister tilted her head to one side and narrowed her eyes in a gaze full of tenderness at his naivety. 'Out of fear, out of anger ... ' She lowered her eyes. 'Out of shame.'

Leo felt the memory of Nardi's words lash against his brain. 'Two on blondie and just one on the skinny one.' Leo was overcome with nausea, just like the first time he had heard them. *Just one on the skinny one.* His Miriam, crushed like that, with no way out. 'Cos this Leonardo guy had gone at it like crazy,' Mannino had said. Leo's imagination rushed to create visuals for his thoughts and he had to close his eyes and shake himself out of it before he could go insane.

'And the bastards are walking free,' Leo said, almost as if talking to himself, his anger making his vocal cords vibrate.

'But who are they?'

'One killed himself in Ariccia. Another is from Torre Domizia.' Leo had to stop for a moment before adding, 'Then there's another one called Leonardo.'

'And why are they not in prison?'

'Cos no one's looking for them!' Leo snapped, then stood up all of a sudden, massaging the back of his neck. The base of his head was in terrible pain because of the tension. 'Lawyers, judges, carabinieri ... The fuck have they done so far?'

Corallina was shaking her head, incredulous. 'But why has Miriam never been mentioned in connection with it?'

'Dunno ... Maybe her family protected her.'

'But she's always on her own,' Corallina objected.

Leo remembered the brief phone calls between Miriam and her mother, the rare times she visited her grandmother in

Olgiata and the lack of communication with her father. Her brother called her a bit more often, but the conversations Leo had witnessed were superficial and Miriam had always tried to sound relaxed.

Corallina let out a deep sigh. 'Does she ever mention Elisabetta's parents?'

'Not a word.'

'There's a lot I don't understand,' Corallina said, lost in her thoughts.

'Me neither. And only Miriam can explain it to me,' Leo concluded. The idea of confronting Miriam was so scary that it took his breath away. 'Gaspare Mannino didn't know that the other girl was Miriam. Maybe the other two don't know either. These animals won't go to prison unless Mannino's story comes out.'

Corallina stared at him for a long time, unable to utter a word that might make him feel better. 'Speak to her,' she said eventually. Her tone contained all the gentleness she hoped her brother would put into his words to Miriam.

Leo nodded in agreement, his eyes gloomy with a mix of emotions that, as time went by, he was increasingly struggling to manage. 'I'll talk to her first,' he said. 'Then I'm gonna find 'em and rip 'em apart.'

On Sunday morning, Leo went to Miriam's much earlier than usual. He had slept very little, just a couple of hours towards dawn, experiencing for the first time something akin to the nightmares that plagued Miriam. He took Corallina's bread with him, since they would not have Sunday lunch together as usual. Before leaving the house, his sister had hugged him tightly, as distressed as if he were leaving for the front lines of a battle. She had said nothing, though: there was no advice she could give him.

Miriam opened the door, happy that he had arrived earlier than usual, but immediately noticed that he looked tired. She stroked his face and told him off for not getting enough rest, and for not shaving. Then she smiled and said that his sister was right: he looked handsome regardless. Leo tried his best to smile back and watched her take the bag with the bread into the kitchen to set the table.

While Miriam warmed up some milk and arranged a few biscuits on a small dish for him, Leo wondered for a moment whether it would not be better to just leave things as they were after all. To give time a chance, without putting that thing between them. As Corallina had said, Miriam did not want it between them. And neither did he. And yet ... He felt a profound bitterness spreading inside himself as he had to admit that the tragedy had always been between them. He sliced the fresh golden loaf, as that was always his job, and they sat next to each other at the square table flooded with the light of spring, which had finally arrived.

Fearing what might happen afterwards, Leo let Miriam eat her slice of bread. Her cheeks had lost the almost transparent paleness of the first time he had met her and her lips were rosy, full, keener to smile. And then there were her eyes, which sometimes got lost in thoughts that shut her down, torturing her, but still always came back to him, full of trust. Leo had fought desperately for that gaze. He had believed that the worst was behind them but now they would have to start over instead, and he felt empty.

'How come you're so quiet?' Miriam asked as she chewed her last bite of bread. She had eaten the entire slice, knowing that it would make him happy. Leo, on the other hand, had not even touched his biscuits and had barely managed a sip of his milk, which must have gone cold by now. 'What's up?' Miriam peered into his face with slight apprehension. She was not used to seeing him looking so pensive.

'I was thinking about the things I've never told you,' he said.

'And are there lots of them?'

'No. But some are important.'

'Like what?'

Leo looked into her eyes. 'I've never told you that I love you, for example. I was too embarrassed.'

Miriam was dumbfounded. He had caught her completely off guard. She averted her eyes and started arranging the biscuits into a circle. Leo noticed that her hands had suddenly started shaking a little.

'I said a nice thing, Miriam,' Leo said to her, as if teaching her a new code that he too had only just learned.

Miriam nodded almost imperceptibly. She stood up and went to rinse her empty cup so as to remove herself from Leo's gaze, and he continued to stare at her from behind. She was scrubbing the cup with excessive zeal – the inside, the bottom, then all over again – in an attempt to gain time, to escape a situation that she was not ready to handle.

Leo got up and came up to her, standing by her side.

'Miriam, things need to be said, when they're nice.' Leo paused for a long while. 'And also when they're not. It's necessary, when two people decide to be together.' Leo was explaining to her as he would a child: the conversation was already hard enough to have, without beating around the bush.

'Okay,' she said, aloof, dropping the cup into the sink. Then she turned off the tap and quickly dried her hands.

Leo grabbed her by the arm before she could walk away. This time, he could not let her go; there was no escaping this moment.

He took a deep breath. He needed air.

'I know that you were there when Betta died.'

Leo had spoken in one breath, amazed that the words had come out so clearly and so steadily. Miriam fixed two enormous, unbelievably wide eyes on to him.

'You were together on the beach.'

Her shock was visible in a movement of her lips that looked like an astonished, incredulous smile. 'No!' she muttered, shaking her head slightly as she weakly tried to pull away the arm he was gripping.

'They left you both there . . . afterwards.' The last word had come out choked: saying it had torn him apart inside.

'No!' Miriam repeated with resentment, as if he had unjustly blamed her for something.

Leo narrowed his eyes to peer deeply into hers, trying to understand the reason behind her extreme denial. 'Why didn't you tell me? Why all this silence?'

'Because it's not true!' Miriam thundered. 'I was in Ettore's room! I was asleep!'

Leo grabbed her other arm and held her more tightly. Rather than reacting, as he would have expected, she stood frozen in place. She was staring at him, terrified, as if he were a stranger.

'Miriam, I don't know what you said, what you told the police ...' Leo was speaking softly, realising that she was scared. 'Maybe all this silence made sense to your parents, but we must be able to tell the truth to each other!'

'The truth?' Miriam whispered, slightly tilting her head to one side.

'The truth, Miriam,' Leo repeated. The word was enough.

'I'm telling you the truth,' she insisted.

'No, you're not, and you know it.'

Miriam lowered her eyes to his hands, which were holding her. She did not speak for a few seconds, then muttered, 'Let me go.'

After a moment of hesitation, Leo did release her, fully expecting to see her disappear in an instant. But she remained still, standing in front of him, arms by her sides. She was looking at him as she never had before, with indignant detachment.

'What do you know about the truth?' she asked.

'I know what one of those animals told about it, Miriam.' Leo lowered his eyes instinctively as Nardi's words played back in his head.

She stared at him, dumbfounded. So, the invader had been talking. That story of abuse, violence and death was no longer a secret between her and Betta. Even that had been taken away from her. She grimaced bitterly.

'You went and took it at all costs, the truth I wasn't giving you, didn't you? And now what?' Miriam challenged Leo, calmly. 'You rummaged, you dug ...' She remained quiet for a moment, then added, 'Just like he did. You're the same.'

Instinctively Leo jerked his head backwards, as if to

protect himself from the impact of those words. 'How can you say something like that?' His voice was crossed by a shiver.

'You wanted to know?' Miriam opened her arms. 'Here I am; now you see me!'

'Miriam, I want to help you.'

'You ruined everything!' Miriam roared, her eyes full with tears. 'Can't you see?' She stretched her palms towards him. 'Just look at yourself! You don't even look like yourself any more.'

Leo held his breath, disorientated.

'The way you're staring at me ... the way you're talking to me ... Have you listened to yourself? You can't even bear to look me in the eye!'

'What on earth are you talking about?'

'I'm saying that you no longer see me now,' she screamed. 'You see me with that monster on top of me!'

Leo tried to grab her arms again. 'That's not true!' he moaned as she wriggled away.

Miriam raised her arms to avoid his. 'Don't touch me.'

'I only want for us to deal with this thing together.'

'We were!'

'No, we weren't!' Leo said, exasperated. 'Denying something doesn't mean solving it.'

'*Solving* it?' Miriam abandoned herself to an incredulous laugh. 'You want to *solve* it? What? The pain? The terror of seeing that all of a sudden they were dragging Betta away and I was alone? His hands hurting me everywhere? The disgust of feeling him inside me, still not having had enough of me?' Her voice cracked suddenly. 'Can you solve the sand in Betta's mouth? Her dead hand? Her dead eyes?' She stared at him. 'Can you?'

Leo looked at her, speechless.

She shook her head. 'No, you can't. No one can.'

Tears were now rolling down Leo's cheeks without him even realising it. Miriam, on the other hand, was now expressionless. All her vulnerability seemed to have gone.

'I swear I'm going to find them and make them pay,' muttered Leo.

'And you think I'd care?' Miriam said, barely shrugging.

Leo ran his fingers through his hair, his head about to explode. 'Miriam, maybe you can recognise them.' He took a deep breath because he felt like he was suffocating. 'They're still free ...'

'But I want to *forget*, Leo!'

'You can't. They have to pay for what they did to you, to Betta ... What if they did it to someone else?' Leo urged her. 'Did you ever think about that?'

'I told you, I don't care!'

'I don't believe you.'

Miriam tightened her lips in a stern expression, her gaze full of resentment. 'I don't want you to talk about this with anyone else. Never. I want you to disappear. Let me live my life, Leo.'

'What life?'

'Go away and don't come back!' She pointed at the door with a definitive gesture.

'I don't want to be without you.' It had come out as a desperate wail.

'It would have ended anyway, sooner or later,' Miriam said icily, then she turned and left the kitchen.

A few moments later, Leo heard the door to her room shut with a sharp thud. He went to sit down, feeling as if he was crumbling apart. He put his elbows on the table and hid his face in his hands. He had just torn down a wall, only to discover that behind it lay a chasm.

Leo had no idea how much time had passed when he stepped into the bedroom without even knocking. At this point, the barriers between them were of a completely different nature: her isolation, her refusal to touch, the kisses they had never exchanged felt like nothing compared to the deep rift that he himself had caused.

Miriam was curled up on her side of the bed, her face partially hidden in her pillow. For some time now they had had their own sides of the bed. This time she had turned her back to him, though, something she had never done before, as if she no longer cared. As if nothing mattered any more.

He went to lie next to her and gently put his hand on her shoulder. She did not pull away. She had given up defending herself. He slowly put his arm around her from behind, pulled her closer to him and buried his face in her hair. He thought that, at this point, he had nothing left to lose. He wanted to hold her tight because he might be losing her for ever, that broken creature he had not been able to make whole again.

'Miriam,' he whispered. 'I'm sorry.'

Miriam said nothing.

'It's not true that you're different to me. I feel different because this is a huge thing and I wasn't ready. Even just the idea that you might think I'm like them kills me, do you understand?'

'Leave me alone.' Miriam turned her head to press her face deeper into her pillow.

'If you don't want to, we don't have to talk about it any more. I swear to God.' Leo waited in vain for a sign, a movement. 'We'll do as you want. Everything as you want.' He pressed his cheek against her hair and lay like that for a long time, listening to her breathing. 'Miriam, please.'

'I want to be alone.'

'Alone to do what? To try to kill yourself like you were doing before?'

'I just wanted to forget,' Miriam said, feeling deep regret for the moments of oblivion that he had given her and were now gone for ever. 'Now it's all over.'

'Nothing is over ... It's just that we need to grow up, Miriam. We're not kids no more ... How can you erase it? You said it yourself: there's no solution. What happened happened. But we can get through it together.' Leo held Miriam even more tightly, with a strength he had never dared attempt before. 'We'll take all the time we need. One year, ten, a hundred ... I'm here.' He kissed her hair as tenderly as he could. 'I'm here with you.'

She withdrew even more into herself, in a feeble attempt to evade his touch, then abandoned herself to a desperate weeping that shook her entire body while Leo held her, his jaws and eyes clenched because he did not think he could bear all that pain. He held her tight, fearing that her sobs might make her snap in his arms. He forced her to turn around and hugged her, not caring whether he was hurting her: physical pain was nothing compared to the force of all that desperation brimming over from depths that he could barely fathom.

Suddenly, she threw herself around his neck and held him with a force that he could have never imagined possible coming from such a delicate body.

'We can get through it ...' Leo said ever so softly in her ear, hopefully, as if confessing a secret that was only theirs. 'You and I, Miriam, I promise.'

She nodded, her face crushed against his neck and her heart full of gratitude. Once again, despite everything, he had not let her go.

11

The Troubling Truth

Corallina heard her brother come back home early the following morning. She waited for a while before getting up. She was focusing on the sounds that Leo was making in the next room, his quiet steps as he went into the bathroom, took a shower and shaved. She was trying to guess his mood, as Leo usually tumbled about the house noisily and carelessly when things were good. Now instead he seemed careful not to wake her up, unaware that she had not slept a wink.

When he went back into the sitting room to finish getting dressed, she was making breakfast and asked him whether he already had had something to eat. He said no and added that he was not hungry. Corallina waited in vain for him to tell her something. She could not decipher the expression on his face, and the fact that he was not talking to her was not a good sign.

'How's Miriam?'

Leo did not look at her as he continued buttoning up his shirt. 'It was a tough night, Corallina.'

She understood from his tone that he was fobbing her off and felt shaken. 'So it's true, what Mannino said?'

Leo nodded.

'Poor thing,' she muttered, lowering her eyes in sorrow. 'And what are you and Miriam going to do now?'

'Nothing.' Leo sat on the bed that his sister had made for him the night before but that he had not slept in and put on his shoes.

'What do you mean, nothing? Did you tell her what you heard?'

'Miriam can't bring herself to do anything about it. She ran home that night and nobody ever noticed a thing.'

Corallina moved closer to him with an incredulous expression on her face. 'You're telling me that her family doesn't know?'

Leo shook his head. 'Nobody knows.' He tied his laces with energetic, resolute motions which betrayed the anger that was eating him up inside.

'But how can it be?' was all Corallina managed to say, in a whisper.

'When they were told that Betta had been found on the beach, they lost their minds. Miriam kept her mouth shut that morning, and has kept it shut ever since.'

Corallina had to sit down. 'I can't believe it... Only a kid and all that grief... all on her own!'

'She was trying to protect herself,' he concluded.

Leo's words hinted at all the horror Miriam had had to face, and everything that had come afterwards. Now that he, too, knew disjointed fragments of that nightmare, they were enough on their own to make him lose his mind. All of a sudden, Miriam's dogged denial and her silence no longer seemed as inexplicable as before.

Leo went to grab his jacket and put it on, his face clouded over by dark thoughts.

'What are you and Miriam going to do now? Leo, you must tell the police what Nardi said.'

'No. Miriam doesn't want to talk about it.'

Corallina widened her eyes in disbelief. 'But that means letting the murderers get away with it!'

'I promised her,' he said drily.

'And what about Elisabetta? Doesn't she deserve some justice?' Corallina asked, appalled, almost screaming with sorrow. 'Leo, you need to make Miriam think straight!'

Leo lifted his eyes for the first time since he had walked into the room. 'We can't talk about it any more, Corallina. Not even between ourselves.'

Corallina saw something in her brother's eyes that sent shivers down her spine. She saw the pain, the sorrow he felt at the thought that, one summer night, his girlfriend had been assaulted, raped and left on a beach, her cousin dead a few steps away and her life in pieces.

Then, she saw a powerful fury darken his brown eyes.

Rendered mute by a spine-chilling sense of foreboding that shook her deep inside, Corallina stared at Leo as he opened the door, and found the strength to ask, 'Leo, where are you going?'

'To work,' he said, slamming the door behind him without even saying goodbye.

Corallina felt the earth split in two under her feet and had to sit down. The shop was closed on Monday mornings, so

Leo was lying. There were still many things that she had not yet understood about her brother. But there were also other things that she did know now, and that scared her.

Marisa Ansaldo too had got up unusually early that morning. Normally, she lay in bed for a while after waking up. From Betta's room, she could hear Stelvio making coffee, his slow movements. Then she heard the gurgling of the moka pot and its smell somehow bothered her. Marisa knew when Stelvio was taking his coffee because the whole house would fall into silence again. Then she would hear him rinse out his cup and the moka pot under running water. When he was about to leave, she would see his shadow stop on the threshold of Betta's room and she'd immediately close her eyes. She did not want to say hi. So, believing she was still asleep, Stelvio would leave without saying a word.

Instead that morning Stelvio found her up and already making herself a cup of tea. Caught by surprise, he stopped on the threshold to the kitchen and wished her good morning. Marisa responded without looking at him and started making him coffee.

'You couldn't sleep?' Stelvio asked.

'I was asleep, but the Frattini kid has been making such a ruckus since six ...' Marisa lied. She did not want to tell him that a strange restlessness had forced her to get up earlier than usual.

'I see,' Stelvio said, nodding understandingly. Children did make noise. Ettore not so much, he thought, but Betta certainly had. She was always making a ruckus.

Marisa and Stelvio drank in silence. Marisa sat at the

table, the hot mug of tea in her hands, and Stelvio stood by the window, sipping the coffee that she had poured him and staring out at the road, which was becoming busier and busier with each passing day. Which, in itself, was not bad for business, but he rather missed the peace of the old times – the peace of early-rising pensioners who slowly made their way here and there, in silence, at most waving hello to someone or exchanging a word with the dustman, who was always glad to take a short break, his hands resting one on top of the other on the end of his broom.

'The weather should be nice today,' Stelvio said, looking up to the sky.

Marisa nodded absentmindedly. It surprised her that Stelvio might think nice weather made the slightest difference to her, since she could not even remember the last time she had set foot outside. Maybe it was a few months earlier, when he had forgotten to take out the rubbish. She had gone downstairs, crossed the road, dumped the bag in the dustbin and gone back inside.

Since Marisa had never returned to the shop, Stelvio had hired a cashier, Maria Grazia, who – Stelvio had told Marisa – had been left on her own with two young children and was looking for a job to make ends meet. In the morning, Maria Grazia took her children to school and then came to work at the shop. In the afternoon, she left them with a neighbour and Stelvio let her clock off early so that she would have the time to pick them up and make them dinner. Marisa thought it a good thing that her husband was helping Maria Grazia out, though lately he had been looking increasingly tired: making do on his own in the shop when he had so many customers and only a part-time cashier was no joke. He had lost maybe fifteen kilos, perhaps even more, and now looked just as he had when they'd first met. Her body too was no longer showing the noticeable curves she had added with age: she had grown thinner than she had ever been, even in her youth, since she, unlike Emma, had always been curvaceous. Now, they ate with no pleasure and without those complicit excesses that had made their bodies rounder over time: a generous serving of spaghetti, plenty of bread on the table, a little sweet treat enjoyed with their coffee as they talked. They did not know it then, but the mark of their happiness had been in those insignificant details that had now disappeared along with the life from before. Marisa looked at her husband – his short hair already completely white and the same figure as when he was young – and thought paradoxically that the sorrow consuming him had also made him somehow more attractive. Unlike her. The rare times she looked at herself in the mirror, she could hardly recognise herself: grief had worn her out and hardened her.

As she finished her tea, she observed her husband rinsing out his empty cup and the moka pot, then fumbling with feigned nonchalance while he tried to hide away the bottle he had drunk the night before, as he had been doing habitually when he thought she was asleep in Betta's bed. Marisa had been looking the other way for so long when it came to Stelvio's new drinking habit that she wondered, with a pang of bitterness, whether anyone else had noticed it too.

'Goodbye, Marisa,' Stelvio said.

'Bye,' said Marisa.

A moment later, he closed the front door and the house fell back into silence.

Marisa Ansaldo started a new, pointless day.

Leo De Maria had never been to Torre Domizia. Whenever he had the chance to go to the beach in summer, he went to Ostia with his friends. It was always the usual bunch, causing a ruckus on the public beach while their neighbours cursed and threatened them because they only wanted to enjoy some peace and quiet. As teenagers, they used to climb on to each other's shoulders and dive into the water, until one day Luca Malerba had hit the bottom badly and broken his neck. Suddenly, they had realised that stupid-ass shit came at a cost, but many had carried on regardless – the stupid-ass shit becoming ever nastier and riskier. Corallina had explained to Leo that boys were like that – that before migrating to his head, a boy's brain spent quite a long time in his testicles. 'And when it finally makes it to his head, it's usually too late,' she had concluded.

When he arrived in Torre Domizia, Leo parked at the end of the high street and realised right away that this was no Ostia: the houses on the seafront were large and surrounded by gardens; the shops were small and their windows were carefully arranged. In the centre of the little squares, there were flower beds with benches around their edges that encircled little fountains with Tritons – a word he had learned from Miriam – spitting water towards a large shell. Even at nine in the morning there were already several old men sitting on the benches, chatting away; these were the residents who had chosen to live out the rest of their retirement in Torre

Domizia, waiting for the next summer when their houses would be once again full with children and grandchildren.

The string of beach clubs was interrupted only by the slopes leading to the small stretches of public beach. Through these gaps, one could sit and watch the sea, which that day was shining blue under a clear sky. The beach was deserted and the bars were mostly open but empty. Music from the radio and the muttering of the TV spilled out from these bars, echoing against their walls and windows. A bored and sleepy town, almost in hibernation, waiting for summer for a new lease of life.

Leo went down one slope towards the sea and headed south, walking along the beach with his hands in the pockets of his jacket, which was zipped up over his sweatshirt, hood up. He was walking close to the shoreline, dodging the few waves that had pushed further in. As he walked, he took several deep breaths: he wanted to find out whether in the fresh air of April he could still smell the rot of what had happened that August. He could not. The breeze smelled pleasant. Violence, screams, fear ... death ... they all felt like things from another world. He had come here to breathe in the smell of those beasts and instead he had found a sliver of peace.

He walked as far as the river mouth, which was almost dry because there had been little rain. There was no way to carry on. So he went up another slope to the road and started heading back. On the opposite side of the road, he recognised the Ansaldos' two-storey house, which he had seen in the newspaper. Out of deep personal respect he did not get any closer but looked from a distance at the closed shutters and overgrown garden taken over by weeds. He rested his eyes on the French windows of the first-floor balcony and wondered which was Betta's room, the room where she had slept her last sleep before going to her death, aged just sixteen. And Ettore's room, where Miriam had slept the last sleep of her innocence. He thought that maybe, like ghosts, Miriam and the Ansaldos were somehow all still lingering here, as life had not been the same for any of them since.

He passed the house and noticed a closed-down beach club on the left, which looked abandoned. He walked on further, lost in thought, and went past another slope down to the public beach. Then past some wooden steps covered in rubbish and another closed-down beach club. A faded sign stuck to the inside of the glass door of the bar read: BUSINESS FOR SALE. Leo let his eyes wander. On the fading blue wall he saw the sign, the name peeling off due to the sea air, and his heart stopped in his chest for a moment. Le Dune. Instinctively, he backtracked as far as the wooden steps and looked down, towards the beach covered in golden sand. The waves were breaking on the shore, docile and foamy, under a glimmering sun that was rising high in the sky. There: he had walked past it and not even realised. He felt insignificant and useless in the face of an evil so powerful as to mark the passage from one life to another, from a before to an after, then to disappear without leaving any visible damage.

He walked on for some fifty metres, pulled down his hood and stepped into a bar that he saw was called Il Pirata. A barman roughly Leo's age was cleaning out the empty ice-cream fridge, jerking his head like a woodpecker to the rhythm of the dance music blasting out of the speakers.

'How can I help?' Mauro Sattaflora greeted Leo affably as he wiped his hands on a tea towel. 'What's it gonna be?'

'A cappuccino, please. And a croissant.'

'What kind?' Mauro pointed to the four dried-up pastries sitting on a tray under a clear plastic dome.

Leo pretended to consider them. 'Plain.'

Mauro nodded with satisfaction, as if complimenting Leo on his choice, then put the better-looking one on to a small dish and started tinkering with the coffee machine to make his first cappuccino of the day. 'Nippy, eh?' he said, referring to the cold westerly breeze.

'Sure is. I went for a stretch of the legs and froze my nuts off,' Leo said back.

'You here on holiday?'

'No, just on my way to Civitavecchia. I wanted to stop cos I used to come here as a kid.'

Mauro turned around all of a sudden and, narrowing his eyes, stared at Leo, setting his unerring photographic memory in motion. '*Here* here?' he asked, peering at Leo doubtfully.

'No, no. Closer to the tower. My folks used to rent a place.'

'Makes sense ...' Mauro nodded with relief. He remembered every single person who had gone through Le Dune over the last twenty years. 'Thought so.'

'I came down this way a few times cos I had some mates around here.'

'So, tell me ...' Mauro challenged Leo as he poured the hot foamy milk into the cup. 'Like who?'

'I used to be tight with a guy called Gaspare.'

Mauro set the cappuccino down in front of Leo. 'Gaspare?' he asked, knitting his eyebrows. He pondered for a moment, visibly annoyed at the fact that he could not remember him. 'What's he look like?'

Leo took a sip from his cup in an attempt to gain time. 'He was a bit ...'

'Hang on!' Mauro raised his hand, wanting to guess without any hints. 'You don't mean Mannino!'

Leo feigned hesitation for a moment. 'Yeah, I think so ... maybe.' He nodded.

Mauro let out a long sigh and rested his hands on his hips. He was still holding the grubby white tea towel that he had been using to dry the cups. 'I only knew him by sight,' he said, serious all of a sudden. 'I know he was from Genzano. His mother rented a place in town every year. But he used to go to the Florida Beach Club, not here.'

Leo set down his cup. 'Must be remembering it wrong, then,' he said.

'For sure. But you haven't heard, about Mannino?' Mauro asked cautiously.

'What about him?'

'He died two summers ago. Someone told me they found him under the Ariccia bridge, half-eaten by boars.'

'No way,' Leo said, bringing a hand to the back of his neck to make a show of the consternation he was struggling to feign. 'For real? Poor Gaspare!'

'Eh ...' Mauro dropped his head. 'That year ... Just forget about it! What a mess it was.' He went back to drying the cups: whenever he thought back to that summer, on top of his sorrow he always felt a great tension mounting inside of him. 'First Betta, then Gaspare, then three mates of mine who spun out and rolled over on Via Aurelia, behind the station.

Carnage.' As he spoke, Mauro swung his head sideways three times, depending on the direction where the episodes had taken place.

Leo was almost startled. 'Right ... Betta Ansaldo.'

Mauro nodded. 'In my beach club. I found her, can you believe it?' His face was now showing no trace of the good mood with which he had initially welcomed Leo.

'I thought it was further down ...'

'At Le Dune,' Mauro nodded. 'They shut it for the investigation and the next year nobody wanted to come down. The only people who showed up came to leave a flower by the fence or to ask their fucked-up questions.' He grimaced. 'But I couldn't take it no more. I could always see her, right in front of me.' He stretched out a hand. 'My mum too, she'd look out of the window and start crying. Forget about it. So Dad and I decided to pack it in, end of. It's all gone to shit.'

'Sorry to hear that,' said Leo, this time in earnest.

'Now I'm here, busting my ass for someone else, and with no contract. Seem fair to you?' Mauro thought back with nostalgia to the times when he used to complain about his father dragging him out of bed in summer to go and open the beach club.

'Did you know Betta?'

'Sure – did you not?' Mauro stared at Leo with surprise. 'Cos Betta was the kinda girl you don't forget, even if you've only seen her once.' He narrowed his eyes at the memory, a dreamy expression on his face. 'What a stunner she was!' He sighed. 'God knows how many times I told her not to walk along the beach to get to the bonfires! The year before I'd caught her sneaking on to the beach so she wouldn't be seen from the road. "Betta," I told her, "it's dangerous, this ain't no joke."' He shook his head. 'Did she listen? Course not. Betta always did what she wanted!'

'So she was going to the bonfires that night ... '

'Yeah, I think so,' Mauro said decidedly. 'I even told that to the maresciallo.'

Leo picked up his cup again and took another sip. 'You got any idea who did it?'

Mauro opened his arms. 'What d'you want me to say?' He shrugged. 'We're all decent people here, you know it ... Guys around here, it can happen with a chick that they say something outta order or even slap an ass ... but then you gotta deal with her brother or her boyfriend, cos you know you fucked up ... ' Mauro paused for a moment, dejected, then grimaced with revulsion. 'But that kinda stuff ... '

'I know,' Leo muttered pensively. 'Can you put the croissant in a bag for me? I'll take it with me,' he added as he pulled his money out to pay.

Mauro did so right away, not finding it at all surprising: that topic would make anyone lose their appetite.

'What about another guy called Leonardo, do you know him?' Leo ventured to ask nonchalantly.

Mauro smiled a little. 'I only know about two hundred of 'em! Leonardo who?'

'Uh, can't remember ... Back in the day, he used to hang out with me and Mannino.'

'Try asking the newsagent on the high street. That's one of the places Mannino used to hang.'

Leo nodded gratefully. 'I'll pop back in next time I'm about.'

'Could be I won't be here,' Mauro replied, now cheerful again. 'I might move to Follonica in June. I'm starting a thing with my girlfriend; she's from around there.'

'Best of luck, then,' Leo said on his way out, feeling a slight pang of envy at the hopefulness he had sensed in Mauro's tone.

'You too!' Mauro Sattaflora said, waving to Leo as he left.

Leo stopped to buy a random newspaper from the newsagent on the high street, and as he waited for the change from his five-thousand-lire note he took the opportunity to ask the owner if he knew a guy called Leonardo who used to be a good mate of the late Gaspare Mannino, the poor young man from Genzano.

The newsagent, who was short of breath but nevertheless loquacious, had known Gaspare since he was a little boy. His mother used to rent an apartment in Torre Domizia every summer, right opposite, on the second floor. He said that when he'd read the terse article in the local paper describing how they had found Gaspare, he had seen him right in front of his eyes, a little boy again, and had almost fainted. Since then, his mother, Silvana, had stopped coming to Torre Domizia, the newsagent added sadly – and who knew: she might have even died of a broken heart, poor woman. As a matter of fact, it seemed that Gaspare had jumped off the bridge, which was a hard truth to swallow for a mother who had raised her son alone, on just her salary as a school caretaker.

Leo pressed harder, saying that he really needed to track down Leonardo, but the newsagent could not recall any young man by that name. New people were coming and going every year and he only remembered the regulars. Then he pointed out, not without a sigh, that he was also getting on these days. But there was one thing he could say for sure: he had been working in that shop for the past fifty years, which meant that, if he could not remember this Leonardo, then he had not been a regular in Torre Domizia. Yes, he was positive about that.

By eleven in the morning, Leo was already on his way back home. He was disappointed, but not too disappointed: he had known from the start that his task would not be easy. At least he had found out a little more about Mannino, and knew that he needed to look for a school caretaker in Genzano. Though this Leonardo seemed to be as elusive as the proverbial needle in a haystack, his instinct as a man told him that gang rape was something you did with people you were close to, people with whom you'd shared more than just a chat and a beer on a summer's evening. It must be people you had confessed a certain weakness to, and who had confessed to having the same weakness in turn. So perhaps that name would not be so unfamiliar to Signora Mannino. Leo had to find a way to approach her and ask her about the people her son used to hang out with during his last summer. Maybe she would remember that someone had come to pick him up on that evening of the 10th of August, the night of the shooting stars? When someone you love died, you cherished all the details, and their last days became especially precious. You mulled them over and over again in your mind. Perhaps, before going out, Gaspare had smiled and told his mother not to wait up for him since he was going to the beach to watch the shooting stars. Instead, he and his two friends who were like brothers to him had started fantasising about what they would do to a pretty girl – if only they could get their hands on one. Then Betta had appeared out of thin air. A beauty you would recognise even in the dark; the kind of girl you did not forget, even if you had only seen her once. Could they let her slip through their fingers? Of course not. It was like a wish granted by a shooting star. Leonardo would make do with the plain-looking one, the skinny one, as he could hold her down on his own. Gaspare and the other would go for Betta instead. Because one was not enough for her. If there was still time and they wanted more, they could even swap, why not? A real feast – if only Betta Ansaldo had not gone and died on them. How rude.

Leo had to pull over in a lay-by and stop the car, his eyes closed and his arms crossed on the steering wheel as he took deep breaths to try to calm down. He could feel the desperation of the past few days transform inside him, congeal, as if turning into a solid core in the middle of his chest. As he thought about it, he could feel a heat, a powerful energy that he was struggling to keep inside – to the point that the effort was making him clench his jaw and his fists until his nails were digging into his palms. This was not anger: he knew anger, he had felt it before. This was different. This was violence.

Leo went home to take a shower and calm his nerves: he wanted to look collected in front of Miriam. He had promised her that nothing would change between them, so he needed to try hard to look normal. Everything had changed, though, just as she had said it would. Yet, admitting that much meant compromising their relationship for ever and losing her.

He was standing under a barely lukewarm stream of water, thinking – he couldn't seem to stop. His mind had come up with images from that night that now would not leave him, not only because they were tragic, nor because he now fully understood Miriam's pain, but because he felt the fury of a male whose female had been usurped. Such primordial emotions made him feel deeply ashamed of himself and he could not understand what they might have to do with the tender love he felt for his girlfriend. The more he thought about that stranger who had had her, the more unbearable he found the idea that he could not have her instead. It was driving him mad: he, who loved her, could not let himself desire her because someone before him had taken what belonged to him. So guilt had been added to pain: despite having sworn to Miriam that he would wait as long as it took, the truth was that he was full of frustration at the idea of how long it was going to take. And at the lie he had told, that he was willing to forget, to let go of that truth that was eating him up from the inside like a parasite. He knew that he could not forget. The two who were left – he could smell them like a starving animal stalking its prey. Unspeakable thoughts came into his mind even when he only imagined laying his hands on them. He had discovered that he too was a beast, and despaired at the thought that Miriam could not love someone like him. He waited until the water from the old heater started to go cold, then stood under the shower for a good while longer, hoping in vain that the icy stream might wash away those terrible thoughts, at least for a moment.

*

Miriam had not gone to the academy that morning. She had stayed at home, wrapped up in her blanket, hoping to catch some sleep that never came. She was missing her pills more than ever before, the pills from the old times that pulled the plug and dispelled everything. It had been her only way to survive for many months: in order to forget, she first needed to die a little.

Then Leo had come along, Leo who could snatch her away from her demons with a word, a smile, the warmth of his gaze, or his rash caresses. At first, she could not explain it. Eventually, though, she had understood that underneath the surface there was a candour in Leo that the ugliness of life had not yet tarnished. He was not corrupted. Leo truly believed that a sunny day could help you make peace with life, that lukewarm pizza bianca with mortadella relieved all pain, and that being vulnerable was a good thing, since vulnerability made love essential. He was brimming over with love, and in order to feel happy he also needed a lot of love in return, as if what kept him alive was that simple virtuous circle. But Leo was also hungry for love because, for some reason, he was convinced that he did not deserve it, that he did not measure up to it. He could not see the beauty of his heart, could not hear the tenderness of his own words, which was why he was always apologising: he felt that he deserved much less than even the little she gave him.

But Leo De Maria too had lost his innocence for ever, now that truth had hit him like a door thrown open by a hurricane. That candour that had survived a bitter life on the edge, the squalor of dealing drugs and the humiliations that had left their mark on Corallina, had finally been snuffed out of his eyes in just a few hours. His desperate promises and his reassurances mattered little: Miriam felt that she had taken the most beautiful part of him away. Leo had been right when he had said that forgetting was impossible. Miriam too had always known it, and this meant that from now on she would only drag him down with her, since she had no way of getting rid of that weight. She felt that she had killed him, just as she had killed Betta. She had held him too tightly to stop him from going, just like that night when she had stopped her cousin from going back to bed, only slightly disappointed that Miriam had not wanted to go with her to the beach. 'I wanted to show you the bonfires. I'll go next week,' Betta had said. Those words played back in Miriam's head all the time and she felt a burning desire to go back and simply say to Betta, 'Good night, sleep tight,' as if she were a child. Then she too would sleep until dawn the next day, eat cake with lemon icing for breakfast again and run down to the beach together for another day in the sun.

At lunchtime, when Corallina got back home, she bumped into Leo at the front door; he was on his way out to go to Miriam's. He said a quick hello, his eyes low and unsmiling, then disappeared down the stairs.

Corallina went inside and put down her work bag by the door. She had just popped in to have a quick bite before leaving again for her afternoon appointments, but she took her coat off and let herself sink for a moment into the misshapen cushions of their old sofa. She tilted her head backwards, resting it on the back of the sofa, and narrowed her eyes a little. Tiny specks of dust were floating in a blade of sunlight that was shining on the terracotta-tiled floor, which was chipped in several spots.

All of a sudden, she noticed a trail of very fine sand marking a barely visible path towards the floral curtain under the arch, in the direction of the bathroom. She held her breath. They were almost impossible to discern, those grains of sand. However, at that moment, she knew with every part of her being that a storm had breached her little home in San Basilio.

Corallina jumped to her feet, pulled out the dustpan and brush and started sweeping frantically, hoping to be proven wrong. But no, the teaspoonful of sand she eventually picked up from the floor confirmed that the wind was blowing a gale and that she had to act fast, lest all be lost. She started pacing the room, massaging her arms to soothe herself. She would have liked to ask for someone's advice, for an intuition that was not just the product of her own confusion. But time was rushing away from her, just as Leo had rushed away down the stairs only a few minutes earlier. So she quickly headed to her neighbour Antonia, knocking insistently, and then waited for her to come to the door in a huff. Corallina walked in unbidden and asked to see the phone book. Antonia warned her crankily that it was out of date before returning to her cooking. She had never liked Corallina much, but tolerated her because she did her hair for free, and she did it so well that her sister, who lived in Trionfale, was consumed with envy.

Corallina opened up the phone book to the letter A and ran her finger down the list until she found what she was looking for. She let out a little cry of relief when she read the name, the number and the address. She thought that maybe Antonia's phone books being out of date was just the stroke of luck she needed: surely the Ansaldos must have sought every way to escape public curiosity after their daughter's death. She wrote down the details on one of those notepads that they gave out for free at the pharmacy and thanked Antonia, who did not even bother replying from the kitchen.

Corallina went back to her apartment and walked into her bedroom to get ready, her hands shaking with anxiety. She looked at herself in the mirror, adjusted her periwinkle turban and smoothed down her roll-neck chenille jumper and her long skirt. Taking a deep breath, she raised her chin to pull herself together, then turned around to find the brown leather bag that best matched her coat. She looked at herself in the mirror once again and paused, unmoving. For a moment, she saw that odious Corallina – her coarse jaw, her thick neck, her thin eyebrows drawn on to her strong arches with a line of dark-brown pencil, her foundation which was already letting through the shadow of the beard she had shaved early that morning. She stared at herself for a while, overcome by the ugly thoughts that were crowding her head, then she suddenly burst into tears, like a humiliated little girl, her hand open, pressed on the mirror to cover up that reflection that was tearing her apart from the inside. Sobbing, she took off her cascading rhinestone earrings, which she adored. Then, still crying, she took off her clothes and tried to console herself with the thought that her Leo mattered more than anything else.

Leo noticed that Miriam seemed to be smiling more than usual when he arrived at her place around lunchtime. She was making him amatriciana, following a recipe from a cookbook that she had found in the bookshop underneath her apartment. She had gone grocery shopping, reading out the ingredients one by one, and – feeling quite hesitant and clumsy – had set out to cook a meal for the very first time in her life. Leo teased her, as was his habit. Still, that plate of undercooked rigatoni in a tomato sauce so thick that it was almost like glue moved him as much as if she had proposed to him. He sat down at the table and ate it all, to the very last piece, with Miriam all the while dying of embarrassment and begging him to leave it since it was awful. Leo wholeheartedly agreed with her on that point: it was so bad that he had to force every mouthful down. Then he laughed and pulled her towards him, putting an arm around her shoulders, as he whispered sweet little nothings to her, consoling her. This tenderness was their way of concealing the uneasiness that they now shared. After lunch, they went for a quiet walk in the early afternoon sun, going as far as the Trevi Fountain, then Miriam walked him back to the car since he needed to be at the shop by four. She told him that she had promised to go to her parents' tonight to keep her grandmother company since she had been poorly, and that she would sleep there too. Leo, not realising that she was lying, offered to give her a ride. Miriam laughed and said there was no need, that families like hers had a driver.

Leo stared at Miriam for a long time with an indecipherable smile on his face before getting into the car. 'So I won't be seeing you or hearing from you tonight,' Leo said. 'It'll be the first time since we've been together.'

Miriam let out a chuckle. 'Are we together? Since when?'

'Dunno. I got no head for anniversaries. That's girls' stuff.'

Miriam stared at Leo and imagined how things might have turned out, had she met him at the bonfires on a summer night, while someone played Claudio Baglioni on the guitar. Maybe he would have not even as much as looked at her: there must have been plenty of girls prettier than her down at the bonfires. Maybe he would have been looking at Betta, like everyone else. Yet Miriam was sure that right away Leo De Maria would have made her feel butterflies in her stomach.

'You are my type, you know?' Miriam confessed.

It was his turn to laugh. 'Sure, as if.'

'I mean it,' Miriam said, nodding energetically.

Leo narrowed his eyes. 'I am?' he asked, a sceptical smile on his lips.

'I swear.' Miriam hugged him in earnest, noticing how lovely he smelled.

'I'm gonna miss you lots tonight, you old bag o' bones!' Leo whispered in her ear.

'I'll miss you too,' Miriam said, taking a deep breath. 'Good night, sleep tight,' she wished him softly, with a smile, then she pulled back to look at him. 'For tonight,' she explained.

Leo nodded. 'You too.' He winked as if to say goodbye, then got in the car.

Miriam stood there on the pavement, looking at the car as he drove off. At that moment, she thought that life had never given her, nor denied her, anything more beautiful than Leo.

At three o'clock that afternoon Marisa Ansaldo was alone, since Stelvio had gone to pick up an order from the wholesalers before running off to open the shop. She had finished tidying up the kitchen while a quiz show on the TV droned on in the background, then she had moved on to ironing and folding the laundry as every so often she glanced at a soap opera on the commercial network. A scene or a fragment of dialogue would catch her attention from time to time, so she would pause her task and stand the iron up on end on its board while she followed the show more closely.

Hearing the doorbell ring, she went to open the front door absentmindedly: the destitute protagonist of the soap opera had just found out that her wealthy boyfriend had been cheating on her, and something in that story had sounded familiar enough to Marisa to make her want to find out what he might have to say for himself.

When she opened the door, the man she saw standing in front of her looked completely unfamiliar. Marisa had almost thrown the door wide open at first, but then instinctively pulled it to, quickly putting it on the chain and reproaching herself for her carelessness.

'Hello?' she said as she peered at him suspiciously. The appearance of the stranger was somewhat disturbing. He was thin but very tall, with broad shoulders. He was wearing a woolly hat, men's trainers and a brown coat with a ladies' fastening. Marisa noticed that his eyebrows were shaven off, and felt slightly troubled.

'Signora,' he said, visibly uncomfortable, as he tried to disguise the deepness of his voice with a musical tone. 'My name is Pietro De Maria.'

Marisa stared at him. 'We don't need anything, thank you,' she said, dismissing him coldly. She was about to close the door when he blocked her, quickly placing his hand on the jamb.

'I beg you, I have something important that I need to tell you,' he pleaded. Noticing that she was startled, he pulled his hand back right away so that she would not be frightened. 'It's a delicate matter.'

'What is?' Marisa asked with annoyance, her expression clouding over.

He hesitated. 'It's to do with your daughter,' he said, taming his voice even more to achieve the calmest tone he was capable of.

'You're nothing but vultures, the lot of you,' Marisa hissed, her voice hoarse with anger as she slammed the door in his face.

'I beg you!' Pietro De Maria said, trying in vain to stop her from closing the door as he hit the door frame with his hand in desperation. 'Signora Ansaldo, you need to listen to me!'

'Go away or I'll call the carabinieri,' Marisa threatened from inside the apartment.

'It's about Elisabetta and Miriam,' he tried once more. He wanted to say more but could not, not there on the doorstep. 'I know some things that are relevant to the case, Signora Ansaldo. We need to talk. Please!'

A few seconds later, the door inched open again. Marisa's eye was peering at him through the crack. 'What has all of this got to do with my niece?'

Pietro looked over his shoulder, as if scared, then leaned slightly towards Marisa. 'I know that Miriam was on the beach with your daughter on that terrible night,' he whispered in a shaking voice.

'You're crazy,' Marisa replied, unconvinced.

'They were together, believe me,' he insisted in a voice that was barely audible. 'But Miriam never said a thing to anyone.'

'Right, and she told *you*,' Marisa replied with a sneer.

'No, not me, but my brother Leo. He's her boyfriend; they care for each other,' he added with a sudden sweetness in his voice.

Marisa stared at him, speechless.

'Since Leo has known this, he's no longer himself. He wants to kill the men who did it. Signora Ansaldo, if the carabinieri don't arrest them first, my brother is going to do something stupid and throw his life away! You have to help me!'

'I've never even heard of a Leo.'

'How long has it been since you last saw your niece?' he reproached Marisa. 'Leo found out that one of those animals was called Mannino and now he's out and about looking for them like a madman.' Pietro De Maria was really struggling to keep his voice down now. And perhaps he was so desperate that he no longer even cared if he was overheard.

Marisa looked at him scornfully. 'You've been coming here ... fortune-tellers, seers, soothsayers ... claiming that you've found out this, you've dreamed that ... You disgust me, the lot of you: you respect nothing.' She closed the door again without leaving him the time to add anything else.

Pietro started knocking on the door loudly with his palm. 'Signora Ansaldo!' He was shouting, struggling to hold back tears of despair.

Not a sound could be heard now from inside the apartment, not even the voices from the TV.

'I beg you,' Pietro De Maria pleaded. 'If you don't do something, he's going to throw his life away.'

Behind the door, Marisa Ansaldo withdrew into an uninterested silence.

'I'll go to the carabinieri in the morning! I have to say something!' He held back a sob, wondering if the carabinieri would ever believe a transvestite from San Basilio.

Then one of the doors behind him opened an inch and he heard a baleful though somewhat sleepy voice say, 'I'll call the carabinieri right now if you don't beat it!'

Corallina turned around and saw half of a stout man glaring at her from behind the door, red in the face with anger. Her head hanging low in shame, Corallina waited for the man to close the door again and then slid a folded note with her address, which she had prepared in advance, under Marisa's door. At the top, she had written, 'Corallina (Pietro) De Maria.'

Marisa unplugged the iron and left everything as it was, in disarray.

She went into Betta's room, which had long ago become her room, and lay down on her bed. Anger had made her stomach turn upside down; she felt nauseous and her head was about to explode. She took a deep breath and closed her eyes. It had been many months now since the last time one of these insolent, shameless beings had come to her door or rung them up trying to sell information or swearing that they had seen, heard, learned, dreamed... With no mercy for the grief of a mother and a father. Eventually, Counsel Custureri had recommended that they change their phone number and have it unlisted, and told them to redirect any self-proclaimed informer to his firm. As soon as he had started methodically reporting them to the police, the stream had stopped immediately, extinguished like a flame in a glass.

However, that strange person who had just told her those things with a desperation in his eyes that had seemed sincere had shaken her deeply. Beneath the wrath unleashed inside her, Marisa could also feel a different kind of disturbance, a chill in her bones. Everything sounded false and treacherous to her ears, yet this time her instinct told her inexplicably that there was some truth in those words. Miriam. What kind of madness was that? What kind of perverted mind could even conceive of the idea that Miriam might have been involved in that tragedy? Marisa had talked to Emma on the phone for a few minutes at Christmas. Yes, her sister was somewhat worried that her daughter was becoming too introverted: Emanuele and she had decided to indulge her by letting her move into the apartment in Barberini on the condition that she attend the academy. Nevertheless, Miriam continued to be listless, indifferent. Emma had confided to Marisa that Miriam was no longer the same after what had happened to Betta. After all, none of them was the same any longer. Marisa had listened without empathy: her sister's insignificant problems sounded like an insult to her grief.

However, the odd things that the man at the door had said had touched Marisa in a way that Emma's words could not. As the minutes ticked past, those few sentences turned into a sort of pang that started softly only to then become sharper and sharper, until peace was no longer possible – it was utter torture. 'He's out and about looking for them like a madman,' the man had said about his brother, Leo. Everything had sounded so desperately real to Marisa, so true. Her mind persisted in trying to make sense of something in the chaos of those broken sentences, those statements that must be without foundation. Because they *did* make sense.

She sat up suddenly as if electrocuted. Then she jumped to her feet, went to the hall, took off her slippers and put on her shoes and her coat, tying the belt tightly around her waist since all her clothes were now too big for her. As she stepped outside, she saw the note on the floor and, after a moment of hesitation, picked it up and put it in her pocket without even opening it. She left the house and flew down the stairs, her heart beating wildly, as if she had overslept, or forgotten something; as if she was afraid that she might not make it in time to an unknown destination.

When Marisa walked into their shop, where she had not set foot since the last working day of August 1980, she stood stock-still on the threshold for a moment, looking at Stelvio. He was holding a little boy in his arms, maybe three or four years old, as he unwrapped for him one of the lollipops that they kept by the till. Stelvio was smiling and praising the boy for something, while Maria Grazia, the cashier Marisa had never met in person, looked at them both happily. Marisa had never made any effort to imagine Maria Grazia – she simply did not care – but now she realised that she was a beautiful woman, younger than Marisa had expected despite already having two children.

'Signora Ansaldo!' Maria Grazia exclaimed as soon as she recognised her, her eyes wide with surprise. She must of course have already seen Marisa somewhere.

Stelvio turned around and his smile died on his lips. 'Marisa, what's happened?'

'You need to take me to see my mother,' she said. 'Now!'

'Is she ill?' Stelvio set the boy down, looking worried.

'No. I have something important I need to ask her. Stelvio, please,' she begged him.

Stelvio looked at the white overalls he had put on only a few minutes earlier when he had opened the shop. 'Sure, sure!' He tried to calm Marisa down while he undid his buttons as quickly as he could and looked around, a little disorientated.

'Go, Stelvio. I'll look after the shop. I'll manage, one way or another,' said Maria Grazia reassuringly, standing up from the stool behind the till.

Stelvio nodded and hastily took off his overalls. In the meantime, Marisa studied Maria Grazia as she efficiently stocked the shelves with the bottles of tomato sauce that Stelvio had just unloaded.

Stelvio Ansaldo did not speak for the first ten minutes of that car ride, hoping in vain that his wife might say something as they drove towards Olgiata. Marisa had clammed up in a hostile silence and was looking out of the window with a pensive gaze that made her eyes look gloomy.

'What happened?' Stelvio ventured to ask. His wife had not set foot outside the house for a long while. She must have a very good reason to rush to her mother, given that she had stopped talking to her after an argument that he had never been able to ascertain the cause of.

'There's something I need to ask her,' she repeated.

'Couldn't you have called her?'

Marisa shook her head. 'No. I need to look her in the face,' she said. Then she did not utter another word.

*

The custodian of Villa Bassevi immediately opened the gate for them and let them in with a big smile: he quite liked Stelvio Ansaldo and it had been a while since they had visited. As soon as Stelvio brought the car to a halt on the gravel driveway in front of the patio, Marisa got out and headed quickly for the steps, running up them, as sprightly as if she were twenty again. Stelvio watched her knock and a moment later the maid had opened the door for her. Marisa slipped inside while the maid stood at the door as she waited for Stelvio and glanced confusedly in the direction of Marisa, who had not said a single word, not even a greeting. Stelvio realised right away that he needed to be hot on his wife's heels – there was a storm brewing and he had better be ready for it.

He was only a few steps behind Marisa when she burst into the bedroom where Letizia had been confined for the past few weeks with a broken femur. Letizia, who was sitting in a wheelchair by the window that overlooked one of the smaller gardens, was startled at the noise, but also at seeing her daughter. The nurse shot to her feet and let the book she was reading fall to the floor, protesting in half-sentences at their manners.

'Get out,' Marisa ordered the nurse without taking her eyes off her mother.

'Signora Ansaldo!' the nurse protested in a huff.

'Go, Giovanna,' interjected Letizia. 'I'll send for you when I'm done.'

Giovanna picked up the book and left the room stiffly, shutting the door behind her with a thud.

Stelvio leaned with his back against the door frame, his hands in his pockets, watching. Marisa slowly walked towards her mother, scrutinising her face. Their eyes were locked upon each other's.

'What do you want?' Letizia asked brusquely.

Marisa stopped in front of Letizia and stared down at her. She was peering into her eyes: she did not know whether she would be able to extract the truth out of Letizia, so she was searching for it in her mother's conscience, scraping away at the wall of appearances behind which she had barricaded her entire life.

'The morning they found Betta, where was Miriam?'

Stelvio was startled. Letizia remained expressionless.

'In Ettore's room.'

'And what did she do when Mauro Sattaflora arrived?'

'Nothing.'

'Nothing?' Marisa tilted her head to one side. 'She didn't leave her room? She didn't ask?'

'No,' Letizia said, averting her eyes and looking outside.

'And you didn't find that strange?'

'Why should I? She could see and hear everything from the balcony. What was there to say?'

'She didn't come downstairs to ask, to see, not even when the Sattafloras brought me back home?'

Her mother remained silent for a long while, as if probing her memory. 'No,' she said with conviction.

'And you thought that was normal ...' This was not a question. Marisa was merely stating the facts, incredulous.

Letizia gave a fractional shake of her bony shoulders, which had been eaten away by her infirmity. 'Miriam has always been very dignified. She was sad, stricken, but—'

Marisa put one hand on the brass knob at the foot of the

bed: all of a sudden, her legs had lost their strength. 'Miriam was a sensitive girl; she reacted like that to the death of her cousin and you thought it was . . . *normal?*'

'Why not? Everyone deals with grief in their own way,' Letizia reminded Marisa pointedly.

'But Miriam was *sixteen*.'

'She has always been composed.'

'Composed?' Marisa repeated. 'Her cousin had just died, and in that awful way, and you thought it normal for her to be *composed?*'

Letizia sustained Marisa's gaze. 'Yes,' she said, almost with pride.

'How was she when she left Torre Domizia?'

'She was pale, tired.' Letizia grimaced imperceptibly with the corner of her lips – there was a lot more that she remembered. 'Pained,' she admitted.

'Pained how?'

'Her cousin had just died,' Letizia said, somewhat sarcastically.

'Don't you dare play games with me!' Marisa roared.

'Out with it, then: ask me what you want to know,' her mother growled back.

'When did you realise that Miriam was also on the beach that night?' Marisa asked Letizia in one breath.

Stelvio took a few steps forward, feeling the need to sit down on the velvet armchair in the corner of the room between the door and the wardrobe.

Before answering, Letizia paused for a few seconds as she followed the thread of her memories. 'I only had real proof when I tidied the room up for Ettore.'

'What proof?' Marisa's voice had become almost inaudible.

Her mother glanced sidelong towards Stelvio and lowered her gaze to conceal her slight discomfort.

'What proof?' Marisa repeated, this time louder.

'There was sand on the floor, on the sheets ... And blood ... And hair on the pillow.' Letizia fell silent and for the first time looked upset. Then she added, 'A lot of hair,' and closed her eyes.

Marisa sat down on the bed slowly, as if her body had abruptly become too heavy and unsteady to drag around. She pressed her face in her hands and shut her eyes, trying to suppress a moan that was voicing this new grief with an indefinite sound. She felt Stelvio's fingers come to rest on her shoulder and instinctively moved her hand to grab his, feeling as if she was sinking.

'Why?' Marisa wailed. 'Why didn't you say something?'

'Because I'd already lost a granddaughter and there was no point in ruining another one,' said Letizia, her voice firm.

'*Ruining* her?' Marisa stared at her incredulously, her eyes as wide as dark wells.

'What happened was not her fault! That was the kind of stuff Betta got up to! Miriam was a respectable girl,' Letizia replied angrily. 'But you think people would understand that? That they would see the difference?'

Her daughter was listening to her, half turned to stone.

'The circle Miriam moves in, they don't forget things like that. It doesn't matter how respectable your family is: you're ruined and you always will be!' Letizia's breathing turned shallow and her voice became thin. 'Would it have been better to damn her to a life of gossip? Of pity?'

'You're sick...' Marisa shook her head, dumbfounded.

'I know how the world works! People only see you for how you appear.'

Marisa raised her eyebrows. 'That's true,' she replied evenly. 'You appeared to be a respectable woman all your life but you were a colossal whore instead. Dad knew it. That's why he married you: he enjoyed life too much to marry an actual prude!'

'How dare you!'

'You were so much of a whore that you're still ashamed of it!' Marisa screamed in her face.

Stelvio surrounded his wife's shoulders with his arm. 'Marisa, let's go.'

Marisa tried weakly to wriggle free. 'You left a girl alone, with no care, with no comfort!'

'She got over it. Miriam is strong! She understood!' Letizia answered with pride.

'You killed her inside!' Marisa screamed. 'But all that mattered to you was for her to appear to be alive and whole on the outside!' She was shaking with anger and sorrow that were consuming her. 'And what about Emma? You didn't think about Emma?'

'Emma would have done the same.'

Marisa flung herself at Letizia but Stelvio managed to hold her back just before she could clench her hands around her mother's neck.

'You're a monster, a disgusting monster!'

'And what about you? You, who let your daughter die because you didn't know how to be a mother? Where have you been for your niece all this time?' Letizia challenged Marisa. 'You don't even know how to be a wife to your husband!'

'Letizia, shut up,' thundered Stelvio. 'Not another word. I won't allow it.'

Holding his wife firmly in his arms, he pulled her away by force.

Marisa turned towards her mother once again. 'Papà would have never forgiven you for this. He would be as disgusted by you as I am!' she screamed at Letizia as her husband pulled her away. She knew that she had struck her mother with the only weapon that could hurt her.

Once they had left Villa Bassevi far enough behind, Stelvio pulled over. He remained quiet, his elbow on the window and his head resting on his hand. He too needed to catch his breath, to recover some lucidity and composure. Driving in that state was impossible. He was shaking inside. The words exchanged between Letizia and his wife had stirred up his grief, amplified it, made it echo throughout his chest and his brain, and to his shame he had to admit to himself that he really did need a drink. Next to him, Marisa was staring out of her window as she tortured her hands and tormented her knuckles: she no longer knew who or what to blame for all the sorrow that punctuated her existence. Days, months, years had gone by and they were still running in circles around the same grief. And now that Miriam's tragedy had been added to Betta's, it all felt impossible to bear.

'How did you hear about all this?' Stelvio asked her.

'Someone by the name of Pietro De Maria came by the house. At first I thought he was one of the usual crooks ...'

'But?'

'But he said that he has a brother called Leo who is Miriam's boyfriend, and he asked for my help. He looked desperate.'

'Help with what?'

'He says that Leo has heard something about the murderers and lost his mind. He's hunting for them.'

Stelvio held his breath. 'Do you think it's true?'

'This Pietro wants to go to the carabinieri and speak up before his brother has a chance to throw his life away.'

'Let's go to see this Leo, then,' Stelvio said with conviction. 'Let's take him to Nardulli, to Custureri.'

'It's only Miriam I want to talk to right now,' Marisa said. 'As far as I'm concerned, he's welcome to kill them,' she added, her words lashing the air.

'But why did Miriam never tell us?' Stelvio sighed.

Marisa grimaced bitterly. 'Because we forgot all about her,' she said, her voice choking with guilt. 'All of us.'

Stelvio did not manage to find any words of comfort. There was some truth in what Marisa was saying: their desperation over Betta's death had sucked them in, pulling them away from everything else, locking them into a selfish grief with narrow borders that had left no space for anything or anyone else.

'Do you want to go and see her?'

Marisa nodded.

When they reached the building in Via Barberini where Marisa had been only once before, many years earlier, the doorman said that Signorina Bassevi had left in a taxi not long ago and he did not know when she might be back. They thanked him, then stood in the middle of the pavement, looking around, uncertain what to do. All this running around was bewildering. It felt as if many lifetimes had passed since they had wandered those streets, young, newly engaged and full of hope. Then, what with the children and the shop, they had had fewer and fewer chances to go out for a stroll in the centre of Rome. But they had never missed it; they had not even realised that time was rushing by, that life was changing. Their happiness had transformed, become the comforting embrace of almost identical days that were yet unique in their own way. They had been immersed in an unexpected beauty that would only reveal itself afterwards, in the time of nostalgia.

'Let's go for a coffee, Marisa,' Stelvio suggested. 'Let's wait for Miriam.'

Marisa looked at the grand-looking bar opposite. Through the window she could see the pretty wrought-iron tables and the elegant chocolate boxes on display. She shook her head and pulled from her pocket the note that she had picked up from the floor as she left the house.

'Take me here, please,' she said, showing it to him.

Stelvio nodded. 'Okay.'

That morning, Leo had rung his boss at home to tell him that he was sick and needed half a day off. At first his boss had complained, then Leo had politely reminded him that he had never been late, not even by a minute, never asked to leave early and never requested a day of leave. His boss knew that he worked hard. Eventually, he had softened up a little and told Leo to get well soon and try to come in on time the following day.

As Leo drove down Via Appia in the middle of the afternoon, headed for the Castelli Romani, he reflected on the burden that all those lies placed on him, on the loneliness to which they condemned him. This was so much worse than keeping his drug-dealing a secret from Corallina: this time he had lied, broken an oath and gone back on a promise. Yet he had not hesitated, not even for a moment, nor had he wondered whether he should turn around. The more he thought about Miriam, the more it became vital that he should carry out his plan.

Despite usually being quite impatient in traffic, Leo queued calmly at the junction for Albano. The other exit led to the lake near Castel Gandolfo. Leo would have liked to take his girlfriend there to see the ducks, eat a porchetta sandwich in an osteria and maybe even go for a stroll by the lake. But no, he told himself, he might never be able to take Miriam to the lake. A body of water like that might remind her of an animal hounding her, grabbing her, using her to relieve his basest instincts and then leaving her to stare at her cousin who had died while pleading for a breath of air. No, they might never be able to go to the lake together. But he had to track down that animal and kill him, or his anger would devour him from the inside.

When he arrived in Genzano, he parked near Piazza IV Novembre and followed the plan he had concocted in his head. He walked into a bar, bought a packet of sweets and asked where the school was. He pretended that he was about to move to Genzano and that he had a young son: he needed to understand how he should go about enrolling him in school.

Though young, the cashier already had a little girl of her own, and so she took his question to heart and told him where the school was. Leo set off in that direction at a brisk pace. He realised that school would be out at that time of the afternoon but he was certain that the shopkeepers in the area would know Gaspare Mannino's mother. He picked a bakery, bought a quarter loaf, exchanged some pleasantries with a cute shop assistant and asked her whether she could tell him where the school caretaker Signora Mannino lived. He explained that he was a friend of her son's and would love to pop in for a quick hello. The cute shop assistant smiled at Leo and deemed it a nice thought. However, she only knew that Silvana lived in the old town and that she always complained about the steep slopes that prevented her from buying more than a few items at a time. Leo returned the shop assistant's smile and sighed, saying that he might have to try another time. The shop assistant gave him a hazelnut biscuit to console him. Leo nibbled at it as he left the shop and headed on foot towards the old town.

Leo was positive that everyone would know Signora Mannino in the old town: surely Gaspare's death must have made her familiar even to those who had never heard of her before. He stepped into the church and sat down in the last pew to wait patiently for the six o'clock Mass to end. Then he approached the parish priest as he was tidying up the altar and asked him if he knew where he might find Silvana Mannino. The priest looked at him somewhat suspiciously and Leo rushed to explain that he had been a friend of her son's, that he was passing through Genzano and that he had come to say hello and try to offer her some words of comfort.

The priest nodded with appreciation and motioned him to follow him. He crossed the nave quickly, reached the exit and from the threshold showed Leo where he would find her, on the ground floor of a pale yellow building at the top of the slope. As Leo thanked him and walked away, the priest blessed him. Leo lowered his eyes and muttered a goodbye.

Leo climbed the large cobblestone steps slowly. At one point, he stopped to gather his thoughts and rested his elbows on the belvedere parapet, looking in the direction of the setting sun. It was almost dusk. The air was damp. He sensed a movement by his thigh, lowered his gaze and met the eyes of a dog, a female with a long golden coat.

Leo smiled instinctively. 'Hello, beautiful,' he greeted her as he stroked her.

The dog wagged her tail gracefully, sniffing his hand. She let him scratch the top of her head and her outstretched neck.

'You hungry?' Leo showed her the bag from the bakery and her tail became waggier. He opened the bag, pulled out the quarter loaf and handed it to her, doubtfully. 'You want it?'

The dog tilted her muzzle to one side and politely grabbed the bread with her teeth, taking it off him. 'But it's too big,' Leo laughed. She simply wagged her tail joyfully in response.

Leo stroked her again. 'Okay, then. You eat it, beautiful,' he said to her tenderly, scrunching up the paper bag and throwing it into a nearby bin.

The dog continued up the steps, her loot firmly in her mouth, and Leo followed her.

When she reached the ground-floor apartment of the pale yellow building, the dog stopped and stared at him eloquently. Leo could have sworn that she had made a motion with her muzzle, as if to say, 'It's here.' He came up to her and noticed that there was no name on the doorbell. Behind the railing, the shutters were closed and a withered plant sat on the windowsill. He wavered uncertainly before knocking. He looked around again, but the dog had vanished into thin air.

When Silvana Mannino appeared at the crack of the window, the first thing Leo thought was that, somehow, that woman looked familiar to him. Her hollow, angular face. Her deep lines. Her hair carelessly pulled back. Her gaze that had no trace of benevolence left in it, after life had tossed her around more than she had been able to bear. Leo realised that he had seen it all before in his mother, especially over her final few years. All of a sudden, he wondered if he had been a good son to her. He told himself that he had tried, though he was not at all sure whether he had succeeded: she had always looked unhappy, just the way Gaspare Mannino's mother was looking right now.

'What do you want?' she asked brusquely, her voice hoarse and guarded.

'Signora Mannino, my name is Leo.' He hesitated for a moment, feeling disorientated: pretending to be someone he was not was harder with her. 'I was mates with Gaspare.'

'So what?' Signora Mannino said, her tone implying that Gaspare had never had any friends, given how he had ended up.

'I heard about the accident and came by to say hello.' He paused for a moment, expecting her to close the window again. 'Gaspare and I used to play together as kids, in Torre Domizia.'

She narrowed her eyes. 'I don't remember you ...'

'People change, signora,' Leo said, opening his arms a little. 'I remember you, though, at the Florida.'

She closed the window again slowly and Leo knew that the door would open a moment later.

Silvana Mannino pulled the door back only just enough to let him in, forcing him to slide through sideways. The door opened directly into a small sitting room, just as in the apartment he shared with Corallina, with the kitchenette at the back past a square table with only two chairs, one tucked in neatly, a sign that no one had sat in it for who knew how long.

'Who told you about Gaspare?' Signora Mannino asked.

'A barman in Torre Domizia who knew we were mates.'

'I see,' Signora Mannino said, and nodded gloomily. She pointed at the table as she wrapped herself tightly in a slightly misshapen cardigan. 'Would you like a coffee?'

'Yes, please. It's chilly tonight.' Leo rubbed his hands together and followed her, squeezing past two armchairs placed next to each other and an old television set. The flickering picture on the TV was showing the news, but the volume was muted. Silvana Mannino had set down on one of the armchairs the knitting she'd been working on when he had knocked.

She pulled the chair out for Leo and motioned him to sit down.

'What's your mother's name?' she asked as she assembled the moka pot at the sink with slow gestures.

'Nadia.'

Signora Mannino reflected for a moment, then bent the corners of her mouth downwards: that name brought nothing to mind. 'I'm really getting on. Once upon a time, I never forgot a name.'

'Mum was a reserved type.'

'And how is she?' After all, even if she could not remember her, they must have exchanged a few words from under their respective sun umbrellas, at one time or another.

Leo wavered. 'She died a few years ago. Cancer.'

'Oh ...' Silvana stopped with a teaspoonful of ground coffee mid-air. 'Really sorry to hear that,' she said mournfully, as if she had eventually remembered that Nadia was indeed that lady, the one with the floral swimsuit. The one who was always telling off her naughty son and did not spare a slap or two when needed. Unlike herself, who had spoiled Gaspare because he had lost his father. Whenever he got up to some mischief, she always made excuses for him. Too many excuses. 'And what do you do now?'

'I'm a sales assistant in a shop.'

'Good for you.' Signora Mannino nodded with conviction. 'And you have a girlfriend?'

'Yes.' Leo smiled a little without even realising.

'She a nice girl?'

'Very nice.'

Signora Mannino nodded once more. 'Good for you,' she repeated. 'It's important. A girl who was not nice really put my Gaspare through the mill.'

'A girl from here?'

'No, from Marina di San Giorgio. I wish she had been from here!' Signora Mannino said bitterly, persuaded that, had she been from Genzano, she would have certainly been nice. 'Gaspare was friends with her cousin. He was another scoundrel. But my son loved him like a brother and wouldn't hear a bad word about him. In the end that bastard didn't even show his face at the funeral, imagine that!'

'But how did it happen ... the accident?' Leo asked in a soft voice.

The lady shrugged a little as she pressed the coffee down into the little funnel of the moka pot. 'Who knows?' she sighed. 'They say he jumped, but I don't believe it. Why would he kill himself? Gaspare was happy. That terrible girl had broken up with him in May, or maybe June ... All she did was stir up trouble and ask for money. And to think that her family was well off ... She took advantage of him,' Mrs Mannino concluded with resignation. 'Her family owns the carousel at the funfair in Marina di San Giorgio – you know the one?'

'Gypsies?'

'No, not gypsies. Sons of bitches is what they are – forget about gypsies!'

'So Gaspare fell out with this mate over a cousin of his? Could he have—'

'No, Leonardo doesn't care about anyone. He only cares about living it up – the funfair isn't enough for him; he wants to be Mr Big Shot.' Signora Mannino shook her hand in the air. 'But he's less than nothing. I told you, he didn't even bother to give Gaspare his last farewell.'

It took Leo a moment to absorb the impact of that name. Leonardo. As anger poisoned Leo, a figure was finally starting to emerge. He made an effort to snap out of it. 'What about her? Did *she* come to the funeral?'

'She did,' Silvana Mannino conceded without appreciation as she waited for the coffee to come out.

When it was ready, she served it in a glass, sat on the other chair and told Leo about the weeks of anguish she had suffered while Gaspare was nowhere to be found, after he had left Torre Domizia for an unknown reason. It had transpired later, in fact, that there was no job at the tourist office. Signora Mannino had even gone to see Maresciallo Nardulli to tell him that she could not get hold of her son, and he had been kind enough to call the carabinieri in Genzano to ask if they had heard about any accidents. But Gaspare had simply disappeared. Her neighbour, Signora Mannino continued, pointing with her chin towards next door, had said that she had not even seen him come in. Not a peep from him, the light always off. And yet, Silvana had spoken with her son on the landline just the night before his disappearance. She remembered that he had sounded strange because he had the flu – you could tell from his voice, which was hoarse and nasal, the voice of someone who wasn't managing to get any rest. Then, months of desperation and nothingness had followed. Since Gaspare was over eighteen, the carabinieri had not even actually looked for him. She could not believe that her son would take off like that for who knew where, leaving behind his money and ID but not a single word of explanation.

Then, in November, a fifteen-year-old girl had jumped off the Ariccia bridge and so they had found Gaspare too, only a short distance away. Silvana Mannino had not been surprised to hear that he was dead – she had already known it, deep down inside. What she could not accept was that he had thrown himself off: such a cruel act from one's child was impossible to countenance.

'But maybe there was something that was troubling him and I didn't understand it,' she admitted all of a sudden, after having been lost in thought for a long spell.

'Perhaps,' Leo said, nodding with an instinctive surge of compassion towards that woman who had raised a monster and could not even imagine it. He wanted to feel rancour but could not manage it.

'I've been racking my brain ... but I really can't make any sense of it.' Signora Mannino shook her head in surrender.

'It's hard to know what's going on in people's heads,' Leo comforted her.

Silvana Mannino raised her eyes to his face and stared at him for a long time, as if searching Leo's features for something that might remind her of Gaspare, something that might give her a momentary illusion that she was talking to her son one last time. 'Always keep 'em close, the people you love. Keep 'em close,' she muttered, as if pleading with him. 'Don't you never leave 'em alone.' Signora Mannino stretched out her hand and, though shaking a little, vigorously grabbed his. 'You can get through anything as long as you love each other; you'll always find the strength.'

Leo nodded vigorously in agreement. 'Is there anything I can do for you, signora?'

'If you happen to be in the area again, maybe come and say hello?' she asked simply. 'Bring your girlfriend too, so I can meet her.'

Leo averted his eyes as he stood up. 'It's getting late; I'd better go.'

'Yes, go now. It's a dangerous road, all bends, and it's dark already.'

Silvana Mannino walked Leo to the door and examined him to check whether he had done up his jacket properly. They said goodbye and she lingered on the threshold despite the damp wind. She wrapped herself tightly in her cardigan and followed Leo with her eyes as he slowly disappeared down the slope, his hands in his pockets and his hood up. She pretended for a moment that he was Gaspare, going down to the town square for a night out with his friends, and smiled inadvertently. Then she went back inside, to continue the wait for a son who would never return.

12

The Storm

Luigi Scansino, aka 'Wheels', the former *wunderkind* of all junkies, had found himself in a wheelchair at the age of twenty-five due to bone marrow ischaemia. The doctors had told him that unless he wanted to go straight from the wheelchair to the grave he needed to forget all about heroin. So, with infinite suffering and regret, he had accepted that he must abandon the joys of shooting up. However, he was still firmly rooted in the scene and enjoyed a certain prestige that came from his experience, his many contacts and his natural predisposition to understand the needs of his customers, to give them the right advice and to sell them decent-quality smack so that they would not go belly-up too young – that would have been bad for business. On his good days he felt like a conductor on his podium as he orchestrated the symphony of the perfect high under the statue of the Virgin Mary behind the San Giovanni hospital. From his wheelchair, he imagined that all his junkies were having a blast, even toasting his health. He had not yet ruled out the idea that, one day or another, he might stop giving a fuck and get the fix of his life. After all, he loathed the idea of waiting around for old age as he sat on his sagging, pruny ass, still attached to those useless toothpicks he called legs.

Nevertheless, that night his judgement failed him in the case of the new girl.

'Are you Wheels?' the girl asked. She was too skinny, but passable all the same. More importantly, she was wearing a puffa jacket that would have kept one of his down-and-out junkies going for a year. It was his lucky day.

'What do you think?' He laughed, banging his palms on his armrests.

'Do you have any Phentatyl?'

He shook his head in a decisive no. 'What d'you need?' he asked, looking at her eloquently.

'I need to relax a bit.' She was staring at him, her hands in her pockets.

'Then I'd recommend a good fuck.'

She looked at him first, then at his wheelchair. Though she was not particularly tall, she still towered over him. 'Do *you* want to fuck me?' she taunted him, looking all serious.

Luigi did not take offence – quite the contrary – and nodded, rather pleased: he could not stand the hypocrisy of pity.

'Raincheck?' he joked.

'What can you give me?'

'Depends on the dough.'

She pulled out of her pocket three 100,000-lire notes, folded in half.

'That'll see you through the week,' he reassured her, stretching his hand out.

She whipped the money back. 'Give me the stuff first.'

'There's no trust in this world ...' He chuckled slyly and nodded to one of his henchmen, who carried all the gear: that way, if the cops showed up, his guys could leg it and he was always clean. The guy was beside Luigi in a trice and whispered a few words in his ear. They came to an agreement and then he disappeared around the corner.

'Have you ever shot up?' Luigi asked with interest.

'Not for me,' she replied shortly.

He sighed disconsolately. 'What's your name?'

She did not answer, still staring in the direction where the guy had disappeared.

'Who sent you to me?'

'A guy I met at Blue Alien.'

He nodded with satisfaction. 'I know lots of people there.'

The guy reappeared and trotted towards them, a paper bag in his hand, the kind usually used for bread. Luigi grabbed it and sent him back to his post with a wave of his hand.

She handed Luigi the money and took the bag at the same time. She did not open it.

'Drink half and take one pill – no more. It'll knock you out for twelve hours, maybe even sixteen, skinny as you are. This stuff will take ya to the stratosphere,' he promised. 'Let me know how you get on with it,' he added as she left.

She slid the bag into her jacket, quickly did up the zip, put her hands in her pockets and went back to where she had come from without saying another word.

When Corallina saw the Ansaldos standing by the buzzer, she slowed down, tempted, just for a moment, to turn around and run away. After her distressing conversation with Marisa just a few hours earlier, she had rushed back home, churned up inside, and had been determined to hide away in the dark under her blanket until tomorrow. Eventually, though, she had pulled herself together and popped out for a last-minute blow-dry appointment with a girl who lived nearby and who had finally secured a first date with the boy she'd been pining for. The girl had left a little note on Corallina's doorbell, asking her to come right away. She had drawn lots of little flowers on it because she was very grateful for the fact that Corallina did not charge her much given that things were tough at home. Once there, Corallina had quickly realised that she had made the right call: chatting away about romantic nonsense as she styled the girl's curls had cheered her up. After all, this was how Corallina got her fix of romance: in matters of the heart, she only shone with reflected light. In the end Corallina didn't even charge the girl, almost feeling that she owed her for that half-hour of frivolity she had so desperately needed.

But now that she was only two steps away from her door, Corallina knew that she could not escape from what was to come and that, after all, the fact that the Ansaldos were standing on her doorstep was actually a good sign. She walked up to them, holding her work bag in front of her legs with both hands. The bag was not particularly heavy, but Corallina was hoping that it might somehow hide the long skirt and high-heeled boots that she was wearing under her coat.

'Good evening,' she said shyly as she approached them.

Marisa and Stelvio raised their eyes at the same time. Stelvio returned the greeting politely, immediately averting his eyes, while Marisa did not say a word, just kept staring at her.

'Would you like to come upstairs?' Corallina said politely, pulling her keys out of her pocket.

'Yes, please,' said Marisa, a hint of tension in her voice.

Puzzled, her husband first stared at the burgundy-turbanned stranger barely lit by the weak light filtering through from the hall, then at his wife.

'This is Signora Corallina De Maria,' Marisa explained, and cast in the direction of her husband the kind of glance which, in the life from before, had meant that he needed to go along with something without asking any questions and she would explain everything later, in private.

'Signor*ina* Corallina De Maria,' Corallina pointed out, with a complicit half-smile in Marisa's direction.

'Signorina Corallina De Maria,' Marisa corrected herself.

Corallina showed them in, apologising as she led the way into the squalid hall and up the stairs. The lift had been stolen, she explained with candour. Stelvio stared at his wife, dumbfounded, and Marisa signalled with her eyes that evidently this was something that would happen in that neighbourhood.

As soon as they walked into the apartment, Corallina set down her bag, turned on the lights and took off her coat. She apologised some more because of the uncomfortable old sofa and suggested that they would all be better off sitting at the kitchen table. She offered to take their coats, but Stelvio and Marisa preferred to keep them on and sat down. Corallina sensed that she had to do something to put them at ease. So she went to the shelf, took a silver-coloured frame, instinctively buffed its glass on her chest, which was made round by the padded bra under her jumper, and showed them the photograph of Leo and Miriam that had been taken during one Sunday lunch.

'This is my brother,' she said reassuringly. She wanted them to know that Leo was a handsome young man and that she had not lied to Marisa when she had talked to her about Miriam.

Marisa and Stelvio stared at the photograph, speechless: Leo was indeed a handsome young man, but Miriam hardly looked like the bright teenager they remembered.

Corallina set the photograph down on the table, glancing at it with tenderness.

'Miriam looks so pale,' Marisa said in a whisper.

'Miriam has been through a lot, Signora Ansaldo.' Corallina fixed her eyes eloquently on Marisa's.

'Please, call me Marisa,' she said.

Corallina nodded. 'She met Leo at a difficult time.'

'Was it my niece who told him about Torre Domizia?' Stelvio asked.

'No. It was me. I had read what happened to your daughter in the papers and later told Leo. I knew who Miriam was. Leo tried to ask her about it but to no avail ...' Corallina searched for the right words; she was struggling to say what she needed to say without sounding indelicate. 'But he could tell that she was ... unwell. She would often shut down, feel very low, stop talking altogether.' Corallina sighed. 'Leo became obsessed with it. He wanted to understand ... So he started asking around, looking for intel from some riff-raff that he knew from before, when he was hanging out with a bad lot.' Corallina immediately raised a hand to mean that they should wait a moment before jumping to conclusions. 'He's on the straight and narrow now, all water under the bridge, I promise you,' she rushed to add with fervour. 'He's working hard and only has eyes for Miriam. Leo has simply been unlucky. He is a good man, and the mistakes he made, he made because of me.'

'Their names, though ...' Marisa said impatiently. 'How did he find out? Who are these people he's looking for?'

Corallina took a deep breath and slowly looked at both of them, first one then the other. 'I'll tell you everything I know, but I beg you ...' Corallina said, her hands joined in prayer and her eyes veiled with tears. 'Please, keep my Leo out of it.'

Marisa stared at her. 'Just tell us, Corallina,' she ordered with a calm voice that hid a stifled cry for help from one mother to another.

So Corallina told them all she knew, beginning from the night when Leo had shown up at the door with a creature in his arms that was as light as a goldfinch.

Leo had turned on to Via Aurelia and headed for Marina di San Giorgio – he could not wait, not even until the next morning. He wanted to find the carousel and then roam the streets, ask around in bars, knock at doors and ring doorbells if necessary.

Only a handful of people lived in that seaside town during winter. How long might it take him to find this Leonardo, from a family of carnies? His brain was under pressure, working at pace as he pressed his foot down hard on the accelerator, fury rising inside him faster and faster, like water in his lungs, drowning him. Leo had already figured out how he would persuade Leonardo to get into his car. How infuriating that his name was so close to his own! He knew where he would take him, how he would make him spill the name of the third one, the one with friends in high places who had nothing to be afraid of in Torre Domizia, even when raping and murdering. He would wipe them off the face of the earth, both of them, in one night – this was not wishful thinking but a certainty. He would not eat or sleep until he was sure that not even the stench of those animals remained. With every passing hour, he cared less and less about the aftermath. Let them catch him, let them lock him away for the rest of his life – he didn't care. This was the only way he could find peace, this much he knew by now. There was nothing else he could do for Miriam but act, that very night, and then never talk about it again, just as she had asked of him.

His gaze locked on the road ahead in the headlights of his Fiat Panda, Leo was speeding like a madman through the darkness towards Marina di San Giorgio, knowing that on the way back he would no longer be the same person. But he had not been the same person since the moment he had taken Miriam into his arms, helpless and bereft of any trust, any desire, damned to exist in a body she perceived as filthy and to see in her own eyes the reflection of Betta's lifeless gaze, the same Betta with whom she had laughed as they ran towards the bonfires. All because of their innocent caper.

'Betta, I swear they'll never see the light of day again.' Despite shaking with anger, his voice echoed through the car like a sob.

It all happened in an instant. A sudden movement in front

of the headlights, a blurred figure standing in his trajectory, no further away than ten metres. Too short a distance to try to stop at that speed, nothing at all really, but his foot instinctively slammed the brake pedal as he steered sharply to the right to avoid the impact. An irrational decision: the car started spinning as if in a spell of vertigo. Leo hit his head a couple of times, in rapid succession, without even realising against what, then he tensed his neck and, his eyes closed, steadied himself for the impact that would end all that spinning, which was fast yet felt slow to him. He could feel every second tick past, and each might very well be his last. He did not feel scared at the thought that he was about to die there, on a random stretch of road that ran along the coast. Yet, in the din of the spinning car, he could hear Silvana Mannino's words in his head, insistent, 'Always keep 'em close, the people you love.' A kind of nostalgia gripped him. In that dilated time he thought about Corallina, about Miriam. Then about his father, who wanted him to be a real man and so on Sundays, when he was still quite small, used to take him to an empty car park in Alessandrino and let him drive. His father, in his youth, had dreamed of becoming a racing driver; he would get in the driving seat and show Leo how to stop dead, how to swerve, how to make the tyres screech. He'd looked like a madman. And when the car skidded out of control he just laughed and said, 'Steer into it and accelerate, Leo! Steer into it and accelerate!' Some time later, he had confessed to Leo that that trick had not quite worked for a friend of his, who had crashed into a wall instead.

And yet, this night, it worked for Leo. The car shook, jolted as if it was about to roll over, spun one last half-turn, then stopped dead. The engine was silent. The only noise came from the keyring attached to the dashboard, which was swinging like a crazed pendulum. Leo raised his hands to his head, not because he was in pain but out of incredulity. For the rest of his life he would always wonder whether that good-for-nothing father of his had not only given him life but also saved it that night.

Leo opened the door and got out, his legs shaking to the point that he was struggling to stand on his feet. He took two or three steps forward, realised that he was heading in the direction of the carriageway he had spun out of and walked back, leaning with his elbows on the top of the Fiat Panda, which was intact. As if he had not been about to die, just a moment earlier. He took a deep breath. His head was still spinning: it felt as shaken as a bag of marbles in the hands of a little boy. His ears were ringing and down below, by his legs, he sensed something rustle. He lowered his eyes and saw the dog with the long golden coat. He was so confused that he did not even find it strange that she had made it all the way there from Genzano. His only thought was that she had almost killed him.

'What the fuck!' Leo burst out. 'You almost killed me there!'

The dog wagged her tail, not at all scared. Leo stretched out a hand to stroke her, repressing a moan caused by the pain in his neck. 'You hurt?' he asked. She wagged her tail again, reassuringly, then offered her head. 'Fuck you,' he muttered, realising that he felt the urge to laugh. He was so happy to be alive, happy that he would no longer leave Corallina and Miriam on their own.

All of a sudden, he heard a voice behind his back. 'Hey, man! You all right?'

Leo turned around and saw a guy more or less his own age, who had pulled over in his car, got out and was now heading towards him with a worried look on his face.

Leo nodded. 'Yeah ... I'm okay.'

'My God, I saw you from the flyover and thought, shit, that dude is toast! You were spinning like crazy!' The guy was staring at Leo in disbelief, unable to process the fact that he was still in one piece. He had turned around to merge on to Via Aurelia and help him out, but now here the dude was, standing on two legs right in front of him. Unbelievable.

'I was going too fast,' Leo admitted. 'Then that dog came out of nowhere ... '

'I didn't see a dog,' the guy said.

Leo looked downwards, left and right, then peered into the darkness behind him. The dog was nowhere to be seen. 'Musta run off,' he said, shaken.

'Guess so. See if you can get your car started. If not, I'll look for a tow truck.'

Leo took a deep breath and got back behind the wheel, leaving his door open. He turned the key and the car sputtered a couple of times. At the third attempt, the engine roared, urged on by the accelerator, as if nothing had happened. He drove the car a short distance, towards the edge of the road, without issue.

'All good,' the guy said. 'You'll need to get your alignment checked, though.'

'Yeah, no worries, as long as I can make it home,' Leo said, getting out of the car again.

'You sure?'

'Totally. Thank you.' Leo stretched out his hand towards the guy and he shook it. 'Leo,' he introduced himself.

'Gianluca.'

'Thank you, Gianluca.'

'Don't mention it. Now go home. Your share of luck is spent for the day,' Gianluca joked.

Leo agreed, nodding with conviction. They went their separate ways feeling that sense of brotherhood that brought together those who had brushed shoulders with death. Leo watched him walk away, get back in his car and honk once to say goodbye as he drove off.

When Leo was alone again, he stood there, in silence. He felt as if he had just got over a high fever, the kind that made your head explode and your skin burn and which on subsiding would leave you reeling, all your energy drained. He was still angry, but the fury that had driven him crazy had abated all of a sudden. Now nothing felt as clear as it had before, when he had believed that there could be only one solution. Or rather, he could still see that solution, but he was no longer indifferent to its consequences. Knowing that her tragedy had turned him into a murderer – how would that help Miriam? And what would happen to Corallina? The selfishness of his plan for a primitive, immediate, uncompromising justice had now come fully into focus.

But he still wanted to get even, despite all that was at stake. He wondered whether it would take more courage to drive on towards Marina di San Giorgio or to turn around and go back home, look Miriam in the eye and show himself to her for what he really was – someone ready to kill; someone who needed her to find another way, some middle ground. He had to make her see that silence was not a price he was willing to pay, because it made him feel like an accomplice in those terrible acts; it burdened him with an excruciating cowardice. He had to find a way, and if Miriam really loved him she would understand: when you love someone, you do not leave them alone.

He rolled down the window and looked around once more, peering into the darkness, then he whistled loudly. He waited in vain for the dog with the golden coat to come back. Eventually, he even started doubting that he had actually seen her. He touched the side of his head and his fingers came away sticky with blood from a wound on his scalp that he hadn't even noticed. He opened the glove compartment, wiped his hands on some paper napkins he found in there, and tried to stop the bleeding as best he could.

Then he got back on the road and, driving carefully, looked for the exit that would allow him to turn around.

Duilio welcomed Leo from the doorman's booth with his usual smile, which died on his lips as soon as he saw the wound above Leo's left ear, red with congealed blood.

'What happened to you?'

'Nothing ... just a minor incident,' Leo played the whole thing down. 'Listen, could I have Miriam's phone number in Olgiata, please?'

Duilio opened his arms to signify that he was sorry. 'You understand ... I can't ... '

'Why not?' Leo looked at him as if he had just spoken in a foreign language.

Duilio swayed slightly. He liked Leo, but the young man often put him in a tight spot with his less-than-orthodox manners. 'It's a matter of privacy ...' Duilio explained, somewhat embarrassed.

'Privacy? I'm always here. It's not like you don't know that I know Miriam.'

Duilio opened his arms again, as if to show off the impeccable suit he was wearing. 'Then ask Signorina Bassevi for it,' he recommended.

'And how do I do that, seeing as she's there now?' Leo asked patiently.

Duilio sighed with relief. 'The signorina came back half an hour ago.'

Leo stared at him, astonished. 'For real?'

The doorman nodded slowly but resolutely – he would not permit his professionalism to be called into question. 'Absolutely.'

Leo smiled at him with such gratitude that the doorman caught himself returning the smile. Duilio could not help but think that, unlikely as their match might be, he really liked that young man for Signorina Bassevi. He had never seen her more at peace in the time she had lived in the penthouse.

Leo thanked him and ran off along the corridor.

'You should have that wound dressed!' Duilio urged him as he picked up the phone to let the signorina know that Leo was on his way up.

Leo took the lift for once. He felt so shaken that it was already a miracle he could stand, let alone go up seven flights on those stairs that looked like the Spanish Steps. He shot out of the lift on the seventh floor and rushed to the doorbell, ringing it insistently even though he knew that it annoyed Miriam. He was tired and everything hurt, but he was so happy that he was going to be able to see her. He just wanted to freshen up, sit in front of her and talk to her. Until morning, if necessary. Let her cry, if necessary. He was even ready to be hit again. Eventually, she had to come around to the fact that he was right, that together they could do the right thing, because he would never leave her alone.

He rang and rang, but she did not come to the door. He even tried knocking loudly, calling her name. He waited for a long time, then went back downstairs grumbling, ready to take it out on Duilio for getting his hopes up.

'She's not in,' he announced, showing his empty palms to signify her absence.

'I'm sure I saw her,' the doorman replied. He was still holding the phone: he had been trying to get through to her since the moment Leo had gone up.

Leo stared at the phone with a sudden surge of anxiety. 'It's been ringing this whole time?'

Duilio tried to conceal his worry. 'Yes,' he said softly, then added right away, 'Maybe Signorina Bassevi is asleep ... Or in the shower ...'

Leo seemed frozen for a moment. 'Gimme the key,' he ordered in a whisper.

'I can't,' Duilio said apologetically.

'Gimme the key!' Leo shouted, so loudly that his voice boomed on the marble that covered the walls.

'You understand ...'

'I understand? What do I understand?' Leo was suddenly beside himself. He marched into the booth and went straight for the key-holder on the wall. Duilio held Leo's arm back with resolve and was about to threaten him when instead, putting forty years of honourable conduct on the line, he took a look at him and gave him the key to Apartment 28.

This time, Leo went up on foot: no lift could ever be fast enough to get him there on time. He went up two or three steps at a time, his strained breathing burning in his lungs. He hesitated only for a moment before putting the key in the door and turning it once to unlock it. He stopped, feeling real fear for the first time. He remembered the way she had looked at him, a few hours earlier, when she had said, 'Good night, sleep tight.' Sleep tight . . .

He flung the door open. The apartment was completely enveloped in darkness apart from the sitting room, where the floor lamp was throwing its dim light on to the sofa. He saw her right away, lying on her back on the strip of rug between the sofa and the coffee table. A body abandoned in a small heap of clothes. She had not even taken off her shoes, her woolly hat or her puffa jacket.

He ran to her, pushing the coffee table aside to make some space. He knelt down and pulled her up a little, sliding a hand behind her neck. 'Miriam,' he shouted, shaking her. 'Miriam, wake up!' He ran his gaze around the room and saw an open paper bag in a corner of the sofa and, next to it, a vial and a blister pack, both empty. He leaned over to grab the vial, sniffed it and licked its opening, grimacing when his mouth made contact with the intense bitterness. He cursed, pleaded with God and shook Miriam again, calling her name. He saw another vial, identical to the first, that had perhaps rolled out of her hand half-empty. He felt the rug to work out whether she had also drunk the missing liquid or whether it had seeped into its fibres, but it was dry. He grabbed her chin between his thumb and forefinger and shook her some more, then he rolled her on to one side and pushed two fingers deep inside her throat, praying that she would vomit. There was no point – her gag reflex was already gone. He called her name again and again, pleading with his late mother that she might help him wake her up. But he was wasting precious time: she too was going to die.

Duilio was standing next to his booth, rigid with worry, when he saw Leo appear at the end of the corridor with an unconscious Miriam in his arms. Duilio was speechless, his hands by his sides. He had never seen such desperation.

'Where's the closest A&E?' Leo shouted.

'On Tiber Island,' Duilio replied quickly.

'Call ahead and say that I'm coming in with a girl who's OD'ing on methadone!'

Duilio was startled.

'Methadone and codeine. Tell 'em that I'll be there in five minutes!' Leo said as he disappeared through the door.

Duilio went for the phone book. He kept repeating 'methadone and codeine' to himself like a lunatic, since he had never heard those words before in his life and would never be able to forgive himself if he were to forget them.

Leo De Maria really did get there within five minutes. He drove to A&E like a madman, despite the wound on his head, the pain he felt all over his body and the completely bald tyres of the Fiat Panda, all the while begging Miriam in vain to stay awake and incessantly asking her why. Why had she done this to him? He shredded what little was left of the tyres when he skidded to a stop in front of A&E. He got out and ran around the car to pick Miriam up again.

As soon as he was through the doors he saw a stretcher and some nurses waiting for them: Duilio had indeed managed to remember those two words.

'I brought the vials,' he said, handing them to a young doctor while the stretcher was being wheeled away promptly. Then he added in a whisper, 'I don't think she's breathing.' He tried to repeat it louder, but the words died on his lips, and in the meantime the stretcher had already disappeared behind the white doors, which were now swinging.

Fifteen minutes later, a nurse came to see him and found him still there, standing exactly where he had been when they had taken Miriam away from him. The nurse's voice reached Leo as if she were talking through a funnel. She told him that they had managed to revive Miriam but that she was still in critical condition. Very critical. The nurse needed a phone number for her family to let them know that they needed to come right away, if he had not done so already.

Without looking at her, Leo said that he did not have a number.

'Who are you, then?' the nurse asked, kindly.

Leo shook his head slowly. 'Dunno.'

This was when she saw his wound. 'What happened to your head?'

'Nothing.'

The nurse gently took him by the arm and led him to see the doctor for some stitches, then she went to ask the security guard at the entrance to call the police.

*

Marisa and Stelvio Ansaldo were still sitting at Corallina's table when Antonia knocked at the door to say that Leo had called, wanting to let Corallina know that his girlfriend was in critical condition at the Fatebenefratelli Hospital and that Corallina needed to go there right away because the cops might be taking him away soon. The three of them looked at each other in alarm as the neighbour delivered her message, unfazed.

When Stelvio Ansaldo walked into A&E half an hour later, he saw a young man with dark hair sitting alone on a bench. He looked exhausted and his gaze was lost in space. Stelvio thought that he had already seen that scene somewhere before, but he was so deeply distraught that he could not remember where.

Corallina ran towards her brother and was about to pull him to her when she spotted the dressing on the side of his head and put a hand to her mouth instead.

'What did you do? Were you both in an accident?' Her eyes were swollen from the tears that she had not managed to hold back as they made their way to the hospital, the Ansaldos having been kind enough to take her with them in the car.

'No, Corallina,' said Leo.

'So what happened?' Marisa asked, standing in front of him. She was pale and her lips were trembling.

Leo raised his eyes. He recognised her right away; he'd seen her in the newspapers. 'She downed two vials of methadone.'

'Did you give it to her?' Marisa asked with wrath in her voice.

'No,' he said, without emphasis. He did not care whether they believed him or not.

Stelvio looked at Leo, then at his wife, then at Corallina. 'Miriam is a drug addict?' he asked in disbelief. The idea that his little niece, who was so shy, so delicate, might have become a junkie sounded to him like science fiction.

'She used to have a problem with sleeping pills,' Corallina explained. 'But she was over it,' she added angrily. 'She was much better!'

'Corallina, she was not better. She was trying to kill herself,' said Leo, staring at a crack in the light blue linoleum floor.

Marisa needed to sit down. Stelvio realised it right away and led her by the elbow to a nearby chair, then stood next to her.

Corallina looked at her brother. 'How is she now?'

'In a coma. On a ventilator.'

'What did they say?' Corallina wailed, looking at Leo then at the Ansaldos, as if seeking a word of comfort from them. 'She'll come to, won't she?'

'That's not the only issue, whether she'll come to.' Leo took a deep breath as he stared at his interlaced fingers, which were shaking. He actually felt as if he was shaking everywhere, inside, outside, as if it were the end of the world. 'The issue is what she'll be like if she does.'

They all fell silent as they each processed the enormity of those words in their own way. Then Stelvio stared at Leo De Maria and remembered. He recognised the desperation as something he too had felt. That dismay, that sense of solitude that took you over when one half of your heart was sinking to the bottom. When you were young and you had only barely dreamed of happiness, barely brushed against it, and then it was torn away from you.

'She'll come to,' he said trustingly, in a steady voice. He still needed to believe in miracles as he had witnessed one, once. 'She'll come to, Leo,' he repeated.

Leo De Maria raised his eyes and met the eyes of Stelvio Ansaldo, who was nodding with conviction. Then he started crying like a child in his sister's arms.

Marisa Ansaldo had just gone to phone Emma in America when two policemen appeared in the waiting room. The security guard, who had escorted them in, indicated Leo with a minimal gesture, having already relayed the rest on the phone. They nodded and waved him away: the matter was now in their hands. As they approached, Corallina stiffened and her heart began to beat so hard that she could feel it in her throat.

'ID, please,' they said to both of them.

Corallina immediately reached for her handbag, and Leo raised his eyes, annoyed. 'Why do you need to see hers too?'

'Sir, you need to show me your ID and mind your own business,' the policeman said curtly.

Corallina squeezed her brother's arm hard and looked at him imploringly as she rummaged through her stuff.

The policemen took both their IDs and stared at them, lingering on the photograph of Corallina, who was now keeping her eyes low. Then one of them left the room to go and run a background check over the radio.

'This Miriam girl – you know her?' the other policeman asked Leo in a strong Neapolitan accent, speaking less formally than the first.

Leo nodded.

'Who is she?'

'She's my girlfriend.'

'And where did she get the methadone?'

'No idea.'

The policeman feigned surprise. 'How's that possible? She's your girlfriend and you don't know where she gets her methadone?'

'Miriam ain't no junkie!' Leo roared in his face, standing up all of a sudden.

The policeman took a step back. 'Calm down or I'll take you to the station without even extending you the courtesy of a chat,' he threatened Leo.

Leo raised his chin in defiance. 'So take me to the station already. That's exactly where I wanna go!'

The policeman looked at him, perplexed.

'Take me there and I'll talk, but only to Magistrate Castagnoli.'

'Castagnoli?' the policeman asked with a frown. 'Who's this Castagnoli, now?'

Leo stared right into his face. He no longer had anything to fear. 'The one from the Ansaldo case.'

The policeman froze. 'And what have you got to do with that?' he muttered, as if it was he who was scared now.

Leo shifted his gaze on to Stelvio Ansaldo, who was staring at him. In Stelvio's eyes he read the hope of a father who had to bridge the unbridgeable with that sliver of justice that he was offering him.

'Take me to Castagnoli and I'll tell him everything I know,' Leo said in one breath.

*

Ludovico Castagnoli had retired in September 1981 and nothing would ever make him shake off the feeling that the Ansaldo case had been the source of all his misfortune. His wife had left him, demanding a generous alimony payment. The party for which he was hoping to run as an MP at the next general election had dropped him. The press still had a dig at him from time to time for how the Torre Domizia investigation had been carried out, casting many shadows on a career that he otherwise deemed to be unexceptionable.

So, in February 1982, after much prevarication and some bouncing around between offices, Magistrate Anita Perrillo – an energetic woman from the Civitavecchia courthouse who was also close to retirement – had seen the three boxes and the stack of folders where her predecessor had gathered all the documents on the Ansaldo case turn up on her desk, out of the blue. She had made an effort to peruse, read, underline a detail or two with her pencil and glance at the photographs, though with no enthusiasm, all the while trying not to give in to the instinct to look away. Eventually, with her usual practicality, she had come to the conclusion that it had taken Castagnoli three boxes and four folders simply to establish that Elisabetta Ansaldo was indeed dead. Outraged, she had called in Maresciallo Nardulli and asked him to explain the reasons behind all the shortcomings and gaps in the investigation. Nardulli had calmly explained that they had done all that could be done with the facts in hand. Anita Perrillo had looked at him with astonishment and asked, 'And what about what you *should* have done? When were you planning on doing that?' Nardulli had left in low spirits: now he was also being blamed for Castagnoli's lassitude.

Magistrate Perrillo had requested further investigations, but the machine was struggling to start up again since there was no one willing to touch that case. Her subordinates seemed to think that the facts were what they were and that the time that had elapsed since the crime certainly did not help. She had argued with everyone over it: with the chief of police, with the commissioner and even with her husband, whose advice was not to take the case too much to heart since she would be retiring in June and then they would finally be able to enjoy their garden in Ischia while doting on their grandchildren. Nonetheless, Magistrate Perrillo felt that she ought to at least try: she owed it to those two parents whose daughter would never give them grandchildren. Then, one day at six in the morning, as she was drinking her coffee while looking out of her window on to the Civitavecchia harbour, she received a phone call that would crack the Ansaldo case wide open.

She left at once for Rome. An office was waiting for her in the courthouse. There, she would take the deposition of Leo De Maria, twenty-two years old, with no criminal record, who allegedly had new information on the Ansaldo case.

When Magistrate Perrillo got out of the back seat of the car the courthouse had sent to collect her, she found Giovanni Fassi, an old colleague, waiting for her outside. As he showed her the way in, he explained to her, almost apologetically, that De Maria would not answer any of their questions but instead was insisting that he would only talk to the investigating magistrate and no one else. Giovanni Fassi hoped that this De Maria would not turn out to be just someone looking for publicity, or he would feel very sorry for having wasted the magistrate's time, but she reassured him that he had done the right thing in calling her.

When she walked into the room, Leo looked at her warily: no one had told him that Castagnoli had retired. Magistrate Perrillo sat down, explained that she was leading the investigation now and looked at him eloquently to signify that things were quite different. She asked him if he wanted a glass of water or a coffee. Leo shook his head.

'I'm here and I'm listening,' she said soothingly. She could see something that gave her hope in the eyes of that young man who looked like hell.

So Leo started from that night in January, when a stranger had asked him for some Phentatyl as he stood in front of the watermelon kiosk, selling drugs.

Marisa was sitting quietly in front of Emanuele Bassevi in the small room next to the intensive care unit. Stelvio had gone to phone Maria Grazia to tell her that the shop would remain closed and to ask her if she would mind putting up a sign on the shutter.

Emma was airborne, trying to get back as quickly as possible and feeling the kind of desperation inside that only Marisa could guess at. Marisa had promised her sister that she would stay by Miriam's side at all times, that she would not leave her alone even for an instant, but the nurses had only allowed her to see Miriam for a moment, through a window. Just long enough to realise the state she was in, almost invisible under all the tubes and machines that were keeping her alive. The doctors had explained to her and Stelvio that there was very little hope and that they should be prepared, despite knowing that there were some deaths you just could not be prepared for. They broke you, and that was all there was to it.

Marisa was reflecting on that cosmic joke in which the De Maria siblings had showed up at her door to tell her the truth just a moment too late, when everything was already in motion. Miriam had not been able to wait any longer – her pain had become unendurable. She had given up before she could be found by Marisa's embrace, before Marisa could ask Miriam to forgive her for abandoning her to all that solitude. Betta had died, and with her indifference Marisa had killed Miriam too – the girl with the tentative smile, whose gaze had lit up easily with astonishment because life outside of boarding school was all a discovery. Miriam, who had not found the words to ask for help, who had kept her secret because she believed that none of them could possibly understand what that damned night had done to her. She was so vulnerable that she had in fact broken.

A faint smile came to Marisa's lips: that expression reminded her that, when Betta was little, she had been oddly fixated on not wanting to throw anything away. If one of her toys broke, she would obstinately get to work and fix it. And she was good at it, she had a magic touch: she glued, pieced together, wedged in and tied up the broken parts. She always showed Marisa her work when she was done, brimming over with pride. Marisa used to call her Fix-It Betta.

'You do it, Betta,' she muttered to herself with a sigh. 'Fix her.'

Emanuele raised his gaze, immediately catching the meaning of those words. He closed his eyes and repeated the same prayer in his head. One, two, a thousand times.

*

A week after Leo De Maria's voluntary statement, Magistrate Perrillo signed the arrest warrant for Leonardo Dagnone, twenty-five years old, co-owner and maintenance operator of Parco Carosello in Marina di San Giorgio. After thoroughly checking the witness statements gathered by Maresciallo Nardulli following the Ansaldo murder, it had transpired that, on the night between the 10th and 11th of August 1980, one Adelina Campisi had seen from her balcony a Fiat 127 parked just past Le Dune. She remembered it, she had said, because it was the only car there, given that the Sattaflora bar was already closed at that time. Moreover, it was an unusual colour, with black stripes down the sides. A quick check had confirmed that Dagnone still owned an orange Fiat 127 Sport with black stripes. It was the same car that Silvana Mannino had seen her son Gaspare getting into for the last time, headed in the direction of Genzano. The story told by Mannino to the drug-dealer Cristiano Cavallari, aka Knight, had been confirmed by Cavallari himself an hour after his arrest *in flagrante delicto*.

During the first stage of Leonardo Dagnone's interrogation, he swore on the head of his entire bloodline – whether living, dead or yet to be born – that he had not been in Torre Domizia that night. He kept repeating this even when faced with the witness statement signed by Mario Spassi, who ran a small grocery shop opposite the market square and who had affirmed that on the evening of the 10th of August he had sold six bottles of beer on credit to Gaspare Mannino, whom he had known since he was a little boy. When shown the photograph of the Fiat 127 Sport, Spassi had also remembered that he had indeed seen Gaspare get into that orange car with the stripes, which had then peeled off at speed. The episode had made an impression on him since that was the last time Gaspare had popped into his shop and some time later Spassi had heard that he had died.

While they waited for Dagnone's legal counsel, he jeered at them, saying that they were trying to frame him with a car that was like countless others, and with the words of a lunatic who had thrown himself off the Ariccia bridge. He kept wiggling around in his chair and shaking his head cheerfully, as if he were at the cabaret. Anita Perrillo took no offence at that, though. Rather, she asked him to make an effort to remember where he was that night. Dagnone sneered and said that he was in Bologna, placing the bomb: she only needed to ask around and she would hear that a guy in a Fiat 127 Sport had been seen hanging around by the station.

This, the magistrate did take offence to. 'Dagnone, this is no joke,' she reproached him.

'You're the one who's joking, not me,' he replied, glancing around the room to garner support: it was clear to him that the magistrate was grilling him for no reason.

'Look, you're in a very serious position,' she warned him.

Dagnone stared at her, annoyed at her excessive confidence. 'Am I?' he challenged her, raising a forefinger. 'So tell me you've found a single piece of evidence on Betta Ansaldo that proves I was there.'

Magistrate Perrillo smiled at him affably. 'No, not on Betta,' she agreed accommodatingly, then stared at him. 'On the other one, though ...'

Dagnone's face immediately lost all vestiges of defiance.

He slowly sat up on the chair and brought his elbows close

to his body. As he assessed whether he should show surprise or keep quiet, he started taking deeper breaths. He was avoiding Perrillo's gaze with feigned nonchalance.

'You have no reason to worry: your counsel is on his way. I'm sure that he's just stuck in traffic,' she reassured him, putting her glasses back on to examine the papers in front of her. Then she politely asked Officer Marini to bring her a coffee and enquired whether Dagnone wanted anything.

He shook his head.

A few minutes later, Anita Perrillo looked at him over the top of her glasses. 'You know, I shouldn't really say this, but your position might be slightly different from that of your friends ... Clearly Mannino jumped because he'd realised that he was in huge trouble.'

'I don't even know what you're talking about,' he replied.

'There is a huge difference between rape, and rape with murder – either a few years, or life imprisonment. But you know that, right?'

Dagnone was not looking at her, but she was certain that he was listening very carefully.

'We know that you shared them out.' She put down the page she was holding and smoothed it out with her fingers, lost in thought, as if she wanted to somehow make it right, erase that carnage. 'The only difference is that when you left yours she was still alive, whereas Betta Ansaldo ...' Magistrate Perrillo let her sentence end in a sigh.

Marini returned with the magistrate's coffee and Anita Perrillo started sipping at it. She could see that Dagnone was wiping his hands on his blue jeans – his palms were sweating.

'Would you like us to open the window a little?' she asked, thoughtfully.

Dagnone was about to shake his head in irritation, but then, unexpectedly, he nodded. Marini obligingly opened the window and then left the room.

To pass the time, Magistrate Perrillo started chatting with Commissioner Fassi and the other colleagues about the lovely April weather that they had been having, though, oddly, the temperatures were a little chillier than the year before. She said that, come summer, she planned on moving to Ischia and enjoying the beach, grilled fish, and pastries filled with ricotta. They reminisced about past trips and memorable meals and Anita Perrillo promised them that as soon as the case was closed she would invite them all over to her place for her speciality, spaghetti with frutti di mare. She spoke enthusiastically, as if it was only a matter of days or weeks, as if she was going to order in the seafood right away.

'I didn't even know her!' Leonardo Dagnone burst out all of a sudden.

Appearing startled, Magistrate Perrillo turned to look at him. She seemed as if she had forgotten that he was there.

'Mizio dragged us into it!' Leonardo shouted, red in the face as if someone were clamping a hand around his neck. 'He had a thing about her and he lost it!'

The magistrate felt many questions rising to her lips like a flood, but she only had a split second to choose the most important one. One of them was still in the wind. Just one.

'Who is Mizio?' Magistrate Perrillo asked calmly, so as not to frighten him, while praying that the door would stay shut and that Marini would not come in to announce that Counsel Ferrari was there.

Dagnone dithered, then rested his open hands on his knees, closed his eyes and took a deep breath. 'Maurizio. I don't know his last name,' he said, giving in.

'Is he from Torre Domizia?'

Leonardo nodded, then dropped the bomb, 'He's the son of the maresciallo.'

Despite the weather being a plague that night, with all that rain that was pouring down, Maresciallo Nardulli was feeling happy. He had driven his wife to Tarquinia to keep her mother company for a couple of days, as she was old and unwell, and now he was headed home. Along the way, he had stopped to buy some arancini from the Sicilian deli and he could already imagine himself spending a lovely evening with his sons watching football on TV. He would go back home, take a nice shower and then go and pick Maurizio up from the station; though it was only a short distance, he did not want the boy to walk in that torrential rain. Commuting to university was already stressful enough. Nardulli knew that his son would have preferred to get a room in Rome, but rent was high, and what with their mortgage, car payments and the money set aside for emergencies there was no way they could afford it right now. As soon as he received the back pay he was waiting on, he would buy Maurizio a small car.

Nardulli parked in front of the gate and ran inside with the arancini tray in one hand and an old paper held over his head in the guise of an umbrella. He was about to put the key in the lock when his younger son anticipated him and opened the door from inside, having spotted him from the window that overlooked the garden.

'Hey, Luca,' Nardulli greeted him as he handed him the tray, setting the soaked newspaper to one side. 'Have you finished your homework?'

Luca cast a glance towards the living room. Two carabinieri had just appeared in the doorway. Nardulli did not know them.

'They said they were from Rome,' his son muttered, while a third appeared behind the first two.

'Has there been an accident?' Nardulli asked, his chest draining of breath.

Looking quite serious, the maresciallo from Rome stepped towards Nardulli, together with the two sergeants. 'Tommaso Nardulli?'

Nardulli was troubled by the fact that, in saying his name, the other officer had left out his rank. 'Did something happen to Maurizio?'

'No,' the man reassured him. 'Where is your son?'

'Maurizio?' Nardulli asked, failing to understand.

'Yes, Maurizio,' the maresciallo repeated.

'He arrives on the seven-thirty train. Why?' He was staring into each of their faces in turn, as if in a daze.

'Is there someone you can leave your child with?' The other carabiniere cast a glance in the direction of Luca.

Nardulli looked at his son almost as if he did not recognise him. 'Him? Why do I need to leave him?'

'When will your wife be back?'

'She's staying at her parents' tonight.'

The maresciallo sighed. 'Can we talk in private?'

It was then that Nardulli understood everything without actually understanding a single thing. He looked at his son and put a hand on his shoulder. 'Go up to your room, Luca. Take the arancini with you.'

Luca tried to protest – he wanted to know too.

'Luca, go,' his father ordered.

Nardulli waited until his son had disappeared at the top of the stairs, and until he had heard the distinct thud of the door to his room closing, then he asked in a whisper, 'What's happened?'

'We have an arrest warrant for your son.'

Nardulli chuckled uneasily. 'Maurizio? You're joking!'

'It's in connection with the Ansaldo case,' said the maresciallo, to make him understand that he was not joking at all.

'And what has my son got to do with it?'

'You tell us, Nardulli. What *has* your son got to do with it?' The other officer was now staring straight at him.

'I investigated that case for Magistrate Castagnoli.'

'How you investigated the case is a matter you will discuss with Magistrate Perrillo later on. In the meantime, there are proceedings against you, with suspension from service effective immediately.'

Nardulli had to take a moment to process the blow. The silence was pierced by the faraway clatter of the express train from Pisa Centrale going through without stopping. 'And what are the charges?'

'Against your son: sexual assault and murder. Against you: aiding and abetting,' said the maresciallo.

Nardulli stared at the three of them. 'You don't know my son ...' He spread his arms out in front of him as if

Maurizio were still there, only a child, and he was squeezing his shoulders, presenting him to them so that they could see for themselves that he was the perfect boy.

'Maybe you don't know him either,' the maresciallo replied with a sigh.

'Impossible,' Nardulli objected, though still politely – it was an understandable mistake; they knew nothing at all about Maurizio.

'If he's innocent, he'll have his chance to prove it,' the officer conceded without conviction.

Nardulli ran his fingers through his wet hair, looking around as if searching for a lost thing that was meant to be right there. He raised his eyes at these carabinieri who were treating him with such hurtful standoffishness. For Nardulli, the carabinieri were a family. 'Can I also be there when …' He could not finish his sentence.

The maresciallo shook his head. 'There's a car waiting outside to take you to the magistrate.'

'So I can't talk to my son?'

'Not at the moment. But you can call your legal counsel.'

Nardulli opened his arms, caught off guard. 'Right now, I wouldn't know …'

'You can call them from the courthouse, in that case. Maybe you'll think of someone.'

As he prepared to follow them, woolly headed as if he were drunk, Nardulli called his neighbour, a widow who had known his sons since they were small children, and asked her whether she could look after Luca for a few hours since there was a family matter that he needed to attend to urgently. The neighbour said that she would be happy to, as she loved his two boys. Nardulli did not call his wife: he wouldn't have known what to say to her. He thought that later on, in the car, he would have some time to work out how better to explain to her that these things could happen, that it only took some gossip, or an inmate joking around, hoping for a chance to spend a few hours on the outside, and all of a sudden you could find yourself in trouble. Maybe he or Maurizio had trodden on someone's toes and they were trying to get back at them. But there was no reason to worry, he would say to her. Everything would work itself out.

It had stopped raining. Two cars were waiting outside the train station in Torre Domizia. Tommaso Nardulli was sitting on the back seat of the one parked at the bus stop, while the other, which was waiting for his son, was parked just a little further ahead. Though he could not see them, Nardulli could picture quite well the carabinieri standing on the platform and waiting for Maurizio to get off the train. They had studied his photograph, so they would be able to recognise him right away and take him to the courthouse in Civitavecchia. Nardulli was sorry that his son had to go through this ordeal on his own: he was all grown up now, of course, but he was still just a boy.

The PA system announced the 7.30 regional train from Roma Termini and Nardulli held his breath, his heart racing as he wrung his hands.

It felt as though an infinite amount of time passed, too long really, but then he saw them. Four carabinieri, one to the right, one to the left and two behind, with Maurizio in the middle, held by the arms, as they all walked briskly out of the station. His son had pulled up the hood of his jacket, tugging it forward to cover up as much of his face as possible. He was hanging his head low as he walked, his gaze fixed on his feet, letting the carabinieri guide him as if keeping his face hidden was much more important than seeing where he was going.

Nardulli instinctively knocked on the window when they walked past the car he was in, trying to draw Maurizio's attention and reassure him somehow. He reckoned that Maurizio had heard him, since he turned his head in his direction and even seemed as if he was slowing down, but then he immediately went back to staring at the ground, his head hung even lower than before. Despite reproach from the carabiniere in the driving seat, Nardulli kept on knocking on the window until he saw Maurizio disappear into the other car.

A moment later, the officer who had been escorting Maurizio got into the same car as Nardulli, on the passenger side. He was panting and cursing as he loosened his tie.

'He even tried to make a run for it, the bastard,' he hissed with his chubby throat in Sicilian dialect.

Nardulli slowly leaned back against the seat, in silence.

Like a father disappearing all of a sudden.

At that moment, a downpour was unleashed upon Torre Domizia.

Maurizio Nardulli did not say a word all night, even when the lawyer that his father had eventually called arrived at two in the morning. Magistrate Perrillo asked, showed, threatened and reassured, but nothing seemed to work. His boyish face remained imperturbable, uninterested: under his shock of blond hair, his blue eyes stayed obstinately fixed on the edge of the desk in front of him. He looked ready to sit there for the rest of his life, feeling neither tiredness, nor hunger, nor thirst.

Anita Perrillo realised that he would be a hard nut to crack, much more so than Dagnone. She knew that, as things were at the moment, the soundness of the evidence of guilt could still be challenged. Nonetheless, she had Dagnone's and Cavallari's statements, Nardulli's attempted flight at the station and all the evidence that Elisabetta Ansaldo's body might reveal about her assailants: they had left traces, some more horrifying than others. Magistrate Perrillo just needed time and perseverance.

Of course, without a confession, the trial would be long. It troubled her to think how many people would be handling the evidence, and to know that Maresciallo Nardulli was so well liked, and by so many – too many – despite his limited talent as a carabiniere. Nevertheless, she was determined to put that young man behind bars and make sure that he stayed there, even if that meant postponing her retirement. She owed it to Betta Ansaldo, and to that poor girl who was lying in a hospital bed, hanging between life and death.

Tommaso Nardulli had been asked by his colleagues to take off his uniform and hand in his service weapon. He was sitting in his shirtsleeves as he listened, speechless, to the story that Anita Perrillo recounted. After following up on all the witness statements and all the evidence gathered over the last few days, the worthless paper that he and Castagnoli had produced in more than a year of investigation had been replaced by two concise, clear, detailed typewritten pages in which everything made sense. Apart from the unspeakable madness of the fifteen or twenty minutes in which the tragedy had taken place, along with his own son's involvement, even Nardulli had to admit that Perrillo's version of the facts was flawless.

At around eight in the evening of the 10th of August 1980, Gaspare Mannino gets out of Leonardo Dagnone's Fiat 127 Sport and steps into Mario Spassi's shop to buy six large bottles of beer, which he adds to his mother's tab, then he gets back in the car. Dagnone and Mannino head to a cheap pizzeria in Maccarese owned by a mutual friend, Gennaro De Luca. After dinner, they try to chat up two local girls, unidentified, outside the pizzeria. At first, the girls seem to be interested but then excuse themselves with some pretext. Mannino turns insistent – he especially likes one of them – but the girl becomes aggravated and dismisses him gruffly. Eventually, Mannino and Dagnone get back into the Fiat 127 Sport, turn on to Via Aurelia and head back towards Torre Domizia, where they have an appointment to meet Maurizio Nardulli, who has recently scored some hashish for a reasonable price and has offered to split it with them. When Mannino and Dagnone reach the agreed-upon isolated spot – that is, the wooden steps of Le Dune beach club – Nardulli is already there, having just arrived on his bike. He is tense. He explains that his father had asked to borrow his brand-new scooter two days earlier and then managed to have it stolen, just outside the swimming pool of the sailing club. He mentions that he has eaten dinner at home and then gone out for gelato in the square with some other friends, who later left to go to Torre del Fratino. It is around midnight and the place is quiet. The bar of Le Dune closed at ten and the Bandiera

Gialla, the last club before the river mouth, went out of business a few months earlier due to unpaid taxes.

They start drinking Mannino's beers and smoking Nardulli's hash, arguing half-heartedly over football, when Mannino confesses with annoyance that the thing with the girl from Maccarese a few hours earlier is still bothering him. Nardulli wants to hear all about it, then tries to cheer Mannino up by addressing a string of insults at the unknown woman. They end up talking about girls. At first, about those who are not very receptive and play hard to get. Then, about those who are keen, easy. They start sharing obscene, explicit confessions. The beers and the hash have loosened their tongues and, since they have precious little to tell from lived experience, they start fantasising instead. They agree that there are so many girls who should be put in their place without much fuss, that men should be able to act like men. They start talking about all the ways in which you can teach a girl what a man can do to satisfy her. Then the conversation moves on to fantasies about non-consensual sex and Elisabetta Ansaldo's name is mentioned. Nardulli has been obsessing over her but cannot bring himself to talk to her. He saw her in the square just a few hours earlier and got so aroused that he is still all pent-up with frustration. But he feels inhibited by her because, although she's only sixteen, she already has a lot of experience, while he is still a novice. He admits that he doesn't feel up to it, that he's scared of being rejected – he knows she likes older guys. Dagnone and Mannino, who do not know her, ask him to describe her. Nardulli undresses her with his words, emphasising her physical features with vulgar tones and expressions, and the three of them feast on her beauty in their hungry heads. They each say what they would do if only they could get their hands on her. They egg each other on, laughing conspiratorially, and agree that, since she is already so experienced, they would not need to take it slow with her. On the contrary, Nardulli adds, Betta might even need more than one of them. The air becomes electric and, all of a sudden, Nardulli jumps up and says he needs to go. He is panting. Dagnone and Mannino too feel quite on edge after fantasising about Elisabetta so much. Nardulli quickly says goodbye and heads off on his bike, pedalling towards the river mouth, since the road is one-way.

Dagnone and Mannino finish their joints and the last of their beers in silence. The sky is getting overcast and the darkness is becoming thicker. The only sound coming from the sea is the breaking of waves stirred up by the current, which is becoming stronger. When they are about to leave, they see Nardulli rushing back towards them, against traffic. He jumps off his bike, letting it fall to one side, and runs towards them, his eyes popping out.

'I've just seen her sneak out of the house,' he says hoarsely, trying to catch his breath. 'She was going down the slope just before the river mouth. She's heading along the beach to the bonfires. She did that a lot last year too.'

'Who?' Dagnone and Mannino ask.

'Betta.'

There is no time to assess how serious their intentions are, no time to think. They stand still, looking along the beach in the direction of the river mouth, but the moonlight is now dim and clouds are gathering. They only manage to see Betta when she passes right in front of them, some twenty metres away, as that strip of beach gets some light from the lamps of the bar.

But she is not alone. She is holding hands with another girl who looks younger than her.

'I'll take the other one,' says Dagnone.

They nod to each other to signify that they are all in agreement. They watch the girls walk past the beach club and slow down. Not wasting any time, they sprint into the dark and grab them from behind.

Dagnone gets on top of the smaller one. Though skinny, she still puts up a fight at first. Eventually, though, she gives up, realising that she cannot stop him. Mannino and Nardulli take Betta instead, though even together they struggle to hold her down. She is tall and strong and kicks at them like a startled horse. The two spur each other on – all the effort it takes to subdue her arouses them even more.

When Dagnone is done with his one, who has passed out underneath him, he quickly catches up with the other two: he wants to watch.

Mannino is now on top of Betta, who is face down in the sand. Nardulli, his trousers half down, is holding her still for him with his knee in the middle of her back. But Dagnone realises that Betta is not moving. He thinks it is weird that she is so still and all of a sudden so quiet. He thinks it is weird that she has passed out, too. He has a hunch: pushing Nardulli away, he forces Mannino off her, dragging him by his shirt. Mannino protests: he is so drunk now that he was struggling to finish, so instead he was just raging upon her in spite.

Dagnone grabs Betta by her shoulder, turning her over.

He cannot tell whether she is alive or dead but says that they need to go. Right now.

Dagnone and Mannino speed off in the Fiat 127 Sport with the headlights off, while Nardulli gets back on his bike and hurries home, against traffic, taking the narrow inner roads. In the morning, Mauro Sattaflora finds Betta Ansaldo's lifeless body by the fence.

When Anita Perrillo had finished telling him her reconstruction of the events, Tommaso Nardulli was gazing into space.

'It's hard,' the magistrate said, fixing her eyes on him. 'It's hard for me to believe that you never suspected a thing. Not a clue. Not a hunch.'

Nardulli raised his eyes. 'Magistrate, do you have children?'

After a moment of hesitation, Anita Perrillo nodded.

'Then it's not so hard.'

'Nardulli, make him confess,' she told him with a hint of sympathy in her voice. 'It's for the best,' she added.

Nardulli looked out of the window. It was dark, and it was raining. It was still raining.

Eventually, at around four in the morning, the magistrate ordered for the Nardulli residence to be searched and decreed that, as well as his son, Tommaso Nardulli should be remanded in custody too, given the concrete risk that he might tamper with the evidence.

Nardulli was not surprised when they told him what the magistrate had decided. He had spent hours sitting in a small room, thinking, and he knew that people did not walk away when charged with aiding and abetting such a serious crime.

Officer Marini, an old acquaintance of his from his time at the Cerveteri station, had come by from time to time to ask him if he needed anything. He was clearly ill at ease, and when Nardulli had asked for an update on his son he had told him that he was not at liberty to discuss the matter, and had said this without regret, as if he thought that both Tommaso and his son were exactly where they belonged. Nardulli was also not surprised when, as they waited for the vehicles that would transfer them to jail, they placed him and Maurizio in the same room, under the vigilant watch of Officer Todaro, who was quick to make it clear that they were not allowed to talk.

Nardulli stared at his son in silence as he sat down on the chair next to his. He could see a hint of a stubble on his chin and that his blue eyes, usually so bright, were now sullen. Nardulli realised that over the past year and a half Maurizio had become a man. Not so much physically: he still looked boyish, making him seem younger than he was despite his toned body. No, something had changed in his attitude. He had become more confident and self-assured, especially with girls; he seemed to be going out with someone new every weekend, even though he was still driving around Torre Domizia on a banged-up old scooter and had to catch the six o'clock train every morning to get to university. You could tell that he had a way with them, that he was turning into a real heartbreaker. Over the last few months, Nardulli had observed all these changes with a certain fatherly pride given that he on the other hand still felt self-conscious with his wife, even though they had been married some thirty years. Maurizio was not like that. He had discovered himself to be different, with a more brazen virility than his father's. That much was evident.

When Officer Todaro was called by the magistrate and had to step out urgently, leaving the door ajar, Nardulli was similarly unsurprised. He took a deep breath and bent down towards his son, his elbow resting on the arm of the metal chair in which he had spent the night.

'When Gaspare Mannino went missing, I asked you at dinner if you knew him, remember? You said you didn't.'

'Because I didn't,' his son said without looking at him.

'Then they found him dead and the parish magazine published a few lines on him, along with a picture from the football tournament that Father Tonino used to organise every summer. Remember? Father Tonino used to name the teams after the beach clubs: Il Pirata, La Vela, Florida ... Florida won two years in a row, in 1977 and 1978.' Nardulli nodded, lost in thought – he was certain that the years were right. 'You and Mannino used to play defence. You were both in that picture: your jerseys, your numbers and even your names. You had your arms around each other's shoulders, standing close together, looking so happy. Father Tonino charged your mother and me five thousand lire for that jersey. Your mother was furious, saying that it was far too expensive.'

Maurizio rested his eyes on him, silent.

'I was leafing through that magazine during Mass, since on that Sunday Father Tonino had decided to labour his point, and I thought it was impossible that you didn't remember Gaspare.' Nardulli shook his head slightly at the memory. 'But then I forgot all about it.' He waved a hand around his head. 'You know how it happens ...'

'What's all this got to do with now?' Maurizio asked with irritation.

'Did I ever tell you, Maurizio, that I wanted to be a train driver?' Nardulli smiled faintly, with tenderness, at the memory. 'Then, when my military service was over, your mother talked me into staying on so that we could get married sooner.'

Maurizio was staring at him.

'I'm no good as a carabiniere. My place was on trains.' He raised his forefinger a little. 'I would've been good at that.'

'You've been a good father,' said Maurizio all of a sudden, averting his eyes. He felt that his father's regret needed a word of comfort.

'That's true,' Nardulli said, nodding with conviction. 'I spent all night asking myself where I went wrong.' He paused. 'And you know what I eventually told myself?'

His son remained still, his elbows on his knees, his eyes on the ground.

'That I didn't do anything wrong,' he concluded. 'And nor did your mother.'

They sat there in silence. Todaro seemed to have disappeared into thin air; the courthouse was suddenly deserted.

'I only want to know one thing ...' Nardulli brought his fingers to his forehead to signify that there was this one issue that was hammering away at him, right there. 'Those bite marks.' Nardulli fell silent: that thought especially, for some reason, horrified him more than anything else. 'Was it you who bit her? Or was it one of the others?' He waited for an answer in vain. Maurizio remained still. 'If it was you, Maurizio, they'll find out anyway. Let me hear it from you.'

Maurizio raised his head a little but kept staring straight ahead. He knew that his father would never look him in the face again until the end of his days. 'When I had her in my hands, I lost my head,' he said with no emphasis, and with no regret. If he had her in his hands again, he would do it all over again. Although he did not say that last part out loud, Nardulli could sense it. He was his father.

Tommaso Nardulli closed his eyes.

He imagined how his wife would scream, had she been here to listen to those words. She, who had carried Maurizio in her womb, nursed him at her breast, rocked him, fed him and combed his hair neatly before taking him to school in the morning, always on time. She who just the other evening had kissed him good night on the forehead before going to bed herself.

It took Nardulli a little while to recover some strength. He felt exhausted after his final ever half-hour on the job, during which he had been a better carabiniere than at any time throughout his entire career. He stood up and left the room, walking slowly along the corridor.

When he was halfway down it, Officer Todaro came up to him.

'Can we go now?' Nardulli asked him.

Todaro nodded and softly led him away by the elbow. 'Magistrate Perrillo asked me to say thank you and that she is sorry,' he whispered to him.

'Only doing my duty,' Nardulli replied.

Anita Perrillo could no longer remember the last time she had managed to catch a few hours of sleep. It surprised her that at her age she could still be on her feet like this, lucid. She felt full of energy, galvanised, in a way even euphoric. In a matter of days, she had cracked open the intense darkness that for almost two years had enveloped the Ansaldo case, which had now unfortunately become the Ansaldo–Bassevi case. She was still struggling to understand how so many adults could have gravitated around Miriam Bassevi without ever sensing her trauma. Maybe it was merely due to the fact that her tragedy had been immediately superseded by an even more ferocious one. There was a lot to be learned from that story about the effect of grief on the soul.

As soon as Maurizio Nardulli had signed his confession early that morning, Magistrate Perrillo had had the Ansaldos called in. They arrived at the courthouse at eight on the dot. Luckily, she had had some time to go home, shower and make herself presentable. She asked Officer Marini to show the Ansaldos into her office and welcomed them with a warm handshake. She enquired about their niece's health, but they shook their heads dejectedly: there had been no good news yet, and every day that Miriam spent in a coma was a step further from recovery. Magistrate Perrillo made a mental note that there were sufficient grounds to add 'personal harm as the result of another crime' to the charges. It was obvious that Signorina Bassevi was in that sorry state because of the psychological trauma she had been subjected to. Dagnone and Nardulli would pay for that too, and Perrillo would not leave her post until they had been sentenced. Her husband was welcome to go and eat pastries filled with ricotta in Ischia on his own.

She invited the Ansaldos to sit down on the sofa next to the window while she sat in the armchair: this was not the kind of news that could be given from behind a desk.

A faint, sorrowful smile came to her lips before she started talking. She knew that, despite the incurable grief that they carried inside, the news she was about to give them would bring them joy, however bitter.

'Signor and Signora Ansaldo,' she said gently, 'we've arrested them.'

Marisa quickly suffocated a cry in the palm of her hand. Stelvio put an arm around her shoulders while an imperceptible spark ignited in his gaze, like an eye coming back to life little by little. They stared at her, incredulous.

'This is only the beginning,' Magistrate Perrillo hastened to explain. 'It will be a long, painful journey.' She looked at them meaningfully. 'You will hear dreadful things,' she warned them. 'But you . . . ' Perrillo hesitated, then corrected herself, 'We are Betta's voice now, and we must stop in the face of nothing.'

Marisa nodded, abandoning herself to silent tears.

'Their names are Leonardo Dagnone and Maurizio Nardulli,' she continued. 'Nardulli and Mannino, the one who died, are Betta's assailants, with all that resulted from it.' She breathed in for a moment. 'Dagnone is mostly responsible for the crimes against Miriam.'

Stelvio was staring at her, bewildered. 'Nardulli, as in Maresciallo Nardulli?'

The magistrate nodded slowly. 'His oldest son.'

Stelvio and Marisa exchanged a split-second glance that expressed all their shock. 'But how can it be?' Stelvio asked, stunned.

Anita Perrillo let out a deep sigh. 'Maresciallo Nardulli has been charged with aiding and abetting. However, if you want my personal opinion, he never suspected a thing.'

Stelvio shook his head. He could not believe it. He had played bocce with the father of his daughter's future murderer and let him comfort him during the first days of his grief. He had put his absolute trust in his investigation.

'Let's speak candidly, Signor and Signora Ansaldo: had it not been for Leo De Maria, we might never have unravelled this knot. Or maybe it would have taken us months, if not years. And you understand that as time goes by and the trail grows cold, memories become more and more slippery ...' Magistrate Perrillo explained.

Marisa nodded to show that she understood.

The magistrate lowered her gaze for a moment: what she was about to say weighed heavily on her. 'I will fight to obtain the maximum sentence, but the justice of the courtroom is not that of parents. You must be prepared for this.'

The Ansaldos nodded. They understood that too.

'What will happen to Leo De Maria now?' Stelvio asked.

'He has confessed to dealing drugs. My colleague in the relevant criminal division has taken into account the situation, the extenuating circumstances, his key contribution to this case ...' Magistrate Perrillo nodded with evident satisfaction. 'He will get off with the bare minimum.'

Again the Ansaldos nodded in unison. They knew that, in his own way, Leo De Maria had demonstrated all of his love and courage with his actions.

'And by the way, that young man has an extraordinary legal counsel, you know? She is one of the toughest, and very practical.' Magistrate Perrillo shifted in her armchair as she played for time and looked for the right words: her code of conduct forbade her from openly recommending a counsel to them. 'You see ... if one needs only to negotiate, then a decent mediator is enough. But when you're going to war, you need a general.' She smiled.

The Ansaldos returned her smile, thankful.

Despite the torrential rain having resumed, Anita Perrillo had the car drive her to the Civitavecchia district jail before finally going back home for some well-deserved rest. Since her visit had not been announced, the director had her wait more than was necessary as a way to express his disgruntlement.

She sat at the metal table and waited for Leo De Maria. When he was led in, the top of his sweatsuit was defiantly open over his white T-shirt, as if he was already used to jail.

'How are you doing, De Maria?' Magistrate Perrillo greeted him.

Leo shrugged. 'Everyone's cool.'

She motioned him to sit down. She had taken a spontaneous liking to that young man. Setting aside his small-time crime, she had been struck by his courage, intuition and instinct. By his rare sensitivity, which was hidden behind an armour that could be breached with just one word, as long as it was sincere. Sadly, now that his criminal record was inexorably tainted, a natural-born investigating magistrate had been wasted for good.

And then there was his ability to love, which had pushed him to tell the whole story, without leaving out a single thing, any detail that might make the facts appear less believable.

Though justice for Miriam Bassevi came at the price of his own freedom, he had pleaded guilty without a moment of hesitation. Almost with candour. Leo reminded Magistrate Perrillo, who was getting on in years, of the modern-day version of a hero from bygone times. Certainly imperfect, but still heroic. The head of the intensive care unit had told her on the phone that the young man had worked a real miracle when he had brought Miriam in 'on the brink', achieving the impossible. If the young woman still had some hope, however dim it might be, it was all thanks to Leo De Maria.

'We've arrested Dagnone and Nardulli,' she told him with a conspiratorial smile. By saying 'we', she was recognising his contribution.

Leo raised both hands to the back of his neck, took a deep breath and returned her smile as if she had freed him from a burden. Then he remained quiet, enjoying the echo of those words in his head.

'You might need to come in to give witness testimony, sir.'

'Sir?'

'Sir.'

'You calling me "sir"?' Leo chuckled.

'It's time for you to grow up, De Maria,' the magistrate reproached him, doing a bad job at concealing her amusement.

'Better if I don't bump into 'em,' he warned her, now serious again.

Magistrate Perrillo took a deep breath. 'De Maria, when you turned your car around to go back to Rome rather than murder Dagnone in Marina di San Giorgio, you made a very clear choice. The only possible one for your future, and for Miriam's.'

His expression changed upon hearing that name. A veil of sadness fell upon his face and he placed his hands on his thighs and rubbed his palms up and down, as if roughly stroking the pain that he carried inside.

'Any news?' he asked, feigning aloofness.

Magistrate Perrillo shook her head. 'I met with the Ansaldos this morning. No news for now.'

Leo nodded slowly, trying to focus on the fact that Miriam was holding on. It must mean something, the fact that she had not given up yet. He kept repeating to himself, so that he would not go crazy, that maybe she had changed her mind after all; maybe she had felt him close by when he was holding her and understood that it was worth fighting on. However, there were moments when he could not believe it and only wanted to scream in anger. He even went as far as saying to himself that he didn't care whether she lived or died, since he wanted nothing to do with her any longer.

'However, I do have some good news for you,' Magistrate Perrillo announced, unable to conceal her satisfaction.

'You do?' Leo asked sceptically.

'Bignoli authorised your house arrest this morning. You're going home tomorrow.'

Leo burst out laughing, incredulous. 'I don't believe it!'

'Well, you'd better believe it.'

'And then what?'

'You'll serve your time under house arrest. Magistrate Bignoli is a reasonable man and Counsel Moroni knows how to do her job. If you behave, you'll be free in a matter of months.'

Anita Perrillo read in his eyes some bitterness at her words.

She realised that the prospect of being free somehow scared him. Especially if it meant being free without Miriam.

'One step at a time, De Maria,' she said encouragingly, as if talking to one of her children.

He nodded without conviction.

The feeling of consciousness came to the surface ever so slowly, by way of a dream.

She was on the beach, but not at Le Dune. The sun was high and the air was mild, still, windless. Miriam looked at the smooth sea, then turned around slowly. Though she was alone, she was not scared. She did not know where to go so she took a step forward, at random. Then she turned around, disorientated. She walked aimlessly for a while, until a young dog, a female with a golden coat, appeared out of nowhere, wagging her tail. She was looking at Miriam with a reassuring expression in her eyes, where tiny specks of gold shone brightly. The dog headed north, showing Miriam the way and turning around from time to time to make sure that she was keeping up, that she had not got lost. Miriam followed her, slowly walking barefoot on the beach – they were in no rush. When she saw the tower, she realised that they had reached their destination. However, it was not Torre del Fratino, the one from Betta's stories. It was the medieval turret from her chess set, but gargantuan like in Alice's Wonderland. She smiled cheerfully.

'Are we at the bonfires?' Miriam asked even though the beach was deserted.

The dog wagged her tail to mean yes, then pointed her muzzle towards the tower – *there*.

Miriam realised that the sea had withdrawn, freeing the path to the open gate.

You can move horizontally or vertically, she had taught Leo. Could he be the king of the tower? Miriam wondered. Wanting to go inside right away, she walked straight ahead, but her feet were sinking into the waterlogged sand. She was scared of plummeting to its depths for ever and turned around abruptly to go back. She thought that she had only taken a few steps, but instead the beach was already far, far away.

On the beach, the dog – her coat shining in the sun as if small diamonds had just rained down on her from the sky – was staring at Miriam, wagging her tail to say goodbye.

Miriam felt a sudden sadness.

There, the dog's eyes were still saying, reassuringly.

Miriam waved goodbye for a long time, then turned around. She walked straight ahead a little further, through the increasingly soft sand that at times seemed to want to suck her in. Step after step, the water was rising around her feet. She looked at the sea and saw it sliding slowly in her direction: it was heading towards her, ready to submerge her. All of a sudden the sky was dark. So she ran, ran, ran. She ran so fast that she barely touched the fragile surface of the sand, which was collapsing under her feet. She was almost flying, with the small fluttering of a butterfly.

To the tower. She crossed the gate and was saved.

She looked behind, towards the beach, which was far away and deserted. Then she stepped into the tower to look for the king.

She quickly climbed the spiral staircase to the top, shouting Leo's name as her voice boomed against the cyclopean walls. Suddenly, the tower started tilting slightly. Caught off guard, she grabbed on to the windowsill of a small arched window to stop herself from falling.

The sky, the sea and the beach were no longer outside. She understood right away that she was in Leo's palm and smiled with relief.

Then a sudden sleepiness took hold of her. She closed her eyes and then opened them again, just a little. Now, instead, she thought that she could see her mother standing behind a large window, and next to her Zia Marisa, who was squeezing her sister's hand in hers, pressing it against her chest, as if to say that they were there for her, together.

In desperate need of rest, Miriam fell asleep again.

At around midnight, Marisa woke up with a start. After a bite to eat, she had collapsed asleep on Betta's bed, still fully dressed.

She and Stelvio had arrived back home exhausted. That morning, they had met with Magistrate Perrillo, who had told them the names of those animals, and they had had the terrible shock of learning that Betta's fate had been sealed by Maurizio Nardulli – a blond boy whom they had often bumped into with his parents over the years, whether at Mass or in the town square. Stelvio had even remembered having seen him play football, one Sunday when he had finally convinced Ettore to go with him to the match. Stelvio remembered that Nardulli had been sitting pitchside, rejoicing over his son's passes, and he also remembered the envy he had felt at that moment. As they were driving back from Civitavecchia, Stelvio had confessed something to his wife, his voice barely able to leave his throat: even though his son played the piano at Carnegie Hall, he had envied the father of that monster, all because kicking a ball around a dusty parish pitch was more familiar to him, he understood it, he could tell whether it was good or not. At first Marisa had felt hurt by that confession, but then she'd understood.

After that, they had been to see Corallina, who was in tears over her brother's incarceration: Leo was good at heart and, though he had made some mistakes, he did not deserve to be in jail. She was crying too because of Miriam, who was not getting any better despite being attached to all those machines that scared Corallina. She was grateful that Signora Bassevi was letting her visit Miriam often from behind the window, on her own and her brother's behalf. The Bassevis were always kind to her, really excellent people. They even wanted to go to the district jail to say thank you to Leo in person, as soon as permitted, since he had done more for Miriam than they ever had in a lifetime. Corallina had burst out in tears whenever she recalled the generous words uttered by poor Signora Bassevi, who was so full of regret. Corallina had tried to comfort her, but Emma Bassevi was bearing the weight of too many errors and kept repeating to herself that it was she who had put her daughter into that hospital bed with her selfishness, with the love of a mother who did not understand sacrifice. 'Without sacrifice, love is nothing,' she had said to Corallina, weeping, as if realising only too late.

Stelvio and Marisa had tried to comfort Corallina: while one got her a glass of water, the other looked for a clean handkerchief, or they simply patted her on the shoulder and said words that might bring her some relief. Eventually, she had calmed down. Then they had told her about their meeting with Magistrate Perrillo and she had cried again, this time with joy.

They had also enquired with Corallina about Leo's legal counsel, given that the magistrate had sounded so positive about her, and Corallina had explained with pride that the lawyer was her dearest friend, one whom she had met many years earlier after ending up in the hospital due to an unfortunate accident. At the time the counsel had still been a student and volunteered at the hospital, so she used to come around often to keep her company. Her name was Giuliana Moroni and she was even better than the lawyers you saw on TV: she backed down in front of no one, Corallina had said with pride. And now she was defending Leo pro bono – which for Corallina and her brother was no small thing, she had added in a voice full of gratitude.

When Stelvio and Marisa had called Counsel Moroni's practice from Antonia's phone, she had said that she would be more than happy to see them that very afternoon, after she was done with her other appointments. They were friends of Corallina's and she felt honoured that they might consider her to represent them.

Stelvio had immediately felt more at ease in Counsel Moroni's office than in the luxury of Custureri's legal firm. It was evident that Counsel Moroni liked to keep all the files relating to her cases at hand, as if they were children that she needed to keep an eye on, listen to and set straight when they were misbehaving. She had boxes, folders and files all over the place: on the chairs, the table, the shelves and even the sofa, like guests of honour. She did not even consider moving them to one side to make room for anyone else. Marisa and Stelvio had immediately wondered where she would put their daughter in that small office of hers that even on that day of incessant rain was brightly lit and had a nice clean smell. Counsel Moroni had two students helping her – both were friendly, cheerful and slightly older than Betta would have been – along with a contingent of cats that kept her company, taking turns to proclaim themselves the custodians of this stack of documents or that pile of papers.

Giuliana Moroni had welcomed them in, taken off her suit jacket and sat down, resting her hands on the edge of her cluttered desk, looking as if she was getting ready for battle. She had stared at them with a faint but reassuring smile from behind her round glasses, then had said kindly, 'Signor and Signora Ansaldo, tell me everything about Elisabetta.'

Marisa had been moved: she had felt as if Counsel Moroni wanted to know everything about Betta in order to decide which was the best spot for her in the room. Betta used to like genuine people, which had made Marisa think that she would have liked this woman a lot, with her intelligent face and her dark, riotous curls falling down to her shoulders.

In the evening, Marisa and Stelvio had stopped by the hospital to see Miriam. Emma was there, as usual, waiting to be let into the intensive care room, even if only for a moment, even if she had to wear a lab coat and a face mask. She could have taken a room at the nearby hotel but she wanted to be close to her daughter, so she had asked for one of those small folding beds from the paediatric unit, which was one floor below, just like the other mothers. When Emma observed them sitting solicitously next to their sick children, she felt remorse at the thought of all the care that she had not given to her babies, and was now inconsolable at the idea that it might be too late for Miriam.

Marisa and Stelvio had told her about their decision to terminate Custureri's instruction and surprisingly she had simply said that she understood. She had even enquired about Counsel Moroni and said that she would talk to Emanuele about her, since Miriam and Betta were fighting the same fight and they would be stronger together. At that, Marisa had not been able to hold back her tears, and she and her sister had held each other tighter than ever before. Marisa felt that that storm wind that had swept them apart was now somehow pushing them towards one other again. They had stumbled about, alone, but now they had found each other again and were holding on together. They were giving each other strength so as not to give in to their shared grief, and they were even asking each other for forgiveness for their respective shortcomings, finally putting to one side all of those misunderstandings that now mattered so little.

Then they had spent some time looking at Miriam from behind the window, so that she would know that they were there for her now, as mothers, as women, and that the net was ready to catch her, if she were to fall.

Marisa and Stelvio had returned home at around ten, protecting themselves as best they could from the pouring rain that had rendered their umbrellas useless. Marisa had gulped down some bread with prosciutto, a spoonful of stewed potatoes left over from the day before and an apple. She had said good night to Stelvio, who was still sitting at the table, and she had gone to Betta's room, where an unbearable tiredness had forced her to lie down without even getting undressed. Just for a minute, she had told herself, but right away sleep had overcome her.

When she woke up, she noticed the glare of the kitchen light on the corridor floor and got up slowly. Her head was spinning a little and she still felt the tiredness in her bones. She went to the window and moved the curtain to one side, wondering whether that torrential rain would ever stop. She could not remember ever seeing anything like it. All that endless racket, the flashes of lightning heralding mighty thunder which shook the earth, that wind which made the trees swing and hurled itself against everything, like an explosion of irrepressible wrath. There had been a few moments of peace, that was true, and for short intervals the sky had even opened up, creating the illusion that the fury had finally subsided. But everything had started up again several hours ago, more violent than ever before.

Marisa left the room and walked barefoot into the kitchen. Stelvio had not heard her come in. He was sitting at the table in front of his empty plate, drinking and staring at what was left in the bottle. Marisa could see the dejection in his eyes and she wondered whether it was the wine he had already had or the little he had left that troubled him. They had both glossed over this vice of his, and she had actually met it with indifference. What could it possibly matter to her whether her husband had become a drunk, now that her daughter, the flesh of her flesh, was dead? At times, though, she had felt anger: drowning his loss in a bottle had felt like a form of disrespect. How could he? How could he get drunk in the face of their tragedy? At other times, she had felt disgusted when she smelled wine on his pillowcase while changing the sheets. Now, instead, she felt her heart open with tenderness towards that man who was alone with his bottle and his grief, which, just like hers, never abandoned him. Stelvio used the warmth of wine to soothe the coldness of his soul because, unlike her, he did not have the option to tell the world that he was too weak to bear that grief. He had had to prop himself up that way, with the bottle as his crutch, so that he could remain standing for her, so that both of them would not sink to the bottom.

She came up to him and he was startled, as disorientated as a child caught stealing, but did nothing. He simply set the glass back down on the table with a slow, guilty gesture, not looking her in the eye. Marisa stepped past him to get to the sink. She poured herself a glass of water and drank it slowly to gain time. She could tell that he was waiting for her to go back to Betta's room, as usual.

Marisa thought back to how Letizia had accused her, during their argument in Villa Bassevi, of not even knowing how to be a wife to her husband. Except, at that moment, Stelvio's voice had resounded strongly in her defence: 'Not another word. I won't allow it,' he had said to Letizia. Stelvio had kept to one side, staying quiet about everything, but not about that offence against Marisa, even though she had hurt him in a thousand ways, and willingly. Marisa looked at him and saw him there, his head hung low, in silence, serving the sentence she had inflicted on him over something for which he had no blame. If hurting him could help relieve her pain a little or release her frustration, that was fine with him: he willingly accepted solitude, indifference and rejection.

What had happened after Corallina De Maria knocked on her door had forced her to leave that house that had kept her isolated from the rest of the world for so long, and it had flung her into a new crisis. It had been a difficult, intense time that had layered pain upon pain, but it had also offered a glimmer of hope. This time, she and Stelvio had faced it together. They had looked at each other, talked to each other and shared silences with the same complicity and common purpose that had been keeping their marriage alive and happy until that tragic night in August. Marisa bent her lips in a melancholy smile. She had known the time of happiness and now longed for it with nostalgia – though not with regret, since they had enjoyed it fully. She and Stelvio had built that life together, year after year, with immense love. In the silence of their kitchen, gathered around the table that had witnessed all their happiest memories, she admitted to herself that still loving her husband did not take anything away from the emptiness she felt over her daughter's absence, and that the comfort of having Stelvio by her side did not belittle in any way the grief she felt.

Marisa went up to him, picked up the bottle, which was almost empty, and the glass, which was half-full, and poured the wine down the sink. She let the water run for a long time, not wanting even the smell to linger. She dried her hands more carefully than necessary as she tried to muster her courage. Then, when she was ready, she went to hug Stelvio ardently from behind, bending over him to encircle his shoulders. She put her cheek against his, her eyes closed. As seconds passed, her embrace became tighter and tighter, as if that contact was causing a new strength to course through her body.

At first, Stelvio remained frozen, as if paralysed by surprise, then he clasped one hand over hers and raised his other hand to her face, to pull her in even closer, to feel her warmth on his cheek, as he held his breath, his heart beating as fast as the first time he had held her.

'I'm sorry, Stelvio ...' she muttered. The words flowed from her chest, her voice painful.

Stelvio chuckled to disguise the lump in his throat. 'And for what, my love?' he asked as he stroked her hair, his hand reaching behind. 'For what, Marisa?'

She could only shake her head.

They stood like that for a while, telling each other everything without needing any words. The memory of the time of silence played in front of their eyes, the time that had exacerbated their pain and left them lost. If there ever had been any fault, in that further silence each finally forgave the other. And that was enough to start picking themselves up, together, with the little strength they had left to survive.

'Let's go to bed,' she said to him as she straightened up, reluctantly breaking that contact in which she had rediscovered a long-forgotten comfort. 'I really am exhausted.'

Stelvio stood up and turned around to look at her. He fixed her hair, which he had messed up a little with his hand, then stroked her face. 'Yes, I'm shattered too.'

Marisa stroked his rough face. 'The drinking ends here, okay?' she cautioned him with an indulgent smile. 'We'll get help, if necessary.'

Stelvio nodded. And at that moment they stopped being afraid of oblivion, which could never dent the emptiness left by Betta. They went to sleep in their bed exactly as they were, fully clothed, pulling a blanket over themselves and holding on to each other tightly, just looking into each other's eyes for a moment before both fell into a deep slumber.

The storm was over.

A week later, while Leo De Maria studied the book on chess that Miriam had given him some time earlier and which he had never had any intention of reading until the infinite boredom of house arrest had hit him, he heard Antonia shout from her kitchen window. This was her new means of communicating with him, having persuaded herself that it was forbidden to knock at the door of a convict.

Leo looked out of the window. 'What was that?'

To avoid looking into the face of an inmate, Antonia instead spoke to the morning air. 'An Emma something or other just rang!'

Leo felt as if he was about to pass out. 'What did she say?'

'That Miriam is awake. She's breathing all on her own. She even spoke.' As she drew back inside, Antonia added bitingly, 'Whoop-de-doo!'

Leo slid down from the windowsill slowly until he was on the floor: his legs had buckled. Then he waited for an instant to be sure that he had understood, considering for a moment whether he should call out for Antonia to ask her to repeat it. Over and over again.

When he had finally convinced himself that he was not mistaken, he raised both his hands to his head and started laughing and crying at the same time.

Miriam had stayed.

13

Another Summer

The season of silence had fallen between Miriam Bassevi and Leo De Maria.

Leo was shut in his little apartment, serving his sentence, while Miriam was shut in a rehabilitation clinic, mending with effort the consequences of her desperate act. They shared the certainty that they would eventually get out, but also the uncertainty over what would be left of their relationship now that everything was different.

Upon waking up, Miriam had discovered that the horror she had been guarding so desperately had come to the surface like putrid water, contaminating everything. Only one truth existed now and it was no longer exclusively hers. She could read it in the eyes of those who looked at her: all boundaries between those demons that had been tormenting her and her everyday life had been torn down. She had hated Leo with everything she had in her for telling the world what had happened to her and Betta that night. For making sure that the invaders had names, as well as faces and voices. Faces and voices that strangers were now, appallingly, asking her to identify. People she did not know were asking her to remember what she had only ever wished to erase, to the point of choosing death. She had cursed Leo De Maria for saving that life of hers that now afflicted her more than ever before, since forgetting had become impossible.

Weeks had gone by, slowly. Without realising it, her nightmares had started to withdraw, like a river that, after bursting its banks and sweeping everything away, eventually goes back to its bed. The horror of that night continued to run alongside her, as black as ever, and yet it no longer dared to breach its embankment. It remained there, threatening, but she could control it, if she wished to. Whenever anguish made her waver, she discovered that she was no longer quite as weak as before, because now the horror had become shared. Something always came along to shore up the banks: her mother's gaze, Zia Marisa squeezing her hand, Zio Stelvio's awkward hugs, the long-stemmed rose that her father had brought to her so that she might always have something beautiful to look at from her bed. But also Ettore's music – he had recorded some piano pieces just for her; and Donato, who was looking after Indira; and Corallina's notes, which were signed with kisses in red lipstick. Counsel Giuliana Moroni often came around just for a chat, having realised that Miriam was not quite ready to tell her story yet. One day, she had made Miriam reflect on how lucky she was, in a way: so many women like her never had anyone to help them get through, to save them. One time that Miriam was feeling particularly dejected, Giuliana had told her about the House of Butterflies, a place surrounded with greenery near Varese where 'women like her' sheltered as they tried to heal from similar wounds. There were special people there: doctors who did not wear lab coats and were always available for a chat, but also women – some younger, some older – who shared the same room, the same pain and the same dismay, and who understood fear, the burden of shame and even the guilt of the survivor. On hearing those words, Miriam had cried tears of compassion rather than self-pity for the first time.

As time went by, Miriam started thinking about Leo without feeling hatred. One day, she even went as far as admitting to herself that she had never really hated him. How could she? He had tried to cure her by sacrificing everything for her, including his freedom. Even if he had made mistakes during their relationship – and Miriam was more and more inclined to think that he probably had not – then he had done so because he cared about her. So Leo's silence, the fact that he had never tried to get in touch with her since the evening he'd saved her life, was causing her great pain.

One afternoon, Marisa found Miriam hiding in a corner of the clinic's garden. She was weeping into a linen handkerchief embroidered with her initials and ringed with little flowers. The handkerchief had been sent by Corallina, who had now taken up embroidery, and Miriam had had the impression that she could smell Leo's hands on it; she missed him terribly.

Marisa sat next to her and started stroking her head, trying to calm her down. 'What is it, darling?' she asked, her eyes veiled with tears. Seeing Miriam like that upset her.

'I want Leo,' Miriam wailed like a little girl.

Though genuinely moved, Marisa could not help but let out

a little chuckle. 'And what's the problem with that? As soon as you get out, you'll get him,' she comforted Miriam with womanly complicity.

Miriam raised her big, desolate eyes to her aunt's. 'What do I have to offer him, Zia?' This time her tone was that of an adult, loaded with unspoken meaning that only another woman would understand.

And Marisa indeed understood. She held Miriam tight, as she would have held her Betta.

A month later, when the doctors said that Miriam was ready to go back home, she called her parents and, with a smile on her lips, said that she wanted to go to the House of Butterflies.

In San Basilio, as weeks went by and Miriam's health improved, Leo was instead becoming more and more furious at her. Now that he had stopped fearing that she might die, or that the overdose might leave her completely impaired, he was free to devote all of his pent-up energy during his internment to being mortally fucked off with his girlfriend, who had wished him good night and then gone off to top herself. He could not care less if, as Corallina kept repeating, she had done it so that her tragedy would not ruin his life too. Leo only knew that if you really loved someone, you never left them alone. So he did not pay any attention when Corallina read him Miriam's letters, especially since they didn't contain a single word about him. Not a hint of a greeting, nor the wish that he might die in that shithole of an apartment where he was serving a sentence that he had copped to save her life. He, who had never been stopped once, not even for an ID check, even when he used to deal drugs. So now he had lost his job, he was under house arrest, he had a criminal record, and if Nardi ever found out that he had been the one who spilled the beans to the cops he also stood a good chance of catching a bullet. Magistrate Perrillo had assured him that they would protect him, that his name only appeared in classified documents, but the fact of the matter was that he would never be able to not worry about it ever again. And for what? For a girl who, now that she was better, would maybe not even dream of showing up for Sunday lunch at her folks' with a guy from San Basilio.

Then, from time to time, after Corallina had gone to bed and he was left alone, melancholy consumed him. So he would lie there on his bed, his gaze lost in space, and replay in his head one of the games of chess in which he had annihilated Miriam. He liked to remember how frustrated she used to get when she lost, but also how impressed she was at his progress in such a short time, especially for someone who had never seen a chessboard before in his life. She used to call him a genius and compare him to famous grand masters. But he could not have cared less about Russian and American champions: all he cared about was that Miriam thought he was good at something. He had already found the love of his life; what else could he possibly need?

One morning in July, while Corallina was making breakfast and Leo was trying to sleep in a little longer so as to have less time to kill with his eyes open, they heard a car honking several times in the street. Leo grunted and hid his head under his pillow. Half a minute later, the horn was at it again. So all the residents of the building looked out of their windows, since the buzzer was still broken and there was no other way of figuring out who was the intended recipient of all that beeping. Corallina however did not look out: since Leo had been placed under house arrest, having visitors had become such a rigmarole that it was not worth the effort.

They heard some chatter coming from the front of the building and then someone laughing. They heard a hubbub of several voices calling out for Leo. Still sleepy, he wriggled out from under his pillow and looked at Corallina, who was staring at him curiously. He got up quickly and went to look out of the open window just as he was, only in his boxer shorts, since the heat was excruciating.

Even before he could spot her, a cheerful voice reached him: it was Berto, who was also under house arrest on the second floor. 'Leo! Your girl's here!'

Leo looked down and saw her. From the fourth floor, she seemed so small in her blue dress with spaghetti straps. Her hair was tied in a ponytail, her face was smiling, and Leo thought that she was more beautiful than a goddess; his heart thumped as if he had just run a hundred metres in seven seconds.

'My God, it's Miriam!' Corallina cheeped next to him, putting a hand on his back to calm him down. She was scared he might have a heart attack.

Emanuele Bassevi got out of the car and encircled his daughter's thin waist with his arm, fearing that weakness and emotion might play a trick on her in that heat.

But now there was no space for anyone else between Leo and Miriam.

They stared at each other like that, from far away. First, they laughed a little, in a daze. Then they made space for the feeling that was rising inside them as they realised that they had both believed, each in their own way, that they would never have a moment like this ever again. The look on their faces wiped the slate clean. Nothing mattered any more – right or wrong, what had been or what would be. They simply stood there and filled their eyes with each other, hungry, because it had been so long, too long. There was a lot to say, but also no need to talk at all.

'What're you two doing, reverse Romeo and Juliet?' Antonia chuckled, though she was evidently moved.

'Juliet needs a good meal, though,' someone bumbled from upstairs.

'Sure, so she gets as fat as your wife,' someone else quipped from downstairs.

'Is she gonna sing?' Old Baldino asked, tickled, since he was a big fan of musicals.

'Who's that handsome man?' Baldino's wife asked, nodding towards Emanuele Bassevi.

'He's cute, ain't he?' another woman agreed from the top floor. 'Like a movie star!'

'If only,' Baldino's wife sighed.

'Why, what's he got that I don't?' Baldino replied in a huff, smoothing his vest over his taut belly.

'The car, Baldino, it's just the car,' a man on the first floor jeered at him, eyeing Bassevi's metallic-grey BMW.

'Why is she not coming up?' the old lady from next door asked.

'She's been ill and it's too many stairs,' Corallina explained.

'He needs to go down, then,' the lady retorted petulantly.

'He's under house arrest,' Antonia butted in. 'If he leaves, he'll go back in jail.'

The old lady waved her hand in the air with frustration. 'Goodness me!'

'Go on, get down there now, we won't tell!' someone shouted at Leo. 'There's no snitches 'ere!'

Miriam shook her head forcefully in Leo's direction to signify that he should not do anything crazy. She blew him kisses to mean that that would have to do for now, then waved him goodbye to show that she was leaving.

Corallina squeezed her brother's shoulder. 'She's going to Varese, that's why she's come by,' she muttered. 'She is going to spend some time in a place with other girls who have gone through similar things.' Corallina fell silent for a moment, on the verge of tears. 'She hopes they can help her ... Also for you,' she added softly.

Leo nodded without averting his eyes from Miriam.

Then it was just a moment.

He turned around to throw on a T-shirt and some sweatpants and flew down the stairs in a flash, barefoot, while Corallina shrieked after him and tried in vain to stop him. When he got down to the street, he was welcomed by the rousing cheer of the entire building and by Miriam coiling herself around his shoulders as he picked her up. She was laughing. She could never have imagined that something like this would ever happen in her life.

When he had her in his arms again, Leo realised that for Miriam he would happily go to prison even for a hundred years. 'Fuck's sake,' he whispered, overcome with love, as he rocked her back and forth and pressed his lips on her ear, trying hard not to cry in front of the whole building.

'Jeez, it's like being at the movies,' said Alberta from the second floor, cheerfully. She was Antonia's daughter.

'I've got goosebumps,' said a tattooed young woman, stretching out her toned forearm.

'So, kiss?' an old lady protested with impatience.

'Ain't youth a lovely thing?' a croaking voice sighed with nostalgia.

Corallina finally made it downstairs, out of breath, and flung herself at Leo, pulling him away while the onlookers continued to protest and plead.

Miriam and Leo held on and kept holding each other tightly, amid applause and incitement.

'Watch out, the cops are on their way!' someone warned from the terrace of the building.

'It's the pigs!' someone else repeated.

'Who called 'em? Fuckers!' Baldino protested.

Miriam pressed a very quick but vehement kiss on Leo's lips and pushed him away, surrounded by jubilant cheers. She kept looking at him as he ran off, dragged away by Corallina, their eyes glued on to each other's until he disappeared inside.

Emanuele Bassevi had been completely dumbfounded as he witnessed the scene. And yet, without even realising it, he had been smiling the entire time.

That morning, Miriam left for Varese. She was still very frightened, but in quite a different way from over the previous two years. The police had shown up in San Basilio but only for their usual checks, since the neighbourhood was tantamount to an external branch of the Regina Coeli prison. Actually, they did not even bother to go all the way up to Leo De Maria's apartment; they just shouted for him from the street and he leaned out of his window to wave, demonstrating that he was indeed right there, bored out of his mind as usual. In reality, he was in such a tizzy that his sister had made him mug after mug of camomile tea to try to help him calm down. So much adrenaline was coursing through his veins that he could not sit still and was pacing the apartment like a madman. But Corallina knew well that it was out of happiness and she was glad not to have any cure for it, as long as it lasted.

Miriam wrote one or two letters a week to Leo from the House of Butterflies. They were not long letters and she would not tell him much about how she spent her time there but simply said that there was always lots to do. She preferred to talk to him about her feelings and the things that she was learning, or that maybe she had already known but forgotten. She was rediscovering new fragments of herself every day, learning that not even the horror she had been put through could erase her true essence. It was still there, hiding somewhere. She needed to dig in, accept herself and her wounds, even the most unhealable ones. She needed to build herself up again and find the strength to look ahead. The secret was love, Miriam had realised: love that saves you, love that bears your pain with you so that it will not crush you, love that heals you. Reading between the lines, she was telling Leo that he had been right, that he had saved her not once but many times. She was telling him over and over again that she loved him so much and that she had gone away also for him: although she could not go back to being the girl she used to be, with him beside her she could become the woman that she wanted to be.

Leo, who found it hard to express most of his feelings in writing, usually simply replied that he missed her and that he would always love her anyway, as long as she never killed herself again.

Marisa started showing up at the shop again. At first it was just to ask Stelvio whether he wanted pasta or rice for lunch, or to pick up a bill that needed paying so that he could come home right away after closing, rather than still having errands to run. Maria Grazia's children were often there, since school was out for summer and she had nowhere to leave them. Stelvio had set up a small desk behind the till and they spent their time there, always well behaved, drawing pictures that Stelvio then pinned on the storeroom door, showering them with compliments, though in truth it was hard even to tell which way was up. Maria Grazia was always friendly with Marisa – too friendly, Marisa would think at times, to the point that she could not help the nagging thought that Maria Grazia might have something to feel sorry for. When she popped into the greengrocer's or the fishmonger's, Marisa always strained her ears to try and catch any gossip or vague remarks. However, as soon as she walked into a shop people just fell silent, out of consideration for her tragedy. So she started studying Stelvio more closely. Now that he was no longer drinking, he smiled more often and he even brought her a new plant from time to time, to replace the ones she had let systematically die of thirst on the balcony. Initially, Marisa had protested: she no longer wanted to look after plants.

After a while, though, she had capitulated. At first, she just gave them a drop of water. Then, she started repotting them when necessary. Eventually, she had started giving them fresh compost when they were looking scrawny and saying a word or two of encouragement to them when they were withering. Though soon she started getting annoyed: could all those plants be Stelvio's way of making amends for something?

One Friday morning, Marisa was waiting to see her GP about her high blood pressure, which she had developed after Betta's death. In the waiting room, she overheard the old secretary say chirpily that she was retiring and going back to her home town. Marisa elbowed her way through the busybodies gathered around the secretary's desk and asked who would take her place. The secretary shrugged: the doctor had been too busy to look into it, though she had warned him that you couldn't find someone trustworthy overnight. As if racing to take the last free seat on a busy tram, Marisa rushed to say that she had someone in mind who would be just the perfect fit for the position and that the secretary should let the doctor know right away. Then she ran off, forgetting her prescription.

For lunch, Marisa made a Caprese salad with buffalo mozzarella and fresh basil from the plant now thriving on the kitchen windowsill. Usually she and Stelvio did not talk much during meals since the silence left behind by Betta kept echoing through the emptiness of the house. However, they had recently started eating together at the table again, and even lingering a little afterwards. And, over the last few days, they had timidly resumed their ritual of afternoon coffee.

On that day, though, Marisa broke the silence after her second forkful.

'Stelvio, is there something you need to tell me?' she asked, not looking at his face.

He was a little startled, as if he had suddenly realised that he had done something wrong. 'It's delicious,' he said with conviction as he chewed his mozzarella.

'Not that!' Marisa replied with annoyance. 'I don't mean lunch.'

Stelvio was looking at her, worried. 'What then?'

Marisa huffed, looking uncomfortable. 'Maria Grazia,' she said, dropping the bombshell.

'What did she do?' Stelvio asked, curious.

Marisa fixed her eyes on him, thrusting her chest out. 'You get along, don't you?'

Stelvio opened his hands. 'Sure.'

Marisa raised a shoulder to signify that it did not make much difference to her anyway.

'Did she say something to you?' Stelvio enquired.

'Should she?' Marisa replied feistily. 'I don't even talk to Maria Grazia,' she added, in a mood.

'I'm not following,' Stelvio said, staring at her, his mouth bent down in a perplexed arc.

'You're not following?' Marisa asked as she smoothed the paper napkin along its fold. 'Fine, if you're not following ... '

Stelvio stared at her for a moment, caught between incredulity and amusement as he slowly started to realise the absurdity of the situation. A relaxed laugh rose from his throat as he shook his head. 'Marisa, are you being serious?'

'Why are you laughing?' she reproached him, upset. 'Did I say something funny?'

'Are you having a fit of jealousy?' Stelvio asked as his amusement intensified.

Marisa dropped her fork and made to stand up; he tried to hold her by the arm, but she wriggled free. She went to the sink and started to rinse some peppers for dinner, scrubbing them furiously.

'How can you possibly think something like that?' Stelvio asked from behind her as he stood up and tried hard to regain his composure. His wife's fury was no laughing matter.

'Do you think that I don't have eyes to see?'

'To see *what*, Marisa?'

Marisa swirled her hand around in the air, still holding the knife which she had grabbed to slice the peppers. 'The way she smirks... Her necklines... Her children...'

'But she must be thirty,' Stelvio pointed out imprudently.

'Oh, that's a problem now?' Marisa nodded several times to show that, as usual, she was right.

Despite his efforts, Stelvio started laughing again. 'What I mean is... I'm not even looking at her!'

'And why shouldn't you look?' Marisa replied, staring at him with her chin up. 'She's pretty!'

'Who cares!'

'So she *is* pretty,' she replied, catching the implication in his words.

'Pretty or ugly,' Stelvio shrugged, 'what's it to me?'

For no reason whatsoever, Marisa started scratching at the skin of the pepper instead of slicing it. 'What about her children? You can't tell me you don't care about them!'

'What's the harm in that? They're cute, and polite.'

Marisa nodded once more, as if she was engaged in a

conversation with herself and all her suspicions were finally being confirmed. Stelvio stroked her head and Marisa pulled away.

'Don't you know that when I open my eyes I only see one woman?' Stelvio whispered to her.

'Save this nonsense for her!'

Stelvio laughed again, despite himself. Though they had been married for a long time, he had never seen his wife in such a state. He forced the knife out of her hands, hoping she would not stab him. 'Come here, leave the poor pepper alone,' he said patiently.

Marisa resisted just a little as he hugged her, obstinately standing with her arms by her sides and looking elsewhere to show that she was not persuaded at all. Then she gave in and put her arms around his waist, only just, before looking at him in the eyes almost as if challenging him.

'I've found her another job,' she announced in a tone that did not leave any room for objections.

Stelvio did not lose his composure.

'With Dr Brosio. It's well paid. Better than the shop. And Brosio is a bachelor. He's well off too, so she might even settle down,' Marisa decided conclusively.

'Okay.' Stelvio nodded. 'But I'll need a cashier.'

Marisa sighed with resignation. 'I suppose that will have to be me, then.'

They stared at each other, the shadow of a smile on their faces.

'I suppose,' Stelvio said.

During the summer holidays, Marisa and Stelvio took the opportunity to freshen up the shop. They made an inventory of the storeroom, fitted new shelves and replaced the old refrigerated counter and the till. It was one way to avoid spending another August thinking about what had been lost from the life from before. During the hottest days they went for walks in the park, their arms linked, and enjoyed the shade of the tree-lined paths. Sometimes, they went for gelato and ate it in silence, since every spoonful came with a crumb of sadness. But when they finished, they always looked at each other and said that it was good. After all, sadness did not always have to be bitter.

A few times, Emma invited them to come and cool down at Villa Estherina, but Stelvio and Marisa preferred to be alone: they understood each other's silences, the sudden gloom that overtook them when memories cruelly lashed their evenings. They knew how to comfort one another: the pain they shared had made them inadequate for any world that was not their own. Marisa had gone from an obstinate search for solitude to clinging on to her husband as she had never done before. It still amazed her that, despite all the hurt that she had inflicted on him, Stelvio kept looking after her with such utter self-abnegation, as if she were one of those poor plants that she had let die of thirst at the time of dereliction.

From time to time Corallina popped in to say hello, to ask for updates on the trial and to gossip about Leo and Miriam's epistolary romance. They would sit at the kitchen table and chat away as they drank coffee, alternating between frivolities and more serious topics. After endless pleading, Corallina managed to convince Marisa to let her do her hair: Marisa's white strands were so *charmant* that they made Corallina giddy. One time she cut her hair, the next she simply styled it, but she would not hear of charging her: Corallina did not take money from *family*. So Marisa simply thanked her and basked in Stelvio's compliments. As Corallina used to say dreamily, Stelvio was the perfect husband. Soon enough, Marisa's hair was so admired around the neighbourhood that Corallina started working two days a week in Appio Latino.

During one of her visits, Corallina confessed to the Ansaldos that she had been looking for a job for Leo, who, according to Giuliana Moroni, would soon become eligible to work outside the house. However, when people heard that he was under house arrest, they would not even take him for a trial. She was starting to get really worried about her brother's future, so much so that she had even considered asking the Bassevis for an introduction, maybe for a job in one of their warehouses. But Leo was too prideful and did not want to embarrass them more than he already had.

So, one evening, as they dined in a silence that was more thoughtful than sad, Marisa set down her cutlery and looked at her husband.

'Why is it that you're thinking it and not saying it?' she asked him.

Stelvio feigned surprise. 'Thinking what?'

'That you might have a job for Leo.'

Stelvio shrugged. 'No need ... I can still make do. And now you're back too.'

'My dad used to say he could make do, too.' Marisa smiled at the memory.

Stelvio smiled back. 'The situation was different,' he reminded her pointedly.

Marisa paused a moment before answering. 'Now that

you're no longer paying Maria Grazia's salary and you don't have to pay me, you can afford to get some help.'

Stelvio took a deep breath. 'I can,' he conceded. 'I could, actually ...'

'What's the problem, then? Is it because of his criminal record?'

'Of course not, Leo made a mistake and he knows it. You'll see that our Miriam will keep him on the straight and narrow from now on.'

Marisa nodded. 'So?'

Stelvio gave her a big smile. 'So we'll call Giuliana tomorrow.'

Leo De Maria arrived at the Ansaldo grocery shop one Monday morning in the ivory Fiat Panda that Miriam had lent him, feeling as tense and embarrassed as he had before his medical examination for military service. Worried that he might be late since he lived so far away, he instead ended up arriving way too early.

Marisa and Stelvio let him in and, as solemnly as if he were being knighted, Stelvio gave Leo some overalls and an apron, then told him that Marisa would take care of the laundry and that Leo would need a fresh apron and overalls every morning, no ifs or buts. The following day, he would find them clean and pressed. Leo cast an apologetic glance towards Marisa, for adding to her chores, then settled in nicely right away. Marisa, for a reason that Leo would understand only much later, was looking amused as she exchanged conspiratorial glances with her husband.

Stelvio had Leo follow him around all morning like a

shadow. He started from the basics, explaining to him that eyes, nose and touch were the most important tools of the trade. He warned him that it would take time, that in a grocery shop the only way to learn was by doing. Without missing a single word, Leo nodded, moved: Stelvio was the first to teach him like a father. Leo had learned very little in school, while the streets had taught him only things that he no longer needed. At the sports shop he had absorbed everything there was to know about trainers, but here, in the Ansaldos' shop, things were quite different. The tidiness, the cleanliness, the pleasant smells of fresh food, the items that Signora Ansaldo arranged in the window and on the shelves with womanly care, her attention to colours, the boxes all facing the same direction, the prices written with beautiful penmanship. The way in which Signor Ansaldo looked at Signora Ansaldo, as if he had married her only the day before, made Leo understand that he wanted to look at Miriam exactly in the same way in thirty years' time.

When they were about to close for the afternoon, Stelvio insisted that Leo must come upstairs and have his lunch with them. Leo objected, embarrassed, saying that there was no need for that, he could grab a bite anywhere, but Stelvio would not take no for an answer. He sent Marisa to make lunch in good time and, at a quarter past one on the dot, they were all sitting around the table. Stelvio told him about the time Signor Balestrieri, Marisa's father, had hired him to work at the shop, and how honoured he had been, since that shop had witnessed all the family history of the Balestrieris, and now of the Ansaldos too. Leo listened with eyes wide in awe: the idea of generations of shopkeepers following one another moved him more than an accession to the throne. Stelvio said proudly that he had poured his whole heart into looking after Ettore Balestrieri's shop, even when life had shredded that very heart to pieces. Leo looked at him full of admiration, then, with his characteristic touch of shyness, complimented Marisa on the stew, which was delicious. Moved for reasons Leo could not understand, she mumbled a quick thank you.

Two days later, when Danilo came to deliver Camastra's bread, Leo De Maria already looked as though he had been born and raised in the shop. He took the baskets of bread and emptied them behind the counter, noticing that the wholegrain ciabattina rolls were missing. Danilo had to double-check and amend the delivery note. Then, unprompted, Leo cleaned a prosciutto bone to perfection while keeping in mind Stelvio's instructions. It was for this reason that, at around nine in the morning, Stelvio Ansaldo did something that he had never done before in so many years on the job: while the shop was open, he took his apron off and treated himself to an espresso at Berardo's, with his beautiful wife on his arm. Leo, swelling with pride, watched them leave the shop.

Her obstinate blindness towards her daughter's trauma had brought Emma Bassevi back from the skyscrapers of New York to the silence of Villa Estherina, where she had found the ideal setting for her atonement. She had blamed her distraction on the frantic life she used to lead in America, yet deep down she knew that the thing she was most guilty of was repeating to herself over and over again that nothing was really the matter with Miriam. Emma had let Dr Mineo – that despicable man – convince her that Miriam's excessive thinness was the consequence of the vain disposition that she had inherited from her. Moreover, Emma had believed that Miriam's inability to tolerate life stemmed from the boredom of affluence, the enjoyment of which had been an achievement for Emma but was a mere fact for Miriam. Out of convenience, Emma had let herself be swayed by Letizia and by her own husband, repressing her anxiety and downplaying Miriam's crisis as teenage awkwardness. It had mattered little that at times her daughter's pain had felt quite tangible to her – that she'd had the distinct impression that something had swept her away. Emma had turned her back so that that something would not even touch her. She had lied, to herself and to everyone else, just as her own mother had done.

It was because of this that Emma could not find it in herself to be as harsh as Marisa when it came to their mother. She could never, ever justify Letizia's silence, of course not, but in that chilling story they had shared in the same hypocrisy. Now Letizia was paying the price of her mistake alone in her room in Villa Estherina, where she was looked after by a stranger as she waited for her illness to finally take her. In the meantime, she remained entrenched in her gloomy stiffness, full of that rancour that had pushed away her own grandchildren. Sometimes Emma walked by her door and, spurred by compassion, opened it an inch to wish her good morning, even calling her 'Mamma', though without any tenderness. She could not bring herself to do more than that – forgiveness was impossible. Nevertheless, she could not forget that she herself had been as much at fault as Letizia.

Maternal instinct had exploded within Emma with all its

might when she had seen her baby, who had chosen to die, being born again in a hospital bed, as vulnerable as in the instant in which she had come into this world. Emma had truly loved Miriam like a daughter when for the first time she had felt the desire to tend to her body, that body which had been ravaged first by anorexia and then by the coma from which she had miraculously woken up. Emma had cradled her baby's head in her arms, while her chest screamed in profound hatred at those who had tortured her soul. It was only when Emma had finally seen Miriam open her eyes, after so many days of hoping, that she had let herself break down, ready to renounce everything, anything for another chance.

Emma had accepted Miriam's hostility, paid for the lack of intimacy between them, and suffered the humiliation of seeing Miriam confide her memories of violence to Marisa before her, her own mother. Miriam had told Marisa of her remorse, that she was the reason Betta had been on the beach that night. Because she had wanted to see the bonfires. Miriam, who had been brought up in that ivory tower where Emma and Emanuele had confined her since she was little, had confessed in despair to her aunt that Betta had died because of her. Because she had said that they should go. How could anyone bear such a burden without succumbing to it?

Afterwards, little by little, things had started to become easier. Miriam had let Emma in a fraction. They had opened up to each other, confessing their respective fears. Emma had begged forgiveness for having been such a deficient mother, and so had Miriam, for the cruelty of her indifference. They had spoken about Leo De Maria, whose name always made Miriam's eyes crinkle. Only a few months earlier, Emma would have been repulsed at the idea of welcoming him and his transvestite brother into her home. Now, Emma played over and over again in her mind the scene of Leo saving her Miriam, who was almost dead, and sacrificing his freedom so that the culprits of those terrible crimes would pay. And, now that she knew how to, she loved him like a son.

So she was living there, in that empty villa in the woods, waiting for Miriam to come back home from the House of Butterflies, where she had gone in the hope that someone might help her become a girl just like any other, beside her Leo. Miriam knew that she would never again be the person she used to be, but she was not willing to lose Leo: she would try that route, and a thousand more if necessary, since life had already taken away too much from her. Emma was full of admiration for the resoluteness born out of love that Miriam was showing.

When Emanuele had called Emma from Turin a few days earlier to let her know that he would be coming to Villa Estherina over the weekend to see her, she had felt her heart skip a beat. They had been growing apart for a very long time, but the events of the past few months had changed them both. She had reconsidered so many things, admitted to so many mistakes to herself. And she was willing to admit to even more to Emanuele, if that might give them some hope of mending their broken marriage. After all, he too could not possibly be the same any more: Miriam's tragedy had stripped them of all pretence and revealed to them their reciprocal need to lean on each other. Even Donato had become more thoughtful, not only towards Miriam but also with his mother. The pain had brought them closer together.

So, Emma was waiting on the patio for her husband, sitting

on the sofa and wearing a pretty powder-pink silk dress that hugged her slender figure, her hair up in a bun that complimented her elegant neck. She tried to read a few pages of her novel but to no avail. Focusing was hard.

When Emanuele arrived, she went to meet him at the car and welcomed him with an affectionate kiss on the corner of his lips. She gently guided him by the arm towards the sofa and went inside to prepare two glasses of cold lemonade. She was smiling when she returned. Then she sat next to her husband and for a little while they simply admired the beautiful sunset that was descending on the surrounding hills as she asked him about his trip and the time when he had taken Miriam to Varese. Emanuele said that Miriam had seemed serene when he had left her, though perhaps just a little self-conscious, and that he had had the impression that the other girls had welcomed her warmly. Though Miriam's stay at the House of Butterflies was free, Emma reminded him to arrange the donation they had discussed. He reassured her that it was already in hand.

Emanuele told Emma that before leaving Rome Miriam had wanted to go past Leo De Maria's place, on the outskirts of the city. Lost in thought, and with a faint smile on his face, Emanuele described to Emma the scene he had witnessed on that street in San Basilio, under the warm morning sun. He confessed how, amid all that squalor, he had found beauty in the choral-voiced reaction of the neighbourhood to the intense look Miriam had exchanged with that young man who could not be further from what her parents had wished for her. He told her about Leo running down the stairs at breakneck speed, despite being under house arrest, just so that he could hold her for a moment, and about the emotional embrace they had exchanged and the chaste kiss their daughter had left with him as a token of her love.

'Do you think it will last?' Emma asked Emanuele, her smile veiled with melancholy.

Emanuele took a deep breath, savouring his lemonade. 'Who knows? They're young.' He shook his head gently. 'But that is not the point.'

Emma stared at him, waiting.

'The point is that ... I envied them.' There was a note of incredulous amusement in his voice. 'At my age, I looked at them and thought, this is what love should look like.'

Emma smiled. She thought that she could read in his words something about a smouldering love that needed rekindling.

Emanuele sighed. 'Emma, I don't think that I can carry on like this.'

'Neither can I,' she rushed to say, with a flash in her eyes that her husband did not see, since he had stopped looking into them years earlier.

He searched for the right words. 'I called Custureri and asked him to recommend a divorce lawyer,' he said in one breath.

Emma lowered her eyes and encircled her glass tightly with her other hand, for fear that it might slip through her fingers.

'I know that I'm at fault,' he went on, 'because of Carola ...'

Emanuele had not even spared her the humiliation of having to listen to his voice utter that name in front of her, but Emma's expression remained impenetrable.

'But if we could end it all as friends, with no unpleasantness ...' Emanuele ventured to suggest.

Emma nodded quietly in agreement. 'Very well,' she said softly. 'I only ask for one courtesy.'

He gave a little nod. 'What is it?'

'I would like to keep Villa Estherina.' She had to pause so that her tone would stay detached. 'I will leave it to the kids, afterwards – you have my word. Nothing else.'

'Very well,' he said without hesitation.

Emma was certain that he would have been willing to offer more, infinitely more. But for her, who had started in that little workshop in Via Pinerolo and had made it so far with her talent, it was enough to know that she would be able to take refuge in this place of peace whenever she needed.

'You're very sweet, Emma,' he thanked her.

She smiled at him.

On a late Sunday afternoon in mid-September, after Marisa and Corallina had prepared a generous meal together, Stelvio and Leo were sitting on the Ansaldos' sofa, watching TV. Leo, betting slip in hand, was commenting with annoyance at the scores from the first day of the season, complaining about his luck: a draw instead of a win, and all those lovely millions that would allow him to buy a house were gone. Stelvio laughed and said that next time he would do better to save his money.

'It's all right for you,' Leo griped. 'Stelvio, I'm getting married soon!'

Marisa and Corallina, who had overheard him from the kitchen, looked at each other with their eyes wide with amazement and burst into laughter.

'Does Miriam even know?' Marisa whispered, amused.

'I don't think so,' said Corallina. 'We'll have to let her know as soon as she's back,' she laughed.

Marisa shook her head as she dried and put away the last of the washing-up. Leo always managed to surprise her – almost a child one minute, then a respectable family man the next. In the shop, he was indefatigable, conscientious and honest to the point that Stelvio already trusted him blindly. But he was also always ready to get in a fight with his older sister, over stupid things like whether his shirt needed to be tucked in or not, as if he were five.

They had spent a few cheerful hours together that day, something to which Marisa had yielded with pleasure, carried away by Leo's enthusiasm: he had wanted to celebrate his sister's birthday properly for once. Everything had been done by the book: there had been a surprise, kisses, hugs, little presents with cards, and a cake with custard and only one candle so that nothing might challenge Corallina's vanity.

Corallina had thanked them, alternating between laughter and tears and waving her hands to contain her emotions, playing the whole thing down since she did not feel that she deserved all that kindness.

'Thank you ... for everything!' she said once more, shyly. Marisa's friendship was a privilege that moved Corallina, especially since the Ansaldos' neighbours never failed to throw out a sideways glance whenever she visited.

Marisa took off her apron and hung it on its hook, staring at Corallina with her lips pressed together in a pensive smile. Then she decided that it was the right time for something else.

'Come with me; I have another gift.'

Marisa beckoned to her and Corallina followed with

cheerful cries of protest – Marisa really should not have gone through so much trouble and it really was too much.

Marisa took her into Betta's room and closed the door.

Corallina realised right away where she was and stopped still in the middle of the room, in religious silence, unable to conceal her emotion. That room contained both Betta's beauty and the emptiness of her absence. Corallina touched Betta's things with eyes full of tears: it was the first time that she had felt her so close by, and so real. Brimming with sincere compassion, she looked at Marisa: Corallina knew that no amount of time could ever heal the grief of a mother whose daughter's life had been so brutally snuffed out. She wanted to say something, but words had deserted her. So she remained silent: no comfort was possible.

Marisa opened a drawer and pulled out a soft parcel wrapped in floral paper.

'This is from me,' Marisa said, handing it to Corallina with a slight nod of her head that expressed how close they had become.

Corallina started unwrapping it with delicate, hesitant movements. Her hands were shaking and she did not want to tear the paper, which was beautiful.

She pulled out of the parcel a crêpe georgette silk scarf with small geometrical corals over a turquoise background, and immediately burst into tears, unable to hold them back.

'It was Betta's,' Marisa said softly. 'I found it while I was tidying some of her stuff and thought that you should have it. She made her dad buy it for her from a hawker on the beach, the summer before she died,' Marisa told Corallina with a smile, lost in her memory.

'It's beautiful,' Corallina said, sobbing.

Marisa sighed. 'That means you share the same bad taste as my daughter,' she laughed.

Corallina laughed too, stroking it as if it were a beloved puppy.

'You can make a nice turban out of it.'

'I've never received a present as beautiful as this one,' Corallina said, disbelief still in her eyes as she stared dreamily at the red corals hugging the azure sea. She remained quiet for a long while, lost in a million thoughts, then she took a deep breath, dried her eyes with her fingers, careful of her make-up, and rubbed them on her dress so as not to risk staining the scarf. 'There's something I need to tell you, Marisa, because you and Giuliana are my dearest friends.'

Marisa smiled with gratitude at those words. After their first, difficult encounter, loving Corallina had been easy. She had a kind, generous soul and knew how to bring a touch of lightness into everything. 'Of course,' she said, motioning Corallina to sit on Betta's bed to talk.

Corallina took Marisa's hand in hers. 'I already know that I won't be there when Leo gets married,' she said in a whisper.

Marisa looked at her with astonishment. 'Where are you going?'

'To Heaven,' Corallina said with the candour of a small child. Then a faint smile came to her lips and she added, 'At least, I hope so.'

'What do you mean?' Marisa asked, alarmed.

Corallina looked for some words that might comfort her. 'I mean that I'm going to meet Betta soon,' she explained.

'No ...' Marisa mumbled, turning pale all of a sudden.

'Only you and Giuliana know. I can never find the courage to tell Leo.' Corallina paused sorrowfully. 'Especially now that he is so happy.'

'Why, though? What's wrong with you?' Marisa, her eyes swollen with tears, was struggling to stop her lips from trembling.

'A nasty disease ... It has spread to my lungs and liver.' Corallina shook her head slowly. 'There's nothing that can be done.'

'But you're so young!' Marisa keened.

Corallina shrugged a little. 'It can't be helped,' she said in a whisper. 'Many years ago, I met a girl – a girl like me – who had been taking hormones. Someone had been giving her these pills, but I don't think he was a real doctor. They worked on her and so I started taking them too. They were so expensive, but they worked on me as well – you should have seen my skin ...' Corallina smiled bitterly at the memory. 'But they made me so sick I had to stop. However, the damage was done.'

Marisa stared at her, deeply shaken.

'So now I have cancer to a breast that I don't even have,' Corallina joked in an attempt to lighten the mood.

'Oh, my dear Corallina!' Marisa shook her head.

Corallina squeezed her hand harder. 'Marisa, I'm at peace. Now I know that Leo has a family, that I'm not leaving him alone.' Corallina looked in the direction of the living room, where they could hear Stelvio and Leo cursing the centre forward. 'You and your husband have welcomed him like a son, and Miriam is an angel, she loves him so much. Even the Bassevis have accepted him. What else could I possibly want?'

'But what about you, Corallina? Don't *you* deserve more?' Marisa replied, her voice shaking with anger.

Corallina took a second before speaking, looking for the right words. 'You know, I can see a positive side in all this.'

Marisa stared at her, confused.

'I think that, perhaps, when I go somewhere else, where Betta is ...' she smiled tenderly '... maybe I'll become who I really am.' She realised that this was too hard to grasp for Marisa, so she added, 'You see, this body suffocates me, and the idea of being rid of it is not as scary as you might think. Of course I would've preferred to stay here with you, with Leo, watch his children grow up ... But if I really must go, I want to believe that there will be something nice waiting for me.'

'You're a wonderful person here too.'

'I know,' Corallina said haughtily, her chin up. 'But I can be much better than this.'

They both laughed a sorrowful laugh.

Corallina looked down at the scarf. 'And, with this on my head, I'll be *très charmant*.'

'And Betta will recognise you right away,' Marisa whispered.

'What do you want me to say to her, when I see her?'

They stared at each other for a long time, their hands clasped so tight that it almost hurt.

'That her father and I are well, and that we love her beyond measure.'

One of the first things that Miriam Bassevi learned when she arrived at the House of Butterflies was that every guest had to learn how to crochet a little butterfly with colourful yarn during their stay. It was a symbol. Each of them would craft a butterfly according to their taste to leave to the women who would arrive after them, since unfortunately they knew that more certainly would. When one of them felt strong enough to leave, she would take a butterfly and pin it on her chest: that was the signal for the others that another one of them was ready to fly off. They would hug her and say goodbye to her, wishing her the best and reminding her that, whatever the distance, she would never be alone again. That moment arrived sooner for some. For others, instead, it felt as if it would never come, their souls having been crushed too much.

On the last day of summer, Miriam put the butterfly she had made in the box. It was as blue as the sea and speckled with golden threads that shone in the sun. Then she took out a white butterfly crafted to resemble the lace of a bridal veil. She pinned it on the side of her heart, then she called Leo De Maria at her aunt and uncle's shop and told him that she was coming home.

Epilogue

Awakening, 1985

Until the last of her days, Marisa Ansaldo reproached herself for not having always been a good friend to Sister Bertilla. It was not that she had completely forgotten about her in the dark time of grief – it was simply that she had put her to one side, confining her to a rare, indifferent thought. Locked away in the gloominess of her house, after the tragedy that had struck her, Marisa had never really wondered what had happened to Sister Bertilla – why she had not heard from her friend for such a long time, a friend who had held her hand during the most trying times of her life: the loss of her first baby, the birth of her other two children, the funeral of her beloved Betta. Then nothing else.

It was only shortly before Christmas 1983, when the blind sorrow of the early days had finally let in a crack of light that had distracted Marisa from herself, that she had finally resolved to call the house on Via Appia Pignatelli where the nun had moved to after retiring. Marisa had been told that she would not be able to talk to her as she was too ill. So Marisa had asked Stelvio to take her to see her friend as soon as possible. But Marisa never found Bertilla again.

The other sisters had explained that her friend had started becoming very forgetful a little while ago, a symptom of dementia that had become much worse after a delicate open-heart surgery. Her mind had become increasingly muddled because of it, her memories turning, jumbled at first, then altered, distorted, faded. The sisters had advised Marisa against seeing Bertilla, thoughtfully suggesting that she should spare herself that sorrow and remember her friend as she was back when they had cared for each other.

Marisa wouldn't hear of it, and had pleaded in tears for them to let her see her, let her hug her.

So, after much insistence, they had taken her to Bertilla. She was in a small room, half-lit, with a window that overlooked the garden. Bertilla no longer wore her veil. She was sitting at a little desk, zealously inscribing unintelligible scribbles in a notebook. The sister who had shown Marisa in had explained that Bertilla, who had been raised by nuns, sometimes believed that she was still a child and that, in the afternoon, she ought to do her homework. Those were her good days, the nun had added, when she was calm and at peace.

Marisa had walked up to Bertilla, her heart full of sorrow. She had delicately placed a hand on her shoulder and whispered to her, 'My dear Bertilla!'

But she had not reacted in any way.

The other sister had whispered to Marisa from behind her back, 'Bertilla no longer remembers that she is a nun.'

Marisa had nodded, swallowing back bitter tears, and called her by her given name. 'Elisabetta!'

Bertilla had raised her eyes. 'Mamma!' she had exclaimed, her eyes as shiny as a little girl's.

Marisa had been on the verge of shaking her head, then, after a moment of hesitation, she had merely nodded yes.

Marisa Ansaldo had eventually learned, at great cost, what a good day and a bad day looked like. She went to visit Bertilla every week and kept her company for a few hours even when she was irritable, aggressive or nervous, or when she screamed at Marisa that she was a usurper, a murderer and a whore. Similarly, Marisa held her hand during her good spells, when Bertilla, or rather Elisabetta, confided to her her dreams of a young woman, her anxieties over her imminent engagement to a young man from the next town over and her efforts to finish her dowry in time. They got lost in conversations about memories from a long time ago that rose to the surface of Bertilla's consciousness, sailed off in an ocean of truth mixed with fantasy and then faded away within moments, dispersing into long silences that let Marisa know that it was time to go, that Bertilla was tired.

When, in early 1985, Sister Bertilla's mind became almost completely absent, locking her into the stillness of a doll, Marisa felt sorry that over the previous months she had never had a chance to talk to Bertilla about herself, that her friend had never been lucid enough to recognise her. She would have had so much to tell her, so much to confide. But Marisa had always feared that a word, an unfamiliar name or an unknown memory might upset her. She had chosen instead to follow the unpredictable flow of Bertilla's memory, the sometimes cruel pranks of her imagination, and simply sit there listening to her and reassuring her to make her feel that as long as they were together, all was well. It mattered little if, come next visit, Bertilla would still greet Marisa as if she were a stranger, or perhaps not greet her at all, or even reject her curtly: they were friends, and Marisa had so much to be grateful for.

So, Marisa decided that, now that silence had fallen over Bertilla, she would have to be the one to do the talking, to keep her company a little.

One afternoon she brought with her a box of photographs. She showed them to Bertilla one by one, even if her eyes, in which the light was so dim, told her that she was somewhere else.

Marisa showed her photographs of Emma and of herself, first as children, then as young women, then a picture from her wedding to Stelvio Ansaldo, who looked so smart that day. She put in front of her the photograph of Ettore's baptism, immediately followed by another one of him on stage, taken as he stood next to the piano and gratefully received the applause of the audience with his hand on his heart.

'When he plays,' Marisa told Bertilla, 'people start crying, you know? My Ettore has a gift.' She clutched the photograph to her chest, brimming over with pride.

Then she showed her a photograph of Betta, her lovely girl who had left them on a gloomy night, falling victim to the wolves, and who would now be twenty-one. 'I named her after you, remember? I always look for her in everything I do,' she confided sorrowfully. 'When the pain is sad, when it's furious, when it's joyous... I'm always here waiting for a sign, and sometimes I'm sure I can see it.' Marisa remained quiet for a moment, then smiled at Bertilla tenderly. 'Sometimes I imagine it instead... Just as you used to do, my dear.'

Marisa showed Bertilla the photograph from Leo and

Miriam's wedding, which had been organised in great haste so that his sister, who was so ill, might share that moment with them. Miriam had only wanted a very simple dress, which made her look even prettier, and had worn a small white butterfly in her hair. Marisa pointed out Leo De Maria, whose face was completely unfamiliar to Bertilla.

'He is a dear boy; you should see how well he looks after the shop, how he takes care of his family,' she said to her. Then she pulled out of the box a snapshot of Benedetta, who had turned one the previous month. 'Isn't she precious?' She smiled, a joyous light in her eyes. 'We all call her Corallina because of her red curls. Nobody knows where she gets them from!'

And so Marisa carried on, again and again, every week. She kept showing Bertilla the same photographs, and sometimes a few new ones, and telling her the same stories as if it were the first time, always adding new details. Sometimes she surrendered to tears, overcome by grief. At other times, she laughed at an anecdote that had popped into her head. In doing so, she was reviewing the images of her own life to fill up the emptiness in Bertilla's, and each time she left with the box in her hands her memories felt even more precious to her.

On a winter afternoon, Marisa stepped into Bertilla's room and, finding her asleep, took off her coat, put the box down on a stool by the bedside table and sat next to her. There was a great silence all around them, a great peace, and she sat like that, enjoying that serenity.

'Marisa . . .' Sister Bertilla muttered all of a sudden, in the thick voice of someone waking up from a deep slumber.

Marisa was startled. For a moment, she thought that she was dreaming.

Sister Bertilla was staring at her in a vague stupor. 'What are you doing here?'

'I've come to see you,' Marisa said, disorientated, as she took Sister Bertilla's hand. A doctor had told her that it could happen sometimes, that there was a remote chance that a person might come out of that limbo for a moment, for just a few minutes or maybe even a bit longer. A little miracle.

'How are you?' Sister Bertilla asked, straining her voice.

'I'm well,' Marisa whispered.

'And my little Betta?' Her tone was suddenly tinged with anxiety.

Marisa hesitated. She wished she had the right answer, both for Sister Bertilla and for herself. 'She's at peace,' she said, with eyes full of tenderness.

Sister Bertilla seemed seized by a thought, a sudden awareness that veiled the tenuous brightness in her eyes. 'Yes ...' she whispered, moving her head in a slight nod. 'She's at peace.'

'And you, how are you?'

'I'm tired.'

Marisa stroked her head. 'Rest, then, if you want.'

'Later,' she said softly. 'Now tell me about you.'

So Marisa told her. About Ettore and his music, about Betta who was now at peace, about their house, which had been left empty but now echoed almost daily with the voices of Leo, Miriam and their baby girl, whom everyone called Corallina and who loved to play in Betta's room. She told her about Stelvio too, how they had got lost and found each other again and how they loved each other even more than before since they both had a huge chasm of sorrow to fill.

'We can shut ourselves away in our grief, Bertilla, or decide to take the good around us,' said Marisa, putting her hand on her box of photographs. 'It's hard. But I need to believe that everything that happened happened for a reason that we cannot yet understand. That one day all will be clear, that what *was* is but a detail of a design that we still don't have eyes to see.'

Sister Bertilla was staring at her, in silence, and Marisa was no longer sure if her mind was still there, but she continued, 'Do you think that one day we'll leave all the pain behind and stop doubting? Will the day ever come when we realise that all that injustice and suffering was just a meaningless speck in the perfect balance of things?'

Sister Bertilla moved her fingers slowly to take Marisa's hand in an extremely weak grip, then she sighed. 'I don't know.'

Marisa knew that she had to tell her something before she was gone, before there was no more time or enough light in her eyes. She bent over her, as if she were about to whisper her most intimate secret. 'My dear Bertilla, I want you to know something.' She paused just for a moment. 'You did not consecrate your life to nothing.' Marisa smiled reassuringly and added in earnest, 'You consecrated it to hope.'

Sister Bertilla smiled too, serene.

'Since what – *what* are we without hope?' Marisa said, just a moment before Sister Bertilla closed her eyes again, slipping once more into her stupor.

Then, Marisa sat there for a long time, next to her box of photographs, as darkness fell outside. Eventually, she stood up and returned to her husband, who was waiting for her.

Acknowledgements

My first thanks are to my agent Laura Ceccacci, for strongly believing in this novel, and to her collaborators.

Thanks to the entire team at Rizzoli, for the warmth with which they have welcomed me, and especially to Federica Magro and Gemma Trevisani.

Thanks to my editor Francesco Deambrogi, for always having the right word at the right time. And for patiently helping me find answers to my countless *whys*.

Thanks to Claudio, Gin and Pandora, the little heroes of this unforgettable journey.

Bringing a book from manuscript to what you are reading is a team effort.

Dialogue Books would like to thank everyone who helped to publish *All That is Left of Life* in the UK.

Editorial
Sharmaine Lovegrove
Adriano Noble
Eleanor Gaffney

Contracts
Stephanie Evans
Sasha Duszynska Lewis
Isabel Camara

Sales
Megan Schaffer
Kyla Dean
Dominic Smith
Sinead White
Georgina Cutler-Ross
Kerri Hood
Jess Harvey
Natasha Weninger Kong

Design
Charlotte Stroomer
Sara Mahon
Sasha Egonu
Luke Applin

Production
Amanda Jones

Publicity
Corinna Zifko

Marketing
Emily Moran

Operations
Rosie Stevens

Finance
Chris Vale
Jonathan Gant

Copy-Editor
Linda McQueen

Proofreader
Jill Cole